"Eloquent on the anguish of reaching spiritual understanding."

The New York Times Book Review

"A strong Southern voice with earthy insights into the intensity and the brooding that drive our innermost feelings."

Richmond Times Dispatch

"A novel that grips and moves . . . a true, haunting story . . . when he describes the Southern landscape, he writes like an angel."

Richmond News Leader

"A human novel, filled with the contradictions and happenstances of contemporary life . . . rich in detail and sentiment and colorful observation. The language is exquisite. . . . The reader accustomed to modern fiction, set in contemporary America, will be forced immediately, and to his great pleasure, to slow down and wander through this epic adventure. . . . Wilson's first novel will undoubtedly be the first unlocking of a rich store of serious fiction accessible to all readers willing to participate in an engrossing pilgrimage of the mind."

The Tampa Tribune-Times

THE QUICK AND THE DEAD

Z. Vance Wilson

BALLANTINE BOOKS • NEW YORK

Library of Congress Catalog Card Number: 86-7899

ISBN: 0-345-34634-3

This edition published by arrangement with Arbor House
Publishing Company, a division of The Hearst Corporation.

Portions of this novel have appeared in the *Missouri Review* and the
Carolina Quarterly.

Manufactured in the United States of America

First Ballantine Books Edition: October 1987

to Linda

From thence he shall come to judge the quick and the dead.

—THE APOSTLES' CREED

I

Luke: Imaginations of the Heart

1

*A*s long as he sought the Lord. In the twinkling of an eye before we heard Mother scream, my father said, "And as long as he sought the Lord, God made him to prosper."

The bull was a red Hereford named Job. We had owned him only a week—or perhaps I should say that a week earlier Dad sold us further into debt to the Farmers and Merchants Bank. To be more precise, he sold us further into debt to the Randolph family, since in that summer of 1941, when I was fourteen, those shysters owned the bank and its mortgages on a full five-sixths of the farmland in Randolph County—yes, *Randolph* County. After Mother died, I found in the store's lockbox some loan statements tied in turnip twine. On that final one those pharisees listed as collateral not only every acre of land and piece of wood we called our own, but even every one of our doomed animals: that year's root hog, Mr. Randolph (a name I'm sure they didn't appreciate) and our six cows, whose great names read like a roll call in hell: Eve, Hagar, Gomorrah, Jezebel, Babylon, and Baalah. My father was cursed with a sense of damnation and it had something to do with women. I've never understood why Mother kept that statement. Maybe like my older brother, Will, she remembered that valley-of-bones farm as a garden paradise, as though it had been Eden. Maybe she blamed the bank for our subsequent divided house. But my worst fear is that she kept that banknote because she blamed herself for what happened that morning.

My twin brother, Doug, and I were walking with my father through the herd, if you can call six cows a herd, listening to him explain how to identify each Hereford. "Babylon," he said, "with those freckles on her nose, is half a hand taller than the other five. Gomorrah has the moon-white spot over her left eye, and Baalah's face is dark red like blood." At a prideful distance Job watched us name his wives. My father planned to make money by leaving Job to service the cows in heat, fattening the calves until he sold them plump and keeping the same bossies until they could no longer drop. I think Mother believed that without that morning's explosion we could have one day owned a large herd and Cedar of Lebanon land.

Maybe so. When we turned from the cows and Job, and circled the cornfield toward the clay road, my father began one of his usual sermons. "This land is ours, boys, and so are these creatures. We must dig and till the soil and care for our stock. And be good, boys. 'A good man obtained favor of the Lord.' As long as we seek the Lord, God will be good to us and we can live here all our lives, and all your children's lives. This property I own I intend to pass on to you, because I love you." As he talked I saw the midmorning sun brighten the green and yellow cornstalks and change them magically into men of straw, leaf-curled figures dried out and blown even by a widow's mite of a wind. Mr. Randolph, our hog, the cornfields, and what I didn't quite understand then, a bull's lust—these three mysteries provided most of our food and livelihood. I knew we would dig and till the soil, care for our stock, and even seek the Lord, but at that moment, boy though I was, I realized that God might not always be good to us.

We passed by the hog pen, the slop bucket half-full and the ground muddy. I grunted at Mr. Randolph, who was as always fatter than the day before, and stood by that hog pen as my father spoke again. "Second Chronicles. 'And he sought God in the days of Zechariah, who had understanding in the visions of God: and as long as he sought the Lord, God made him to prosper.'" Then we heard. Mother was screaming. We stood frozen. We had heard her raise her voice, fighting with Will. But we had never heard her scream.

Will's latest rebellion had begun innocently enough. As the eldest, Will had inherited King Solomon's portion of responsibility, teaching his kid brother to split wood, hammer and nail, paint, feed the hog, plant, bale hay, weed, shell pecans, and harvest the peaches, but even though seventeen he was still about as free as a swaddled babe. He'd been out Saturday night, and Mother was worried he'd been dancing, and if he'd been dancing, then he'd been drinking, and if he'd been drinking, then he'd probably been up to something worse. Mother had tried to reason with him, give him a choice, she said, but Lucifer is Lucifer and lust is lust, truths she had not admitted to herself until that Monday morning. Maybe she had a premonition about his womanizing. After he came back from the errands in Wedowee and strolled into the kitchen, she waited until my sister, Belle, lugged the wash out. Then she turned from the sink and confronted him.

"Will."

"Yes'm."

"Do you need to talk with your father?"

He was flippant, as usual. "He preaches enough now. Why should I talk with him?"

"You know what I mean?"

He occupied himself with a stray kitchen knife, refusing to look up at her.

"Do you need to talk with your father about getting a girl in trouble . . . or about disease?"

Whatever skirts Will had chased, with an upbringing like we got, he felt guilty enough without her asking. Her sudden words sounded like God's condemnation of his soul, which Will never took gracefully. He yanked a kitchen chair from the table and heaved it across the room and kicked the door. "Goddamn you, Mother, leave me alone!"

Now in 1941, in Randolph County, Alabama, a curse meant something. Curses were rare, they were words that still possessed power, they conjured a vision of hell and fiery destruction before the Lord. Mother sagged against a chair, almost fainting from the sacrilege and disrespect of his words and from their sudden anger.

But my mother was not a madonna, nor a southern belle with the vapors. She was a farm woman. She quickly collected herself and untied her apron, threw it on the floor, and marched right up to him, slapped him across the face and grabbed his ears. "Young man, you don't talk like that to your mother!" she shouted as she twisted his ear. He didn't move. She could never make him admit pain. "You sit yourself right down here, Mr. Man-about-town, you've got a lesson to learn.

We can't let such words fall from the mouth of a son of mine."

She pointed to her chair. At seventeen he really had no choice but to sit down and he knew it, especially with the Dark Ages temper his father had. She rammed a bar of soap into his mouth and rubbed it on his tongue and broke it into pieces on his teeth. "You never talk like that again, son. God should cut out your tongue."

The lye tasted dry and sticky, with an aftertaste of ashes. He tried not to swallow, and for a moment he thought he'd vomit. Puke came to his throat, but he swallowed it, and with it bits of soap as vile as spoiled milk. He choked, which made her stop, righteously triumphant, but he could tell it was just because her arm was tired. He would get her. He hated her with love's passion. She might treat him like a child, but he would give her no pleasure in it. He stood up, suddenly knowing the worst he could say, looked down on her and spoke as calmly as he could. "Are you finished, whore?"

It worked. That her son, her eldest, after he had been defiling himself with lewd creatures, should call his own mother . . . She started screaming.

Hearing my mother scream harrowed my very being. I was only a fourteen-year-old boy, and her awful screaming tore through me like the sound of pharaoh's chariots. My father and Doug ran ahead of me, and I shouted after them and followed with a vision in my mind of my precious mother tortured by some unknown convulsion, her hands white on her stomach and sweat around her eyes. Belle ran around the corner of the house. Dad jumped onto the porch at the same moment Will swaggered out.

"What's wrong?" Dad was breathless.

"It's her mating call, I guess."

In a moment my father burst back out of the house, fists clenched, eyes narrow and dark. Will did not run. In that whole county, sometimes I think over the whole face of this dry-bones dusty earth, Will's unthinking temper was bested by only one person—my father. Indeed they were too much alike. Neither saints nor blackguards can abide each other's close company.

Dad grabbed Will by the collar and dragged him toward the hog pen. Mother followed, her face tear-streaked. Mr. Randolph squealed and scurried to the other side of the pen as Dad flung Will into the mud, then knelt and grabbed the back of his son's neck and rammed the boy's face into the slop

bucket. Broken, half-chewed, dripping corncobs plopped into
the mud, and a pink gruel of kitchen garbage rushed up Will's
taut neck and stuck on my father's hand like fresh vomit. The
hog stink was murderous. Doug and I held each other. "Filth,
Will, your life is stinking filth! Don't ever speak to your
mother like that again!" He jerked Will's head from side to
side like a clapper in a bell bucket. Some slop stuck in Will's
hair. The rest spilled into the mud.

"Enough, Robert," Mother said.

"Sin." Dad turned to her with unseeing eyes. But he let go.

Will rolled onto his butt and then collapsed like a wounded
soldier in the mud, staring through the mess at the sky. For
one suspended moment the bucket teetered on its edge and
then it fell over, empty. Dad rested on his hands and knees,
and Mother stood above them, guilt-stricken. Doug, Belle,
and I waited for speech, for some word that would restore
us, for a simple sign that would release us from our frozen,
silent fear. But nothing. The sickly pink slop sat on Will's
face. I expected to see worms crawl toward his ears. Yet his
blank eyes denied knowledge of his condition. I wanted to run
to him and wipe his face clean and wash him human again,
but I dared not touch his humiliation or walk in front of my
kneeling father. Then Will began to cough and spit, to come
alive again, and with each rasp his eyes started to burn like
torches, suddenly remembering what had happened to him
and who was responsible for the filth on his face and in his
nose and mouth. He had never suffered a moment so humiliating. He was gasping with rage. He jumped up, stared at Dad,
spat into the mud next to him, and ran past us toward the
house.

"Will, honey," Mother said, repentant. "Let me tend you."
But he stormed on without answering and slammed the door
behind him, to lock himself in his room. "Robert, Robert," she
said.

Dad pushed himself up and slung the mud off his hands. "I
shouldn't have," he said. "I let my anger get away."

With their words we finally felt we could move again, that
slowly our lives and their safe habits would, God willing, return to us.

Belle whispered to me, "I thought he'd kill him."

Doug walked over to Mr. Randolph and scratched the hog's
head.

"We can't let him sass," Dad said.

"But the soap and then—"

"It was too much. Yes, it was too much. I will tell him that soon enough, when he calms down and gets control of his senses."

But then two shots exploded in the house. My stomach came to my mouth. Quicker than any of us could scream or finish our thought—*he's killed*—the front door shattered into splinters and Will stood in the yard, my father's shotgun uncocked and smoking, two shells in his hand poised over the open barrels. He dropped the sixteen-gauge shells in, clicked the chamber closed, and looked up at us.

"Will, what's wrong with you, son? Put that away this second," Mother said, pointing at him.

Any sorrow Dad felt he now repented of. His hands began to open and close into fists, fists begging to bend the shotgun's steel around his profligate son's neck. But the hidden parts of my father's mind and soul must have known that his first son had inherited from him at least one affliction—anger at the world. Such anger was not safe, even among blood kin. So he stood still and let Mother try to talk sense into the boy.

Will slowly walked toward us with the gun pointed at our heads. Those eyes were not his own.

"Get control of yourself," Mother continued in a quieter voice. "Think of what you're doing. We're sorry, honey, but we love you. We only want to do what is right in God's eyes. You can understand that, can't you?"

But he kept walking toward us, steady and slow. Doug carefully stepped around the pen and stood in front of Mother. Watching him, and without really knowing what I was doing, I stood in front of Belle, even though she was two years older than I. I will never forget Will's eyes. The silence of the moment felt eternal, longer than any space of time I can remember, longer than any space of time I can imagine. I said to myself, "Bless the name of God in heaven," when Will stepped right past us, and on and past the pen, straight into the near cornfield, on and over the stalks like a suicidal warrior charging the Philistines. The cornstalks tried to stand back up, but half-bent and torn they seemed signs of our family's slaughtered, piled-up bodies in rigor mortis. None of us moved. We were ashamed of our fear that a son and a brother might shoot, but still thankful we were alive.

Dad didn't turn around to watch Will. He stood with his shoes sunk in the humiliating mud, his fists still white as bones and his eyes staring blindly ahead. When he had punished Will and listened to Mother's sorrow, he had struggled with his contrary soul. But when this rebellious Lucifer challenged him again, I saw in that set face and sure hands a newfound, singular will. I knew he would not listen now. He pulled his feet from the loud-sucking mud and marched directly in Will's path, trampling each bent cornstalk with Will's same blind vengeance. We ran after them.

Will stomped toward Job like an ancient soldier phalanx-trained to march straight and fearless into the enemy line, filling in the gaps. Dad followed him with the same savagely even pace, as if he were the second wave and the enemy were common to both. Mother hurried ahead with Doug. I knew we were ruined. Our house divided, our farm destroyed, our lives split apart forever.

"Stop, Will!" Mother shouted. "Stop it right now. You've got to get hold of yourself."

When Will burst from the cornfield, the cows loped away from him as soon as he came within twenty yards, but the new bull, Job, from some unknown instinct as possessed and dumb as Will's and Dad's, stood ground. Job had not been doing his duty for more than a week, though blessed with six wives, and now he suddenly faced a crazed boy charging him with a gun. Job hesitated, then at the last moment leaped and came toward Will, who jammed the barrel ends into the bull's eyes and pulled both triggers. Job never even touched Will: the shot blasted the bull's face to the side of his shoulders and felled him instantly dead. There was a soft flop on the grass, then an endless echoing of the double blast through the woods. Belle stopped and dropped to her knees, but I kept running. Dad and Mother and Doug stood a few feet from the bull as Will tossed the gun down and stared at the blood-splattered broken head of the great beast. His eyes were blown off his white skull and blood swam over his brains, spilled like white worms on the grass. Will turned to Dad with tears in his eyes.

My father's rage, like Will's, was blind, but unlike Will's, unspent. He reached down to the ground and grabbed the smoking hot barrels of the gun. Will stood above the ruin of our family silently watching him and waiting. Mother cried out, "No, Robert!"—but she was too late. Dad lifted the gun by the barrels, its heat scorching his hands, and clubbed his son in the head.

* * *

What happened on the road to Damascus? A man named Saul journeyed there gripping letters to the synagogue asking for help in his personal quest to stone sons of the way. He walked on the King's Highway almost 150 miles past the sea of Galilee, with the taste of dust in his mouth, dust that tasted of death. Christians ask the world to believe that a blinding light and a voice converted him.

Why Saul? Why did this particular man become the apostle of Christianity? Not, as the prophets might suggest, because he was a good man who observed the law, nor because he was a bad man who observed the law. It was the anger in his soul, the anger at life, an anger that filled him with radiance as he watched the stones break skin and soon crush Stephen's skull, an anger that allowed him to lap up the blood of a martyr with his righteous tongue. But later, in the horrific darkness after the voice and the light, his companions had to lead him by the hand to Damascus. Christians argue that Saul's murderous anger was stripped to nothing, into which God could move with a new soul, the one of love, the one Christians call Saint Paul.

By the time Doug fetched Dr. Brown, Dad had disappeared. No one mentioned it. While Doug and Belle stood outside the bedroom door, I walked through the shattered doorway to the porch and saw Dad just as he wandered into the woods. We were to keep compresses on Will's head, Dr. Brown said, to wake him up every so often and not to move him; he would do just as well here with my mother as at the county hospital. And it was just too dangerous to move him to Atlanta. Will should be in and out of consciousness, he continued, more than likely all right in a few days, more than likely undamaged. But, yes, there was a chance he might die—a slim one; and a greater chance—still slim, though—that he might have brain damage. "And Mattie," he said as he left, "I pray God has not turned his mercy from Robert Treadwell."

Mother didn't answer. All night she waited by the bed.

Staying awake as long as I could sit up in my father's bedroom chair, I listened to the wind lament the empty doorway. Somewhere in my soul I feared for Dad as much as for Will. I prayed silently to God that He would restore blood unto my brother and watch over my father, who had lost himself in the wilderness; and that once Will and Dad were all right, He would help us to follow His commandments forever. But as I fell asleep, in my memory I saw six cows and I named them— Eve, Hagar, Gomorrah, Jezebel, Babylon, Baalah—all widows now, easing toward Job, their dumb eyes full of wailing. And I saw purple bruises coming from Will's left temple across his face, like an angel of death passing in the night.

The next morning I awoke in my own bed. I quickly began to dress so I could check on Will: sleep had not made me forget. Through the window, however, I saw Dad coming up the red road. With burnt hands, he pushed a wheelbarrow full of dead leaves, twigs, and pine straw. Again and again, for the next day and a half, he would push that wheelbarrow along the clay road from the forest to the house, his head bobbing up over the bare hill first, followed by his sweat-stained shirt and his burdened soul. The hump of kindling in the wheelbarrow strewed its leaves into the wind and over the road behind him like a trail of Israel's palm branches. Every time at the curve between the barn and the front yard, he set the handles down and tipped the wheelbarrow up on its front lip until most of the tinder fell out. He jerked the wheelbarrow away from the pile and with a shovel spread the leaves and twigs and straw into a mat across the road. Then he disappeared back into the wilderness.

This first time I saw him, on the morning after, I wanted to scamper outside because he was alive and had not run away. Strange how even at that age I worried he'd one day run away. I could grab his arm, hug it, and tell him that everything would be all right now: Will would live, we'd find another bull, and all of us would live happily. But just as I buckled my belt, I stopped. The worn black line across the brown leather at the hole where I fastened the buckle looked like the bruises worn across my brother's face.

I looked back through the window and saw the strain in my father's forearms and the disregard for his hands, the focus in his dark eyes, and the meticulous care he devoted to the mat he began to spread across the road. His suffering through these details did not gain my sympathy. They were suspect. This man, my pathetic father, had clubbed my brother in the head. It could have been myself. Or Doug. My father had tried to kill his own son. And suddenly I felt like killing him.

The night before, leaves had blown in through the doorway and scattered over the wet floor. I stepped over them and into my parents' bedroom. Will lay with his head to the side, eyes closed, but his bruised white face was turned toward Mother, who sat in a stiff-backed chair beside his pillow, sponging his face with a washcloth and rubbing his bare wrist as if the cool wet rag might somehow heal the wounds of his distant mind. The skin was puffed up under her red eyes, their blood lines like the jagged edges of the broken leaves. Belle knitted in Dad's chair.

"Dad's outside," I said.

"Yes."

"How's Will?"

Mother looked up at me. I was not sure she knew me. "He's been awake."

She seemed rigid and strange, unconcerned with my life. For a moment I hated Will, too. What was happening to me? I left, and spent most of the morning watching my father on his knees as he spread the kindling into a mat, or easing back into the bedroom to see my semiconscious brother and remote mother. All of us simply waited and watched, as still as the wet leaves on the floor.

The afternoon of the next day, the sawing began, like hissing out and in through clenched teeth, at two dissonant pitches, or like the anguished heartbeat of an exiled Judas. When he was satisfied with the mat of kindling, Dad pushed his wheelbarrow into the barn and returned with two sawhorses cradled under his arms and his leather-strapped toolbox slung over his shoulder. Then from the woodpile he lugged long, nail-scarred boards. He popped the nails out of the wood with the hammer claw, measured and cut the first long slab, and started sawing boards to match it, the two-pitched hissing drifting across the yard and fading into acceptance. From a distance Dad looked as sick as Will. He had not eaten since the blow, nor shaved, and if he had slept, it was on a pine-needle forest floor. Belle carried some country ham and biscuits to him, but he didn't recognize her, he only sawed, with the slow, numbing strokes of raw hands. She left his plate by the toolbox.

Later on Belle came from the bedroom and told us that Will had been awake for a while, didn't remember a single blow but could take soup. Mother said we were to sweep the floor, change the sheets on every bed, polish any silver and brass in the house, and scrub down the kitchen. She didn't mention the door.

An hour later I was bent over my bed when the sawing

stopped. My heart shuddered for a moment and at first I
didn't know why. Something had happened: it was the silence.
The cut ends of the six slabs across the sawhorses glistened in
the sunlight, and the sawdust speckling Dad's arms and piled
at his feet sparkled like fresh snow. He stacked the miraculously clean boards neatly beside the mat. I thought then that
he planned to build a hut with a twig-and-leaf floor, maybe
even a thatched roof, and live in penance away from us, like a
hermit. Doug left the brass-polishing and joined me on the
porch to watch.

The construction took two more hours, until the blue in the
sky began to darken into a muted sunset. First Dad picked
four boards about nine feet long and a half-foot wide. Then he
hammered and nailed an L-shaped piece on the ground next to
the mat, the angle of the two boards right and level and the
long nails flush into the wood. He secured most of the uneven
slabs across the square so that he made a platform, but then he
lifted one end and dropped it on the mat. A few leaves flew up
in the air and then circled down again as if in despair. Now it
was the base of a square box. He made three more squares like
the first, pulled them on top of the base and fastened them
with diagonal nail cuts from the fourth and top sideslab to the
third, the third to the second, and second to first. The height
then was about half the width. He didn't even step back to
admire his handiwork, though. He carried his toolbox into the
barn and for the second night walked down the red road into
the woods.

Doug and I looked at each other. "A cow pen?" he said.

"Can't get in it."

"Who knows?" He picked up the plate of ham and biscuits
and tossed them into Mr. Randolph's pen. "Here," he said,
"eat a little of yourself, ol' boy."

When I awoke the next morning, Dad was sawing from the
center of the top board down to the floor, and then again, a
parallel cut, so that he knocked out a wide entrance to the
square pen, which now, as Doug had guessed, appeared to be
an animal cage. Then he perched four of our brass candlesticks on the edges, one on each side, as if his work were somehow holy. He must have stolen the candlesticks out of the
house while we were asleep. Leaning against the oak tree was
the shotgun. Beside it stood a kerosene can. As I dressed I

thought that the blow he'd delivered had damaged his son's brain less than it had damaged his own.

I sleepily stumbled to my parents' bedroom and, when I knocked, recognized in the tone of my mother's voice the love that for the two days previous I'd thought was lost. Doug and Belle stood at the end of the bed, smiling at Will, who moved his eyes to me as he opened and closed his hands. Like my mother's voice, his eyes were his own and they knew me. Thank God they knew me.

"Won't Dr. Brown be surprised?" Mother said. "Luke, come over here, honey, and look at your big brother. Doesn't he look good? Why, in a few days he'll be up and at 'em, feeding the cows and tending the—and . . . well, eatin' more vittles than I can cook." Mother slipped her arm around my waist as I came to her bedside chair. I so longed for everything to be all right then, for our family to be restored and for life and love in all of us. Will's eyes moved indeed, watery but knowledgeable, and thankful. He tried to push himself up in the bed but grimaced and stopped, then touched the bandage on his head.

"A little while yet, son. You've got to go slow."

Will took her hand, slid it up his chest, and kissed it. He whispered "Mother," which moved her to cry, so sleepless she was. For that simple moment it seemed all was not lost.

But one more time. It was another shotgun blast. At the end of those three days, one more insane act sounded like a trumpet call announcing that my father would never for the rest of our lives allow such simple, pure moments. Another shotgun blast.

Mother looked up at Doug. "He does not have the courage to kill himself," she said. "You go. I've had enough."

I could not believe her words. She called Belle back as Doug and I scurried to the porch to see the mystery solved, in the broken face of a hog. As Dad dragged him by his stiffening legs, Mr. Randolph's blood-splattered face stared at us with vacant horror. We were farm boys raised on the rightful murder of animals, for man has dominion over the beasts of the field. But this was cruel, unexpected slaughter. With a sixteen-gauge shotgun. And to me, feeding Mr. Randolph corn and scratching his muddy pink head had made him a pet. Seeing his mangled face with its shocked dumb eyes killed me. I truly hated my father then. He was no savior and he was no prophet, only a sinner, and I wanted nothing to do with him.

Some of Dad's strength was gone, so he had to jerk and tug the carcass inch by inch to the mat. As he pushed Mr. Randolph through the pen's opening, the broken snout folded back under the wood like a split-open hose and blood spurted from the hog's head and throat into the pen. Dad reached down and lifted the snout over the floorboard and then pushed the hog into his contraption. Blood and brains covered his hands. He stared at his hands, and then let loose a long, anguished cry.

"Why persecutest thou me!"

Doug and I stood on the porch. Dad walked around the pen wiping his bloody hands on the wood and muttering, "Yes, yes, I know. It is hard to kick against the pricks." Then he stepped to the tree and unscrewed the cap of the kerosene can. He poured the fuel over the mat surrounding the pen and shook the rest onto the carcass and bloody, brain-covered floor. From his pants pocket he pulled a long kitchen match, struck it on the bottom of his shoe, and tossed it toward the mat, its flare falling like a comet into the stitched leaves and twigs. For a moment silence reigned. Then, with the loud whoosh of a gas heater, the flame ignited into a holocaust. The whole earth seemed afire. The crackles and knocks of the blaze shocked my heart. Mother and Belle hurried out to the porch, stunned silent before the suffocating blanket of heat and the burning sky. Dad, by the tree, stared into the center of the fire. We watched and waited. In the air soon breathed the sweetest smell.

2

Christians believe, from the Old Testament's story of Abraham and Isaac and from the New Testament's God and Jesus of Nazareth, that fathers sacrifice their sons out of love. This idea is false. I don't know why Abraham strapped his boy to a primitive altar, but I do know that he had another son, older and darker, against whom he turned an unloving, deaf ear as he sent him into sacrificial exile. Since he didn't cast Ishmael out because of love, I also have to question his motivation with Isaac. And the story of Christ—what love was there in that slaughter? If God did indeed love Jesus, wouldn't the Christian thing to do have been to die instead for His son?

In four days Will was well enough to stay on his feet. While the old man went to Wedowee to lose our ruined farm back to the bank, Will packed a burlap bag, dressed himself in his Sunday suit, and called the four of us to the kitchen. Will sat Mother down and explained that since he was a week from his eighteenth birthday and was going to be drafted anyway as far as he could judge, he'd just as soon leave right away; he could send her money from the marines. Given what had happened between him and his father, surely she understood. Belle immediately tried to talk him out of his decision, but her tears and pleading could not persuade him to stay—he wasn't going to listen to reason.

Mother surprised us. Anticipating him, I assume when she lay sleepless during his recovery, she had decided that leaving might indeed be the best solution. If he didn't bring the subject up, she would. It might save the family—splitting the two Samsons for a while. She still had three at home and she could no longer control Will. Besides, like most people, she didn't think we would actually enter the war. So she said yes, you're right, go on—quickly now.

And he did. I couldn't believe it. He stood up, saying, "I've got to catch the bus then."

"There's no use—" Belle began.

"None," he said, interrupting her. He wanted to keep the final scene short, but Belle fell into his arms, where she stayed for the longest time, sobbing. He stroked her hair and whispered into her ear, but nothing he said calmed her grief. When she finally pulled herself away, he turned to Mother, who was waiting for him. Their strong embrace forgot her role in his awful humiliation. They held each other fearfully, like two innocents who stood alone against the legion of devils out in the world, and inside my father.

In the yard Will took Doug and me aside. "It won't be long," he said, shaking Doug's hand and then mine. "While I'm gone, you two take care of Mother, you hear?" He tugged on Doug's hair as he admonished us. And then we waved goodbye as he walked down the road to the highway. None of us cared what Dad would say when he came home—perhaps he expected it, too. Fighting off my tears, I hurried inside, stunned by how quickly he had decided to go. A moment before he disappeared around the curve in the clay road, I turned to see his figure through the window, still a strong youth, setting off, one lucky son who had escaped the old man, at least for a while. One day, I decided, I would follow.

Will's enlistment not only kept our family tentatively together, with the old man still the head, but also gave that Judas an unobstructed campground on which to test the evangelical spirit that struck him in the woods. That vision—he himself said it was like the blinding light that smote Paul on the road to Damascus and that it led him to build his little bonfire—from then on kept bursting into our lives with an inexorable vengeance. He didn't drag us on the road to tent after tent, but we did say goodbye to his family in Wedowee, and with a loan from one of his brothers we became tenant farmers in Cusseta, one county to the south.

Tenant farmers. The very idea was insufferable to my mother. Her history explains. Her mother had died when she was young. Her father then married a virago, who persecuted my mother and her sister until one day they ran away to their grandparents, who, against their son-in-law's will, kept the girls. These grandparents—the Kings—were immensely proud people, Cleburne County farmers who had slaved their way out of poverty to own their land and their animals. My mother was given the same landowner's dream and was taught the same work ethic and the same pride. She thought death was better than tenant farming. But it was all we could do—a small cabin on the Ray farm in Cusseta.

For all the swallowed pride and energy that Mother gave to keeping the family together and starting over, my father gave none. He was convinced he had been struck by God, but he had been given no direction, no instructions to set off to Nineveh or to cross the Red Sea. His only solace was that the Bible said Paul spent three years in the desert before he reappeared as the greatest of evangelists. Dad was not able to say to himself, "I know what His will in my life is, and I am going to evangelize." But he did evangelize, eventually, and like every other evangelist I know and the biblical fathers Dad so often spoke of, he sought out the innocent. In doing so, he brought down upon our house for the rest of our days on Earth a curse as hard as the Benjamite's stones, and as dry as the bones of dead dogs.

His first campground was a schoolhouse. When the Cusseta schoolmarm up and married in September, Dad volunteered to take her place. As a young man, before he met Mother, he had actually studied for a teacher's certificate in Cleburne County. He was able to add and subtract and recite enough chapters of the Bible to impress the other men in town, who only knew a few verses, which they could declaim but not write. He still did some of the tenant farmer's work before and after school, but he gladly let most of the chores fall on Mother and us.

He had other matters to attend to.

Dad was waiting to charge our souls for Christ. In the fall he concentrated on what was expected of a one-room schoolteacher—the three R's, plus moral instruction and heavy-handed discipline—but all the time he was watching us for signs. Soon we gave him reason to hope: we were fourteen-year-old boys who spent most of our waking hours dreaming, ripening our imaginations every day.

By early October Doug had discovered in the vast wilder-

ness around Cusseta a secret place where we could escape
after chores. He quickly led me upcreek from old Fort Cusseta
(Horseshoe Bend is forty miles away), leaping over fallen trees
and weaving through the vine-strapped seedlings and honey-
suckle until coming to a rare clearing between two branches
that flowed into the Osinappa. The branches made a peninsula of the level ground, and the one side accessible by land
turned toward the thickest reach of the forest. Magnificent
beeches and tulip poplars—they were giants—arose from the
banks of the circling waters. High above the clearing, their
dwindling leaves stitched before the sun a green-gold, trans-
parent ceiling, sheltering the hideaway and infusing it with its
own special light, and the fallen tulips spread over the ground
like a Halloween bed of candy corn. It was our own place,
where we could give play to our imaginations. "Here," my
twin brother said in his best Indian warrior's voice, "we'll
meet here by the giant trees that climb to the sky of our an-
cestors. Here we will council against the white man. Here we
will know our courage."

Each afternoon we stole away, readying ourselves for our
surprise attack on Fort Cusseta. Young braves, we knew, must
prove themselves before the elders of the tribe, so Doug imagined three blood-brother trials. First and simplest, we had to
keep secret. Indians knew the value of surprise and the curse
of a loose tongue. After I cut my initials, Doug carved his into
the beech bark with his Buck knife. With our hands locked
over each other's wrist, we swore eternal secrecy. And then
between the initials he scratched a broken arrow and said, "So
we will never forget what will happen if we break this sacred
vow."

Then we had to prove we could survive in the woods. I don't
remember what excuse we managed, but we slept overnight
and built a fire to keep the animals away. In the morning
when I woke up, Doug knelt next to me, staring far into my
eyes. Then he opened his hand. Five berries curled in his
palm, red and violet beads.

"Wait a second," I said. "They could be poisonous."

"Courage," he said.

"But why?"

"It is our only food."

Like a fool I ate, playing the game, but I was sure that any
moment the wine of the berries would kill me. Doug popped
his five into his mouth and, grinning, chewed them as he
pinned his hazel gaze onto my worried face: the world could

not poison him, his eyes said. We lived, and then boasted to ourselves that we young braves could survive in the woods forever.

Third and finally, we had to show Crazy Horse daring. Every afternoon at the bend in the branch, a sleepy water moccasin, ready for winter, emerged and slid onto a wet flat rock to sun his copper body. He curled into a brown, slack circle, the yellow edge of his soft underbelly glistening in the light. He was our last trial. If we could grab him behind the head, then his fangs couldn't get us and we could sacrifice him to our mission.

We stood behind the clearing's side of the beeches, downstream from him, then tiptoed in chorus to another pair of trees, waited, and moved again, until we reached unseen the silent white tree trunks by the water. The snake didn't know we stared at him. As he watched the sleeping moccasin, Doug's eyes burned with a fire intent on consuming it, without regard for its quick strike. We were so near, I could see the yellow skin around the mouth of its flat head lying still in the middle of this brown curl of venom. Waiting beneath those lips, the forked tongue could strike us like lightning.

Suddenly Doug leaped—headfirst toward the rocks. I saw the quick flick of the black tongue. Doug's knuckles cracked against the rocks and his face sunk into the mud as the snake darted away and swam under a submerged tree root. I pulled my brother from the water by his feet, all the time watching that root for the moccasin to come after us, until I could lean Doug against the tree trunk. He was stunned, but there were no marks.

When I washed his face, he looked at me, panting, and said, "I wanted you to cut the *X*, brother, and suck out the poison."

I gladly gave up snake-daring for the fort. Doug never let our failure to milk the moccasin drown his imagination. With the Buck knife he drew plans for the attack in the dirt and crushed pokeberries into a bowl of war paint, which he gooped under our eyes and in wavy chicken scratches over our ribs. We whooped and hollered in a dancing circle and then darted tree by tree toward Fort Cusseta. At the creek we crawled behind a stand of rocks and spied the hundred-year-old rotting barricade, in our imagination populating the jagged, crumbling four-foot walls with sleeping Indian warriors. Doug motioned me downstream for my rear action, while he would charge over the front and take their fire. We locked hands over our wrists in mortal love, and then he scampered away. I didn't move but watched him dart across the creek, his quick body gliding over the rocks and through the air of what he had created, the absolutely certain presence, for himself and now for me, of a fort and a forest, the people within them and the Buck knife and war-paint trail of courage.

After I reached the downstream end of the fort, I peeped over a rock and gave the long, descending call of a screech owl. A whippoorwill answered. Then I counted to fifteen and just as I slipped up to the wall I heard his vicious shriek. As I hurdled the wall, I saw him astride the other one, whooping and filling the hot air with singing arrows and skull-crunching tomahawks. One hand beat his chest with each shot while the other fired the stone-smooth weapons. In his sides he took the furious fire of the awakened fighters, still keeping his wounded stance above the field, daring one and all to take aim. But I was now there to turn them toward me as I whooped my way through the coonskins. One of my arrows thumped through the leader's throat. I tossed three men off my back, one of them crushing the attacker in front of me. A bullet grazed the side of my head. Finally we fought only a few feet from each other, in hand-to-hand and knife-to-knife combat with the last, strongest survivors. When we stood before each other, we screamed from the depths of our lungs and locked hands over wrists again. Quickly, before reinforcements could come, we scalped our prizes and took off, leaping the walls and racing through the vines and trees toward our secret clearing up-creek. I was exhausted, but the glory exhilarated me.

Then, just as we reached the tallest beech tree, I saw Doug grab his side, fling his head back, and fall, rolling through the leaves over and over and over again until he stopped, under the broken arrow, facedown in the crook of his right arm, his left arm slung straight ahead, palm up. "Doug!" I shouted, tumbling down beside him on my knees. I turned him over. He tossed his arms to his sides and kept his eyes closed, his chest heaving from the run.

"I'm dying."

"Doug!"

"I didn't tell you." He swallowed, struggling for breath and final words. "They got me . . . one too many. I'm dying, Luke . . . I'm dying."

I combed the wet stringy hair off his forehead while streams of sweat rolled from his red, exalted face onto his arm. A line of beads gathered along his lip, and his throat beat his heart's pulse. His breathing was hard. This imaginary death made his eyes and exhausted face seem beatific, from the sinews of his heart to the sweat on his brow.

"You'll be all right."

"No, I'm dying, I tell you." He lifted his head toward me for a moment, but it fell back to the ground, his hands on his chest. "Water."

I stumbled to the creek and cupped cool water to bring him. But with my back to him I drank first and then let the water leak through my parted fingers as I knelt there, wondering.

I felt stupid and dull. Should I have chosen to die, too? I'd never even thought of it, certain no number of coonskins could overpower me. But Doug's imagination was richer than mine. If how he lived had to be heroic, then so did how he died. He was attracted to the drama in death, for this final sweet goodnight he pulled off did indeed climax all of it—the secrecy, the poison berries, the war council, and the attack.

I hurried back, my hands folded as if I held a butterfly. He raised his head and drank as much as he could, but most of the water ran down his quivering chin. "One last request," he whispered.

"Anything."

He dropped his hand from his chest to the ground, reached to his side, and unsheathed his Buck knife. He lifted the brown handle toward me.

"Yes."

"The X, like the . . ."

I wrapped my hand around his forearm and gathered his wrist to me, but he pulled it back. His eyes were closed when he said, "You first."

I turned my left wrist toward me and stared at the blood veins far beneath my skin, small blue creeks etched on the map inside me, where I never dreamed of going.

"Even after I die," he said, "you will feel me live."

I touched the point of the blade to my wrist. It didn't cut. I tried sawing, but my skin folded under the cold steel. The fear still kept me. So I swung the handle straight up and drove the point down. A sharp sting shocked me. For a moment I thought I had cut my hand off. Then I looked down. A drop swelled around the point like red ink on paper. The circle widened until a stream flowed off my arm. I felt dizzy and too warm inside, but I pulled his arm to me and quickly cut an X in his wrist, the blood from the deep slashes running down toward his elbow. He didn't grimace, but raised his wrist toward mine and opened his eyes.

"Brothers," he said.

I set my cut into his and felt the warm flow of his blood into mine, our foolish selves forever met in the flesh.

3

Our favorite recess game at school was paddlecat. The ball was rubber, its surface so nicked by the paddle and fingernails and the bark of the pecan trees in deep right field that its flight could not always be trusted. The last schoolteacher's paddle, with a few more holes carved into it for speed, served as the bat. At fourteen Doug and I were the oldest kids in school and so we always balanced the teams out.

One January afternoon, contrary to his usual practice, my father the schoolteacher stood and watched us play. We didn't mind the cold at all, not when we were playing paddlecat.

We had time for only a five-inning game, and after four the score was tied 13–13. Doug and I were responsible for twenty-four of the twenty-six runs; both of us had hit for the cycle. In the top of the last inning, with one out and three men on base, I pounded the ball from the schoolhouse plate clear over the orchard, past the point of the right fielder's even considering it. I doubt the Babe himself could have hit the ball an inch farther. I laughed all the way 'round, even danced a little jig on either side of third base before I touched it. I was so confident my team had it in the bag that I told the next boy to make an intentional out so we could be sure to play the inning before recess was called. My father, though, looked intent on seeing the game through to the end.

In the bottom of the inning, the other team immediately scored a run on three consecutive singles, but followed their success with two quick outs. Doug was on deck, so we had a chance to win it before he could bat. But an error loaded the bases, and after waiting through three intentionally bad pitches, Doug hit the ball out of sight; I suspect he hit it even farther than I did.

After scampering past third, however, Doug ran in place in front of home plate, where our team had positioned our youngest, most awkward and pathetic player, Timmy Lee, a short kid with bifocals and big feet. Two of Doug's teammates—Ricky Smith and John Bob Brown—ran from behind the welcoming committee at home plate and tried to push Doug toward the black-and-white pentagon, but he shrugged them off and kept running in place, with this unearthly grin from ear to ear.

"Come on, Doug, score!"

"Pigface, Doug—you're a pigface!"

"Knock it off, Doug—don't give it to 'em."

But he did. He waited for the three-man relay—that was how far he hit it—until the sorry little catcher firmly held the ball. Then he slid into Timmy Lee's tag, presenting the boy with his greatest lifetime thrill, a heroic, game-ending play.

For all of the fall and the first part of the winter, as the rivers of childhood ran through Doug's veins, Dad had slowly watched and waited to see if his view was as God promised. I don't know when he determined that God had pledged him a fellow prophet for a son—perhaps in the woods during his vision. Perhaps sometime in the fall, while he was waiting for God's directions, Dad saw in my twin, and not in me, an overflowing love for people like Timmy Lee, an innocence about the ways of the world, and a remarkable imagination the secret Indian games only whetted—three testimonials to the prophet's current in Doug's blood. Dad had never openly consented to the conventional religious life of Cusseta—Sunday School, Training Union, ice cream socials, revivals—but Mother still insisted and he didn't object, waiting in his desert for the propitious moment to introduce the true religion.

That afternoon after Timmy Lee's heroics, the first week in January, he asked Doug to stay after school. Doug sat in the green pew that faced my father's platformed desk, his reader and notebook in his lap. The sun behind him shone on my father's face and cast his shadow against the corner blackboard. Dad turned in his chair. On his desk two gray metal bookends framed a primer, six *McGuffey's* readers, and an Alabama Institute farming handbook. Flat on his desk lay his thick, worn Bible, and in his hand he fidgeted with a ruler that underneath the inches quoted the Golden Rule.

"Put your books down, son."

Doug set them beside him and sat up, worried that Dad was finally going to chastise him for our cut wrists. But Dad kept silent, simply measuring Doug with his eyes.

"You know it speaks in your blood?"

Doug hesitated. "Sir?"

He turned the ruler in his hand. "Some are born to it."

Dad was giving his fourteen-year-old son's dumbness words. Just as my father had yet to find a way to tell himself he was an evangelist, Doug had not said to himself, "Doug, you are different, you have an imagination, you are willing to wager your imagination against the real world, you are born to a special life." If Dad had not spoken to Doug at that age, life's deceits and the natural human defense that shuts away risk taking might have interfered and withstood the evangelical spirit and saved him. But my father didn't want him to withstand.

"Here." He handed Doug his Bible and gave him his first assignment. "Isaiah. The burning coal. The chariot."

And that was all he said.

Doug took it from there. He read Isaiah three consecutive times, and to give himself a break read Ezekiel and Revelation before returning to Isaiah at the beginning of the spring, when he gave up paddlecat for good. There were, of course, other ramifications for his fellow students, but giving up paddlecat disturbed us most of all, for there was nothing as bad as a lopsided paddlecat game. I tried for a while, batting my weak side, righty, but I was still older and stronger and my side always won going away. Then I pitched to both sides, grooving the ball into everyone's wheelhouse and simply listening to the frenzied screaming and life-or-death arguments. Some bolder kids tried to taunt Doug back with cries of "pansy," "sissy-wissy," and "preacher man." Ricky Smith kept up his chorus of vulgar accusations, trying to get him angry enough to show us, but Doug paid no attention to Smith or any of the others and they got bored with it. Soon I quit, too, and wandered after him out to the orchard, where he read during recess, and sat against a nearby tree.

When the Bible was not on his lap, he seemed a simple daydreamer against a spotted pecan tree, with his legs arched and a half-eaten apple on his chest, his eyes roaming the clouds for figures of his imagination. But most of our free time his head bent over those onionskin pages. I could barely hear him, but I knew he mouthed out loud, as if he wanted to memorize the whole book. When he was called, then he could follow with the promise of rough places plain or the judgment to come down and sit in the dust. What figures need he imagine? He could simply lean against the tree every day or sit by the nearby waters or read the nights away under the kerosene lamp, the word of the Lord in Isaiah's voice.

The call came in June.

The early June day began with our usual ritual. (It was one week before school was out and my father's first and only experience as a teacher was completed.) After the predawn chores, we walked three miles along the Osinappa out of the forest to the railroad tracks, tiptoeing on the rails with wingspread arms. "One day I'll walk these all the way to the sea," Doug said.

"And keep right on going?"

"Why not? 'And thine ears shall hear . . .' What is it? Don't tell me. . . . 'And thine ears shall hear . . . a voice behind thee, saying, This is the way, walk ye in it.' Isaiah 30:21."

With a drowning brightness, the sunlight streamed down the hill that led from the tracks to the schoolhouse. We filed up the stairs by age, Doug and I the last and least dirty of the boys, passing my father, the teacher, who as usual left the farm later than we, in the buggy, alone, so he could finish his chores and meditate on his lesson plans, or so he told us. He greeted each child as he or she paraded into the white light billowing over our inkwell desks and the pews behind them. All of us were happier, now that school was almost over. I smiled at him and walked halfway up the aisle before I realized Doug was not right behind me.

Something was wrong. In the doorway, Dad simply rested his hand on Doug's shoulder and stared at him. Doug returned his gaze with the same firebrand intensity. They did not embrace, but the light of their eyes—I know this now in retrospect—partook of the foolish death of fear that martyrs must know when they wager together for the unseen.

"Good morning, class."

"Good morning, Mr. Treadwell."

He stepped up onto the platform that stretched across the front of the classroom, and waited, lost in his meditation on my twin brother. The sun cast his long-legged shadow across the floor to the institution-green wall. For a moment I thought he might dismiss the rest of us, but, recovering himself, he gave us the sign and we began reciting "The Lord's Prayer." Then we sang "Alabama the Beautiful" off-key. The first, second, and third grades tumbled up to the pews by his desk as the banging and chattering of the school day beginning kept up for a moment, until finally the room quieted down, as each row began its separate work.

In the back corner Doug and I were supposed to be memorizing a poem, but Doug was distracted by the way my father had greeted him and by the way something mysterious within him had responded. I tried to get Doug's attention, worrying that it wasn't healthy messing with the old man's eyes, but he kept staring out the window. Anytime Dad could look up from the first lesson, he did, studying Doug's attitude. Stalking his prey. But he did have to teach those in front of him, the sons and daughters of the people paying his salary.

"Password?" he asked. He had given a special word to each group that came forward.

"A-be-ce-darian," they answered.

After Dad explained what a chimney sweep was, Jessie Lee Chambers read from his *McGuffey's*. I had nothing better to do than listen.

" ' "Now," says he,' " Jessie Lee read.

" 'Said,' " Dad corrected.

" 'Said he,' " Jessie Lee continued, " ' "if I's take it, I's shall be a thief—and yet no b-b-body sees me. Nobody! Does not God see me? Could I ever again be good? Could I ever say my p-p . . ." ' "

Dad tried to help. "You say 'em every night."

" ' "P-p-p . . . p-p-p . . . prayers again to God?" ' " He continued reading. " ' "And what should I's do when I come to die?" ' "

" ' "I." ' "

"Sir?"

"Never mind. What is he talking about taking?" Dad asked.

"A watch." There was a chorus of answers.

"A gold watch," Martha Pearl added.

"It p-p-played pretty tunes, it did," Jessie Lee said.

"And should he take it?"

"No way, nohow," Billy answered.

"Why?"

"It's one of the Ten Commandments," Martha Pearl said.

"If you don't steal, Billy, does that mean someone will reward you?"

"No way, nohow, 'cept maybe your mommy—if'n she ever finds out."

"So if no one can see you do it, why not?"

" 'Cause God can see you," Martha Pearl answered.

"What do you mean?"

"God is like a Big Eyeball, you know. In the sky. He can see everything."

"And you know what that is, don't you?"

Billy moaned.

"A cross for Martha Pearl," Ginny said. "She always gets the crosses."

At the corner of the platform stood a blackboard on an easel, and on it Dad had chalked his own special grading book, and by each child's name he wrote either an *o* for what he called "rocks of offense" or a +, cross, for what he called "imaginations of the heart." The *o* was for misbehavior, even a misspoken word. The + was for spiritual insight. Doug led the class in crosses, going away.

Ricky Smith, who was the leader in "rocks of offense," sat in front of Doug and me. As my father got up to give Martha Pearl her cross, Ricky turned around and grinned. "Pigface," he said.

Doug sat up in the pew.

Ricky jammed his index finger up his nose, and then quickly turned around before my father could see him. Neither Doug nor I, though, would have dreamed of calling attention to Ricky Smith. He was younger than both of us. And even if he were older, I would not have because I was embarrassed, not only because my father was the teacher but because he was the fool he was, scratching on the board his stupid symbols for our stupid answers. Doug would not have pointed the boy out because he routinely forgave Ricky Smith every one of his nose-picking vulgarities.

Both of us turned away from Smith and from the group in the front and halfheartedly drilled each other on the assignment—Longfellow:

> *Trust no future, howe'er pleasant,*
> *Let the dead Past bury its dead;*

Act!—act in the living Present!
Heart within, and God o'erhead.

I stopped reciting. Once again Doug wasn't paying attention. He thought only of my father's hand on his shoulder. The Longfellow faded away and we gazed out the bright window together, at the green orchard, the house and the fields at the fold of the trees in the forest, and beyond, at the burning blue piedmont.

"Password."

I grimaced every time I had to say it. "Repentance." Doug, however, shouted it. We were the only ones in the last group.

"What'd you think of the Longfellow?"

Doug answered, "Awake and sing, ye that dwell in the dust."

My father smiled and stepped once again to the blackboard, chalking up another cross for the young Isaiah.

Algebra 1 was out the window that afternoon. After the morning's episode at the door, I should have guessed. Dad sat down again, folded his hands, and looked at us. "Put your book down," he said. "I want to tell you a story."

From my side I felt the wings inside Doug move like a shadow toward him. "Yes, go ahead," he said. "I'm ready."

"A good boy grew up far east of here, in Brunswick, Georgia," Dad began. "As a child his only bad habit was hunting rattlesnakes, sneaking away at night to Rattlesnake Island, just offshore from Jekyl, with an old colored man named Mr. Seth. They stuck their legs through stovepipes and carried a kerosene lamp over the swamp in search of the diamondbacks. All the way over the narrow water, to the beach at Jekyl, sounded the quick, beady rattles and then *ping, ping . . . ping . . . ping* as poison fangs broke against the stovepipes. And then Mr. Seth's wild voice: 'Hey, Mr. Rattl'r, sho' nuff you's dead!' as the boy chopped its head off with his hatchet and tossed the wiggling body into Mr. Seth's burlap bag to take home for dinner.

"The boy married a local girl named Sara. They were childless. He went to bed every night at eleven and slept until two or three o'clock in the morning, when he suddenly sat up wide awake, as if he were called by a trumpet blast. He dressed and rode his horse to the beach, where he dismounted and walked along the water's edge staring at the stars. A voice or sound seemed to call him every night at nearly the same time. The horse always wandered home, where Sara would find it the next morning, stable it, and wait for her husband.

"One morning after such a night under the stars, he came home to Sara and said, 'We must go.' He gave her no explanation. Nor did he offer reasons to his or her parents, his brothers and sisters, or the people of Brunswick. And so he took his wife, Sara, and left his family and set out to the west, finally into Alabama at Palestine, in the northeast corner of Cleburne County. On the way they gathered up with them a colored woman whose man was long gone and her little son, a dark-eyed boy who looked like a baby Mr. Seth.

"From the moment he set his first seed down in the red soil, he and Sara prospered. But even amid this prosperity, Sara was sad, not because she'd moved so far from home but because she did not have her own child. Before long she could not look upon the colored boy without tears. And then her husband began to wake up again and rise from his bed early in the morning. He walked through the fields under the stars, until one morning as before he came to Sara and said, 'We shall have children who number as the stars.' He heard her laughter into the afternoon as far as the south forty where his head was bowed over the plow, the laughter she cried at his words.

"But how Sara laughed when nine months later he lay the boy child in her fifty-year-old arms! They named the boy after her laughter. But one day Sara came to him. 'The colored boy shall not be heir with my son. Cast him out.' And it was grievous to the old man when he told this boy and his faithful mother to wander once more because they were not heirs to his promise. The promise would come from the loins of the other child.

"And then one night he woke again. He sat up stark awake, got dressed, and hurried into the fields under the stars, where he could not believe what God told him. But he knew to obey. Early the next morning he packed the bag, slung it over his son's shoulder, and gave him the hatchet.

"He led his son up the road toward Sand Mountain, listening to the steady young footsteps in the dirt behind him.

" 'It is not myself,' he muttered, 'who provides.'

"The old man soon stopped and motioned his son to the side of the road, through a cluster of trees to a field. The son

hitched the pack off his back and the old man slipped it open.
Piece by piece they set in order the kindling on a cleared circle. And the man sent his son with the hatchet to the edge of
the woods to search for clean, dry, dead limbs.

"The old man laid the wood in an ancient pattern and un-
strapped from the back compartment of the pack a strong
rope. He drew from his pants the bowie knife and looked at
his son.

" 'My father?'

" 'Lie down, my son.'

"He tied the rope around the boy's neck, his waist and feet.
One last moment his eyes turned to the cold heavens, for a
promise and a voice. But there was nothing."

My father stopped, kept silent for almost a minute, and
looked directly at Doug. "Later, on the way down the mountain, the man wondered about his son. He thought that until
then, until the snaps of that fire and the smell of the burning
flesh of the ram miraculously sent by God to be sacrificed in
place of his son, he knew not his own seed. It is more, he
thought, than sacrifice, more than leaving home. It is a miracle. It is going up the mountain without your son, and coming
down with him.

" 'My father,' the son said to him"—these were Dad's closing words—"as the boy looked at the space between them,
'Who is this other man who walks beside us?' "

I wanted to scream. I was upset and worried about the blaze
in Doug's eyes. "People don't act that way today," I said. "If
you hear voices like that, you ought to be locked up in the insane asylum. The man is crazy. Doug, do you hear? The man
is crazy! His son should have shot him. Just like Will should
have shot you, Dad—do you hear? And besides, if you intend
that we all ought to be Abrahams or something now . . . well, it
is unrealistic to bring him into our times and put him in our
clothes. And anyway, I don't care what God did in the Bible,
He wouldn't do that these days because He doesn't tell us to
do what is wrong, and He sure doesn't speak in voices. Not to
you, not to Doug."

My father didn't answer. Instead we sat quietly in front of a
class given up its work to watch us. The afternoon sun cast our
shadows high on the wall. Doug, with his hands on his knees
and his back rigid, began to sway like a teetering Egyptian
statue, oblivious to the presence of any other human being in
the room save our teacher/evangelist. My father's hands were

folded, his elbows on the desk; in his eyes a terrible fire burned toward my twin, whose eyes answered the call with their own quivering rapture.

They set me apart. I was a brother and a son but could only watch my father hypnotize his soul. It was as if I lay away from them on a wooded hillside far within the wilderness, spying the two of them embrace and dance around the firelit altar below, where he had forged his golden calf and entreated his son to worship it. It was idolatry. For me to step into their camp was death, because I was not one of the initiated. I could not whoop or wail, I could not risk my life believing in his poisoned idols and promised lands. But in their burning eyes they loved each other. They believed they could move mountains. I feared that Doug would step over the edge and plummet down the pitiless crevice.

Then Doug jumped up from the pew and hurried to the front of my father's desk. "I know where Abram is," he said, turning the Bible and flipping the pages to Isaiah, stopping to read the headings, then flipping again, as if he searched for a word in the dictionary.

Dad dismissed school. I turned toward the front so I wouldn't have to see the glances file by, but I felt them, the cornered eyes fascinated by yet another Treadwell family scene. I heard Ricky Smith guffaw as he kicked the platform, and then he blew his nose—probably into his hand.

When everyone was gone and the room was quiet again, except for the crinkling pages of the Bible, Dad said, "Of course Abraham lives in our time, Luke. Do you think God intended his story to count only for the Israelites? All the prophets and kings live with us, in this very room. And we live in their time. We can imagine ourselves living in almost all times and in all men. We are Moses and Samuel, Micah and Matthew, Peter and Paul. God is not I was or I will be. God is I am."

"But things don't happen that way today," I said. I tried to talk loud enough to make Doug look up from the Bible. "The ram was just . . . a lucky chance probably, which they took for a miracle. And anyway, if God sent the ram, he sent it to one man who was father of his race, just like the Bible says. He didn't send it to you, Doug—listen to me! We never hear stories where the ram didn't show up. If you go around thinking God's watching over your every stupid move, Dad, what's to keep you from jumping out a window? Or killing Mr. Ran-

dolph? And Isaac is not just going to lie down and let his father kill him. No matter what you think. His instinct would
fight."

"I found it!" Doug called out. His face glowed with discovery. When he lifted the Bible, his hands shook so much that
the drooping leather binding flapped like the arching wings of
a swallow. " 'Who raised up the righteous man from the
East,' " he read, " 'called him to his foot, gave nations before
him, and made him rule over kings? He gave them as dust to
his sword, and as driven stubble to his bow.' Isaiah 41:2." He
shut the book quickly, the deep resonant sound of the big
Bible slammed closed giving his lawyer's bearing added authority. He had closed the case before the jury. "Isaiah," he
said, as proof again.

But then his body began to shake in earnest. He ran to the
middle of the room and banged a desk lid. He whirled around
and ran toward the door and pulled it wide open, then hurried
to a window and pushed it even higher. His face was luminous
and his hands moved with the speed of a darting bird. "Sometimes I see," he said, "like the stars."

"Yes, son—yes," Dad said, standing up.

Some invisible electrical shock continued to shake Doug, as
if a great creature rested its hands on his forehead and made
him quiver. He stopped, he forced himself to stop, then
pushed his back against the wall so he could call across the
room to us.

"At night, after I pray—"

"Yes, son. Amen."

"When the whippoorwill calls—"

"Praise God."

"I see the golden fields of Sharon lie before me, and crossing over them I see a procession of prophets and kings. I
see Abraham and Jacob, who carries a white ladder, and I see
Moses, Joshua the trumpeter, and David, with a slingshot over
his shoulder and a crown on his head. And I see I-sai-ah!
Daddy! I see Isaiah, with Jeremiah and Ezekiel and Daniel
behind him, the three arm in arm, dancing in sackcloth after
Isaiah. Then I see Him bearing His cross and I feel His
wounds and I cry. The screech owl cries with me; I hear him
weeping for His scars. Oh, I have been there, Luke. You must
believe me. Daddy, you know I've been there. I have seen the
stars as the seed of Israel, I've wrestled with the angel and
stood before the giants of the Philistines. The chariot flies me
to Babylon and into the lion's pit where I have wept at the foot

of the cross, His sweet precious blood falling to my lips. Oh, I go with the Lord every day."

And then, suddenly, he seemed to calm down. His breathing slowed. It was gone as quickly as it came. I was shocked, having unconsciously chosen until then not to believe how far gone he was. The bull, Mr. Randolph, my father's "crosses," the Indian death, Isaiah—all this I had not put together.

Dad came from around his desk and said, "He that loveth father or mother more than me is not worthy of me." Then he stepped off the platform for the first time that day and walked toward his son, who met him in the middle of the classroom and embraced him. Doug cried.

As I watched them, a depression descended over me, sitting on the platform, barren, suddenly unsure, and alone. I quietly slipped to the door, remembering that he had passed me by for Doug that very morning. Though I had told myself I hated him, I felt a sudden emptiness—my father would never turn to me.

I hurried down the hard, dusty road over the railroad tracks to the humid woods. As I walked into the steaming wilderness, I began to understand that I, too, was different, that I was at a point in my life when I needed to tell myself what the difference was. These people—these visionaries (now I was lumping Doug with my father)—changed too quickly, as if a cloud's shadow passing over were an answer to prayer, or a sign. One moment they seemed normal human beings and the next they were crazy for Christ, spouting some nonsense about their visions, building a fire and destroying everything. And then they came back, exhausted, but calm, still human beings—which was why I doubted this visionary business. I explained to myself that there was no permanent change worth mentioning— my father was the same man, basically, and I assumed Doug would return to normal, though a part of me was very scared. He would still try to live in this world, but right here and now, I said to myself, I have discovered *my* God—he doesn't intend us to open and close like day lilies. We lived by common sense and decency, the deep-rooted trees that made man able to love his fellow man and God. This was in the Bible, too. I could look it up.

But I still felt empty. I decided to tramp toward Fort Cusseta. The way was rougher now, for many reasons. I was a half-foot taller than the fall before and had to climb where once I ducked. The undergrowth tangled and confused my path. And June's humidity was stifling. But I reached the fort soon enough, sweat running down my legs, and it stood, as always, still and alone, but with a few more planks hanging out of it like crooked tombstones.

As I stepped over some fallen wood into the yard, now much smaller than I remembered, the heat settled over me even more closely. It slipped into every piece of wood, old nail, and hinge, and then up over the fort like the roof of a stove. It came down from the treetops and spread over the windless earth. Sweat then rolled into my eyes and off my chin, as heavy as drowning water. I couldn't breathe. The temperature kept rising. The heat would soon burn me into ashes. I couldn't breathe. I began to trot, hoping my movement would bring cooler air into my lungs. But I felt like I was trotting under water.

Then I ran. Only running full speed gave me fresh air. I darted around and over the fallen trees and vines, some of them catching me and ripping my skin. But I kept running. Something without words inside me knew where I ran. I could not have said, 'Doug will leave tonight,' but I knew he would. I could not have said, 'Though you are betrayed, you will embrace him,' but I knew I would. I could not have said, 'It is a question of death,' but I knew it was. I fell on my knees in the same spot he fell, only a few feet from the creek. I rolled through the leaves over and over again, the earth, my sweat and bloody scratches stinging like a bed of nails, and I grabbed the candy corn tulips and beech leaves and squeezed them, remembering what he had said.

"I am dying," I said aloud.

I looked at the faint X on my wrist and then pushed myself up to my knees, grabbed the trunk of the beech tree, and, almost crawling up its side, like a blind man I rubbed the fading scratches of Doug's broken arrow.

That night I heard him get out of bed. The burning in my body had kept me awake. I had been listening to the dark chorus of incessant crickets through the open window between us. He stood up already clothed in his blue jeans and red checkered shirt. Beside the white wall he waited for a moment, a strong, God-assured shadow, balancing himself before his crooked journey. When he turned toward me, I pretended to sleep. He quietly pulled his sheet up and folded the edge neatly under the pillow, then in his socks tiptoed to the end of the bed, knelt, and slipped from under it a striped apron bundled and tied together with twine, the bulk of the sack my father's outlined Bible. He sat on the floor and swiveled to his boots, lifting his feet and, with his thumbs gripping the inside seams, jerking until the heels clicked into place. Standing up by the mantel over the fireplace, he pocketed a box of kitchen matches and stopped: he had his Buck knife.

Out of the chorus of crickets a dove called. Five low, echoing notes, like the lowest breath of a flute, carried from the darkness of the woods through the window and into both of us, the second fatal note, inhaled, a little higher. Doug stepped to my bedside gripping his sack and the Buck knife. I kept my eyes closed but felt him hovering over me, trying to decide. I had tried my best to save him, to keep him from my father, and when I could no longer keep him, to speak against my father's voice. All my efforts were vain. Why witness his foolish exit? Why force me, when he knew, to look into his eyes? But he did, because he was my father's son, and all our lives our father had forced his will on us. He sat on the bed and shook me. I pulled up, wide awake, and leaned against the headboard.

"Please give this to Mother," he said, slipping a note into my hand. "Explain to her, please—that Abram had to follow the call. And I want you to have this." He laid the Buck knife in my palm as he stared at me.

"Why should I, brother? Why not Dad?"

He dropped his wounded gaze to his hand. But he was not my father, only his son, and my brother. We had lived together. I could not help myself, I loved him so much.

"Doug," I said, and I embraced him, the sheathed knife against his back.

He let go of me, stuck his heels through the open window until he held the ledge, and then took a backward leap into the night. As he jumped, the dove called again. It seemed two, maybe three, whispered notes came to me before I heard him land on the earth and tumble, then get up and run. I stared at the knife and then at my wrists, the scars by then faded and much smaller, like an *X* of trickled sand. Suddenly I jumped from my bed and squatted at the window, knowing he was gone, and there I saw him—as the last fatal note of the dove sounded, I saw the shadow of my brother disappear into the wilderness.

4

*E*arly the next morning Doug's body was found in the Chattahoochee River, washed up on a sandbar at the bend south of the mill. After we were told, Belle stayed with Mother while Dad and I journeyed to Lanett, stopping at Aunt Cora's first, asking her to hurry to her sister's side while we went to the county hospital. Cora's husband, Uncle Warren, came with us. The sheriff and Mr. Schnedel, West Point's undertaker, met us at the entrance and escorted us to the dimly lit basement morgue.

Doug lay half-naked on a table. His body was unnaturally white, so tossed and bathed in the current that the waters polished his skin like smooth white pearl, except for a crooked line of scratches that cut up his left leg, and a purple bruise, like a birthmark, that darkened the side of his face below the left ear. The awkward weight of death had already dropped the back of his knee flat against the table. The skin on his neck and face stretched in horizontal lines away from his nose and mouth, aging him into a still, unfamiliar creature. Only his eyes resisted. They bulged up out of his head. "What have you done to me?" they asked.

I wanted to take two coins from my pocket and cover his eyes. I turned and walked in a stupor to a wall of the room, listening to my shoes echo on the floor like ticks of a loud clock. The wall was dull white and cold. I had known. I could not explain to myself, but I had known he would die. The gasps erupted uncontrollably from deep in my guts and spewed up through my lungs and into the unjust air. My face pressed flat against the wall and stayed there. I had known it would happen.

"Mr. Treadwell, this sure's a trag'dy," I heard Sheriff Johnson say. "I know it must be hard on you and your'n. You saw the bruise? A Bible was on the rocks. Can you beat that with a stick? A Bible. I guess he was tryin' to swim across. Maybe he fell in—but that bruise must be from hittin' a rock or somethin' 'n' then conkin' out. He held tight to that Bible 'til the end. You have any idea why he run away?"

"No."

My stomach, my chest, my jaw—every part of me—hardened. I turned around. Under his dark coat the sheriff's gun rose high on his suspendered chest. His coat buttons hugged his paunch and his white hair was combed straight up off his forehead and then down in long, plastered coils.

"Is there anything else we have to do, Siler?" Uncle Warren asked.

"You understand, Mr. Treadwell?" the man continued. "I'm tryin' to 'xplain best I can. We got boys that run away all the time and this never happens to 'em. Why, they'll reappear a few days later, a little worse for wear, but nothin' serious. Your son musta just slipped or something—I betcha he could swim that river anytime. Just an accident, ya know, like God was lookin' the other way this time."

My father stared at him with dull eyes. Mr. Schnedel worriedly shook his head, trying to get the man to stop talking.

"I'm sure Mrs. Johnson sends her sympathy to your missus," the sheriff continued. "We knows a few of your cousins up Wedowee way—Homer Treadwell, and Leon, too. Your wife—she comes from Cleburne County, don't she? My daddy knew hers—'fore she went away, he did."

We rode in Uncle Warren's car back to his house. He assured us that Cora would persuade Mother to come there—we might as well stay until the women arrived. But when we got out, while Uncle Warren was going inside, Dad took me around to the other side of the car, wrapping his shaking hand halfway around my neck. "You know the bend they're talking about—below the mill?"

"Yes, sir."

"Come get me when it's time." He didn't explain what time he meant—he couldn't finish. He set off across the driveway and down the street.

Uncle Warren was right: both Cora and Mother decided that Mother—a Cleburne County King—should not entertain callers in our shack in Cusseta, a shack that symbolized all that was depraved about her husband, Robert Treadwell. Cora insisted we use their house, and though it infuriated Mother that she was left with only the kindness of her sister and brother-in-law, she accepted, telling the Ray family to spread the word among the Cusseta neighbors, no slight to them intended. Word of that decision was out in Lanett and West Point even before Mother and Aunt Cora arrived. I was busy taking the fourth batch of food to the kitchen when the car pulled up late in the afternoon. They had been to see Doug's body first.

Mother didn't even ask for Dad, knowing all too well he wouldn't assume his duty. The last time, after bashing Will's head in, he had run into the wilderness, and even before she came through the door and saw he wasn't there, she suspected he had run away again. She hugged me when she came in, and then gave way to Belle. Both of them spent that evening and most of the next day in her sister's bedroom, preparing themselves for the body to lie in state, and assuming that they would stand there alone, without the boy's father.

The next morning Uncle Warren finalized the arrangements with Mr. Schnedel, and telegraphed Will. He even telephoned an army friend in Washington, but there was little hope of contacting my oldest brother anytime soon. Mother hoped that Doug's death would free Will to come home to us during our sorrow, and to be taken away from the planned island hopping across the Pacific. Losing two sons would kill her, she said. But Uncle Warren explained that the chances he'd even hear in less than two weeks were slim, and that there was no chance he'd be sent home. Uncle Warren was right. By August Will was on Guadalcanal.

Without asking anyone, I left in midafternoon to drag Dad back to his duty attending Mother while the body lay in state. He had had his chance to stay out overnight and ask God what went wrong. It was time he returned. I would make him. I walked two blocks from Uncle Warren's house and then turned before the town circle so I could avoid as many food-bearers as possible. I kept my head down and felt the unsympathetic heat bead on the back of my neck as the sun cast my shadow behind me. A block before the mill, I turned onto a parallel street that took me south, until past the edge of town I crossed the highway and trudged up the dry dirt road that led to the rise overlooking the river.

Halfway up the road on my right I walked by a gray shack. On one side some tall weeds grew out of a rotting pile of tires. Chickens began to squawk at me, and two sleeping mutts, their bony heads flat on their brown legs in front of them, consented only to lift up to see I wasn't worth the trouble. From the long, dark porch stretching across its front, an old black man, his gray hair and beard circling his head, watched me, shook his head, and shouted, "No man I's ever seen dat bad o' way!" I kept walking. When I mounted the cleared bank I looked upstream first. Past the nearby clump of mangroves clogging the riverside, the mill's top floor and turrets were burdened by a sultry dull sky, and the brief white smoke from its three tall stacks died into the haze.

I looked downstream. At the far edge of the clearing, my father sat on the spotted riverbank, a distant, small figure with his legs balled up in his chest and his hands clasping his ears, a line of trees beginning beside him and, beyond, in the middle of the brown river, three sandbars scattered with stones, one where Doug's body had washed up. A steady, cicadalike but muted noise drifted from his direction.

I took a few steps down the hill, uncertain, but still drawn toward my father, seeing more detail the closer I got. A purplish color spread across the back of his neck. With his knees pressed against his chest, he rocked forward and backward in time to his faint moaning. His hands were not grabbing his ears but yanking between them a rope he had jammed into his mouth. But even with this wiry rope cutting his lips and teeth, he kept that muffled insect shrieking, like some ancient, mourning Israelite willing to gnash his teeth and pull out his hair.

I stood in front of him. At first he did not recognize me. His eyes seemed larger than half-dollars, swollen into blank, grief-stricken circles, and when he finally let go the rope, blood oozed from his mouth, blood cut out of his insides.

Then he knew who I was.

"My son, my beloved son, would God I died for him."

At dusk a warm breeze came, softly blowing the curtains full and lifting them like loose sails until Belle lowered the windows. She and Mother stood beside the coffin as people filed by. She often touched Mother's arm to strengthen her, and Mother worked hard to maintain her composure. Her eyes greeted people with a dull sheen, her jaw was stiff and her mouth short and tight, and the thick powder over her face pasted her into a hardening white cast. But the edges of her eyes betrayed her, hovering at the point of collapse and promising that if they fell, the cast would break before a rush of grief.

About eight o'clock the minister from Wedowee came. He was Mother's favorite minister—a former suitor, Will once said. A tall man dressed in a dark suit, on his hand was a golden ring, and a white monogrammed handkerchief peeped out of his coat pocket. It took Mother a long, confused moment to see and know him and decide that with him it was appropriate to weep. The edges of her eyes quivered and gave way and he held out his arms so she might fall into them. She turned her face back and forth in his chest as if she wanted to burrow through and hide in what her Bible called "a sure and circumcised heart."

"Oh, Preston, why?" she sobbed. "In God's name, why?" She gripped his arms as she tried to stand up and compose herself. "I'm sorry, I just can't. . . ."

Belle slipped her a handkerchief.

"God be with you, Mattie. 'In my father's house are many mansions. If it were not so—' "

"Oh, Preston, thank you. It's so good of you to come. Let me go in here for a moment." Belle and Cora followed Mother to the bedroom.

I stood at the corner living-room window, the whispering breeze barely touching my back. The minister stood by the coffin and stared at my painted twin brother; he had a serene glitter on his face, as if to say, "This boy pressed toward the mark of the high calling." But did the man not see those eyes? This preacher, whose life it was to comfort the afflicted and assure us of resurrection—did he not see? A nervous, sharp pain overwhelmed my chest, saying it didn't matter. Nothing whatsoever mattered. My heart beat those words, "Nothing matters, nothing matters." Not the life Doug and I shared, that imagination we carved into our hearts, not the faint X's, one still throbbing on my wrist and the other cold and decaying on his. Nothing matters.

Mother came back, followed by the two women, and

slipped her arm through Reverend Sellers's as they gazed down at the corpse. "I'm better now," she said.

He took her hand and patted it. "He looks beautiful," he said.

I wanted to puke. Mother smiled and turned to the next person, the cast on her face even whiter.

I looked out the window over the oleander bush to the driveway and the yard. Four men I didn't know stood in a circle by a fig bush, smoking. One man laughed and pushed another's shoulder as if kidding him. I thought I heard him say, in a muffled tone, "Come on, show us."

The man who was pushed brought his cigarette to his lips. Suddenly he opened up, arched his tongue, and pulled the cigarette completely into his mouth, all of it, including the ash. The three looked on in disbelief. It seemed as if he'd swallowed a burning coal. Then he brought the still-burning ash out on his curled tongue, took it from his mouth, and blew a perfect smoke ring into the face of the man who had challenged him. The three slapped their hands on their knees and laughed. One looked over his shoulder at the house, checking to see if their disrespect was seen or heard.

My father surprised all of us. Somewhere between the moment I led him away from the river and the moment that night when he came into Cora's living room, bathed, groomed (though his lips were swollen and blue), and dressed in his only suit and black tie, he discovered and kept a calm, direct tone, with a blank expression on his face, quietly repeating for most of the time, "It is God's will." One time a lady turned away and flushed, but I couldn't hear what he had said to her. I did hear, though, what he said to the minister. Even with his mouth and lips torn up, he spoke clearly, in that same calm, direct tone, as Reverend Sellers stepped toward him just after he spoke with Mother and Belle.

"Full well ye reject the commandment of God," my father said, "that ye may keep your own tradition."

By the next afternoon, at the graveyard, I had suffered enough well-wishers. At the end of the graveside service, before Uncle Warren took her, Cora, and Belle home to Cusseta, Mother turned and came to my father and me. We had retreated to the other side of the flowered coffin, out from under the striped tent and away from the crowd. A black veil, draped from her round hat to her chin, so darkened her face that it hid the look she gave him, but the tendons of her neck hardened like roots of trees.

She moved one gloved hand to his. He stared at her without speaking. She turned and followed Warren, our family's defense finally over.

No one else came to us, because my father had made his reputation as a crazed fanatic. After Mother left, the townspeople milled around and looked at us, trying to decide, finally whispering among themselves, 'It isn't worth trying to say something to him.' Only Mr. Schnedel waited, but ten yards from us, while the graveyard cleared of people and the slight wind died.

A mockingbird perched in the ancient, gnarled oak next to the plot and began to sing. He would sing a phrase, full-throated, and then in midmeasure switch to another song that imitated a sparrow, then a cardinal, and a bird I didn't recognize, cataloging all the ways he knew to mock the world. Two black men soon appeared from the other side of the graveyard, next to the hill, carrying shovels. They seemed surprised that three figures and not just one waited by the oak, but they walked up to us and nodded, speaking for a moment to Mr. Schnedel. He stood by them as they let the coffin down with ropes and pulled up the closed side of the tent, which conveniently hid from the mourners the brutal reality of the waiting mound.

The first dirt fell like hard rain. But soon it fell softly and the mockingbird stopped, to listen. The blades cut like scissors into the dirt, swung, and scattered it softly into the ever smaller hole, falling with the sound of drummed fingers. We left when it was packed down.

". . . Thy will be done, through Jesus Christ Our Lord. Amen."

On the sultry June evening after the funeral, we opened our eyes after my father's prayer and looked upon a supper table permanently unbalanced. Will's place was set again, as it was every meal since he had gone to war, but the chair next to my father's was empty, the table where Doug's setting should be was bare. When my father sat down, a distracted look to his eyes enlarged behind his thick spectacles. His hair showed more gray and his jowls were more pronounced, hanging like wineskins. For a moment he tried to speak, but he stuttered, shook his head, and then shut himself back up in his confused thoughts. At the other end my mother seated herself on the front third of her chair and folded her hands in her lap. She kept her brown hair in a bun and wore a black dress. Her eyes turned toward the empty chair, but without focus, like the worn eyes of an ancient statue. Belle looked handsome that night, with high cheekbones and raven hair, but when she looked at Mother, her red eyes widened with fear, like a cat facing headlights in the night.

"Be strong," Mother said.

After the prayer there was a long silence. I could not keep from accusing him. "My brother's blood," I said, "is on your hands."

Another moment of silence passed.

"Luke," Mother whispered. I recognized the tone, and the expression on her face, which said, "Not now, son. We must keep our family together." She tightened her lips into a nervous circle so small a coin could cover it. I didn't believe she'd take my father's side. She couldn't. If Will sat at this broken supper table, he'd tell her.

"It is," I said. "Will would say the same thing, and so would you, Belle, if you weren't scared. His blood is on your hands." I pointed at him, feeling a sense of righteousness strengthening me. "The damned teacher, you had to force him to learn your way."

"Please, Luke," Belle said, answering me. "Why now? We've just put him in the ground. He wouldn't want us this way."

"Crap, Belle. Yes he would. Why don't you face the truth?"

When I first accused him, instead of answering, my father tried to eat, fiddling with his fork as he carefully chewed, his lips still swollen. My words demanded a response, but he let them drift unanswered into the silence. But when I yelled at Belle, he looked up.

"It is the will of God," he said.

I wanted to kick the table and rush him until I could pin him beneath me and take my fingers and press them against his eye sockets and dig and dig until I gouged out those fiery, lying eyes that were responsible for this pain, for those false funeral words, those thorny abominations that had supposedly seen the grace and favor and glory of the Lord.

Then Belle began to defend him. His smug righteousness was deceiving her, as it had Doug. "You talk like Doug had no will of his own," she said. He didn't have to run away."

"You sure as hell don't know."

"Luke!"

"Come on, Mother. Has Dad loved us? He doesn't want to make us happy, he wants to make us dead. You think you're the world's savior, Dad. Will supports this family, anyway."

"Oh, yes, Luke," he said. "Oh, yes. Will sends us his money. He makes the cash in this family, and with every cent he makes, he stores one more moth-eaten and rust ... rust-covered treasure of what you call 'love' and what you call 'duty.' Let the thieves break in!" He was finally breaking. His hands gripped the table. "All of you love costly spikenard—anoint your feet with it. You love the black ledger. You set this table with righteousness and all of it is corrupt. Your coins compare not one iota with the dust off Doug's feet—"

His voice broke. But he leaned over the table and pushed himself up, drawing a long, loud breath. "He didn't forget God. He didn't pretend death didn't exist. He didn't say, 'Oh, I'll do something about that tomorrow—tomorrow I'll find an answer.' He looked to God for the present. I'll tell all of you something: you could live to be as old as Methuselah and all your days in the eyes of God would mean nothing, absolutely nothing, compared with the one night that boy spent on the road to Christ."

First Mother's eyes and then her lips tightened. At the same time her jaw began to protrude and her face lost color until she wore that now-familiar hard white mask. He had finally gone too far. And she didn't need many words. "Our son, Robert, is not on any road. He is dead."

No one answered her.

He immediately realized what she meant, as if she had said, "You murdered him." She had finally cast aside the hope of a family restored, and she wept.

Belle came to her. "Mother, Mother." She held Mother's head on her breast and stroked her hair. Mother wrapped her arms around Belle's back, her sobs buried in her daughter. Belle looked at us. "Why? Why do you have to do this to her?"

I turned on my father. "Can't you see? Look at your wife and daughter. All this about Methuselah and the will of God. Your stupid dreams. Mother is destroyed—that's all that means anything."

But Dad wasn't listening. His eyes turned toward our sorrowful mother. He looked through her and out to the imagined horizon. Then he lowered his head. "Doug," he whispered. And sudden rivers of tears poured from his eyes, a quick, surprising, and quiet flow that streamed down his heavy cheeks and onto the table and his lap. Mother turned her head from deep within Belle's breast. I stopped talking. His grief made me feel my own bone marrow guard against the anguish in my heart.

But I went for the jugular. "What is this? Tears? Don't you think it's a little late, Dad?"

Our father lifted his face and looked at me. An unseen wind moved over him. He stood up and with the back of his hand slapped over the empty chair. "Doug had the courage! He knew and he followed, even if it meant giving up his family." He grabbed the edge of the table, spilling salt over his plate and onto the floor, and began scraping his shoes on the wood, wiping every grain of dirt off his soles. "I shake off the dust of my feet!" He hurried by the fallen chair without looking back and threw open the screen door into the night, the door swinging back behind him and banging once, twice, and then no more.

5

*A*fter uselessly waiting three months for Dad to return, in the fall of 1942 Mother moved us out of the Cusseta shack, and with a loan from Uncle Warren bought a small grocery store, with a house attached, in Lanett. Belle met the store customers, Mother took phone orders, and I delivered the groceries in a truck Uncle Warren lent us. The whole enterprise felt doomed—one adult and two teenagers the total work force. But Mother was determined never to return to a cabin like the one in Cusseta; if she had to work all day and night, she was going to pay Warren back, keep shoes on our feet, and stay in the house, where a Cleburne County King belonged. With Dad gone, we were all the more devoted to Mother, and eventually, with Will's and my army paychecks signed over to her, we kept the store going and our fatherless family got by. In four years Mother paid off the principal of the loan, which satisfied her pride and gave her, living in a small, gossipy town as a woman whose husband had abandoned her, a much needed self-esteem.

In 1946 Will returned a war hero. He had never lived in Lanett, but the town of course adopted him and put on a parade in his honor. Mayor Tom Lanier's declaration esteemed "all the brave boys from all over this great land of ours," but especially Lanett's and West Point's new hero, William Stearns Treadwell, recipient of the Purple Heart for his valor in the Pacific. The Veterans of Foreign Wars marched, and the high-school bands from Lanett and West Point played. The Daughters of the Confederacy sponsored an all-day picnic on the lawn of the First Presbyterian Church, where the parade finally ended when Will's and Mother's rumble-seat roadster, strung with multicolored streamers, arrived to townwide cheering and applause. Will even gave a speech. A month later Belle married a bricklayer named Raymond Bonner; they lived only a mile from Mother, and Belle still helped her in the store.

By that time I had been sent to Germany. In her letters Mother kept me informed about Will's new civilian status in Lanett. After his honorable discharge, he entered Mr. Schnedel's furniture business, and a year later Mr. Schnedel talked him into studying undertaking as a way "to come up in the world" (Will's words, Mother said). He embalmed at nights and over the weekends. Then, with the extra money he was making, he bought some farmland near Pine Mountain, where he hoped to start a cattle business also. His ambition, at least from my perspective, was startling. And, my God, given what had happened on our Wedowee farm, why would he want to start a cattle business?

I was discharged to the army reserves in 1948. I went to the state university year-round on the GI Bill, majoring in philosophy, and finished early, in the spring of 1950. Mother set me to work in her store again until I could decide what to do with myself, philosophy not the most marketable pursuit in Alabama. With the developing crisis in Korea, I was worried my army unit would be called up any moment, which made any career plans seem foolish. But I tried not to think about another war, only about some way to go with my life, however halfheartedly. When I had been home a week, Will proposed a Saturday-afternoon picnic in honor of my graduation. After four years of courtship, he was engaged to a girl named Susan Mordew. He and his fiancée also invited her sister Elizabeth, whom I hardly remembered even though we had gone to school together. She had just come back from New York, where, Will said, she bombed out as a dancer.

An event I must mention, however, occurred before the picnic. The Friday evening before this brother-and-sister outing, I had to drive down to Eufaula for Mother, trying to collect an unpaid bill from a family that had moved from our street. On the way back I stopped at a Langdale all-night café. It was around midnight. Two unshaven, squint-eyed men fell into the neighboring booth. Both were too drunk and exhausted to recognize me. The shorter one was a cousin of the Browns on Fifth Street, twice removed, one of Will's buddies, but I wasn't sure who the other was and I wasn't going to ask. After five minutes I was riveted to their conversation.

"Guadalcanal," the man said. "A Purple Heart."

"And the keys to the town?"

"More than City Hall, Old Gooseberry." He laughed. "He has the master key to every box of sugar in town." I considered leaving, but the second man, the taller one, spoke again.

"Who is this Susan Mordew?"

"The sea dog's ward. Susan's parents died when she and her sister were young. Admiral Mallery was named their guardian."

There was a pause, and then the same man continued.

"Will's marrying her in June, I think. A complete transformation is supposed to take place. He will shed his snakeskin and forget every garter and every smile and sit in his church pew as righteous as Elmer Gantry."

"He is righteous now, isn't he? Righteousness is just looking righteous."

The first man sneered. "I think he believes it, though. I really do. Like marriage converts a man. That's it—he's waiting for a goddamn conversion. . . . Pooh!"

I escaped, backing out of the booth with my head down and skipping the change at the cash register.

The next afternoon was sunny and warm. Will escorted the sisters, arm in arm, down the Mallery mansion's side stairs. He looked captivated by the one on his left—Elizabeth—a tall, sylphlike, smashing woman. She wore a sherwood-green blouse with an oversize red collar and baggy black pants—an outlandish getup for Lanett, Alabama. But she pulled it off. She glided down the steps like a long-legged crane flying across water. Will laughed at her, seemingly so caught up in her radiance that he held her hand along the crooked path, and at the dock, where I prepared the rowboat, he mimicked spreading his jacket over the river, just for Her Highness to prance on.

"Ah, such a gentleman!" she said, turning to her sister. "Are you sure you don't want to give him to me?"

"No, I think I'll try him out for a while. Maybe later."

From the first, Susan had impressed me as a dutiful person, valuing the family, the flag, and the church, as she was taught and as Will would want, at least for appearance's sake. She carried the picnic basket from Will to me, and I secured it dead center, high and dry. She didn't dislike Will's horseplay; she just didn't know how to respond. She was beautiful, too, in her own way. Her latest permanent pressed her brown hair over her ears and back from her pearl-smooth, oval face—a Botticelli oval, with the same short eyelashes. With Elizabeth's hair she would have resembled Botticelli's Venus. But she didn't. That windswept, languid look was more the younger sister's.

"You remember Elizabeth, don't you, Luke?"

I stood up. "Yes. Of course." She shook my hand, which surprised me. In Lanett, ladies didn't. "It's good to see you again."

"Yes. High school—really, it's so embarrassing."

We waved to Admiral and Mrs. Mallery on their back porch and took off, Will and I gently rowing from forward, the sisters side by side in the stern. It was going to be a great day. A few afternoon clouds floated overhead, but none of them darkened the steady sun, cradled in the bluest of skies. The air, even above the water, was touched with the warmth of spring and with the smell of its searching pollen. We rowed to a cleared rise on the other shore, directly across from the house.

The moment before we touched the far bank, Elizabeth sprang up in the stern and snatched the wicker basket. After catching her balance with a hand on Will's shoulder, she took two steps to the bow and, like a fawn, leaped to the shore, leaving the three of us precariously gripping the boat as she gamboled up the rise, laughing like a little girl. Will swung the oar like a baseball bat, but she sped away long gone, high and dry, and his jerking strikeout almost dumped Susan and me off the other side. Laughing, I tied the boat as Susan and Will ambled up to a great oak tree, where Elizabeth had already spread the red-and-white checked cloth over the grass. She leaned long-legged against the trunk, her blouse half-unbuttoned and her pants bunched up at her knees.

Will sat beside her, Susan and I opposite. In a few moments Susan spread a Balthazar's feast: fried chicken, ham and cheese sandwiches, deviled eggs, cole slaw, three-bean salad, a cold squash casserole, iced tea, and some dessert Susan had hidden. Elizabeth was little help in arranging the food, but Susan seemed pleased to be in complete control. In the middle of the glorious repast, Elizabeth slipped off her shoes and tip-toed out in front of us, turned, bowed, and announced she was Sleeping Beauty come awake with a kiss. Then she started to hum the Tchaikovsky music (Will clapped) and she danced like a halfway decent ballerina. I was mesmerized. The spontaneity! We applauded as she twirled and tiptoed with winged arms and an arched, swanlike back. She stopped and said, "Grand Jeté!" and leaped that leap where those unnatural creatures turn in midair and land with an arched back on one foot, the other one extended and pointed parallel to the ground, balanced by arms spread out like a swan dive. What kind of woman was this?

After she sat down, no one broke the appreciative silence for a while, until Will spoke to Susan. "Luke was off to Eufaula last night, trying to collect Mother's money."

I groaned.

"I told you, Luke, that no one in this whole valley is going to pay a bill as long as Mother gives them credit." He tugged on a chicken leg.

I couldn't believe his vulgarity. We row across the river with two beautiful women, the sun comes out on a glorious banquet, and my brother begins a conversation about the mud and slop of our family—and his solutions.

"Surely they must pay something," Susan said.

"A dollar a week."

"I see."

"You must tell me about your plans, Elizabeth," I said, trying to change the subject. But Will insisted.

"Now, you're impartial, Elizabeth. You've been away and you really don't know our family situation that well." She glanced at her sister. "Susan and I are trying to persuade my Mother to sell the store and move out of that house into a smaller place. The store still loses money. I make up the losses—"

"And so do I, and Belle and Raymond."

"That's what I meant, Luke, you know that. Don't be so defensive. Just listen for once. You see, Elizabeth, the money the store loses could just as easily support her in a smaller place, and the extra money we save could be invested. Besides, she has no business being in that store all day by herself, what with the—"

"Belle helps her."

"Belle has a husband to look after."

"I'll say this to you, Will, until I'm blue in the face. Mother needs that store to occupy herself. It is work for her, whether or not it loses a few pennies a week, and that work is crucial to her well-being. The little money we spend is worth it in order to keep her busy and alive." When I finished, both of us looked at Elizabeth, who for some reason Will had declared the arbitrator. Her judgment was unexpected.

"Let her go find your father."

"Not the right answer," Susan said, smiling. She had learned that subject was taboo.

Will didn't smile. He set the chicken bone down and with a napkin slowly wiped his mouth. Elizabeth was clearly innocent of malice. But such an idea, that our maligned mother should search for our prodigal father, triggered an automatic and excessive response in Will, as if a tap on his folded knee would invite him not just to kick, but to kick someone's teeth in. Even after eight years, Will did not forgive, nor did he forget.

Elizabeth was obviously shocked by the way he looked at her. She continued to lean against the tree trunk and watch Will as he turned to stare at her with the eyes of a stern father. The long, visible muscles in Elizabeth's neck tightened at the collarbone. She was learning something about her new brother-in-law.

"I can't believe," he began, "that you said that. How could you be so unmerciful? The very idea—"

But Susan was not going to let him get started. "Look," she said, pointing across the clearing. "Shhh! Be quiet. Look, over there."

Will glared at her for interrupting.

"Oh, please, Will, look. Don't be a spoilsport."

I heard the call—"Chewink. Chewink. Drink you tea"— and searched through the bushes at the bottom of the rise. "Drink your tea"—high, low, higher. I couldn't see it. Will and Elizabeth found it, though both their faces looked unimpressed. Will was merely being patient with his fiancée. Susan had stopped Will by picking a readily available bird, I assumed, claiming it was rare enough to warrant the interruption.

But maybe I was wrong. I just wasn't sure about her. Her oval face kept completely silent and still with a wonder I surely didn't feel. I looked again. I caught a quick movement and then its head. He was on the ground, not in the bushes—that was why I didn't see him. He was black and white and reddish orange on his flanks, and I think I caught orange eyes as he hopped, scratching his way through the grass. I had him in my sights when he sang—or warbled—so fully his throat shook. For a moment, and then he was gone.

"My tea song," Susan said.

"Stretch," I answered, unfolding and standing. I shook my legs awake and strolled toward the water by myself, pleased to see Elizabeth respond. Some movement might free us from Susan's bird watching, and, more important, from the doom of an argument with Will about our father. Mother had told us that ever since Dad had run away, approximately every four months he sent her a postcard, most of them postmarked from Atlanta. He was an evangelist, she told me once, with a disgusted look on her face. She had not given up her strange hope that he would one day forsake his idolatry and come home. But as far as I was concerned, he was dead and gone. Good riddance.

"Dessert, Luke."

"Oh, my God, more?"

"I baked it just for the picnic," Susan said. She cleared away the leftovers so the apple pie could stand alone in its sugary majesty. Much too soon we had to sit again, but this time Elizabeth stayed across the way from Will, not shoulder-to-shoulder with him against the trunk of the oak. The three of us gave Susan the necessary compliments even before Will took up the knife to slice the pie.

I didn't really know Elizabeth. When Dad left I was fifteen, and though I graduated from high school before I enlisted, anytime I wasn't in class I was working for Mother. I only remembered that Elizabeth was blackballed. All my classmates, especially the girls, called her an Atlanta snob. (When her parents were killed in a car wreck, she and Susan moved from Atlanta to live with their godparents, the Mallerys.) She didn't play any sports or belong to a club, and worst of all she didn't care. In the afternoons she either went home or went to some music or dance lesson, nowhere else. How gawky she looked, a long-legged crane, walking knees forward, followed by flopping feet. And that was all. I went to war and forgot who she was. She went to college and New York. If I had known her that picnic day as I grew to know her, I wouldn't have bothered to get up and stretch, and I would have interrupted Susan and told her to watch her bird alone. Elizabeth was no less stubborn than Will was.

"Now tell me, Will," she said, "surely you know the answer to this question. Why did your father leave?"

The knife hovered over the pie. I glanced at Susan; she was as helpless as I was. " 'Leave,' Elizabeth? He didn't 'leave,' " Will answered. "He ran away. A coward and a traitor runs away because he doesn't have the courage to do his duty or to face up to what he's done."

"How long have he and your Mother been married?"

"I have no earthly idea."

She looked at me. "Thirty-three years," I said, "on Christmas Day."

"When he left?"

"Twenty-five years."

"Twenty-five years hardly seems like a betrayal to me," Elizabeth said.

"It seems especially so to me," said Will.

"But if he was such a coward, as you say, how could he have made it through the first five years, or seven, or fifteen? Cowards show their stripes much earlier than twenty-five years. You're a war hero. A man doesn't fight through twenty-five battles and then become a coward, does he?"

"So when we run out of experience, we run away?"

"No, when we run out of spirit, we—"

"But, Elizabeth," Susan said, "he deserted his wife."

Will swiftly cut a deep slice in the pie. An apple sliver hung on the knife tip. "Deserted, yes. He abandoned his wife, he murdered a son, Elizabeth—that didn't happen in the first five or seven or fifteen years—and he left three children fatherless."

"Children? I don't know how old you were, Luke, but *you* were already in the army, Will. Eight years ago. What were you, nineteen? Did you ever think his leaving was better? Maybe it was. For your mother and for him. Maybe he needed to set off in order to find himself."

I had never heard my father defended. By anyone. Elizabeth was an outsider, who in the comfort of her own life could imagine other motives than the real ones, like an abstract theorist. She could easily say it was better for him to disappear, that he had not abandoned his family but gone in search of himself. She could say whatever she dreamed up, because the pain was not hers. That was the difference. I had seen this brother bashed over the head, bloodied, half-stunned for weeks, and with my own hands I had touched another brother laid out in a morgue, his flesh, which was my flesh, cold and sticky, stinking of formaldehyde. And since then I had wandered through my own life wondering where in that past, when the rain descends, the floods come, and the winds blow, I could find rocks on which to build.

There was a moment of silence, in which the tension grew. Elizabeth pivoted her legs from one side of her to the other and folded her feet as far back as her hips. Leaning one hand on the ground, she tilted her head with childlike innocence until her hair fell and touched her shoulders. No matter how wrong she was about my father, there was something about what she said, and who she was. I had studied her eyes, innocently. They were dark blue. Deep within them, at the end of a nave bathed in the light of slender, blue stained glass, brightened by the unearthly white light from a clerestory, I imagined I saw a small candle burning. I was sure it was there, if only a dancing flicker, far beyond the surface of her eye. I wanted to be still and listen to the breath of my soul, and then my footsteps, echoing like heartbeats, as I made my way there. She had said he might find himself. And I might find myself with her.

Will finished cutting the pie. He stared at the knife he still held, unable to break himself out of his vengeful memories. Susan took the pie server and gave each of us a slice, but all the time she rotated the pie and scooped out the pieces, Will never moved from that same oblivious position, legs crossed, head bent over the gleam of the blade. "Thank you," Elizabeth said, though Susan didn't offer the dessert, she shoved it.

"I don't think you understand," I said, "especially about my twin brother. He and I were my father's pupils, and my father indoctrinated him, not with any kind of formal belief but with some shallow, irresponsible attitudes about religion. My brother ran away one night because he thought he was doing the will of God. And he drowned when he tried to swim across this very river."

"I knew . . ." Elizabeth began. She shifted uncomfortably, as if she finally realized she had gone too far. "Well, I knew he had died, but I didn't realize that he . . . here."

It was then that Will finally looked up, pulling himself out of his trance.

I watched the knife. Elizabeth and Susan were startled by his eyes, and then his slow, vicious words: "He was a murderer from the very beginning!" He turned the knife in his hands, grabbed the point, and then I heard it, like an arrow released into the air, as it flew high over Elizabeth's head. I quickly caught sight of it in the air, and because every thrown knife should, I expected it to hit a tree trunk and vibrate. But it gleamed in the sunlight a second, like a spear, and then tumbled over and fell into the river—the river where my brother had drowned—sinking to a grave in the bottomless mud.

6

One of Dad's postcards came the day before Susan and Will were married. The edges were serrated, and in the bottom white border a message read: "The Southern Railroad Says Hello!" The train, however, obviously said goodbye. The camera caught a brief diagonal glimpse of a hopper, a tank car, and a fast-fading flatcar, but the caboose stretched across most of the picture. The conductor, in a dark blue uniform with a French general's hat, leaned out of the crow's nest to wave. Dad drew a cartoon character's balloon out of the conductor's mouth, to make him speak. "There shall be," it said, "a highway out of Egypt."   Without looking at Mother, I turned the postcard over. It was sent to Will at Mother's address, and it read: "Take, I pray thee, my blessing."

"As if he cared."

"I wrote the Atlanta Y," Mother said, staring at me.

"Why?"

"Well, Will *is* his son."

"But really, Mother, you couldn't want that."

"I needed to try. I won't mention it again." She bent the card and stuffed it into her purse. The morning sunlight, angled through the window, pointed to new and craggier lines on her face. There was the sense of weight pressing down, a weight that began with her black pillbox, sitting squarely on her hair, and delved down somewhere deep within her, where she still resisted.

"I guess I don't feel the way I'm supposed to about the wedding," she said. "Full of joy; isn't it? Happy? Well, I don't. I don't feel jealous, either, jealous of another woman. Even though all mothers say they're gaining a daughter and not losing a son, they don't mean it. They don't mean a word of it." She didn't even gesture to emphasize "a word." "I'm relieved, I really am. Will has had no business staying a bachelor as long as he has and no business stringing that girl along. He's been pampering himself, our own little Robert E. Lee."

I picked up Will at his new house on Eighth Street and drove him to the church, where we waited for an eternity in the choir room. He looked like he was going to puke. Once when he turned toward me I thought he was going to say he couldn't go through with it, that it was all a trap, that he really didn't love her. But he stopped, and held his head between his legs. When the minister came in and prayed about the vow and the holy occasion, I said, "Amen."

Will said, "It's now or never."

In the first row, flanked by Belle and Raymond, Mother sat with an erect and formal bearing. Will had bought her pearls to wear with her navy-blue dress. She gave us the slightest private smile. But her husband wasn't by her side for this second marriage, the first of a son, and no amount of jewelry or flowers nor the devotions of sons, could substitute. Uncle Warren and Aunt Cora sat behind them, and stretching back through the pews were the Randolph County relatives, who didn't care if Robert was there: a Treadwell wedding was a Treadwell wedding, and they felt the family obligation.

Will was still in terrible shape. "The aisle, Will," I whispered. He stared at me. "You're supposed to watch the aisle."

I saw my words plunge into his head and rattle around, until suddenly they sparked some kind of recognition and he looked up, just as Susan and Admiral Mallery came to the back of the church. They were a radiant couple. Admiral Mallery wore his ancient uniform, with epaulets an inch high on his shoulders, a sword strapped to his side. No one dared ask him to leave his weapon at the door. The bride's beauty—it was stunning and clean and simple—suddenly composed us. Smiling, she seemed in complete control of everyone in the room, making her slow, stately way past the murmuring people. Everyone smiled in response. As she came closer, I saw a necklace at the base of her neck, in the slight indentation where her collarbones met below the veil. It was a rose leaf, and in the noonday light streaming through the windows, it glimmered.

Halfway through the service the minister led the people in the Lord's Prayer. With all the eyes closed, we deceived ourselves into thinking we had tiptoed off stage for a few minutes, where we could change roles, relax, and forget who we were until the lights came up again. I spent the time studying Elizabeth, whom I had never seen so formally dressed. We had dated throughout the spring and she'd always worn casual clothes. When I dreamed of her—which was often—I never imagined her a lady at a formal affair. The picture painted in my mind caught her midair, in baggy pants, the aching second before her grand jeté touched this dull earth.

Now she wore a romantic Gainsborough hat like the other bridesmaids, but like them only in the sense that the hat was the same shape and made from the same material; the others couldn't wear it the way she could, with a cockeyed flair. Her light-blue dress fell tightly over her breasts to a high waistline. Her sleeves ended in fitted cuffs. And she seemed born into the pumps on her feet. No seamstress could dream of a more beautiful model. I realized then that there was something about her—and it wasn't simply her incredible body—that encouraged her to suit herself to this new set of clothes, or to her informal getup, or to any set of clothes or occasion or speech, like an actress always searching through her repertoire of roles.

The reception was at the Mallerys'. Most of West Point and Lanett came, as well as sizable portions of LaGrange, Lafayette, and Roanoke. The Treadwells were in full force. At one point in the afternoon, my father's oldest brother, Leon, put his arm around Mother and escorted her to the yard, where they talked under the oak until too many people bothered them. I wondered how she endured his sight. Our Treadwell genes were so dominant that every man in one generation looked the same as every man in the generations on either side. When Leon embraced her, he easily could have been mistaken for my father. She didn't cry, and in a moment she left him, smiling and nodding, a paragon of charm.

A green-and-white tent bigger than our house spread across half of the Admiral's yard, but all its food wasn't enough. Inside the house, silver punch bowls beckoned from every other corner, and all afternoon white-suited servants offered enough hors d'oeuvres to feed me every week, I guessed, for about seven years. I hadn't realized that a man in the navy made so much money, or that a woman from Mobile could bring so much with her. Nor had I understood what my brother had become. The war-hero status was thankfully passing, but in the meantime he had made his connections. He was even building a weekend house on their farmland so he and Susan could have two places, not ten miles apart.

The wedding ceremony was easy compared to the rigmarole afterward. At the church we took pictures in every possible permutation. Then at the house we went into the living room to stand on the reception line. With our backs to a great bay window, we suffered through a procession longer than common civility should demand of people on any occasion, whether it be a marriage or a coronation. The part of it we could see began in the foyer and stretched along the wall to us, then bunched up at the first refreshments (the punch was nonalcoholic—Susan and Will were Baptists). The conversation was repetitive and boring, through no one's fault except whoever dreamed up the idea of a reception. One of my Randolph uncles said I was next (that comment became the chorus). Two of Mother's friends had the gumption to mention Sharon O'Flynn, the first-grade teacher.

One of Will's friends—I had seen him at the Langdale Café—pumped my sweaty hand, winked at Elizabeth, and said, "If you can't dance." I didn't understand.

The afternoon sun burned through the bay window. Susan finally explained she needed to rest a moment, which left the assembled hordes to belly up to the food instead of to us—which was just fine.

But then came the cake ritual, one more folly we insisted upon before we could smile with satisfaction and say it was over, we had done it right. I stood aside and watched the two of them peacock through it, arms locked, mouths agape, bodies posed for the camera. Three local businessmen stood nearby, each of Irish descent. One of them said, loudly enough for the couple to hear, "May you ever give a kindly greeting!" Then the talk all around me turned to toasts and blessings, so I ducked my way toward the back of the crowd, having made my obligatory toast the night before and having no interest whatsoever in embarrassing myself further. I needed fresh air. I had done my duty. The last phrase I heard was "May the road rise up to meet you." I pushed through the door, past a few stragglers in the pantry, and finally out of the kitchen to the side stairs and into the sudden daylight.

I became aware of a presence before I identified who it was.

I looked toward the road and then back to the river. Elizabeth leaned against the corner of the latticework, by the stairs that led down to the path to the dock, where when we returned from that picnic in April she had drawn me aside and said, "Your brother. How can my sister . . . surely she realizes?" She had kicked off her shoes and tossed aside that Gainsborough hat, and she hid her hands behind her hips, which kept her shoulders nestled in the corner while her waist pushed foward, seductively. She was rumpled, from the heat and the crush, and she stayed in the shaded corner like a wise cat. A long devil-may-care curl fell over her face. She didn't bother with it when she saw me.

"These are times—" I said, "the cake, the how-do-you-dos, the first-name basis—when our due recompense as humans should be no more than quick and painless death."

"I knew there was something I liked about you, Luke."

I walked to the edge of the stairs. The sun burned like a demon on the opposite side of the house; on the shaded porch the heat was still intense. At my back I heard a few ripples in the river and a crow's cawing. The air would be refreshing at the riverside, where she and I could sneak away and stroll among the tall grasses, laughing at the fame and beauty of weddings. Then we could keep on going, if she was willing. Her eyes were slightly glazed, and then I caught the strong smell, and a taste like burnt wood watered in my mouth.

"A swig."

She hid the tiny silver flask behind her when the porch door opened. Every matriarch within would have condemned her to hell. We had stolen some together before. She followed suit when I returned it, and then held it again behind her back, daring me to come and find. I stared at the stray curl, and the press of the day weighing on the bridesmaid's composure. A pink flush colored her face. When my brother snatched up that kitchen knife and tossed it high over this woman's face, in a way I knew why. My brother was sick, compassed about with a pride and vainglory that this woman kicked against, as no woman or even a man should, he believed, because of his rod and staff, his glory and crown. But there was more to it than that, at least for me, as I felt myself swell up and want to press against her. I knew a blasphemous desire, a wicked boasting of my heart, to cut her open, to cut down her groves and remove her high places and break her images, merely because I am who I am and I wanted to cleave to her regardless of the ensuing hell and destruction. When I bent over, I paused at her lips, recklessly prolonging the moment until she kissed me, softly. I reached for the small of her back and pressed her to me.

She pushed me back, my arms leaning against the lattice-work on each side of her face. "My, how the lamb becomes a lion."

And then, quicker than an angel, she was under my arm, and gone.

II

Elizabeth: Nothing Is True for Everyone

7

*E*lizabeth dated Luke for the rest of the summer, but in September, just as he had feared, his reserve unit was called up and in less than two weeks he was shipped to Korea. She missed him, especially since he was the only man in the valley capable of carrying on a civilized conversation. Their sensibilities in such a wasteland made them kindred spirits, but if he had asked her to marry him that summer while they were dating, she would have refused. It was just too early in her life to marry. She could not abide the thought of a husband and children. She could not stay in Lanett, Alabama, either, nor did she want to return to New York, at least for now. She wanted to see other places. At first she assumed it was the usual yearning anyone her age knew, but the longer she stayed in the mansion by the river, with nothing to do, the more she believed her need to see—to see nothing less than the rest of the world—was desperate.

By December she persuaded Admiral Mallery to send her to Europe, in the company of two elderly ladies, all expenses paid. Their first stop was Paris. She rested two days before she got in touch with an old girlfriend from her one year at Agnes Scott, who gladly took her along on an excursion, a full week from Paris to Reims to Amiens and back, during which time Elizabeth did little else but wonder. Simply wonder.

Never in her life had she known an experience like the one she had the first morning in Reims, when she walked up from

the Marne and turned the corner of the boulevard to see and
to stand as a human witness to the great facade of the cathedral. She promised herself that as much as a human being
caught in time could, she would try to remember every detail.
But there was too much, much too much. The sculptured por-
tals, the windows, the arches, gables, the gallery and the
towers—there was more than she could grasp, more than was
humanly possible, just on the outside. And one tour around
the inside exhausted her. For almost an hour she rested in the
nave, staring at the two rose windows, each nestled in the most
glorious arch that man ever found in his soul to offer to God.
The lower arch that encompassed the smaller rose window,
along with the lancetlike arches of the gallery above it,
pointed to the greater rose window above, heavenward, where
the Apostles attended the death of the Virgin, and Christ,
along with the sun and the moon, accompanied her soul to
everlasting life.

As far as Elizabeth was concerned, heaven was here and
now in the great arch that gathered the lower one, the gallery,
and the two achingly beautiful windows together, and then
proceeded, column by column, down the nave to the altar as
only something essentially supernatural could do. Later on,
still stunned, she tried to sketch the face of the Smiling Angel,
but she was far more intrigued by a statue she found an hour
before dusk, hidden in the north transept. In the midst of all
the overwhelming transcendence, it was a comfortable detail
she could grasp, as a human. Eve, her face astonished by a
sudden intrusion, petted a gargoyle she clutched to her
breasts.

The next day their train approached Amiens at sunset. And
Elizabeth could not believe what she saw. Two days in a row.
It made her wonder if whatever was spiritual in life (she didn't
want to say God) was trying to communicate with her. Or was
it Beauty? The cathedral stood on a hill overlooking the town.
At the exact time the cathedral was first visible, the sun, low
enough on the horizon to be a clearly outlined, burning orange ball, shone in a direct line through the rose window
down the nave and out the incredibly high chevet windows to
the railcar where she sat, gaping. Studying the cathedral after
that first experience with it was senseless; it was best left
alone.

When she returned to Paris, she couldn't sleep. She sat up in
bed the first night back and thought. The distance of her trip

from Paris to Reims and Amiens was the same as a journey from Lanett to Montgomery to Birmingham and back. It made her sick. What reason was there for Alabama even to exist when a mere two provinces in France glowed with more art and culture and history—and beauty—than Alabama could possibly imagine, if it even cared?

An ache of homesickness, however, did smite her in Paris one night about three weeks later. She was double-dating. Her date was a fastidious, bowlegged, full-of-himself army lieutenant who spent the first half of the rainy evening pontificating on the shortsighted Marshall Plan, and the second half describing in detail the Chinese technique of brainwashing. He expected her to be impressed, not only with his brilliance and his money but with his good looks. Elizabeth sniffed out the goat in him. Toward the end of the evening, he tried to suggest, with as much grace as a Patton tank, that she come home with him. She shook his hand instead. After he was gone, she locked the door to her room and stood by the window for a few minutes before undressing. The rain hadn't let up all day. She could barely see the dark spire of Sainte-Chapelle and the lights of the Court of Commerce and Le Pont Notre-Dame. If her date had been a different kind of man, perhaps then, she thought. Lovemaking could be spiritual, too, she told herself.

She stayed in France through the winter and spring of 1951. Admiral and Mrs. Mallery continued to pay for the entire half-year junket, believing the two older ladies chaperoned her everywhere. Susan objected to the extravagance, but only to Will. He agreed that the Mallerys were indulging a spoiled young woman who was merely delaying the inevitable: figuring out whom she wanted to marry.

One day Elizabeth suddenly left her traveling companions in Paris, without explaining. She spent the Mallerys' money only on food and cheap accommodations—so cheap, in fact, that most American ladies would have passed them by. But for Elizabeth it was a matter of pride. She might not know who she was, but she knew she wasn't an American lady. From Paris Elizabeth traveled through the Loire Valley to Bordeaux, and then across to the sea. She wandered around Provence for a month until a week of rain came, and with it memories of home. At Saint Tropez she locked herself into a room with a Gide novel. She was so moved by it that for the next three days she roamed along the beach, wondering who she was and where she could find whatever it was she wanted to find.

Then a telegram came, forwarded to the embassy in Nice by her two older friends in Paris. It was reason enough, finally, to go home. Susan and Will's first child—a boy—had been born the first week in May.

It took a week to get to Alabama, and the time change coming back was worse than going, so even after a day's sleep in her own bed she was still exhausted. Will left for a business trip to Dothan before she could see him, but his absence was reason enough for Susan and her baby—his name was William Stearns—to spend the night at the Mallerys'. Elizabeth occupied most of their first day together—it drizzled all afternoon and evening—simply introducing herself, cradling, feeding, changing. Susan took the baby upstairs to put him to bed about the same time the Admiral and Miss Margaret retired. Elizabeth stayed downstairs by the living room's bay window.

It took Susan a long time to get the boy to sleep. For a while Elizabeth watched the raindrops roll like crystal-clear pendants down the tall glass of the window until they gathered into rivers along the bottom edge, and dropped off. As the rain slowly ceased, dim beacons of house lights began to spot the far shore of the river. She was tired. Taking care of a baby felt like forty-five minutes of nonstop dancing. But before she went to bed, she wanted to sit in this bay window, the most beautiful part of the house, and relish its charm, and her sense of being at home.

And yet she found herself thinking of Paris. She had left France exactly one week and two days before. She lived again in West Point–Lanett. But now that she was here, she felt a sudden desire to be there. She didn't want to stand at this plain, boring window; she wanted to stand where she'd once stood, in the bell tower of Saint-Germain-des-Prés. To her right wouldn't be the darkening street of Lanett, Alabama, but Saint-Sulpice, and in the distance the Luxembourg Gardens. Straight ahead wouldn't be a dirt town but the Eternal City lights, and to her left not the Chattahoochee but the Seine and the Île de la Cité. What was wrong with her? What was this uneasy desire to be in a place other than where she was, or to live in a time other than her very present? It was a momentary mood, she told herself; she was glad to be home.

But she could not convince herself. There was a great contradiction within her. She remembered how from Saint Tropez she'd written a long letter to Luke, narrating a story about herself in Paris. She told him that she had met a French girl one evening at Le Café des Deux Maggots on the boulevard Saint-Germain. They had talked for a long time and decided to meet and talk again the next night because there was something mysterious about the way they so quickly responded to each other. The next evening they had walked down to the Palatine, over to the School of Medicine, up the rue Dalphine to the river. They continued to join each other for a week. Elizabeth had never known such a freedom to speak, with a sincerity possible, perhaps, only in strangers. She told Luke about it, and told him about the book:

> At the end of the week, she told me I had to read this book. It was a life-or-death matter. I had France in my blood, she said, but I wouldn't really understand until I read it; then I could cast doubt aside because doubt was all. Doesn't seem to make sense, does it? I have read it here in St. Tropez and it does, though. Even though the book was published in 1926, Gide just died, and all the newspapers in France are full of articles about his lasting contribution, etc., etc.

She was lying to Luke. This French girl she'd met at the café was actually a French student named André. He was a short, dark boy, ferretlike, with small hands and feet and a nervousness calmed only by an endless parade of cigarettes. This sincere exchange of souls Elizabeth remembered was actually a week of his talk alone, in French and in broken English, about the world and French literature and politics and morals. He could quote from any of the newspapers in Paris. The way he talked, though, made Elizabeth believe that she was not falling into the role of devoted disciple, but that she, too, was talking, personally agreeing with his every opinion, fascinated by their collective insights. And when he said they should make love because only philistines objected on moral grounds, she agreed. Of course. Why had she not seen? What was wrong when two people, willingly, without deceit, without the encumbrance of outdated morals, decided they wanted each other? And she thought she loved him.

He did not touch her as they weaved through the crowds on Saint-Michel. To touch her would admit more than either wanted to at this point in their relationship. He kept talking, sometimes quite loudly so that she wouldn't miss what he said, but he never mentioned where they were going or why, because it was simply a physical act—she should understand—of little significance, like combing her hair, he had suggested at the café. The night was warm enough to stroll forever. Thousands of Parisians ambled along, in search of their evening leisure. A few looked traumatized, as a few always will in a great city, and Elizabeth kept away from them to protect her mood, and her determination. Past the Cluny they turned onto a side street and lingered at the cinema, where the projectionist sat propped in an open door, reading, while his machine clicked away behind him. Then André pointed to the balcony at the end of the street. They watched the movie for a few seconds, until he casually led the way into his building. Out of the corner of her eye, Elizabeth detected a movement in an open room to her left. A small black rabbit sat up and stared at her. Then a few more peeked out from behind a chair. André smiled, but Elizabeth didn't understand what he said. All the furniture, and most of the floor, was littered with rabbit pellets.

The circular staircase was a dying remnant of the building's more prestigious days. The paint on the banister had peeled off. The gilding on the carved balusters accompanied them upstairs like a choir of tin putti, and at each of the first two landings a beveled window overlooked a courtyard illuminated only by the lights of the surrounding rooms. Tall weeds grew up from the courtyard and tangled the rusted chairs circled around an unused table; atop it a cat waited for movement in the grass. Someone had left laundry on a line strung across the second floor—three dresses. In the half-light Elizabeth imagined three headless victims, let stand for public instruction. In the hall she told André she needed to go to the bathroom first. He showed her his door and motioned a few doors down. There was no seat on the toilet. And the toilet was filthy. It reminded her, for some reason, that she hadn't given a thought to the possibility of getting pregnant.

He was casually undressing when she came in, standing like an exhibitionist in front of the window, smoking another awful cigarette. The whole city stank of that same cigarette. He smiled as he saw her, but turned back to the window and finished undressing. Then he flipped through one of the newspapers on the table next to him. At least ten coffee-stained papers cluttered the table—no books. Unwashed dishes held the papers down. On the single chair was a half-eaten loaf of bread; a bottle of wine perched on the floor. A spotted mirror hung opposite the bed. The room was small enough as it was, but the clutter made it intolerable. She began to undress, but André stayed by the window, stark naked, engrossed in some article. It was just as well. She had never completely undressed in front of a man. The ash of his cigarette was ready to fall.

André wanted to enter her quickly, but she persuaded him to go slowly for her sake. He never asked her if she was a virgin, he just continued to go on, as if he were reading another article in his precious paper. At the end of the day, his beard was wicked. He drove into her neck and would not relent even when she tried to tell him. He wanted her to relax, he said. But he grew impatient. The taste of his mouth began to choke her. The cigarette taste was so stale she felt like vomiting, though she tried her best to get used to it. Very little about the experience was satisfactory. And then she felt a great swelling begin inside her. It had nothing to do with sexual pleasure. It was fear. And with it came a voice crying, No, it was not time, and if she let herself continue with this travesty of lovemaking, she would suffer so much she might not live. She had never known such a scornful voice from within her. A denial. Warning, warning her that she did not know herself.

His scorn was monumental. He stood at the end of the bed haranguing her without concern for anyone else in the building. How dare she stop! How dare she say no! She was a slut, a whore, a prostitute. She did not deserve his body. He was sorry he had even touched her vile skin. One day she would make love to a baboon and have his child—that was his curse on her. Then he turned to the window and went into a great Gallic deep freeze. Elizabeth left Paris the next day.

In Saint Tropez she decided André probably liked the Gide book so much because of Gide's name. But still, he was right. The book affected her. It made her forget any sense of the divine in cathedrals. And it made her ashamed of the way she had acted in bed. It had been an involuntary denial. The next time it wouldn't be, she told herself. But she did not completely understand why she lied to Luke about her French friend simply to tell him about the book. Luke was important enough to her to make sure he realized how significant she thought the work was, and yet she made up an elaborate lie about her life in Paris in order to tell him. She could have said,

"Luke, read this book," or "I found this book in the library."
But, no—instead she created this outlandish story of a girlfriend with whom she had a great spiritual affinity, as if it were
important to her to let him know that she had a spiritual affinity with someone, and that someone had given her a key to
living. Why did she do it? Was it because she found herself
spiritually attached to Luke while knowing that though they
had come close to making love once or twice, she didn't want
to with him? Why not with him? He was attractive enough,
and he never tried to force himself on her. He loved her—she
knew he did.

In the letter she went ahead with the novel, telling him the
plot, highlighting the unjustified murder, and then making her
point.

> But earlier in the book two characters named Bernard
> and Laura are talking. He says that nothing in the world
> exists that is not the subject of doubt, and therefore
> doubt might be all that does truly exist. He explains that
> he is keeping a journal in which each page is divided by
> a line. When he has an idea, he writes it down on one
> side, and then immediately writes an exactly opposite
> idea on the other. He goes on to say that he loves her
> (she answers that love is not important to her), but here
> is the passage I wanted to show you: "Nothing is true for
> everyone . . . that if, in order to act, we must make a
> choice, at any rate we are free to choose . . . and the be-
> lief that becomes true for me (not absolutely, no doubt,
> but relatively to me) is that which allows me the best use
> of my strength."
>
> Luke, I am tired of acting, or not acting, to suit a false
> notion—that something can be true for everyone. Noth-
> ing is true for everyone. Doubt is all that truly exists.
> What I must do is see the contradictions—oh, how I
> have seen them—and then choose what is the best use of
> my strength.

When Susan hurried back into the room, flushed with mother-
hood, she interrupted Elizabeth's reverie.

Since the day Will and Susan became bone of their bones
and flesh of flesh, Susan had discovered who she was and
where she belonged and thus she stayed firmly planted in the

middle of the road, by the side of her husband, her son in her arms. Susan never wandered the way Elizabeth did, even before she was married.

The day after Will and Susan returned from their honeymoon, she rearranged one of the bedrooms into an office, as everyone expected, and she took over the family finances, which no one expected. For the next month she met with the architect once a week until she was satisfied with the plans for the farmhouse and certain that Will's wishes were met to the minutest detail. When the farmhouse was finished, she didn't mind packing the clothes and food every Friday afternoon to spend the weekend there. Sometimes Will came back to town at odd hours when there was a death, but he was becoming more interested in cattle and she wanted to encourage him in his interests. She believed each individual needed to be personally satisfied before a marriage could be fulfilling. A few times she questioned the amount of work Will did away from home—in the office, at the funeral home, or with the cows—but she told herself that she'd rather have a worker than an idler. When she became pregnant, she worked four months on the two nurseries, home and at the farm, wallpapering them blue because she somehow knew it was a boy. (Will laughed at her, but she was right.) And they were the best nurseries ever created. Only the best.

On Elizabeth's first day back, Susan more than once implied she wasn't going to judge her sister. Elizabeth was younger than she was, reason enough not to judge. Not everyone came to a sense of purpose at the same time, Susan believed. Elizabeth would find an aim for her life someday. In the meantime it was Susan's turn. She had never been happier. She explained to Elizabeth that she enjoyed taking care of her husband, and when he was gone she enjoyed trying to imagine what he was doing, from inventory to baling hay. (She did not think about embalming.) She loved humming a tune to her baby boy, loved feeding him and tickling his cheeks until he smiled. She made his world. When Susan leaned back in the window seat across from her sister, her oval face glowed. The rose-colored tint of her skin reminded Elizabeth of all the paintings she'd seen of the Madonna—the ones she couldn't stand, the ones that turned her from religion—when Mary's eyes were illuminated at the cathedral altar by the flickering sea of votive candles.

"Now, my sister, sit down if you're not too tired," Susan

said. "You've finally come home. Now we have a chance to talk again—alone and uninterrupted."

"I'm sorry I wasn't here when William Stearns was born."

"Oh, I can tell you all about that for days and days. You'll regret giving me the chance. But—you've come home."

"Yes."

"Well, tell me. What happened? Out with it."

Elizabeth sketched a brief itinerary for her.

"Did you go to Versailles?"

"No."

"No? Why not?"

"I wasn't that interested."

"You went to Paris and you didn't go to Versailles? They'd never get me out. Poor Will, he'd suffer. Well, what did you do, then?"

"Walked a lot, I guess. I just enjoyed walking."

"You couldn't be gone that long without seeing something big—you know, something magnificent."

"Cathedrals."

"Yes, cathedrals."

"There was a rose window at Reims. . . ." She stopped, hesitating. She was tired. She also suspected—it was terrible of her—that Susan wasn't truly interested but had asked from some sense of politeness. Elizabeth didn't want to think about that window, not after André. Before she went to bed with him, she'd thought there might be a connection, but not now—she knew better now.

"I don't remember a tongue-tied younger sister. Of course you've been gone so long you might've changed. And you might not want to tell me about your escapades—or who you met?"

"No, no one. I was alone most of the time."

"I thought that—"

"I was with them for a while, in the city, but away from there it was safe to travel alone. No one bothered me. Of significance."

"I don't know if I believe that."

"Really. I met a few people, but . . . nothing."

Susan waited, but Elizabeth didn't continue. A long silence passed between them, until Elizabeth spoke again. "I really came home to see Stearns. I want to hear about the birth. We haven't had time all day and I don't know what to say yet about my trip. It will take me time, Susan. I'm still not sure I know where I am. You understand? I don't. Please, you tell me—for now. Really. I'd rather hear you. I can sort out my trip later."

Susan smiled. She narrated the story of the baby's birth, a story that in family circles and even around town was gaining popularity. Will had been so nervous in the waiting room that he'd kept his hat on the whole time. Elizabeth patiently listened to her sister's long story about the people who saw him in there and tried to give him a hint about it, though she wasn't interested in the details everyone else thought humorous, such as the condition of the hat itself or what the nurse and another waiting father and Dr. Morris had said. While Susan was laughing, Elizabeth searched above the horizon, which was cleared of rain, for the first star of the night, a diamond pinned to the sable cloth of the universe. As the story continued, the stars came out, thousands of stars, pure and safe from the confusion below.

There was something in her sister's story, however, that began to affect Elizabeth. It was Susan's tone of voice. The story itself unfolded as any other such story would, no matter how singular the Treadwells imagined it to be. But what impressed Elizabeth as different from her life, regardless of the cathedrals she had seen or cities she had promenaded through—or the man she had lain with—was the conviction in Susan's telling. She sounded happy—no, almost joyous.

"It was the strangest feeling, Elizabeth. As soon as the contractions started coming with any force, they put me completely under. It—I mean they—just happen to you. I don't care what you've heard. They happen—out of your control. I said, Stay calm and relax and breathe, but you do what your body tells you to do. Then they simply drug you into oblivion. It's too bad in a way.

"And, Elizabeth—I know I'm not supposed to say this, but when I was awake enough they gave him to me, the nurse did; she laid him in my arms and I looked down at this baby, Elizabeth—I know I'm not supposed to say this, but he was a real live human being and I wanted to say, 'What do I do now?' My God, it was the strangest feeling! I'm glad I didn't speak, of course, but here I've been preparing myself for this child, oh, so long, and suddenly he's snuggled at my breast and I don't care how much you think you've prepared yourself, it was still such a shock to have him real live and wonderful in my arms and know that he was ours and we would take care of him."

Elizabeth, paradoxically, felt old. Her older sister spun that rose-leaf necklace around her finger and chattered endlessly on like a young girl first in love. One moment she laughed at Will's hat, and then she jumped to Stearns's smile, or the dimple that giggled just like his daddy's. Elizabeth's daily existence suddenly seemed only a perch by the window, her crooked hands folded on her lap, where she would watch the river and the sky and experience life as memory, nothing more. André was a man of the past. Luke would be, too. What was wrong with her? She was a young woman, but the joy radiant in Susan's voice seemed inaccessible. She would not find another human being who intrigued her. Her blood would never feed two heartbeats. Her mind would never experience the ripening of a pregnant body, and surely not of a soul.

When Elizabeth looked up, Susan was smiling, her face radiant.

"What are you thinking of?"

"A day later, when they brought Stearns in, I don't know who was more helpless, the baby or Will. But I'll never forget that moment, sister. I curled the blanket back from my son's face and my husband just stared at him, stunned. The baby looked so old and wise; his skin was wet and red and wrinkled, and his tiny hands were scrunched up into fists. Will just didn't know what to say. Here was one of those moments in life and he didn't know what to say. I could feel all three of us swelling with wonder. I pointed to his Treadwell features and we talked for a moment, but soon we eased back into silence. I know I was tired and drugged, but when Will gave him back to me, every part of my life, Elizabeth—all my breath and my heart's blood—seemed fulfilled. Oh, I know. I know how I'm getting. I'm sorry. I can't explain it more than that."

They sat in silence until Elizabeth said she needed to go to bed. They walked up the stairs together, embracing outside Susan's bedroom. After she bathed, Elizabeth sat on her bed and began to comb her hair as she stared into the dresser mirror. Her reflection was a weary woman, weary unto death, even with her face freshly washed. She was dressed in a nightgown, that woman in the mirror, combing her hair before she would plop into bed for a long sleep. In the past year she hadn't had to get up early and hustle to work. Not since she'd pounded New York streets night and day, bathed in a dream that she could dance.

It was time to cut her hair again. She hated for the hairdresser to wet it down, because she was the only one who could comb through the tangles without committing Chinese torture. The woman would begin by saying, "Oh, it'll be no problem." Then, "Your hair is so thick!" Then, "Your hair is such a mess!" And finally, "How can you do this every day?" Thank you, world. She set her comb down. If only untangling her hair were the most difficult problem she faced.

On her way to the bed, she stopped by the window, which looked east from the back of the second floor. Unable to distinguish the river, she turned off the last light—the bedside lamp—and returned to find the dim moonlight glimmering on the river's muddy surface, and the few scattered lights across the way approximate to the shoreline. There were hundreds of lights along the Seine. Many a night she had strolled behind the cathedral, and once or twice she'd ventured down by the water, though the lower promenade was risky, what with drunks, thieves, and worse. She claimed other great rivers, too—the Hudson and the East rivers, and for one day the Thames. The Chattahoochee was the only river of significance her sister knew.

Susan jokingly called her trip "the Grand Tour." She was right. Elizabeth knew two European capitals. She'd sampled delicacies (in one restaurant, Le Pied du Cochon, her escort had treated her to pigs' feet. She didn't have the courage to tell him she could have stayed right at home in Alabama if she desired any single part of a pig). She'd climbed Notre Dame's north tower and knelt through ancient masses. She'd met handsome men who spoke words like *beaucoup* and *ce soir* and *le coeur*, not *y'all* and *sur' nuff*. She'd witnessed more of the world than most people in this town would see in their and their children's and their children's children's lifetimes. Susan had stayed home, by this river. And now Elizabeth was home again, and she felt broken apart, sick, and terribly out of place. A voice in the back of her mind told her she was tired and too hard on herself. Go to sleep, it said. But it was true. Susan seemed whole, healthy, happy to live where she did every moment of the day. All because of her love for this man Will Treadwell. And this son.

But Elizabeth did not covet her sister's way. She did not believe that a woman found her only fulfillment in childbearing, or in sacrificing for a man and those children she suffered to squeeze out into the world. She hated the very idea of sacrifice. What she wanted from her sister's life was its sense of fulfillment, its excitement, even in this backwater place. What

happened to a woman when she was married, when every
night a man like Will came to her? He was a handsome man.

A strange desire came over her then to strip herself naked.
She wanted to yank away her nightgown and stand at the
window, stripped and naked to the earth and the stars, barefoot before hell and heaven. Then she would dive, far into the
night, flinging herself uninhibited into the cool, liquid air, her
arms extended into her most mighty dance, until her naked
breasts split open the rush of that river. Then she would know.

8

*A*dmiral Mallery died in the fall. For the rest of the season and into the winter, his widow, Miss Margaret, did nothing but grow old by the living-room fire. At first she carried in a ladder-back chair and, with her patchy hands folded in her lap, searched through the flames for a glimpse of four spit-polished stars. Then she gave up moving the dining-room chair and asked Elizabeth to slide the soft wing chair across the room to the same spot, where she sank into the cushion like a waif and listened to Elizabeth play all her requests, one by sentimental one, listed in the *Broadman Index* under "Heaven": hymns such as "Beautiful River," "On Jordan's Stormy Banks," and "Jerusalem the Golden." Finally, she was in a wheelchair. She barely indented the seat, a flesh-going-to-spirit whose aged hands turned yellow, pocked with stains.

Even in all its despair and suffering, the months with Miss Margaret sustained Elizabeth. After the evening and two days she spent with Susan and the baby, she couldn't shake a depression that gripped her in a vise through the rest of the summer and the fall. She slept late and took afternoon naps. She ate too much and sneaked gin. She sat in a chair on the dock for hours. All she found worthwhile to do was read. But then the Admiral died. Elizabeth found him facedown in the yard; he had been headed for the river. Suddenly she was given an overriding purpose: to comfort a widow who even at her age had never expected the hands of death to wrench from

81

her the person she'd lived with for sixty-three years. Elizabeth helped with the usual tasks relating to the funeral, the estate, and to the deceased's personal belongings, but Miss Margaret seemed most consoled by what Elizabeth did best—play the piano. If hymn playing was how best to help, Elizabeth was more than willing to sit for hours and play whatever Miss Margaret desired. She felt useful. And, in a way, transfigured.

One January morning Miss Margaret sat in her wheelchair more silent and still than on any day without the Admiral. "Play 'Wayfarer,' honey," she whispered to Elizabeth.

Somehow that part of Elizabeth wrung with melancholy seemed to flow from her heart through her fingertips to the keys of the upright, losing itself in the C minor of "Wayfarer"—transferring her out of body into the sounds she gave to the old woman.

Miss Margaret sat straight up. Elizabeth finished the refrain and began another verse, startled by the invalid's sudden motion and apparent strength. Out of the woman's sorrow and weakness came a shockingly strong singing voice:

> *"I am a poor wayfaring stranger*
> *While traveling thro' this world below;*
> *There is no sickness, toil, nor danger*
> *In that bright world to which I go."*

Then she stopped singing, as abruptly as she had begun. Elizabeth played the melody again, with her left hand, and glanced at her guardian mother. "Are you all right?" she asked.

Miss Margaret didn't answer.

Elizabeth closed the fall board and settled the afghan from the woman's lap to her shoulders. Her aged hands were folded across her chest, fingers locked beneath her palms, as if any moment they would respond with the rhyme ... "here's the steeple, open the doors and see all the people." Now that her eyes were closed, though, head slanted on the backrest and her mouth open, Miss Margaret's face, yellowing and aching, looked more familiar. The wear of the years was more understandable. But Elizabeth hadn't taken three steps to the door, on her way out for the mail and a vigorous walk, before the woman spoke. "I see."

Elizabeth turned around. "Miss Margaret?" But her guardian mother didn't answer her. She was asleep, but speaking. "And there's little Martha, would you believe? How different you are. And over there, who? Why, Mr. Julius. And here is Adelia. . . ."

Elizabeth waited, her attention suddenly, and fearfully, awakened. "Miss Margaret, can you hear me?"

"Come, Adelia, come here, my darling. How I've longed to see you."

"Miss Margaret?"

"Come now, you come."

Adelia was Elizabeth's mother's name.

But Miss Margaret gave no more, falling back to sleep with a faint gurgle in the depths of her throat. This person's present life is nothing, Elizabeth thought; she has given in to her memory, where she found, for a moment, my mother. Even all these years—it still seemed unfair. Her mother hadn't been much older than Susan when she died. Elizabeth drove the thought away, took her wrap and her beret from the hat rack, and eased the door closed behind her.

After reading the return addresses, she stuffed the mail in her coat pocket, pulled on her mittens, and hurried across the street to start her daily walk. Sometimes in Paris she'd walked all through the day and evening, from the Cluny past the Louvre up the hill to the Sacre-Coeur, down to the Champs-Elysées along the river and then Saint-Germain to the Jardin des Plantes, its zoo, and its 1734 Cedar of Lebanon tree, where she rested until supper. But at home she walked only to the business section, over to the river, and back on the other side of the street, keeping away from the more frequented areas because she hated to stop and politely listen to another woman's squawking, and coming back quickly because she didn't want to leave Miss Margaret alone very long. The wind was brisk. She pushed her cap down over her ears and shuddered. Sometimes Alabama was too cold, too gray, almost as a revenge against human expectation. As she walked, Elizabeth stared at the tops of trees, where, except for a few pines and magnolias, the uppermost black twigs grasped for the sky like frayed electrical wires.

At the stop sign she crossed the street and stole past the Historical Society. She glanced at the river—it was even higher than yesterday—and started back, cutting through Peter and Mary Vredenburgh's backyard. There was a letter from Luke in her pocket. He had probably heard about the Admiral: his fourth consecutive letter without an answer. Once, and only once, he mentioned how few responses she sent, laughing in

his self-effacing way about the amount of time when he had
nothing to do but squat in some mudhole and write letters—
he was apologizing for loving her. If he weren't in a war. . . .
But she would write him—tomorrow.

In a few moments she was back. It was only a short walk,
but it always helped. She lingered outside the door to the
house. She didn't want to disturb Miss Margaret's nap. She
folded her mittens and unbuttoned her coat, wondering again
what dream it was that welcomed her mother. Elizabeth
hoped that the windows of the dream opened onto a meadow
sparkled with fresh dew, where her mother and Miss Margaret
would stretch forth their arms to each other and walk under
the veil of the morning star. That was the dream the old
woman deserved.

After she opened the door, Elizabeth hung her coat up and
turned to see Miss Margaret in the same sleeping position in
the wheelchair. It was only then that Elizabeth realized she
was dead.

Sometime in midwinter a thaw came. Everyone called it a
"surprise" thaw, though Elizabeth remembered sixty-, even
seventy-degree spells almost every February she had lived in
this outback. It was a "surprise" thaw because though it happened regularly, it wasn't supposed to happen, according to
the human wish that Nature will give us clear signals. Nature
even seemed to fool itself. Some stray strands of forsythia
blossomed and bent back toward the muddy earth to root
again. A few daffodils came awake. Pear trees began to flower,
and here and there a hint of peach.

Elizabeth took advantage while the warmth and the song
and the smell lasted. She first tried the lounge chair on the
back porch, but the wind at that height chilled her bare hands
and feet. She couldn't abide the prospect of shoes in this
weather. She took the chair, her stationery, and her book
downstairs to the middle of the yard, where the sun was direct.
It felt over seventy. The river only crawled along in the heat,
its surface warm and windless, and the house hid her from the
street and the neighbors. No better time or place to write the
letter to Luke—finally. She paused at the first sentence,
though, and looked up, waiting for some emotion, which had
grown within her for days, to discover words. That feeling
pricked her like a bursting seed. It had something to do with

this midwinter thaw, as if the ground within her were easing and she would force up a new self that would live forever. But she couldn't pin it down, she couldn't understand it, she couldn't say it.

She returned to the letter: news first, of course; Luke would be anxious to hear her perspective. With their part of the inheritance, approximately seventy percent, Will and Susan had begun an education fund for Stearns and purchased an additional 300 acres adjoining their farm. Will was trying to persuade Susan to sell the house in town and move to the farm, where he was expanding his calving business. (He'd also bought a leviathan of a bull, some monstrous humpbacked Brahman—he even named him "Brahman"—who was supposedly a superior animal: "resistant to cattle ticks," Will boasted, "and'll eat any grass and live through heat worse than hell.")

Admiral and Mrs. Mallery left Elizabeth $20,000. She decided to give Luke only the facts, at least for now: there was a request, not an injunction, that she invest part of the money and use the rest to finish her education; there was a clearly worded injunction that Elizabeth be unable to withdraw any amount over $1,000 without a countersignature from Susan, which in effect meant from Will. And finally, Will campaigned to sell the house to Mr. Schnedel, who was sure to convert it into a funeral parlor, an idea that made Elizabeth want to vomit.

At this point Elizabeth set her pen down and let her book and the letter fall on her lap. There was much more to say, but she questioned whether she could speak directly to Luke. His sensibility matched hers, and in this land his was the only one. He, too, wandered after a dream of a different place; whenever they knelt beside a fire in this wilderness and talked, the only two civilized creatures, their words were common and immediately understood. She wanted to tell him how she felt about something new in her life, about a new self, a new direction. But the more she let him say "Yes, you're right—of course—I completely agree," and "I understand—yes, something new," even if he said so in a letter sent from some politician's war, the more she encouraged him to come back to his alien home and ask for what she could not give.

She picked up the pen and went ahead. Her sensibility was far from aristocratic—she was writing the words so she could hear them herself, and profit by the thought that went into writing them; she was using him in the process, plain and simple. But she would worry about using him later. She narrated the story of Miss Margaret and then finished the letter:

At the time I felt like I was in the presence of something profoundly mystical. Here she had died by my side, and spoken. Is this how you feel, Luke, living your life on the edge of death? When men all around you are killed? Please pardon me if I am asking questions I have no business asking, considering the fear you must know every beat your heart takes—and in between.

For a few days I felt immensely generous. My soul wanted to burst open my rib cage and envelop the world. How fortunate we two orphans were to know the Mallerys, I told everyone. How necessary it was to live a life full of love—to give all you have to God and your neighbor. You'll laugh, but I felt like running down to the Presbyterian church and demanding they make me their first woman elder. I was ready.

But in another few weeks it changed. Of course it changed. First of all, it is the contradiction I've written about before, as if my soul—I'm not sure I want to call it that now—refuses to settle on one thing. This so-called soul knows that being an elder in the Presbyterian church would by definition keep me far from the truth. But here for a moment I had thought of myself as a disciple worthy to rival Paul—this scares me, this tendency of mine, sometimes to change rather quickly.

But as Bernard says, the belief that becomes true for me is that which allows me the best use of my strength—anytime and anyplace. If today I want to be a Presbyterian elder, and tomorrow I want to dance in a burlesque, so be it. Remember, Luke, that nothing is true for everyone.

                                 Love,
                                 Elizabeth

A month later Elizabeth spent a Saturday with Will and Susan and Stearns at the newly enlarged farm. In the afternoon she went with Will to feed his cows. As they strolled across the yard and up the long surge in the land to the first forty, Elizabeth occasionally looked back over her shoulder at the southwestern sky, where a gray curtain of rain, bordered in black by the sun, fell from high, tense clouds. Every moment the rain darkened and widened its reach. "All night long a storm can rage over there," Will said, pointing in the opposite direction, to the northeast. "It'll wake you up stark naked in bed. I mean the lights boom everywhere, like a battlefield. But nothing comes. Not a drop." Then he pointed to the threatening curtain. "It does come from there, without much fuss. We'll have to hurry. Catches you out sometimes."

After a few minutes the field ended. The trees curved by a muddy green lake that the state of Alabama paid Will to build, where the black cows waited, at the edge of the uncut, darkening woods. Their hindquarters were firm and muscular, but each pair of hocks seemed too bony to bear the downward thrust of such massive body weight. Farther out in the field, appropriately distant, the new Brahman watched them move toward his cows. Amid the great mountain on his back and the leviathan horns, Elizabeth found the two small holes that were his eyes, gray like the coming rain, close to white, to the absence of color. Every pendulous part of him appeared unknowable, a creature governed by an age-old instinct that willed one thing—to revenge any insult Will and she made against his territory.

Will smiled, reading her thoughts. He led Elizabeth toward a long wooden trough and metal storage bin and began yipping until the Anguses (he was crossbreeding) swung their heads and ambled in his direction, where two brown-and-white blocks of salt plunged into the earth like ancient monoliths.

Will had never been happier about his work—he said so himself—and Elizabeth thought he had grown handsomer from the more frequent farm work. The bulge had eased off his belly, while a sleek tightness gripped his back and shoulders and a sunburnt cast colored his leaner face. All the Treadwell men wanted leaner faces. Susan needed to tell him, though, to wash his hands. Elizabeth watched the cows nuzzle the wrinkled salt blocks and hover around the trough. From a distance she always thought cows were beautiful animals, especially the spotted ones, with white faces and feet, and full, rounded shapes. But close to them she saw the mess around their mouths, behind, and underneath, and she smelled them. Nothing was worse. One's wide, speckled tongue curled from its muzzle and licked the salt. Elizabeth turned away.

"You put the bull up in the fall—around October," Will said as he busied himself with some feed sacks in the bin. She didn't answer. " 'Til at least January. Prices are better in the late summer, you see. Yip now, come on, darlings!" A sharp busting sound scared her. Will plunged his knife into a feed sack and lifted it over their faces, the cottonseed cake pouring like grains of sand over their hot snorting. "Quickly now, honeys, before it rains. Almost the last time, with the grass looking so good." Will lifted an ear for Elizabeth to see. "Swallow fork. You nip a sideways V in each." With two fingers like scissors, he pretended to cut the cow's ear.

"Does it hurt?"

"She screams."

Elizabeth walked toward the lake. A faint gray cloud cover closed in on them and suddenly she felt the heavy, threatening air circle about every move and thought. A cow raised her head from the trough at the sound of thunder. Elizabeth watched Will. He was still slightly heavier than Luke, but his assured air was so different, especially outdoors. He finished with the feeding, closed the bin, and for some reason pulled back the skin above a cow's eye; whatever he did, he did economically, confidently. Lightning struck near the edge of the forest. The cows startled, bewailing their fate. "We better go," he shouted.

As she came toward him, the sky darkened and the rain began. She folded her arms under her breasts. Before she could object, he took off his flannel shirt and covered her head with it, lightly circling her shoulders with his arms. "Will," she said in a complaining tone.

"I don't care about getting wet. I don't want you to get soaked." He cradled her tighter, his chest naked against her side, and walked her across the field. In a few moments the rain fell so hard she forgot about objecting again, both of them grasping at each other simply to survive the downpour. She put her arm around his waist and encouraged him to hide under the shirt, too, and together they marched through the fast-sinking mud. The noise of the storm turned her hearing within her, as if she were listening to a seashell, and the steady sight of only grass and mud made her more conscious of the other ways she knew who she was: the taste of rainwater, for one—clear, pure water falling from the country sky. As she felt her hand hold on to his naked, wet skin, she imagined herself kissing the lips of a man risen from water. How smooth his wet lips were, and sticky his skin, clean and beaded. The fragrance of the wet earth rose from beneath her, and the smell of cows came with it, and the smell of his hands. She felt herself resist, but soon she was used to it.

Susan met them at the door. The farmhouse was a modernized slave quarter with a breezeway left intact through the middle, where the two drenched sojourners shivered in the towels she threw at them.

"What are you trying to prove, bonehead, that you can catch pneumonia? I told you two not to go out there, didn't I? That rain tears across the field every day. Both of you'll probably be bedridden for a week. Take your shoes off, Elizabeth, and put some of my clothes on—and bring your wet ones back out here. You, Will—to the garage. I'll bring you some dry ones and a switch."

In the bedroom Elizabeth kept the lights off, listening to the storm. She picked up the clean underwear and blouse Susan had selected and slowly dressed in front of the full-length mirror. Lightning struck nearby, shocking her. A tree cracked, stunned still for a second, and then achingly creaked, faster and faster, until Elizabeth heard a thud, the feather brush of leaves, and silence. Her heart was beating against her ribs. Stearns cried, but Susan's footsteps came quickly. She felt threatened, hiding in the only house for a square mile. Nothing protected them from the dark sky and its thunderheads. The wind had a forty-acre head start before it reached them, and the rain could attack from any direction. But the fear excited her.

The thunder subsided, giving way to a steady hard rain. Instead of the lightning flashes staggering the room, an even gray tone settled in through the window and across the mirror. The skirt and the blouse were ridiculously big. From the time she began dancing, Elizabeth remained slimmer than Susan. Her long, muscular legs, slender arms, her small breasts—every part of her fit into a narrow frame. Susan was fuller. She was also a mother.

As Elizabeth stared at her baggy figure in the mirror, she felt odd wearing her sister's clothes, the clothes Will knew intimately, as she had known his naked side hurrying through the storm. She slid her hand across the waist of the skirt until it played with the bottom of the blouse, and then eased toward a place between her breasts, where the material was loose. She bunched it up with a sudden tight grip. Then she let her fingers wander from there to the base of her neck, and on, caressing the smooth muscle, pathway to the ear.

In June Will sold the house in town and moved his family to the farm. Two weeks after moving in, Susan mailed over a hundred invitations to an open house. Elizabeth stayed over the night before. The two sisters got up at dawn and slaved in the house until the sinks were mirrors and there was enough food to feed two counties.

It was not a happy day, though. Susan was in a bad mood. In the morning, when Stearns wouldn't stop crying, she yanked him off the floor and shook him, and then held him out to Elizabeth and said, "Here, you take him." She slammed the door to her bedroom and stayed for at least thirty minutes. In the afternoon, as they were dusting, Susan complained that Mr. Schnedel took advantage of Will, working him both in a furniture store and in a funeral parlor and yet making it clear from the beginning that Will would never be a partner in either enterprise. When they finished the housework, around four o'clock, they showered and dressed. Elizabeth pinned her blond hair at her nape and wore a blue dress, and Susan matched her own hair with a brown outfit. A few minutes before 7:30, the sisters found their way to a couch in the corner of the living room, where they plopped down, anxious about what they forgot, and more ready for bed than for an evening of standing, smiling, and trying to remember names. Will had gone to town for more ice, and taken Stearns to Mother Treadwell's.

"Now when I want ice," Susan said, "or milk or butter, or I want to cry on Mattie's shoulder, I have to drive twelve miles to town. Twelve awful miles, and back! All because Will has gone off his brain's track about fat, ugly, filthy, stinking cows. My goodness, you would think a boy raised on a farm, once he saw the rest of the world, would have sense enough never to go back. But no, not Will. He's suddenly been converted to fields covered with cow pads—that's his paradise." Then she grimaced. "Oh, my God, I forgot that soufflé!" she said, running off to the kitchen.

Elizabeth didn't budge. Susan would imagine soufflés sinking every ten minutes for the entire evening, and when the party was finally over, she'd worry about something else, probably whether to wash the dishes before going to bed or leave them until tomorrow morning. And Susan was particularly nervous about the wine Will had convinced her to make available; he didn't care, he said, what the ministers of the gospel and the regulars of the front pews thought. Elizabeth wasn't going to bother with soufflés, dishes, or wine. Here, in the moment before guests would arrive, time was suspended like a bridge between the morning's great rushing and the shouting noise of the evening. She kept still, atop that bridge, listening to quiet waters softly swirl.

She especially liked the room's country motif. She loved the look and the feel of wood, in the ceiling's crossbeams and in most of the furniture—the corner cabinet, a chest, a trestle table beside her with an apothecary drawer in it. Wooden window shutters stretched the length of the walls. Three were open. The sun set on the opposite side of the house. The cool, bittersweet shadows of evening edged toward the warmer field and the darkening forest. This quiet moment was not perfect, though. It could not deny the day. Elizabeth had never heard Susan so complaining. Susan nowadays was never happy, even with the housework and its most insignificant details, sniping all day at Will and her and even the baby.

Something must be wrong with their marriage. The tone of Susan's voice had changed. Will had lost himself in the farm. Elizabeth remembered how jealous she'd been when she first came home, how Susan had seemed fulfilled, caught up with her baby and her husband. Elizabeth had imagined that the only way she could find some sense of herself was to cuddle a baby in her arms and love and be devoted to a man like Will. For the first few months after Elizabeth's return, Susan did keep talking of Stearns, as if her life were still joyous. But then, once in a while, she commented on what to everyone else was obvious: Will was staying away from home. Elizabeth had once summoned the courage to ask Raymond if Will was playing around. Raymond had told her that none of Will's friends had seen him at the Langdale Café or the pool hall—everyone in town would know, anyway, he said, winking at her, as if he thought she deserved a warning, which offended her. Susan, against her better judgment, had begun to complain, sometimes bitterly, even to Mother Treadwell, who understood better than anyone. It was still a mistake to mention it to Mattie, though, no matter how close to her heart the problem was. Elizabeth understood by the way Mattie carried herself, after almost ten years alone. She held her lofty head proudly through even the most trivial part of the daily routine at the store. She didn't mention Robert, or her dishonor in town. And no one dared question her, her sense of pride and self-sufficiency radiating as clearly as any strong words she could say.

Susan returned with two glasses of ice water. After she handed Elizabeth one, she dabbed at her nervous temples with a handkerchief and sat down again. A curl hung from her permanent onto the back of her neck, but Elizabeth didn't want to upset her more than she already was. In a few minutes she'd catch it in a mirror. "I hope Will is serious about the expansion," Susan said. "This is such a strange house. It'll take me a month of Sundays to grow accustomed to it—nothing is in its proper place. The absolute first thing we must do is close in that stupid breezeway, to make an entrance hall, maybe, and then add two rooms in the back. There's so much more we need."

"There are only three of you." Elizabeth knew she had made a mistake even before she finished her sentence.

"Well, there's only one of you over there in that mansion. Do you think twenty rooms are enough to do whatever you're doing with yourself, Elizabeth?"

Elizabeth laughed, a little nervous about Susan's sarcastic tone. "Yes."

"Are you sure? Maybe we should expand there first. We could build out from the back porch. In one corner a little piano room, for that music, and then in the other a dance studio—you must start dancing again—and maybe in between an art studio. I think you should take up painting, and then—"

"Enough, Susan, you've made your point. One room will suffice. Or maybe none."

"I'm not sure any amount of space will suffice, as long as . . . well . . . I might as well say it, you don't have some purpose."

"Purpose." Elizabeth wondered if that word didn't imply something else. "Purpose. I'm not sure that is the question. Or that there are such questions."

"You should go back to France. People can talk that way and get away with it over there, where there is no sense of morality." Susan mimicked her. " 'Purpose. I'm not sure that's the question.' Who do you think you are, Elizabeth? It's not that way here and you know it, yet you sit around in the mansion and indulge yourself as if there were nothing else in life but leisure and a few books, your stupid dreams, and gin. Yes, I know about that."

"I'm not trying to hide it, Susan. Why don't you simply say you want to pick up your family and move home and kick me the hell out of there? I don't mind your saying that. It makes perfect sense. I don't care. I *don't* care. I don't plan on staying, I just don't know where I'm going, and it has nothing to do with purpose—only a place to go."

Susan didn't answer but looked away with an angry sigh. Elizabeth felt her own hot wave of disgust break through her. She massaged her face, listening to her breath touch her hand, and tried to calm down. She didn't need to put up with Susan's pettiness. She didn't have to spend a whole evening and a day helping her prepare for her petty open house, when Susan didn't even want to live here. Elizabeth wanted to go. But not just home. She had to pick herself up and get on the road and never come back.

A car pulled into the garage. Will was back. It was 7:45. Then the doorbell rang—the first guests.

Susan stood up and turned toward her. "And I've seen the way Will looks at you."

Elizabeth shuddered. Before she could answer, Susan huffed away indignantly, until she opened the door and suddenly transformed herself into a sugary hostess whose accusation seemed no more significant than a bar of soap. She was so happy, so absolutely pleased that Barbara and Bob Rogers were the first to arrive; and after them, that Mary and Steve Heath could make it; and then the next couple, and so on, doorbell after doorbell through the evening. She made a person think that adultery—if that's what she really meant—was a minor imposition on her party: two fewer people would enjoy her hospitality.

Elizabeth waited on the couch, still disbelieving. The way Will looks at her? Finally, after five or six or seven arrivals, she stood up, but she felt too dizzy to move. Steve Heath asked her if she was all right, but she gained enough balance to thank him and excuse herself to go to the ladies' room, she said. Maybe Steve would worry enough to tell Susan, who might worry that she'd been too harsh, especially when she found her spick-and-span bathroom forever stained with Elizabeth's innocent blood, which she wanted to let from her wrists just to spite her wicked sister. But that was a childish idea. Elizabeth went straight to the guest room. She intended to pack her overnight bag and walk home, and afterward walk west to nowhere and never return, never even send a postcard.

Zipped into an inside pouch of the bag was her flask of gin.

The drink burned, and it burned again, and a third time, until the unseen hands that gripped her head every time began to tighten. She turned to the dresser mirror, but her image looked the same, no matter what vicious thumbs dug into her brow. Gin. She had no capacity and she knew it. But she didn't drink to hold it. She folded her nightgown and stuffed it into the bag and wandered to the bathroom in search of her cosmetics. The bathroom blurred—first the sink, then the towel rack, the mirror ... She held on to the door. She would go home later. *The way Will looks at you.* Susan had said that. Elizabeth couldn't believe it. She would go back to the party and find some way to sin, except it wouldn't be sin—that was just a word she used, left over from her childhood. "Nothing is the same for everyone," she quoted. But whatever she did, it would be within Susan's sight. And not something silly. She wanted to sin, really sin; she loved the very thought of sinning, and the worse the better. Something evil, something unpardonable—that was it. Something no one could forgive her for.

She sat down on the floor and leaned against the bed, her brain dizzy. For a moment she believed she was dying, fading far away from the fever of this life she was beginning to hate. Then a vision of a man came to her, half-André, half-Will (yes, it was Will). He wore gloves. They were walking somewhere green, in the Luxembourg Gardens, maybe, or this farm through the forest toward a hidden place, where the ground was covered with spongy green moss and shy spots of violets and trilliums. There they lay down. All around them tall pines rose up, taller than she imagined they could grow, and slanting light came through the forest ceiling, each sunstroke painted at an angle that made her ache. Finger by finger he tugged until his gloves came off. He cupped his gentle hands and laid them on her, gently massaging, and kissing her, and gently loving until she knew the truth of sin, the part of herself she was taught to deny. She felt the air circle and flutter through her as she had never dreamed possible; felt that the very earth was alive if only she'd touch and taste and know. Then there was a blackness. . . .

Down the hall the toilet flushed. She woke up. Her head hurt. She tried to gather herself together as Kay Donaldson walked by, glancing in and smiling. Had Kay noticed her the first time? Elizabeth didn't care. She really didn't. She felt a little more stable, though she didn't know how much time had passed. She'd try again. Damn Susan. She made it to the kitchen, where she picked up a glass of white wine. She felt a little sick. All she needed the wine for was to hold the glass. It actually helped her balance. Leaning against the wall, she surveyed the people, clustered in many more groups by then, chatting about this recipe and that fabric, this woman and that child, that and this and this and that, until she felt sicker. Insects buzzing. She was too shy, though, to sin. A few years ago she wasn't. That was a loss, a terrible loss. She heard a man's voice—it was Steve Heath again, with eyes that were dead giveaways. He was married, too. She ducked under his arms and through the door to take up a post in the breezeway, where the night air seem to relax the hands around her head. She wasn't that bad off, thank God.

This *was* a strange house, she thought. Brick pilings elevated the floor almost four feet at one end. Against all advice, Will had chosen not to underpin, believing the circulating air better in hot weather. He only wrapped the pipes. Another roof, at a different angle, came off to form a front porch. On one side was the living room, kitchen, and guest room, and on the other two bedrooms: she could stand smack-dab in the middle and still feel the night air curl like kitten paws around her neck and soothe away the gin. Everyone would comment about the breezeway. Elizabeth smirked. Every supposedly discriminating person would whisper that the arrangement was as ridiculous as Susan feared every discriminating person would think. The breezeway wasn't ridiculous—Elizabeth liked it and knew creative people would, too—but she guffawed because Susan was so concerned about what her fellow upstanding citizens would think. They were probably more indignant that it was once a slave quarter, though they didn't tell her.

Elizabeth heard voices behind her. At first she could distinguish only a circle of burning coals in the darkness. When the lights swung back and forth like signal lanterns, she realized they were cigarettes burning and that the circle was of men. She immediately felt out of place and resentful. If she sashayed down the walk and showed herself, they would make a gentlemanly fuss over her and she'd never discover what men talk about in those primitive circles they form, far from female hearing. She wanted to know. And the prospect of overhearing pleased her—at least that was sinful, if only a little. She strained to listen, but the gin had dulled her hearing. As quietly as she could, she stepped closer, until she detected words, cocking her ear toward them.

"Those days are over, aren't they? It happens when they put that ring in your nose."

"Shoot."

"Who owned the place?" It was Will's voice.

"Some vice-president of GE." Elizabeth could match a face to this voice, but she couldn't remember the man's name. Just as well. His face was ugly and vulgar. Brown teeth smiled under his pockmarked nose, and black hairs grew like grass in his ears. Did men like this one dominate those private circles?

"And?"

"Well, it was the middle of the night. I saw the full moon when I went to bed but didn't ponder it, as dead tired as I was. But we realized afterward. There's a connection, I tell ya, and it ain't just with bitches and bossies—it's with our own, too. That full moon comes out and strange things happen. Watch your women then, or bet your booties you'll lose them. Well, to make it short, we didn't expect it. There was a pasture at the end of the rows of houses for them prize bulls, and in the middle of the night one of the cows we put in there that very goddamn afternoon, she came in heat.

"The cowboys woke up before the roof hit the ground. They jumped out of them bunks and were on their way before I knew what happened. Maybe he'd be finished by the time they got there, they said. It had happened before. I never heard the crash myself, but one of 'em shook me awake and said, 'Stop jerking off, boy, and get your pants on. We got big problems.'

"The road was white with moonlight. As I ran I heard the bellowing. Long, moaning sounds like a foghorn. And then shorter and quicker. I couldn't believe the houses. Those things were built with concrete, and if the bull had any sense, he would have gone out the open end and pushed over the barbed wire. 'Cept we're dealing with a dumb brute, just as dumb as every penned-up horse that won't leap a fence. So the bull gets so frigging hot he butts the wall down. I swear to God. It looked like a tornado had cut clean across half the house, one wall crumbled and the roof collapsed on it, the other wall still standing. And his face was mangled. Blood dripped down off his nose, and I thought I saw bone. I couldn't stare in his face for long, though—it was too awful. Besides, I got there too late."

"Oh, come on, Luther."

"I did. He was already finished."

"All this and you're goin' to tell us you didn't see it?"

"I tell you what I did see, besides his mangled bloody face. The biggest goddamn . . ."

Elizabeth hurried to the other end of the breezeway and down into the safety of the silent yard. They could finish their story alone. For a few moments she paced back and forth in front of the house. She didn't want to think about it. If she let herself, she felt disgusted. Her stomach turned from the very thought—or as much from their attitude, their vulgar laughter. The night air slowly settled her and eased the gin's grip. She kept walking, telling herself she was not drunk—that though she wouldn't feel better until tomorrow, she wasn't drunk—until she rested against the side of the house and took refuge in the night sky. The sprinkle of stars, dancing stars, feathered the dark firmament. The half-moon turned its silver purity away from the vile earth. She had never studied the constellations, but now she wished she knew every one by name so she could occupy herself, announcing, one by one, the people of the heavens. Even though her feet were forever planted, holding the earth for fear, she wanted now to stay with those heavenly symbols as long as she had breath. But she heard party voices vibrating through the wall, insects buzzing. Not the voices of the gods. Nothing could protect her.

"It's a beautiful sight, isn't it?" Will stood on the steps.

She didn't answer.

"You feel open out here," he continued, turning the palm of his hand toward the night. "You can stand where you are, Elizabeth, or better, far out in the field. Lift your hands up and feel all around you, turn and turn and turn, and feel how open it is, and then you can stare ahead to the forest, pointing, and see the trees stand up like giants." Elizabeth swiveled toward him to get a better look. This was a Will she didn't know. He looked more relaxed, a little like Luke, but carved into a fuller substance, with sloping, muscular lines. Luke was always too monkish. "And the trees keep on going, to the dark blue horizon, Elizabeth, blue on blue, and up until the stars come out, and the lady moon, and somehow you feel more a part of it than you do in town, no matter how small a part."

Elizabeth didn't know what to say. These words—from Will? She stood still, looking at him, and then away, up at the night sky. She was confused. His words washed her soul with purifying water. Maybe he knew she had heard Luther and wanted to come and tell her not to be offended.

But it was not only Luther's offense. Luther's was insignificant, unintended. Susan was the one. Susan had accused. Did Will know? She was confused because she suddenly became aware of Will's presence in a way she had not felt before.

He kept his distance and did not speak again. How wise not to. She was beginning to understand who he was, and could forgive him his faults. He was a much more sensitive man than the one she first met, with that knife that was simply his father's scar—she should have realized. Susan couldn't fathom his desire to live at the farm, but Elizabeth could, especially now, after what he'd said. He was recognizing where his own stars and their voices were, and he knew that life was not worth living without them. And they didn't even have to confirm it to each other, only stand nearby, and keep silent.

A few of the guests began to leave. Will spoke with them, and Elizabeth sneaked by and returned to the living room, where she hid in a corner chair. Steve Heath was drunk with wine, but harmless. After the first guests left, most of the others departed in the next half-hour, leaving only the perpetual stragglers, the ones who'd rather stay away from home. Elizabeth still didn't feel tired, so she decided to leave. Someone could give her a ride home; she surely didn't desire Susan's indulgence another night. She wandered through the room, seeking someone to ask, and stopped at the kitchen door.

"But she's your sister." Neither Susan nor Will saw her standing there.

"All she thinks she needs to do is jump up and dance and the world will forgive her. And you like it."

"She *is* different."

"And she's my sister, Will. And don't you think for a second I haven't seen."

He didn't answer. Tension infested the air. Susan didn't need to start in on *him,* too. Once was enough. Elizabeth wasn't angry, only resolved to break away for good. She pitied her sister, whose life had stooped to such pettiness.

"Look at me." His voice flared. "Look at me, Susan! I am sick and tired—"

Susan turned and saw her. She burst away from him before he could finish, and, unbelievably, marched directly past her own sister into the living room to assume a pose that nothing was wrong. A couple turned their heads at the shouting, taking their cue that it was time. "Oh, you're not going, are you?" Susan said. "The night's still young."

Will's anger, however, did not leave his face. He stared at Elizabeth. "Get your bag. I'm taking you home."

"I will make it on my own."

Will touched her hand. "I said I'll take you."

She went to the bedroom and then walked to the door with him. "I am taking Elizabeth home," Will said, staring into Susan's face.

She didn't answer.

Will opened the car door for Elizabeth and then backed the car out. When he turned around, he floored it, the tires squealing for almost three seconds. They sped along the blacktop like rapids breaking past a riverbank, and she was happy, happy in the desperate ache she felt at being alive and traveling somewhere, anywhere—to any other place. By the time they reached the State Line Bridge back into West Point, he had his hand on her thigh. "What is the use, Elizabeth," he said, "if my wife is going to be suspicious no matter what? Tell me—what is the goddamn use?"

Elizabeth let another hot draw of gin burn down her throat. "Then you haven't been cheating on her?"

He stared at her, smiling ever so slightly. At the mansion he was out of his side of the car as quickly as she was hers, and when he took her arm he led her past the side stairs to the backyard and the trees lining the river. The stars were hotter now, closer to the earth. The stars had come down to tell her that, yes, she could make a new self, and that this man was a different man from the one she first knew—look, he had made himself anew.

She let him pull her to his chest, and she felt his strong hand grab her hip and softly knead it. Then he fumbled toward her blouse, jerking at her bra and kissing her ear. She would let him. She heard a voice that said this was unpardonable, that no one could forgive her for it, and she loved it, the sound of that voice, for she would let him and she would love each moment, the strength of their passion, the strength of their sin. What the hell.

III

Luke:
Letters from Home

9

I arrived in Korea during December of 1951, with the Forty-fifth National Guard. Another two years of attacks and counterattacks along the 38th parallel would follow, with the most savage fighting centered around the Iron Triangle, where my division was first sent.

I was very lucky, however: I didn't stay with my division, because, of all things, I could type. Most boys couldn't care less about their high-school business course, but my mother was obsessed with mailing legible bills and letters and thus insisted I type them for her, and since I was obsessed with my own hormones, I didn't especially care to spend my few extra hours pecking at the keys with two fingers. So I mastered the old Royal, never dreaming that this skill—women's work— might one day save my life. My army buddies tried to humiliate me when I was transferred, but every one of them would have traded places. I felt guilty about my luck only long enough to realize I wasn't stupid or sacrificial enough to volunteer to change jobs. My only claim to service beyond the call of duty was that I was one of the few Van Fleet didn't ship home after a year: male typists were not easy to find.

I was sent to Munsan-ni. I worked in a small concrete building painted the same brown as the mud and the few trees nearby, with four windows, each positioned in the exact center of each of the four walls. My window looked out on one small tree that bordered a stretch of checkered rice paddies on the edge of town. Every day our negotiating team helicoptered to the tents of Panmunjon to wrangle with the Communists about the last and greatest obstacle, the prisoner-of-war issue. I waited with nothing to do but read and monitor a few military and press reports until the team returned; then I typed into the early morning, either the day's proceedings, copy after copy, for military and not press purposes, or letters back and forth from negotiator to general to senator to negotiator.

All this time we were close enough to the Iron Triangle to hear the muffled thunder of bombing along the northern horizon, which all the more made us feel the utter uselessness of each successive negotiating session. I would type conversations in which the Chinese lambasted us as munition merchants and warmongers, while the U.S. preached about civilized countries and criminal behavior, and not more than a few miles away from this ridiculous talk stood the cratered, bloody hills with names like Elko and the Hook and Old Baldy and Erie, and when we ran out of good names, places like Hill 347 and Hill 395 and the No-Name line at the depths of the Communist offensives. Here the Chinese began another murderous drive timed for the American election, and then, in the final senselessness of the war, one U.S. company after another—King, Love, George, Fox, Able—was wiped out defending a worthless plot of ground called Pork Chop Hill until we retreated, sixteen days before both sides suddenly, as if everything were different, signed the armistice.

There were times when I almost lost my sanity: alone at my window in the middle of a languishing afternoon; early in the morning, unable to sleep, listening to a dog howl like an unbeliever strapped across the rack. I accept that a man experienced in combat cannot allow a behind-the-lines typist the pressure to go insane. Only twice was I in the bunkers, I never flew over the Yalu River, and I didn't suffer the indignities of those demonic camps in the North. And I am not even arguing that if I had been sent to the front line, I would have had that steel rod in my guts necessary for murder, or the acceptance of being murdered. Nevertheless, hour after hour I stared out that boring window and felt a growing pressure of the mind. It was a sameness in the middle of death, as if death didn't matter.

Two or three times a day, a procession of the wounded and dead crossed the yard to the Red Cross tent conveniently staked next to our building. Since my unit had long since been sent home in exchange for fresh meat, the men were mostly strangers to me, but all of them were human beings who couldn't understand any more than I could that they were simply part of the skyrocketing body count—the numbers, that is: the same ten figures arranged in a different way every day—while we tried to negotiate what the politicians considered an honorable armistice. Could anything honorable come out of one stretcher after another?

One difference, perhaps, between myself and the other men—the living men, that is—was that they had contact with what they could call reality: letters from home. Oh, I had letters from home, but they were not anchors to reality. They didn't describe the new farmhouse my brother was building, or remind me of his cranky, irritating habit of humming after he sneezed. None of them tasted of Mother's sugar-sprinkled apple pie, or told of her letting loose at the washing-machine service man until he backed out of the door. And no one bothered to tell me of my nephew's two new teeth that kept his mother up all night. This daily trivia was what every soldier desired. Each picture took on overwhelming significance, binding the man, through all the shrapnel and strafing, to some hope that he could make it back to the radiance of the mundane.

No, the letters I got talked of other things. Unreal things. Three of them, in particular, reminded me that there wasn't much for me back home—no hope nor joy nor love. Only the troubles of my family.

My father wrote one of these three letters. I was shocked when it came; its very arrival seemed unreal because my mind had sent him away into the community of the dead. Fifteen pages scratched in tiny script, with dashes for periods, were written over four months; each entry had a date, as if it were a diary. The letterhead of the first page read *The Atlanta Mission House.* He began without a greeting or an apology or even some innocuous questions, but with two quotes, one verse in Acts and the other in Galatians: "After that many days were fulfilled," and, "But I went into Arabia."

At first glance these verses made no sense. I expected "For by grace are ye saved" or "For God so loved the world," evangelical injunctions in keeping with what we had heard about him. But a little study explained. The half-verse in Acts follows Paul's conversion, the quickest of conversions; the writer of Acts gives the impression that once the scales were dropped from Paul's eyes, he ran to the synagogues and pronounced Jesus to be the son of God; and that after he was lowered from the Damascus walls in a basket to escape death, he sped off to Jerusalem. The miraculous story, then, from blinding light to Barnabas's introduction to the apostles, seems to take no more than a few weeks. But the verse in Galatians, "I went into Arabia," explains that after his blinding on the road to Damascus, Paul spent at least three years in the desert (the "many days" of Acts) and did not begin his evangelical missions until he'd had this time to fast and pray and, as my father suggested, to find himself and his true mission.

My father spent much longer than three years in his desert, and after a while, he wrote, there was no doubt in his mind that he, too, was going through a similar process of fasting and prayer in preparation for four great missionary journeys God had in store for him. But at first he was full of doubt. In June 1942 he'd banged out of our tenant farmer's shack and headed toward the Chattahoochee, tossing his wallet into deep water. All he could do was recite the Lord's Prayer over and over again. He stayed with the river for days, hopeless and hungry, until along the crest of the bank he found his first rusted fishhook. He clawed up worms, tied his shoestring to bamboo, and fished for crappie. From a junkyard he took a small rack to lay across the fires, where he sat for hours, hearing nothing. The dead fish eyes were glassy.

A bum tried to rob him. He almost killed the man, believing that it was he who had killed Doug. When he realized that his own sinful hands had tried to murder a man, and that Christ said that the least of them was He Himself, my father beat his head with a rock until he fell to the ground unconscious. He could not tell how long it was before he returned to his senses. He only remembered waking up, a long ways away, in front of a face bathed in steam.

It was a man named John Barker, an old, infamous railroad engineer in Atlanta. The steam rose from the tracks in the downtown Atlanta railroad station. Below the headlamp of his engine, he had constructed an open wooden book and had painted on it JOHN 17:7, "Thy Word Is Truth." He persuaded my helpless father to sign on with him, traveling by slow-moving local freight train from Atlanta to Spartanburg, South Carolina, and back. Dad not only signed on, he stayed with Barker for seven years, learning about evangelism and about the operation of a train. After two years the train company was paying Dad, but like Barker he distributed his money to the poor along the tracks and stayed in the mission house in Atlanta and the YMCA in Spartanburg. He also implied he sent money to Mother.

Along with the writer of Acts and the Gospel writers, he had no more to say about the experience of praying and fasting in a spiritual desert. On the fifth page he asked me to close my eyes, as if I were in some tent revival, and imagine what it was like bringing that big engine into a small town like Winder, for example, and seeing, even in winter, the bundled field hands atop their pickups, waiting for Barker to preach. Mechanics, grocerymen, and shop salesmen made pilgrimages to the station, and colored people waited on the outside edge of the crowd. Dad said he sat beneath the cab window and held Barker on his shoulders—even at his age it wasn't hard, because the man's sermons never lasted longer than ten minutes. The sermons always finished with a rhythmic challenge to the crowd.

"I bring the message o'er the rails, brothers and sisters. Repent and be saved!"

"Amen!"

"Believe on the Lord Jesus Christ."

"Amen. Praise the Lord."

"Repent and believe on the Lord Jesus Christ and the cold winter will give way to the Balm of Gilead, your sins'll be forgiven, your soul'll be healed, and you'll mount up not on this earthly train but on a celestial one, chugging its way to heavenly glory, brothers and sisters." Barker always pulled the train whistle at the end. "Amen."

"Amen!" the crowd shouted. "Hallelujah!"

The rest of the letter, as expected, was more speculative. My father realized that this railroad engineer succeeded as an evangelist because he did the work of the Lord in a memorable way—in the same way, I suspect, that Paul's "thorn in his side," whatever it was, might have captivated sinners scattered around the Mediterranean. For seven years, then, my father searched for what might distinguish him. If he were crippled, perhaps, or maimed, or in some way terribly different from other people—if his eyes burned with a fire no one could deny—then sinners might pay attention, even if for the wrong reasons. When they listened, he was convinced they would be his.

He knew it would be a matter of how he preached—or, better, how he didn't preach. He wouldn't preach, really, not in the conventional way, but he would imitate Christ by the purest method possible, telling what he called "modern parables." He had always loved the parables—he had drawn boxes around them in his Bible. They were stories, and stories appealed to people of the South—and to all people. These parables helped him see Christ as a person, walking along rows of corn, like a farmer, talking about the sower and the reaper, the given talents, the watchmen waiting or the prodigal's brother. If Christ were alive, Dad remarked, and wandering these same fields of Georgia, he would be a storyteller.

And with that thought, the casing began to burst. He still resisted, he made a point of saying, knowing all too well that I would remember he had told a story before, and that my brother was dead. But one day in a late fall, on the way back to Atlanta, with the engine stopped, he stared across a pasture to the edge of a forest. It was almost evening and the changing woods stood in the shadows, while the fast-setting sun lighted the tops of the trees like the flames of candles. In his soul he felt the need to rise up from the darkness of his years into the burning fire. He quoted Hebrews: "Our God is a devouring fire." Then God told him he had to throw himself in. There was no other way. No matter what had happened.

Beyond those still, incandescent treetops, a few buildings of Atlanta edged up toward the reach of blue, but as the sun dropped to the earth, its flames seemed to set fire to the city. He watched as the burning gold and dark red and purple of the sunset sacrificed Atlanta to the wrath of God, who had flooded the earth, who had burned Sodom and Gomorrah, drowned the Egyptians, and leveled the walls of Jericho. God had also threatened to burn Nineveh, but a prophet who had tried to hide saved the city.

In the Atlanta railroad station, my father said goodbye to John Barker. He skipped across the way to another track and caught the Boston-to-New Orleans home, with the incredible idea that since he finally understood what God had in store for him, Mother would be so impressed as to hear the voice of Jesus, too, and join him on his first missionary journey. This trip home was narrated in the second letter that vexed my bones, thousands of miles away in my Musanni tent. All of

Mother's previous epistles intended to instruct and comfort, any news that would jar eased over with a pasty sentiment she felt would nourish me during the long hours of war. But instead of fussing over her underfed son this time, she confessed her anguish to him. I was shocked: this my mother, a farm woman, a Cleburne County King, who knew that children, no matter what age, should not share in the private life of their parents. In those three months after Doug died and Dad ran away, and in the ten years he had been gone, she had not discussed her barest feelings with me once.

She began by flat-out announcing that the old man came home to enlist her as his disciple. But before she could tell me what the man actually had the gumption to say to his very wife—they were still married, she reminded me—she was compelled to let me in on a scene from their early marriage. She had recalled the episode more than once, including the day before he came back. Her tone was bitter—how ironic it was that she remembered that stormstruck summer night, when she was pregnant with Will. Could I understand how she felt in the pit of her stomach when this long-absent prophet popped in the door and began preaching at her?

They lay awake, hand in hand, listening to the stormy sky convulse and yet not rain. She stared at the flashing ceiling. "He's kicking," she said. "I've never felt him kick like this, Robert."

He immediately knew the obligation to be male. Rising from the bed, he stood at the window, where the winds threatened a tornado.

"Do tornadoes come at night?" she asked.

They didn't have a cellar. He'd take them to the middle of the house and lie her on the floor, with him on top and the child down. Wasn't he supposed to open all the windows? He looked foolish, trying to act like his father, the calm, grown man.

Then he jerked from a nearby explosion. It cracked open a pecan tree right next to the house. She got up and stood next to him.

The sky seemed helpless, convulsed in a fit before a truth greater than itself. No other cracks of lightning cut down to the earth—it wasn't that clean and simple. The flashes and thunder far exceeded heat lightning—it wasn't that, either. No, it became much more—a fire all through the night sky, a burning, a booming like the stars themselves exploding. She watched for light and began counting, but four more flashes lit up the sky before she heard the first strike. Or sound hit first. There was no sense to it, only fear, as all of the night sky shook uncontrollably in a fit of fire, blast, and roar, and none of her husband's male and rational ways could do anything about it. And there was still no rain.

"Come back to bed," she said. He led her there. "The baby's stopped kicking. Maybe he knows something we don't."

When he pulled up the sheet, she rolled onto her side and rested her hand on his naked shoulder. The storm hadn't let up, but he seemed calmer, too, resigned to the night as it was. "I believe," he whispered, "I believe that when you marry, you marry forever. That whatever happens, you're with each other in some way forever, in this world and in the next, for whatever is."

Between the memory of that night and her story of my father's return home, Mother drew a long, perfectly straight line across the page. Then she began again, without further comment. She had heard the noise outside on the porch and then the sound of the doorknob rattling. She got up from bed and decided to turn on the overhead light and make as much racket as possible, hoping the burglar would be scared away. But then someone was knocking. When she saw who it was, she knotted her housecoat's belt another time and lifted her nightgown's collar higher on her neck. She unchained the latch and walked away from him as he entered.

"How did you know I was coming?" he said.

"I didn't."

"The light was on."

"I was reading. I read books now that I don't have a husband. You come back like a thief in the night."

"I didn't want to be seen."

"And what makes you think I want to see you?"

"Nothing makes me think you want to see me, Mattie." His anger broke out, not fifteen seconds into the room. "I couldn't begin to pray to God that you would halfway consent to even talk with me. Why, if it were up to you . . ." He caught himself. "I wanted to talk to you."

She sighed, and breathed deeply before she answered. "How old are you, Robert? Let me ask you that. And how long have you been gone? How long have we been married?"

He frowned. "Stop it. We decided that was unfair."

"We didn't decide any such thing and you know it. But talk. Go ahead, I'm willing. It's the least I can do." She spoke with less than conviction. "Sit down."

It was not until he pulled a chair from the table that a sense of the past rushed over her. Here he was again, her husband. His waist was slim, his hair grayer. His eyes still burned bright. This dinner table—in Cusseta—had once been their very life, ringed with fidgeting children and the abundance of labor. She had bossed the children about everything from manners to dessert, while he sat at the other end, the acknowledged king, even though every family member knew how much of a failure he was at playing master provider. Wasn't that really one reason he ran from them? Wasn't he being truthful by not sitting there the rest of his life, like most men, and living a lie? No, she thought, he wasn't being truthful.

He narrated his years with the engineer, Barker, from the moment he woke up to the man's face until he thanked him that very day for his wilderness of locusts and wild honey. He was no longer obligated to farm work or banks or a school board. Or a family, she added. Yes, he said. He'd had these years to do little but read the Bible again, and to read it in a new way. "There is a message," he said. "The truth comes from the parables."

Mother sat quietly and listened to him go on about this parable and that, and about all the biblical stories. After the first few minutes, she didn't move, her hands folded in the lap of her housecoat. It was hard to believe the man had returned home to talk about his own confused ideas. She finally had enough. "You told a story to Doug and Luke in the schoolhouse."

"I was coming to that. I knew you'd ask, and well you should."

"Well I should."

"I didn't mean it like that, Mattie."

"But what's the difference, Robert?"

"There doesn't seem to be, I know. . . ."

"There certainly doesn't seem to be. I have my suspicions. What have you ever done with your ideas other than impose them on others? Is it any different now, ten years later? Do your ideas matter more than ten years you've been gone? You want to take those parables and walk the streets of Jerusalem until they declare you king, just as you wanted before. Your pride is what matters."

"God rules the unforeseen, Mattie. I didn't tell Doug to jump out of his window and hide in the woods. I didn't want him to. Can't you believe me now? I didn't lay the Chatta-hoochee down in the wilderness, cut it out of the rocks and run it to the sea just for him to drown." He waited for her to re-spond, but she kept silent. "Teaching was power for me—you're right. It let me make the boys into disciples. Now it is love. I'm not scared to say that word. And one other thing. I am forgiven."

Her lips tightened. "There is nothing else you could have said that would more convince me you haven't changed at all. What you've just told me makes no sense. You should go to your grave seeking pardon. The moment you feel you are for-given is the moment you show your pride."

A long silence followed. My father looked away from his wife, across the dining room.

"Tell me about the children."

She told him, gladly. She didn't understand why, but sud-denly she wanted to rescue the conversation. She told him story after story, most of them repeated from her letters. Belle's husband was the best bricklayer in the valley. His fa-ther, Ben Bonner, had been a rumrunner during the Twenties, but Raymond seemed to have survived any bad influence. They had a beautiful garden and a new house and she hoped for special news any day now. She wanted nothing else more than that special news. She was worried about me and Will, but she stopped her letter a second time, drawing a line directly across the page, and skipping below it to their next conversation.

"Why did you send me money, Robert?"

"I didn't need it."

"What made you think I did?"

"I had no idea one way or the other. I just sent it."

"But weren't you saying something?"

"I guess I was."

"You want it both ways, Robert. But I have made it on my own for ten years. I am not willing to let you have it both ways. I have more pride than that now."

I had my own reverie then, reading her letter in my tent. I imagined—because I had seen her do the same with me—that the corner of her mouth turned into a half-smile, and how when he saw that smile, he hated it. And I imagined that when they were courting, Dad first noticed it one day when he walked with her to the edge of the woods on his father's farm, still within sight of the house. Even then he didn't want to live a common life. My father never wanted to be thought of as common. Instead of carving a heart into the beech tree, he cut an X with arrow heads on all four ends—surely he taught Doug that sign. In each space between the lines, Dad placed one of their initials so that their love would be boundless—it would merge with eternity, not the confines of the human heart. Then he leaned her against the trunk and brazenly framed her face in his hands. He would not say what the common lover would say. He had rehearsed his words.

"You are the most beautiful woman whose heart has ever been alive."

She gave him that crooked half-smile and lowered her eyes. "Don't say that. It fills me with too much pride. And it's not true."

He was terribly disappointed, I am sure. He wanted her to let loose that maidenly humility and like a queen of Sheba give in to all the world of his love. But she didn't think that way. And when he did, striving not to succumb to commonness, she gave him that crooked smile. He was such a fool, it implied. It was a doomed marriage.

"Are you still at the Atlanta Y?" she asked.

"You haven't told Will?"

"You've sent postcards, Robert, remember? Everyone in the family knows you're in Atlanta. Will assumes you're preaching at the Mission House and other places—I guess. We sure don't talk about it, whatever you think."

"No one would find me if he came there."

She didn't respond.

"It is for you to say, " he said, pausing. "But I want you to come with me."

Mother stared at him without changing her expression. The moment knew the tension of one long awaited, from his vision of a fire burning the city of Atlanta until then, when she finally heard the words he had come to say.

When I read about this request, that she go with him, I felt a sudden grief of mind. Our lives are beyond our control. There are patterns, perhaps, which we live without understanding, if we can even think of these forces as patterns. With this thought of a life beyond, defying every decision we make, I sensed myself lifted up and carried thousands of miles across the sea to loom over them.

Who were these people? A man and a woman, simple human beings who sat at the dining-room table, the overhead light casting their reflections onto the polished veneer of cherry wood, a couple like all other couples in time, married thirty-five years but unable to live together the last ten. Her hands were blanched from the work of laundry and kitchen, and cracked from the unnourished clay she dug in her garden year after year. She was not slender, but for a woman her age her carriage was firm and straight, twenty-five years after Doug and I were born. In the last ten years she had gained a greater pride in herself—because he had left home.

He was a man like many other men, with salt-and-pepper hair and a broad, muscular back, raised on a farm. There was no curve in his sitting. His shoulders dropped straight to the same width waist and down past large, rubbing thighs to the ground he gainsaid while he walked. That was the problem. He numbered himself among those whose bodies beg for answers and yet fight against them all their lives.

"That is a bargain I refuse, Robert."

He waited.

"A woman of my generation marries only once. You are right in assuming that. I made my choice almost forty years ago. I have lived my end of it and I am proud. I will not falsely humble myself now."

"I am not concerned with the past."

"Of course you're not. You've come home to strike a bargain for the future. I tell you I refuse. On the one hand, if I say yes, you get from me my blessing, I go and do your 'work of the Lord.' Or—better yet—if I say no, you get your great sacrifice, your great and glorious sacrifice. You stay here, suffering because of my wishes. I tell you I refuse the whole deal, Robert."

"I didn't consider the second choice," he said. "I will not stay here."

She stood up. "Fine. Then go on your own. I may be your wife, but I am not your handmaid."

A last letter to mention—one of her few—came from Elizabeth. It was in the middle of a June afternoon. The horizon was punctured with trails of billowing black smoke. Elizabeth seldom answered my epistles, and epistles they were—long diatribes about a soul at war. A part of me, of course, understood her neglect, though I didn't want to admit it to myself. She was skittish, I reasoned; it would not have surprised me in the least to read "Dear John," she had married someone else, and "My dearest Luke," she was already divorced. She prided herself on her surprises. This letter was another one. It was first postmarked from Saint Tropez, then forwarded through Washington. Admiral Mallery had apparently sent her abroad. She told a story of some girl she met in Paris who introduced her to a Gide book I had not read. She insisted on the wisdom of a phrase from that book, "Nothing is true for everyone." Here I was, in the middle of a war, torn against my will from a woman I loved and wanted to marry, and she writes about her little jaunt to France and some trite dialogue she picked up out of a weak-thinking Frenchman's book. But I had my own phrases, too, culled from a philosophy major— did mine sound just as trite?

I looked up to my window and to the single tree, greatly disappointed. Why not at least say, if only once, "I wish you were here, by the waters of the Mediterranean, where we could picnic again under the sun, friends and lovers. I would dance for you"? Or say that she imagined herself here with me, walking along the edge of the rice paddies I'd told her were beside the building. The rice paddies. I could put that phrase of Gide's in one ancient field after another—"Nothing is true for everyone" in the first field, "Nothing is true for everyone" in the second, and so on—and say, "Look at these, Elizabeth, they are all the same, year after year, decade after decade, because there *is* something that is true for everyone. The very fact that you can say that nothing is true for everyone, the very fact that you can deny, simply means that you are alive, and if you are alive, there is something that is true for you and everyone who is living now, and who has lived, and will live, if we let this earth continue to be peopled with humans."

I thought of Heidegger. "Nothing is true for everyone" is inauthentic. It forgets what has been. It is blind to genuine potentialities. It evades choice. It is what Heidegger calls "the forgetting of being."

IV

Elizabeth:
A Particular
Examination of
Conscience

10

*E*lizabeth knocked on the door to Atlanta's Priscilla Worthington Home in September 1952. She was alone, and without the usual required papers—a doctor's certification and a letter from a family minister. Mr. Standard, a minister from the West End Methodist Church, telephoned to warn Mrs. Benning that the strange girl was coming, explaining that he had given Elizabeth the information because as a Christian and a minister of the Gospel, he wanted to help, but let there be no mistake, he could not speak to her character. "You never know," he said over the telephone, "about these girls that walk in off the street. . . . Yes, you're right, Mrs. Benning, no warning, nothing—just came right in the front door. By the way, Mrs. Benning, she says she can pay."

In her office interview Mrs. Benning began by telling Elizabeth that she was not the first girl to try to get in improperly, but even if she did have the appropriate credentials, which she did not, Mrs. Benning repeated, all the beds were filled. The woman became more interested, however, when Elizabeth showed her the $999 she had withdrawn from the bank. Mrs. Benning lectured Elizabeth, saying that she had sinned, but that God would grant forgiveness if she asked; and that her pride was wounded and she was agitated, but she seemed like she wouldn't be any trouble. Unlike the others, who were bent on lying in, her desire to work as long as she was able was excellent. And, frankly, she was not underage. Though it was quite an unusual procedure (Mrs. Benning reminded Elizabeth of what Christ had said—it was the reason she was in this business), she decided to let Elizabeth show up unannounced and work as long as her condition allowed. She could sleep with the maids. Elizabeth gave her the money, a portion for the initial payment, and the rest for safekeeping.

For three months after Elizabeth had made love to Will, she didn't have a period. She had worried about pregnancy from the beginning, and after the first month she assumed it was true because it ought to be, considering what she had done. She thought she felt her breasts grow and her stomach move. She never threw up, but that didn't mean anything. She did not go to a doctor. At the end of the ninetieth day, she called the West Point bus station, went to the bank, and walked out of the mansion by the river the next morning, without even locking it. As soon as she arrived in Atlanta, she chopped her hair off and removed most of her makeup, so as not to call attention to herself as she tried to decide what to do. Then she found a complete stranger, the pallid Methodist minister named Standard. He promised as a disciple of Christ not to share her confession with anyone else, so she told him the whole story, including time, place, and characters. He was shocked, but after he realized she could pay, he told her where Simpson Street was. And said he'd pray for her.

For the first two weeks in the Priscilla Worthington Home, Elizabeth watched her fingernails be bitten away, frame by frame, as if she were studying a newsreel of someone headed for destruction. She could calm herself only by making beds and scrubbing floors and dusting until complete exhaustion finally overwhelmed her. It never occurred to her that she might be wrong about her condition.

But she was. Her period came on the 106th day. It was long, aching—she suffered immense pain for over a week. But it told her she could walk out the front door, make no excuses, and reenter the world. Escape scot-free. For the rest of her life, only the people in the house, Reverend Standard, and Will would know. And anyone they told.

But she did not want to leave. She couldn't understand why, but she didn't. Someday soon she'd have to, for her mistake would embarrass the others, but she had no desire for freedom. At first she told herself she was needed. One of her jobs was to play the piano for Sunday morning and evening services and for Wednesday night's prayer meeting. Once when she missed, the girl who substituted was awful. Mrs. Benning made a point of telling Elizabeth that the Priscilla Worthington Home had never known piano playing as elegant as hers. Mrs. Benning—Sarge, the girls called her—seldom gave such compliments. But it was not the piano playing. She was kidding herself. Late at night, alone on her cot, staring at the antiseptic white ceiling, Elizabeth could admit that she had nowhere to go, nowhere she wanted to be. Every option—back to New York, to Europe, back home—no place felt right.

Her one friend on Simpson Street was a girl named Mary Phillips, who came from Louisville, Kentucky. Every day Mary's face grew prettier, unlike Elizabeth's. She hardly had a chin, just a checkmark below her mouth, but her nose was a pink button and her eyes the color of almonds. Because she was a devout Catholic, Mary felt as alien from the others as Elizabeth did because she was older and, later, because she was living a lie. Each of them thus felt a double estrangement, not only from their families but from living in exile. In the back of the house, a dark stairwell led down to the pantry. When Elizabeth wasn't working, the two of them sat out of sight, side by side, their arms touching. There was always a fusty smell—Elizabeth associated it with hiding.

"Daddy owns the largest Chevrolet dealership in the state," Mary explained one day. "He comes down here to Conyers with the archbishop—there is a retreat house at the Trappist monastery. When I told Daddy, he wasn't worried about me; he was worried everyone would find out about him." Mary leaned her head against the banister and paused. She couldn't look at Elizabeth. "He knows so many people in the Church, even in places like this, so when he came in May he decided to send me to a Protestant home."

"A sin worse than death?"

Mary didn't laugh.

After a few weeks of meeting on the stairs, they traded their shameful stories. Neither mentioned them again. Elizabeth realized that Mary was shocked about her sin with Will, unaware of the familiar reach of evil. But unlike the stereotype Elizabeth held of Catholics, Mary never moralized, and thus their friendship solidified. At times Elizabeth actually grew jealous of Mary's pregnancy. The father had run away, but Mary still bore great hope for her child. She was determined to keep it. Never before had she stood up to her car-dealer father, but on this issue there would be no argument, she said, her tiny chin set firm. If God wanted her to pay for her sin, then she would; her penance was a glorious suffering, for she was to bear a child, God's greatest gift. Sometimes Elizabeth romanticized that same vision for herself; a woman alone with a fatherless child, wandering through the world. There was purpose and a place in it. Except now there was no child.

For two days, once, they weren't able to hide away and talk. When they met again, Mary wore her bright yellow print dress, which Mrs. Benning frowned upon. A bow tied it under her swelling breasts. By then Elizabeth had known for over a week that she wasn't pregnant, but she had not found the courage to tell Mary. Before Elizabeth could speak, however, Mary gave her a book they had been talking about and began on a story herself.

"One night when I came home, Elizabeth—it had been going on for over a month by then—I felt as filthy as a pig. I didn't think I could wash off any of the filth; I thought my sin was eternally caught in the very pores of my skin, and that anytime I sweated, a milk-white glop would ooze out of me and reveal to the world just how wicked I was. I ran a bath of steaming-hot water. I wanted to sneak downstairs and boil four huge pots of water to make the bath even hotter, boiling hot, but I was afraid my mother'd wake up. I wanted to mortify my sense of touch. I closed my eyes and concentrated on every sin of touch I could remember, from my first memory until then, forcing my foot into that water until it ached so much I almost screamed. And then my other foot, and my leg. Oh, my God, Elizabeth, I never wanted to touch another thing in my life. If I could burn away my own skin. . . ."

Afterward Elizabeth believed her friendship with Mary and her decision to stay at the Priscilla Worthington Home were more than coincidences. André had once said to her that the most important things in life happen to you by accident. But at this point in her life, she was willing to consider that more than accident might be involved, though she still didn't want to use the word *God*. She could just as easily have paraded out the Simpson Street front door, free as a vestal virgin, and walked through the world until she found the proper distraction—another André, perhaps. It was naïve of her to say she had nowhere to go. She had plenty of places to escape to, but staying a while at the Worthington Home had turned out to be more momentous. She'd met Mary Phillips, and Mary Phillips gave her the book and taught her about mortification.

Elizabeth had never imagined she would believe again—no, not after Paris—nor that she might learn from someone younger than herself, and a Catholic at that. But something in her responded to the idea of humbling one's senses and oneself. She had been so self-indulgent about Paris and André and, most of all, about Will. The thought of him and that night by the river physically sickened her. But after she began to read Mary's book, she forgot about that awful sin for days, all because of the supposed accident called mortification, a singular idea that she began to grip as tightly as she had the idea of Paris. Coincidence. Accident. But maybe a gift from God.

On the first Friday of October, Elizabeth received a letter from Mattie. Denying herself, she decided to wait until Sunday afternoon to open it. She would pray about it until then. The usual routine that same Sunday—"the procedure," as Sarge called it—was suddenly changed after dinner, when Mrs. Benning rang the bell at the head table and stood up to make an announcement. If she sat when she touched the bell, the girls were dismissed. But if she stood, everyone froze. Elizabeth waited in the corner by the stack of dirty trays.

"Mr. Sellars," Mrs. Benning began, pausing to clear her throat, "our minister this evening, has been taken ill. Our prayers are that it is not serious. We will, of course, go on with our usual procedure, though at this time I am unsure what arrangements will be made. I have been in touch with the Atlanta Mission House. They tell me there's a layman who happens to be a very good speaker—he might be able to come over, but I don't know yet. Come to the chapel, though, at the appropriate time, and if no one can preach, Elizabeth Mordew will lead us through a hymn sing, won't you, dear? That might be a pleasant change." She rang the bell again and most of the girls rose to leave. It was around 2:30.

"Keep it short, Elizabeth," one girl said, nudging her.

"First and last verses," another added.

Elizabeth smiled and proceeded with the work of clearing up. She thought about Mattie's letter as she stacked the plates and bowls, gathered the silverware, and brushed the crumbs into the pocket of the white jacket she wore. The napkins had to be fresh, the short fork with the dessert spoon above. The flowers that day were chrysanthemums. While she finished, Elizabeth made her particular examination of conscience after the noon meal. She asked God to give her the grace to remember how many times she had fallen into the particular defect she was working on—namely, bearing false witness. As she ticked off some exaggerations she had indulged in that morning and during lunch, she discreetly touched her hand to her pocket, where she was keeping the letter. Then she went to her room and stretched out on the bed and opened it. Finally.

By the time she finished reading, she felt utterly humiliated, far more so than she had ever imagined possible. Reverend Standard—the man she had confessed to—had telephoned the Methodist minister in Lanett and asked him to find out Mattie's address. Elizabeth assumed he had chosen Mattie because she'd told him what an understanding, loving person Mattie was. The misguided man wrote Mattie and told her that he had helped Elizabeth in a terrible time of need and that he had pulled strings to get her into the Priscilla Worthington Home and that he was praying with her every day and wouldn't Mattie like to send a contribution to his church and to the home as a way of showing the family's appreciation?

Mattie wanted to know if this story was true, and if Elizabeth had left unannounced because of it, and why Elizabeth hadn't come and talked with her instead. And then, unbelievably—Standard must not have completely explained—Mattie had asked Will to go fetch his sister-in-law.

Elizabeth felt she deserved it—her due recompense. Then she laughed. She laughed when she imagined Mattie talking to Will. She could see his face when her own mother naïvely asked him about it—how he would suffer! There was no way under God's heaven that Will would show his face at the Priscilla Worthington Home; the most he would do would be to drive to Atlanta and go home and tell his mother that Elizabeth had left. How Elizabeth would relish, in a perverted way, seeing Will, especially since she wasn't pregnant! She would rub his face in it. But she was shocked at herself—at how quickly revenge cut through her studied mortification. Then she cried.

Elizabeth had thought she would take a nap, but she spent the rest of the afternoon at her little bedside table, praying first, and then writing the letters in response. She placed her hand on her breast and prayed that she would learn from the experience, would not harbor the need for revenge, and would be truthful. Her hand, however, hurt from gripping the pen so tightly. She told Mattie it was a lie that she was pregnant, but said she wouldn't be back in Lanett for the foreseeable future; Will and Susan could do with the house as they pleased. Then she ripped up three long, unsatisfactory drafts to Standard because not one of them was good enough—she seemed incapable of a tone of righteous indignation. She left the stationery and the pen on the table to await her return from the evening chapel service.

The chapel was nothing more than a converted sitting room in the corner of the rambling, gingerbread house that the Priscilla Worthington Association, Inc., called their home for unwed mothers, though there was no sign on the street, or even a street number (the mail was hand-delivered to Mrs. Benning). Elizabeth began playing the piano to let everyone know it was time. She always picked a funny, spry one to start. The atmosphere of the occasional chapel was not only dingy but stuffy and prisonlike. A row of staid portraits lined one wall. Only one was of a woman—Priscilla Worthington herself. One look at her horseface and it was easy to see why she lived a life of virtue. All the other pictures were of men dressed in high collars and the cut of righteousness. More than once Elizabeth had thought that Will's portrait belonged on that wall.

Someone said that the layman was coming. He had called to say he would be a few minutes late, and Sarge was panicked, her procedure threatened. She sent word to keep singing. Elizabeth hoped he didn't show up; she was tired of sermons. Now was the time for her to leave the home, she realized. Mattie's letter had decided for her.

Sarge and the guest walked in during "Will There Be Any Stars?"

Will there be any stars, any stars in my crown,
     When at evening the sun goeth down?

When Elizabeth saw the man's face, she missed a complete measure. Some of the girls' voices faltered with her; a few stopped altogether. She rescued the hymn in the next line, staring at her own hands alone on the black and white keys. At first she could have sworn it was Will's face. The man looked so much like Will and Luke, with dark, deep-set eyes, moles on his neck, the loose skin that had already formed jowls, and that same Treadwell stroll, as if his balance were perpetually doubtful. It had to be the father.

When she looked back up at the two of them, the man was staring at her. Sarge looked terribly worried, as if the few words of courtesy she had exchanged with him had tipped her off to some danger he presented. She was protective of her girls, especially in their condition. But Elizabeth wasn't concerned with Sarge; she was assuring herself that the man looking at her didn't know her. Mattie had not asked *him* to come get her. She steadily returned his gaze until she was sure she was safe. He definitely wasn't looking for her, thank God. And then she realized that the Atlanta Mission House was one of the places he was evangelizing—all of them had said he was an evangelist in Atlanta.

He and Will almost looked like twins, not father and son, though the closer she inspected the man, the more gray she saw, and a slight stoop that Will didn't have. He was leaner, surprisingly. When she finished the hymn and sat down, she didn't know what to feel. Of course his face, because she had assumed it was Will's, brought back her guilt. But she had always been intrigued by what was unsaid in that family, and after Mrs. Benning made a brief, worried introduction, she listened, carefully.

"Thank you, Mrs. Benning. It's an honor to be here.

"I'd like to tell you a story, ladies, a simple one that won't take too much of your time. I'm sure you have better things to do than listen to me."

Elizabeth heard nervous laughter behind her. He was mistaken: they didn't have one single better thing to do in the whole wide world because they didn't have a choice: they couldn't deny Mrs. Benning, nor their swelling bodies. Robert's irony was certainly unintentional, but none of the girls cared to be reminded, however mildly. Elizabeth felt sorry for him, off to such a bad start.

"There were two sons of a LaGrange, Georgia, mill owner," Robert continued, "who lived in a white-columned mansion half-hidden from the road by a tall hedge and a choir of guardian oak trees. In the mansion each son had many rooms. The older son—our hero—was the picture of perfection, almost without blemish, a gentleman and a scholar, soon to be a pillar of society and of the church, a true Christian. He made a list of his goals each month, and every day drew a bank ledger to examine his sins and good deeds. He also gave ten percent of his allowance to the First Baptist Church of LaGrange. His only fault was that he believed his father favored his younger brother.

"When weighed in the balance, the younger brother was found seriously wanting. He was a constant worry to his father, lacking judgment, motivation, and sometimes even respect. If he stayed through the school day, in the afternoons he played eightball, not baseball. One night he stole three hundred dollars from the safe in his father's home office and gambled it away in a poker game with colored folk. When the police raided the bar's back room, they found him drunk and half-naked in a sea of his own vomit."

Elizabeth glanced at Mrs. Benning, whose eyes were already glazed with anger. By the way Sarge sat, pressed into the back of her chair as if the speaker were a filthy, contagious disease, Elizabeth understood that Robert Treadwell would never speak at the Priscilla Worthington Home again and wouldn't even make it through this sermon if Mrs. Benning could figure out a way to stop him. He probably didn't care, though, if Elizabeth judged the tone of his voice correctly: it was confident and unconcerned with social niceties, social hyocrisies. How refreshing to hear an honest voice, who when it said that the man was a wastrel, illustrated the fact, whether or not Mrs. Benning wanted to believe men could be half-naked, drowning in their own vomit.

"Sorry, ladies, if I've offended you, but you must know the truth. His father kept it from the papers, but he aged twenty years in a night.

"One afternoon the older son stood in the library and stared at a gold-framed portrait of his brother. 'Golden boy,' he said to the silence of the books. 'Father does nothing but forgive him, no matter what he does. There is no justice.'

"At that very moment his father pushed open the door and shouted, 'He's gone! He's run away.' The older son turned to see the man's pale face and shaking hands trying to show him a letter. The boy had run away to New Orleans, it said, and would never return to such a shallow existence as his father and brother led. The father looked at his eldest. 'You must go, you have to. You must bring him back. He's your brother and my son. He doesn't understand what he's doing. Go, take the money, search everywhere. Please find him.'

"And so the eldest son set out over the endless roads toward New Orleans. It took him days. The heat was stifling and the air wet and heavy. The back of his shirt stuck to him and the sweat from his forehead stung his eyes. The more he thought about it, the angrier he became. There he was, half-killing himself in search of a boy better off left to muck about in the pig slop of his own degenerate, selfish life. Why go after him in the first place? There was no justice.

"For the first time in his life, then, the eldest son turned from his father's will. He would show his father just what it meant to disobey. At a small coastal town due east of New Orleans, he paid the fare on a ferry across a waterway. He breathed the salt in the air and smelled the dead fish. How his lungs rejoiced in the anticipation of sin! As he walked out onto the dock, a swarthy man came up from a trawler, smiled, and said it was a friendly game below. Why not? he asked himself. Here was the sea and he was far far away from his father. It was his own life.

"He almost fell off the ladder squeezing down into the ship's room, where the tobacco smoke stung his eyes and made him cough. The men circled a green tablecloth stitched with numbers and designs. He was smart enough to take only a small swig at first. The man on his left helped him learn the game, and he won two of the first five, showing a one-eyed jack to win the second. He would use his father's money to begin with and keep the winnings as his own. It wasn't fair to his father to use his money like that, but when had his father been fair to him? He played the game and drank his fill until early in the morning, when he became very confused, ladies. He felt like he'd been tossed overboard. At first he didn't realize he had fallen asleep, until a hand clawed his shoulder and shook him awake.

" 'So who are you, kid? Gambling and illegal possession—we'll have to take you in, and you'll surely pay for this!'

"He didn't understand. 'I am my father's son,' he heard himself say, his tongue drier than hard clay. It was a voice from somewhere inside him. 'And I love him. Take me. I am guilty.'

"He was sent to a dark, damp prison. I ask you to imagine yourself straight into his soul. For him there can be nothing more horrible. He feels the humiliation of the stinking walls staring at him as if he is just another bum sitting there in a stupor. It is more than humiliation—it is sin, and it is disobedience, even death. We can believe, can't we, that this young man thought he might die?"

Elizabeth felt every muscle in her body concentrate on his words; she leaned forward in her chair, lost consciousness of those around her, and pinned her eyes to him the rest of the way. He was a godsend. His family couldn't understand because he was too close to them. But she could. There was something truly honest about this man. What he said was true for all brothers and sisters: Will had never understood anything Luke did, nor did Susan understand her. And Elizabeth whispered to herself when Robert said it was more than humiliation, that it was death.

"What, then, must we do?" Robert asked. "In the gutter or the pigsty, wherever each of us feels is a place worse than death, we must cry unto God. In the prison our hero lifted up his head and knew he wanted his father's mercy. 'I cry by reason of my affliction,' he began. 'Hear me. Out of the belly of hell I cry. The waters compass me about, even to the soul; the depth closes me round about, the weeds are wrapped about my head. Yet thou has brought up my life from corruption, O father. I will sacrifice unto thee with the voice of thanksgiving. Salvation is of my father.'

"When the jailer came, he didn't explain, but only gave our young hero an envelope and told him he was free to go. It was money. He used it to have his car fixed and to buy a black shirt, so if he forgot his sins he could look on the blackness and remember. He drove quickly to New Orleans, with his windows rolled down all the way. The warm wind whipped across his face. He sang himself hoarse. The earth had never moved so greenly, the fields were burdened with fruit, and the sky reached beyond the brimming clouds.

"He found his brother quickly, as if it were meant to be: every morning the younger one showed up at the sewage plant, where they hired day labor to clean pipes. When he found him, he thought the boy'd aged twenty years. His young blond hair sprouted on his face in uneven, dirty tufts and dark sagging pouches hung below his eyes. Before he spoke to him, the eldest looked at his own black shirt to remind himself. His brother turned his sick eyes unto him and said, 'I would eat the corn husks pigs leave over. The servants in our father's house are better than I.'

"During the drive home, the eldest felt a great prideful swelling in his heart. He had turned from his father and fallen into disobedience, selfishness, and jealousy, but he had realized the sin of his ways and bowed before the Lord, a repentant son. He hoped his father would understand just how much he'd been through.

" 'Let me be a servant,' the younger brother said. 'I am not worthy to pick up the crumbs under the table.'

"The eldest replied that it was for them to do the will of their father, whatever it was, no matter how inscrutable, but he thought to himself that if the boy were his son, he would set up a program by which the boy could work his way back into good graces.

"As the eldest stopped the car, they could see their father coming toward them with his arms thrust open, as if he had been waiting all this time. The youngest fell on his knees, but before he could mutter a syllable of his speech, their father lifted him up and wrapped his arms around the boy's shoulders and wept. 'My son,' he said, 'it is a day of great rejoicing. You've come home.' And then he turned to the eldest and embraced him. 'Thank you, my son, thank you.'

"The father gave a feast in his honor. It was a day La-Grange has never forgotten. No one will tell you he didn't have the time of his life. Their father gave them new clothes and sat them in places of honor. He positioned long tables spread with checked cloths across the lawns and hired a hundred people to roast the pigs on open spits.

"It was almost dusk when the eldest couldn't take it any longer. He tried to calm himself. He had sinned and been thrown in jail, yes. But he had repented, he almost shouted aloud, and then he did the will of his father. It had not been easy tracking down his brother. And now he had to come home and be treated to the same favor that profligate was given. The exact same way. What about his own self-respect?

"From the steps of the back porch, his father saw the boy walking away. When he caught up with him, the boy only stared at the ground. 'I admit I sinned on the way,' he said, 'but I brought him back. I gathered him up from the pig slop of his sin and brought him back to you. Don't you understand that?'

"The father nodded.

" 'And I? You have only taught me that there is no just reward for what I have done. What is to keep me from sinning wildly if he is given the same chair and the same table? It makes me want to kill you,' he muttered. His jaw was set and his fists tight.

" 'Yes.'

" 'It is not fair,' the boy said again.

" 'No,' his father answered. 'It is not fair.' "

And then Robert finished. "God have mercy on us all, ladies."

* * *

Elizabeth was stunned by the ending. It was radical, this business about justice and mercy. Neither Will nor Susan nor all the other pharisees in the world who falsely called themselves Christians understood; they thought not in terms of repentance and mercy but only of justice—ways in which they could distinguish between themselves and other people. But the rain fell on just and unjust alike. Robert's point—and God's—was that mercy was all that counted; it, too, fell on just and unjust alike.

Her faith felt suddenly renewed. Will and Mattie and Luke and Belle were no better than their father, no matter what he had done. Will and Susan were no better than she was, no matter what her sins. The Gospel proof was in that very room: the only difference between pregnancy and virtue—between the girls in that room and the judgmental ones on the outside—was the difference between two men's semen, or between two women's timing, nothing else. Everyone has sinned, but the girls on the inside were rained on. She was sure she understood exactly what Robert meant. It was radical, for sure. All a person had to do, to realize just how radical his words were, was look at Mrs. Benning biting her lips.

"Thank you very much, Mr. Treadwell. You may leave, girls." And with those abrupt words Mrs. Benning, huffing with disgust, canceled the usual invitational hymn.

Elizabeth was angry. Mrs. Benning wouldn't dream of allowing this man to save one of her girls—no, not this man who happened to speak the truth—and most of the girls seemed to agree with Mrs. Benning, hurrying out of the room in obvious embarrassment. A few waited, but Sarge pointed to the lingerers with her crooked forefinger and reminded them that she had said they could leave—*now*. The girls skulked away.

Sarge marched to Elizabeth and squeezed her shoulder twice. "There's no need. I'll see him on his way." And then she turned to Robert, her hands crossed slightly above her waist, as if she were prepared to sing. "I'll send someone for your coat, sir."

"I know this man's family, Mrs. Benning," Elizabeth said, coming to Robert's side and smiling at him. She should have guessed how different he would be. No minister who'd ever stepped into the Worthington Home looked like him. He didn't wear a suit or tie, nor were his shoes polished or his hair waxed into place. A tiny hole peeked out from under the collar of his blue shirt; his frayed jacket was a size too large; and the material on the front of his pants, around his knees, was rubbed thin. It was a wonder Mrs. Benning let him in. "I will be glad to make sure he gets his coat, and I'll see him to the door," she continued. "There's no need for you to bother. I know you have pressing responsibilities."

Sarge obviously did not want to spend one more second with the man if she could help it. She had never been so disgraced in her house before, a man insensitive enough to tell such a brutal story to wayward girls. "Thank you, Elizabeth," she said. "Mr. Treadwell." She turned toward him before she left, hands in singing position. "The Lord will judge the wicked."

Elizabeth and Robert waited through an awkward moment after the woman barreled off. All these years she had heard about him, in Susan's offhand comments, in a few of Luke's stories and Mattie's jokes, and of course in Will's infamous tirades. It was hard to believe this man was the man. He was an innocent.

"I didn't have a coat," he said. He looked suspicious of her. He had heard her say she knew his family.

"I apologize for the way—"

"Oh, please now." He put his hand up to stop her. "I understand, I'm used to it." He began to stroll toward the opposite side of the room, where the hallway led to the front door. He didn't know who she was, and he wasn't going to ask her about his family. Elizabeth walked beside him.

"How long have you been at the Mission House?"

"Oh, I don't work there, though I stay with them a lot. I really don't have a job per se. I go back and forth between them and the prison and the hospital."

"Doing what?"

"Helping."

"Is the story about Margaret Mitchell's roses true? I've always wanted to ask someone."

He laughed. "Strange, isn't it, that that is what people want to know about the penitentiary? Yes, there is a beautiful row of them along the edge of the main building. When she died . . . well, you've obviously heard the story."

"Luke told me."

He paused, staring at his feet. He did not impress her as a man who had given up thinking about his family. "You know my son?"

"My sister married Will. But I haven't seen Luke in two years."

"I see. I thought that perhaps ... your condition ..."

Elizabeth blushed.

"I didn't mean ..."

She was flustered, meeting him in this place. She felt like telling him the truth right away; she needed to tell someone the truth. "You know he's been in Korea?" she said.

He nodded. "I've written him."

Mary Phillips interrupted them. Because she was Catholic, Mary never attended the services, but on Sunday evenings helped Mrs. Benning by typing a few letters, answering the phone, or entertaining any late visitors. When she spoke, her face tried to appear impassive, but throughout the brief interchange she kept her eyes fastened on Elizabeth until Elizabeth realized her friend was trying to tell her much more than what she said: that there was a man in the front room waiting to see her.

"In the front room?" Elizabeth repeated, stalling for time.

"He wouldn't tell me his name. Shall I say you're sick? I can easily do that."

"My goodness, no," Robert answered. "I must be off myself. There's no reason for me to interrupt." He, too, seemed anxious to escape.

"Please don't," Elizabeth said. "Let me, Mary. Would you mind talking with Mr. Treadwell a moment? I'll go speak to the man and be right back. He probably has the wrong Elizabeth. Please stay, Mr. Treadwell. It's very important to me."

Neither Mary nor Robert looked pleased with the suggestion, but Elizabeth hurried down the hallway before they could object. She had no idea who it was. She walked into the front room to see Will, his back toward her. When Elizabeth had read Mattie's letter, if she had stopped and thought for a moment, her mind would not have closed itself to this possibility. But she had not allowed Will even the sensitivity of suffering guilt.

He turned around. Although she had time to reason out his appearance, she thought only in terms of the supernatural—not coincidence, not logic. Since the night of the party, some mental shock about what she had done—making love to her sister's husband—had created its own false evidence about reality and run her out of Lanett. The awful experience was one known by many other people, who in response made a few promises to themselves, which they promptly forgot. Life continued. But the blow had pummeled Elizabeth harder than a bull's charge into her solar plexus. Up until then, she decided, the way she had lived was absolutely wrong. Her dancing, her time in New York, André and André Gide and the Eternal City, even Luke: all nothing. For three months she had found no way out of the darkness, though she never changed her mind about what happened. All she could do was listen to Mary Phillips on mortification. In such a condition, Will's coming was not a mere coincidence to Elizabeth. No, it was more than that. Robert was there at the same time. No mere coincidence.

Will's fingers inched around the rim of his hat. A rosebud was pinned to the lapel of his navy blue suit. The promise of a dewlap in his neck was more pronounced, and all she could think of after staring at him for a moment was how rich he looked. His face was as similar to his father's as identical twins' faces to each other, but here was the one, nattily dressed in the big city, while the other, because he valued the spirit and not the flesh, wore a borrowed jacket.

Will cleared his throat before he spoke. "I came to help."

Elizabeth sat down. A table lamp cast a taut, dim light over the floor between them. He kept staring at her. She looked away to the window, where the dark had already descended over the world she had renounced since last she saw him. But she could still feel his presence, waiting silently across the room. The window curtain blurred the streetlamps and the few headlights of the cars swimming through the ocean that began to swell up around her. She would drown. The walls would crack until the water filled her lungs and down she would drift, wrapped in the ooze of twisting weeds.

"I know you didn't ask me to come here, Elizabeth, and you probably didn't want me to. I could not abide myself, though, knowing what happened. I did not want you to suffer alone."

"Does Susan know?"

Will paused, weighing his answer. "Yes, she knows. It was wrong to keep it from her."

"It was wrong to keep it from her."

"Be easy on me, I beg of you. I asked a lot of myself to show up." His shoes turned pigeon-toed as he fiddled with his inside coat pocket. And then mechanically, like a youth who has practiced hours before the mirror, he stepped quietly across that no-man's-land of lamplight, kissed her on the cheek, and set a business-size envelope on the couch beside her, retreating as quickly and awkwardly as he'd come. "I have brought this for you. It's only meant to help."

She deserved it. She had only been playing games with the idea of mortification until Mattie's letter arrived. She deserved the great tidal wave she expected, sweeping up from some mysterious weather conflagration hundreds of miles out in the ocean and moving in, rolling into an immense crest that would break over them and shatter her to pieces. Maybe there was another life afterward, when she could begin again.

"Now don't be proud. Don't be a fool." He gestured; the back tongue of his tie flopped to the side. He had forgotten a tie pin. "I brought it to help. I don't care what you do with it, so don't think I'm trying to buy you out or something. I just didn't know what to do and it was the best I could think of."

"I am not pregnant."

He lifted the back of his hand to his lips and, trying not to be obvious, bit some loose skin. "I beg your pardon?"

"You heard me." She saw the uncertainty in his eyes and smiled. She had not considered the predicament he would be in. If she was not pregnant, his confession to Susan, if indeed he had made one, was necessary only in the moral sense. Otherwise he could have simply insisted that he took Elizabeth home after the party because he was angry and felt Susan had treated her wrongly. His infidelity would have been undetected, and thus fallen in line with all his other hidden adulteries.

"I don't understand. Are you sure?"

"And I don't want this filthy money of yours. I am not going to touch it. If you want it back, you'll have to pick it up yourself when you're finished. If not, I'm sure one of these girls will be glad to dispose of it for you." Because she could at first think of nothing other than this reckoning of her own worthlessness, her reaction to the envelope was delayed. But then she asked herself what he meant by offering it. She might think his presence compared to a supernatural visitation, but he was still the same self-centered man. She simmered over her answers, lost patience and endurance and any sense of mercy. It was a much greater insult to her than the original sexual crime. She had imagined—rarely, but still sometimes—that it wasn't a crime, that he loved her. But now—this money. Her anger burned away all other emotions save one, which made her forget that she believed all people were equal sinners.

"Why don't you come home, then, Elizabeth?"

"I . . ." She hesitated at the evil in her thought.

"I'm sure all of us could patch our lives together. I know it would be hard."

"You want us to repeat it, is that it?"

"That's unfair."

"I will not come home, because I am in love." She listened to the sudden silence. It was indeed not she, not the Elizabeth Mordew she knew, who had spoken those words; but Elizabeth liked the sound of them, anyway, and the absence of sound in response. It was what he deserved. "Yes, that's right, I am in love with a man I met up here."

"I . . . well, three months, Elizabeth . . . I—Susan and I are happy for you." A wrinkle came to his eyes, which were darkly suspicious, and distracted by his uncertainty. He had lost control of the situation. He, too, felt the wave.

She looked at him defiantly. "He is here. I was talking to him in the other room when Mary came to get me. I'll go after him. The two of you should meet." She stood up.

"But there's no need . . . I really don't think . . ."

Turning toward him in the doorway, Elizabeth measured the man with eyes of acid. "It's the least I'd do for you."

As she glided from the front room back to the makeshift chapel, her mind cast out any thought about what she had said and what she was about to do. She was simply not going to think about it.

Robert was sitting on her piano stool across the room, elbows on knees, leaning forward in conversation with Mary, who was making her point by slapping her left hand's palm with two fingers of her right. Her face was red. Both of them acknowledged Elizabeth's arrival, but rather impolitely kept talking.

"But doesn't it still come down to the individual's experience of God?" he said.

"No, it does not. If it did, I might walk out of this house with a shotgun and shoot my neighbor and explain to the world that God told me to do it."

"Not within the confines of the Scripture."

"But I might think so—the way I read it. And if the individual's experience is the final authority, then who is to say I read the Scripture incorrectly. No, the Church must interpret the Word for us."

"But the Church wrote it. How can the Church truthfully interpret itself?"

Elizabeth's resolve was fading. She interrupted. "Thank you, Mary, for staying with Mr. Treadwell. I'm sorry to have taken so long." Both of them deferred to her, reluctantly.

"Oh, we've had quite a time talking. This young lady is fascinating. You ought to tell your Church to make you a priest."

"Until now I had only suspected you were crazy, Mr. Treadwell. Now I know you are." Mary laughed, and turned to Elizabeth. "Did he leave?"

"No, he's waiting to meet Mr. Treadwell, actually—if you don't mind. The three of us can sit and talk in the front room. Can you spare a moment?" Elizabeth met Mary's questioning gaze again. Since Elizabeth had told Mary the story of her sin, Mary was wondering if the man in the front room was the one. Elizabeth couldn't explain just now; she was caught in the undertow and she couldn't pull herself out or keep from tugging Robert in. Besides, had she asked either of them to swagger into this house where she had run? Was she supposed to keep them from meeting?

"He wants to meet me?" Robert asked.

"Shall I join you?"

"No, Mary, but thank you."

"Are you sure?"

"Yes."

"It was a pleasure, then, Mr. Treadwell. When you're ready to convert, please look me up. In the meantime I'll pray to Saint Jude for you. He watches over those in desperate straits."

Robert laughed gaily. "I accept the prayers of all people."

Elizabeth led Robert quickly to the front room, staying a stride in front of him to keep from talking. What kind of man did Will assume she was bringing? With his pride, Will would only be able to picture a weak-kneed city sissy, in horn-rims and a polka-dot bow tie. He would point to the man's looks and reassure himself: she'd been so jolted by his masculine power, he would think to himself, that she had to run around quickly and pick up whatever she could get because she knew nothing could ever compare.

The envelope was gone. Will stared through the corner window at the watery darkness of night. He turned around, the arrogant judge. When he saw Robert by her side, every muscle in his body went limp.

"What in God's name?" Will swung his arms behind him and tightened his lips. His face turned colorless.

Robert stopped a few feet from the doorway. "Elizabeth?"

He, too, tensed up, as hard as a rod. "Elizabeth? I don't understand."

She didn't answer. She felt the swelling rise from far away. Somewhere the great curl was forming, with the wave arching its back and threatening to break, crashing over the trough of her life.

"What in God's name—my own long-lost father." Will's lips twisted into a sarcastic grin. "Of all people."

"My son."

"I can't believe this. I trudge up here believing I'm going to help Elizabeth and who do I find but the devil himself. How many years has it been?" Will laughed. "Here is a case of the blind leading the blind if I've ever seen one. The prophet and the dancing girl." Robert lifted his hand to quiet his son, but his gesture only made Will keep talking. "Still the king, is that it, old fool?"

"I'm trying to tell you something."

"And what's that?"

"I don't know what you mean. I've never met Elizabeth until now. What do you think . . . ?"

Will stared at her, but she still kept silent. "Her sister is my wife. And she is here—in this place."

"I gave the sermon here tonight."

"The sermon."

"Yes, son, the sermon."

"Was it the same one that killed Doug?"

"Will!" Elizabeth said.

Robert rubbed his fingers together hard enough to catch on fire. "I have prayed, son, that when we met again—for I knew someday it would happen—we wouldn't start up where we left off."

"And why not? Tell me what has changed?"

"Ten years."

"Nothing. Considering."

"Mattie told me about your heroism in the war, and your family and the new farm. I dreamed we might sit down together. You could tell me about all you've done and what you've thought." As he continued, the tone of his voice changed, cracking and having to pause, the words spoken stored inside him for years. "About your son, too—who he looks like and how he lies down when he sleeps. And I had hoped that someday at least one member of my family might wait for a quiet moment, when no one else could overhear, and whisper, 'I understand.' Or if no one understood, 'I forgive you.' Vain hope, I realize. It is sinful for me to imagine such a scene. But I am weak."

Elizabeth thought he was going to cry. She laid her hand softly on his forearm. Surely his family would understand after all these years. Surely time had worn the hard edges smooth. And then in the midst of the silence that fell over them, Elizabeth broke out of the trance that had carried her from the original shock in the front room to the chapel and back. What she had done was terrible. She had deliberately manipulated and deceived two men in order to revenge herself on one.

"You might as well kiss him, Elizabeth."

"But he's telling the truth, Will. I was lying—we just met."

"You keep winning 'em over, right and left, Dad. As long as they're children and women."

"I told you I met her this evening, and she just said she was lying. But I have no reason to justify myself to you, anyway, or to anyone for that matter."

Will took two steps closer to where they stood, within an arm's reach. "Well, you know what, Dad? I have imagined this meeting myself many a time in the last ten years."

"Not in the way he has, I'm sure."

"You're absolutely right, Elizabeth. I remember lying in a hospital bed in Honolulu, staring at the ceiling for weeks when I heard my brother was dead. My own wounds meant nothing to me. There were cracks in the plaster and no matter what time of day I stared at them, they outlined my brother's face. First I saw his profile, and then some picture I remember of him when he sat bareback on a horse and whooped like an Indian. Soon I saw his face in an oval frame, as if he were already a family memento, and then like a pair of binoculars my mind focused in on his eyes, only his eyes. Did you ever look into his eyes, Dad, and realize what you had done? I knew it was your fault—I didn't have to wait for Luke and Mother to tell me. I dreamed of taking my rifle with one single bullet and jamming it into your face.

"So you see, I've thought of this meeting today and I didn't imagine myself saying 'I understand, I forgive.' "

"Will, please." For a moment she had hoped that her sin would not be so terrible, that they might end up reconciling. "I didn't mean for this to happen—I don't know what got into me. I was angry, and I lied. Believe me."

"And then I came home, Dad, to two lonely, broken people. My mother was abandoned, as she had been when I left, in a house too large for her, with a business to keep. And Luke. He is a casualty of the whole episode, too. We forget Luke. He's never been able to do a lick with himself since then. So you see, the situation at home didn't make me feel any better, either. It made me feel even worse, for however the two of them try to hide it, they have never been the same since then and never will be. There is nothing in my mother's emptiness or my brother's uselessness that teaches me to say 'I forgive. . . .'

"And you're right, Dad, I have a little boy now. And I've made a promise to myself: my son will never in his life meet his grandfather. I will die before I'll let him learn one lesson from you.

"And now, after ten years, I walk into this house—"

"Will, stop."

"I walk into this house and who do I find but—"

"Will, I said—" But she could not stop him.

"My father. And what is he doing? Whoring around with a woman like this."

"You—you—" Robert choked. "You're the whoremaster!" He stepped forward and hit him. The sound stunned all three of them. Blood came to the corner of Will's mouth and lingered, gathering more of itself from the broken inside of his cheek until it was heavy enough, shaped like a tear, to roll down the crevice of his quivering chin. Unaccountably, Will smiled. His smile showed the blood on his front teeth, and then gave way to a sneer. His fists relaxed, as if he had struck his father and released his anger, not taken the blow and the humiliation himself. Slowly, with dramatic arrogance, he turned the other cheek.

"I forgive you," he said.

Elizabeth pushed herself between the two men. "You, Will, of all people!" she shouted. "You have no right whatsoever, you hypocrite! The very idea—"

"What's wrong—"

"Don't interrupt me again, Will," she said. "I'm sick and tired of your arrogance. The very idea of you accusing him of whoring! My God, don't you have any shame?"

"Are you sorry I'm not suffering enough, woman?" He crammed his finger into the corner of his mouth and held it before her, bloody. "Is this not enough? Are you angry that

your surprise didn't humiliate me? I came here knowing I had
sinned against you, Elizabeth, and I came intending to do
something about it. But I don't track all over the place like this
murderer proclaiming myself Jesus Christ, son of God. Then
to strike his own son, as he has done to each one of us all our
lives. And you, Elizabeth, to seek your revenge with this old
man . . . I can't believe it—it's too perfect." Will stepped
around her toward the door, but she dug her hands into his
shirt and yanked at him.

"Listen for once, Will. I lied. I said I lied. You know I'm not
in love with him—I only met him tonight."

"Leave me alone." He pushed her away, but she followed
him into the hallway.

"He doesn't even know me. He's completely innocent of all
this." The door banged shut. He was lost in the night. Elizabeth stood by herself at the edge of the darkness, until she
whispered, "It's what you want to believe."

When she turned around, a group of girls were huddled together in the hallway. Two were murmuring. Another giggled.
"If you don't leave us alone," Elizabeth said, "I'll have to claw
out everyone of your goddamn pregnant eyes."

"You'll have to get out of the Priscilla Worthington Home
with language like that, Miss Mordew."

"I plan on it, missy. I plan on it, especially since I am not
pregnant. You hear me? *Not pregnant!* So leave."

"Oh, we will. But we'll be back—with Mrs. Benning."

"Bring her, then, you little gossips."

Robert stood in the middle of the room, not a half-step from
where he'd struck his son. Tears filled his eyes. Elizabeth went
to him, but he did not respond. "My God, I'm sorry." She was
drowning. The water finally broke, filling her mortified lungs
until the weight collapsed her. She wrapped her arms around
him and fell, crouching at his knees. "My God, I'm sorry."

He did not move, except to grab his right arm—the one that
had struck his son—with his left hand, just above the wrist. "O
my God, this hand, cursed be . . . it was fierce and cruel. O
Lord Jesus. Why must this hand strike my sons?" Robert
broke from her embrace, following his eldest son through the
door into the night.

"If thy right hand!" he screamed, disappearing.

V

Elizabeth: The Mountain Mission

11

Within five minutes after Robert ran out of the Worthington Home, Elizabeth had packed her bag, suddenly convinced that there was no alternative but to follow him. She had not been struck down on the road to Damascus, nor cradled in the belly of a whale—she couldn't even say it was a religious experience—but she knew that she had to find that man and, for now, find her life with him. On top of the small nightstand by her bed lay the diagram she had sketched to help her with the particular examinations of her sins. It struck her to the quick. Each line represented a day of the week, and each, because she was expected to improve, decreased in size from Sunday to Saturday. How laughable her petty little sins seemed—a note here that she coveted one girl's sense of humor and another's wealth—and how utterly terrible her self-deceit in thinking there was any improvement! There was no improvement. She was a vile, selfish creature, as sinful as Judas Iscariot. She stuffed the paper into her pocket and carried it with her. She didn't bother with the money she had left with Mrs. Benning.

Robert had hurried straight to the Atlanta Mission House, squeezing his right wrist all the way and asking himself just what was profitable for a man. It wasn't a long walk—past Sacred Heart and the hospital to Ellis Street. In the dark he didn't have to acknowledge any of the wandering faces he passed, only push on, to cast away his sure damnation.

"Is it profitable for thee?" A clear, strong voice inside his head asked the question.

The doors were always locked early, but he had been given a key because he was designated a responsible person who had freely helped for months—enough time to know where he could find what he needed.

The Mission House lived in fear of fire. There were rules about smoking, of course, but the men who migrated to the mission's doors were addicted to every drug available, whether it be bought over the counter, kicked out of a machine, or murdered for in a back alley. And they had little interest in being careful: the rich were careful. Though army cots, chairs, and folding tables took up most of the building's space, some of the more farsighted volunteers took extra precautions in the small storage room in the basement. Robert knew what was there. At the entrance he passed by two drunks as if they didn't matter in God's kingdom, letting neither of them in and not even hearing their curses. He slithered down the stairs without seeing anyone else. (One person noticed him, and Elizabeth was on her way there, fortunately.) The door was unlocked. Across from the food tins stood the two extra fire extinguishers, and the ax.

It was a wedge ax, with a handle about two and a half feet long. He picked it up and knelt down on the concrete floor.

"If it offend thee," the voice said, "cut it off. It is better."

By then he had almost choked the circulation to his hand, but when he laid it out on the concrete he felt a tingling rush of blood come back to it, recoloring the skin. For a moment he loved that hand. More than his own life he wanted to protect it. It was well made and beautiful. Inside he felt a quiver come over him, and before he could raise the wedge with his left hand and let it fall, he imagined what the pain would feel like when the brutal steel shattered the bones of his own hand and the warm blood fled until his very heart gave way.

"What is profitable for man?" the voice asked. "If it offend thee, cut it off. It is better." The hard and demanding voice challenged him.

He gripped the handle with his left hand, and without looking drove it down onto the ringing floor.

The ambulance took him to Grady Memorial Hospital. After he was moved from the emergency room to a public ward the next morning, Elizabeth and the train engineer John Barker maintained a vigil, waiting across the bed from each other. The strange engineer had simply shown up—Elizabeth had no idea where he came from. His starched white shirt was as stiff as his posture, and his small black bow tie also boasted no creases. He sat like a courthouse statue beside one of the two windows in the green-walled room, a Bible in his hands. Elizabeth had the impression his eyes saw through her.

After a few days recuperating from the pain-killers, Robert was strong enough to explain what God had told him to do: live as Christ bade men to live; take nothing for the journey; dress simply and preach repentance. This was his new revelation.

"Amen," Barker answered. "God be praised."

How ironic, Robert continued, that after ten years of false starts here and there, he was driven to launch this missionary journey by Will, who in turning his cheek mocked all that Robert believed a man should be—an imitation of Christ. Without his son's severe blow to his soul, he would have continued in Atlanta half-committed; but now, he had his mission.

Given the guilt she felt, Elizabeth might have followed him even if he had gripped the steering wheel of a car with his one remaining good hand and a bottle of booze with the three fingers of the other and renounced Christ for a sex jaunt to the West Coast. There was no chance whatever that she might say this wandering for Christ was perverted nonsense; by then nothing in her life was perverted nonsense. And there was no chance she might say she belonged back in Paris in the nicotine-stained hands of a younger man. No, for reasons she couldn't explain, she was bound to an old man. And if he was bound to Christ, so was she. She needed to believe.

He saved her from speaking about her guilt. "When Adam and Eve sinned," he said, "two things happened. The first was that they were exiled to the kingdom of death, where he was to sweat when he worked in the field and she was to suffer pain in childbirth. But the second was the redemption of the kingdom of death by Christ. Without the first, the second could not have taken place." She wasn't sure what he meant, but he was excited that she wanted to come along—there was a look in his eyes.

And thus they began—that quickly. John Barker didn't object. He carried them on his train and dropped them off in Greenville, where they walked northwest on State Road 447 toward Caesar's Head, two foolish pilgrims facing a fourteen-mile path up the mountain, or a night under the stars. He was sixty-three and she was twenty-five.

Not until halfway through the walk did Elizabeth stare across fields of harvested corn and up to the horizon of the silent blue hills waiting for snow and find herself unwillingly wondering not only why she felt this need for a complete life—these were the words she gave to the desire in her chest—but also why she imagined the complete life had anything to do with Robert. She forced herself to stop doubting, however. It was only the first day and her will was still strong enough to resist the questioning. The trip had just begun, her mind reasoned. She needed to give it—and him—a chance.

The journey worsened as the day went on. A salesman who gave them a lift drove so fast around the mountainous S curves she got carsick. He had to stop so she could retch in the woods, and instead of waiting for her and Robert, the salesman sped away, shouting an obscenity about Robert being too old to make love to her. She reminded herself she had wanted mortification. Robert helped her back to the highway and the last two miles of the journey.

In Caesar's Head they checked into a boardinghouse at dusk, and it wasn't until noon the next day that Elizabeth felt human again. By the time she hobbled downstairs, Robert was returning for lunch, his Bible, because of his hand, pressed between his right arm and his side as he walked. His injury seemed to have no effect on his rather remarkable stamina. Mrs. McMillian, the boardinghouse proprietor, served them a cold meal on the back porch. The weather was mild. Elizabeth massaged her thighs and stared at Caesar's Head, a ship's prow lurking in the nearby sky. Robert talked. "God is watching over us, Elizabeth. This morning Mrs. McMillian got the newspaper and showed me the advertisement for a maid she put in just yesterday, saying God was using us to answer her prayers. Isn't that amazing? And she said that even though we were fools enough to walk from Greenville, we had a responsible look about us. I told her you'd work for about a week. Are you willing to be a maid?"

"What makes you think I need to stop?"

"Shouldn't we tell each other the truth, Elizabeth?"

"And you? What are you going to do?"

"I'm going to walk around the streets talking to people about Christ. Where I'm led."

She didn't argue. For a week both of them rose before

breakfast and helped Mrs. McMillian prepare it for the other boarders. Then Robert stuffed his Bible into place and disappeared for the day into the streets of Caesar's Head, preaching the Gospel to all who would listen. He blessed Mrs. McMillian and Elizabeth as he left. "All the saints salute you," he said, "Second Corinthians 13:13."

Elizabeth nodded at him, never waving goodbye, and then joined Mrs. McMillian in each morning's holy war against boardinghouse filth. Only a man would think this work was preparing her for greater tasks. They cleaned, purified, scoured, sanitized, and even spiritualized that sprawling house until it sparkled brighter than a holystoned ship's deck. All done according to a ritual. Beginning with the bedrooms, Elizabeth dusted every wayward corner and unseen ledge—on top of the four-posters' side rails, along the windowsills, around the paws of the straight chairs, above the mirrors, the headboards, and the eight-foot-high doorframes Elizabeth believed past praying for. Then she changed the daily-pressed sheets, being sure to make tight hospital corners that would please Mrs. McMillian.

"The Bible says cleanliness is next to godliness," the woman said, "and dirt is cast out into the streets."

Elizabeth rubbed the mirrors and windows to a squeaky shine while Mrs. McMillian zealously polished the beds, dressers, and wardrobes in every room. Each day she paused in the room she'd last rented, beside an oakwood crib. She stroked the smooth louvered slats. "This was made in London, Lizzie, and crossed over with the Clarks of Donegal. And passed on to me. God has shown me great favor." She said so every day.

Elizabeth began to feel stronger, no matter how wrong Robert was about her endurance, and she was again ready to live—she still hesitated to say the words—as Christ bade men live. She didn't really mind Mrs. McMillian or the work; it helped her to concentrate on the task at hand and not ask questions about the past or the future. Each evening she knelt by her bed and tried to pray. She wanted to know what she was doing. Her knees felt as stiff and prickly as straight pins and the muscles in her back almost paralyzed. But she liked the pain—somehow it made the prayer seem more authentic. Speaking words never helped much. Yes, she remembered that when she thought she was pregnant, she'd cried out and felt a small quiver somewhere inside, telling her that the other side of the closed darkness was not empty. But even then it was her tears, not her words, and in no time—as soon as she thought about it—that significant quiver was gone. Speaking words in her prayers, even "Our Father," always felt like she was talking to herself.

When Mrs. McMillian gave her some money in the middle of the week, she put aside a little and passed the rest on to Robert without telling him what she was going to do with her portion. The next afternoon she hurried to a flea market and bought a cheap gold necklace. That night with a nail file she cut nicks in the chain and tied it around her thigh. She didn't want it so tight she'd have trouble taking to the road again, but it had to be tight enough to let her appreciate its presence all day long. It worked. While she labored Friday morning, she felt the slight but constant irritation in her leg. Then she could pray. There was an honesty about pain.

Friday night one of the boarders, who up until that supper had eaten in silence, asked Robert who they were. Robert answered that his wife was dead, Elizabeth was his daughter, and the two of them had abandoned their home for a journey into the mountains to preach repentance. The man immediately changed the subject.

It was the first time Robert had said Mattie was dead. The repulsiveness of the lie sickened her, like watching a knife cut open the belly of a dead fish. But it was necessary. In a way Mattie *was* dead to him. (He had told Elizabeth he'd asked Mattie to join him in Atlanta and that she'd refused.)

Another boarder followed with a story of a new Cadillac he had seen that morning in Greenville. "If I had all the money in the world," he said, "I'd be right smart of cars."

"There is nothing like the shine of chrome to make you want to stand up and shout," the first man said. "When it sparkles bright as a good spittoon, it warms my heart."

Robert interrupted. "Maybe the way to truly love a car is to save all your money, buy it, and then give it away."

The man laughed. "Then I wouldn't have it."

"Would you have us give up all our most valued possessions, Mr. Treadwell?" Mrs. McMillian asked.

Elizabeth answered: "Abraham offered up his son."

"Oh, Elizabeth, there you go again. Why, just this afternoon we were picking up in the sitting room and this young lady accused me of hoarding my daughter's piano books."

"My God," the man said, "piano books!"

"Why do you keep them?" Elizabeth asked.

"They're mementos. I wouldn't dare throw them away."

"They're not being used anymore. You said yourself no one ever plays."

"They have great sentimental value."

"I'm sure there is some little girl in town who could use them."

Mrs. McMillian shook her head. "My goodness, girl, aren't we sassy tonight? But you're right, I guess. Someone's daughter in town might use them, while over here they're just an old woman's silly memories." She tightened her lips. "Yes, you're right. God has shown me great favor and I ought to share."

"They're probably out-of-date," the first man said.

"Why do you say that?" Elizabeth asked.

"What?" Mrs. McMillian answered. "That I ought to share? I thought you just said—"

"No, I mean that 'God has shown you great favor,' " Elizabeth said.

"He has blessed my labor," Mrs. McMillian answered.

"But are blessings always good things?"

"My girl, I think it's time you read your Bible. Look at the riches of Abraham—you mentioned him yourself. And the power of Joseph, who ruled over Egypt. And the spoils of Jericho and David's kingdom. These were gifts of the Lord."

"But Christ said not to store up treasures on earth, where moths and rust do corrupt," said Elizabeth.

"Haven't you trained your daughter well, Mr. Treadwell. All she can do is mimic you," commented Mrs. McMillian.

Her words stunned Elizabeth. For the rest of the meal she didn't speak, and afterward she went upstairs early, though Robert tried to persuade her to take a stroll with him and talk about what Mrs. McMillian had said. "I don't need you to explain," she responded.

In the kitchen Mrs. McMillian even took her by the elbow and said, "I didn't mean anything by it, girl. Don't wear your heart on your sleeve."

Still, she wanted to be alone. After her bath she sat by the window and examined the scars from the chain, which, though no deeper than needle scratches, nevertheless hurt. They cut a small circle around her thigh, etching her own crown of service. But service to what? Or to whom? "Mimic," Mrs. McMillian had said. She mimicked him. Like a chimpanzee. She stared out the window at the sight of Caesar's Head darkening with the coming night. Dusk wore away its definitive lines until the bald ledge, like the prow of a mammoth ship buried beneath the rocks and silt for eons, suddenly burst through the mountain. Or maybe it was a ship going down, with bow tipped to the sky.

What was she doing? On the road the first day, she had told herself to quit asking that question. Time would tell, she reasoned. She had to give herself, and him, a chance. But did her own decision to come have anything remotely to do with God? Did she care? Night fell over Caesar's Head, and when she couldn't see the mountain anymore, she got up and went to bed, without kneeling to pray.

Robert had told Mrs. McMillian they planned to leave on Sunday; instead of attending church, they would take to the road and pick God's ears of corn, as the disciples had done. After only a few chores Saturday morning, Mrs. McMillian took Elizabeth's hand and led her upstairs to her own third-floor corner rooms, which she always kept private from Elizabeth and everyone else. All the way up she didn't speak. Elizabeth was worried: perhaps because Mrs. McMillian felt guilty about her comment at the supper table, she had decided to share her secret life and would expect a sympathetic response.

When they entered the sitting room, Elizabeth noticed a landscape painting on the left, dwarfed by a garish gold frame. It hung over a high-backed Victorian couch covered with protective blankets. Opposite the couch a parade of family portraits, nestled in lace, topped a secretary, and crammed into the dormer was a cabinet cluttered with whatnots—glass figurines, china, a scrapbook, needlepoint, calendars, and an old Bible. Mrs. McMillian unlocked a small door in the corner and, stooping, she and Elizabeth squeezed into an attic space in the back of the house. She turned on a chair lamp, whose light spread over a dark green, dusty trunk. With another key she unlocked it.

"Come here."

Elizabeth knelt beside her as she raised the top, the hinges creaking open. She carefully lifted two white quilts out, a few mothballs bouncing on the floor like marbles. The noise startled Elizabeth. Only a silver box tied with red ribbon was left. Mrs. McMillian untied the ribbon and slipped off a pressed cotton cover. Circled by its chain lay a large golden locket in the shape of a heart, pierced in the middle by a star-bright diamond.

"It took me years to save up the money for this, Elizabeth.

It's fourteen-karat and that's a real diamond. I never cut corners on boarders, Lizzie—you know me better than that—but each week I've laid aside a little nest egg until it was mine. Now let me finish before you start in on me." She undid the locket's tiny latch. Inside, a gold thread bound three curls of hair: one gray, another blond, and the last brown.

Elizabeth gripped the side of the trunk to steady herself. She felt nauseated again. She was overreacting, but she couldn't help it. She didn't want to know. It was unfair of Mrs. McMillian. The cord that ran from inside her neck down to her bowels felt ready to burst open. Two powerful, slimy hands grabbed it, and squeezed and kneaded it like clay until she felt as though her inner organs were oozing between someone's fingers.

Mrs. McMillian touched the blond lock. "This is Martha's baby hair. I kept it the first time we got it cut. When your baby grows up, it's almost as if you lose the most important part of life forever. This gray is my John's. The day before he died." Then she fingered the brown. "Martha's John. She gave it to me after he shipped out. She was so distraught when she heard. You know, they didn't have any other children and he was still a bachelor. . . ."

Elizabeth didn't think Mrs. McMillian knew where she was. The woman kept staring at the locket and talking to it. There was another presence in the room, a new presence, but it wasn't in the memento. Elizabeth suffered its presence in every foolish word the woman spoke, in the very air, in her own guts.

"Nothing we own means much by itself—you are right there. We should give away about half of what we own. So much junk. But when I was young, none of these things meant anything to me, not like what they mean now that my time approaches. No—don't. You're good, but I don't want to hide from Death. God is good to us, and we live on until He decides."

Mrs. McMillian paused, contemplating her tears. She draped the locket around her neck. Elizabeth fastened it for her and retreated to her tight grip on the side of the trunk.

"You don't know what it's like. I'm going to die wearing this locket. When people come by, I want them to see it open on my breast, with these three curls visible to the world. 'Here is a woman who lived for them,' they will say. It will be a sign to all. Death can take the rest—the house, the crib, the silver,

the insurance policy—shoot, you're right, it doesn't mean a
whit in God's eyes. But when they prepare to shovel the earth
over me, my soul with my Maker, Martha will seal this locket
as the coffin is sealed. I'll carry it to heaven. Surely God respects my wish."

Elizabeth could not speak to the woman. She had left her
own past and taken to the road with an old man only to find
herself kneeling through a long, unwanted silence with an old
woman, the two of them alone by a dusty trunk in the far
reaches of a strange and damned house. But for the first time
on her journey, she suddenly felt a sense of purpose, which
came upon her unannounced, as if all her efforts to find it, by
their very nature, were in vain. And the purpose she sensed
was not to preach repentance, as Christ instructed, but simply
to gaze down upon this presence in the coffinlike trunk. It was
Death—not the lace-and-flower death Mrs. McMillian knew,
but death by brutal hands that choke the heart, the darkness
that falls like a hammer on the brain, the weight of gravity
that flattens the muscles, and the worms that feast upon man.

Elizabeth wanted to leave the house that very moment, but
she knew she would not escape. She gripped the sides of the
trunk and looked into it. The white quilt Mrs. McMillian had
tossed aside lay like a burial pall. Elizabeth saw her own body,
arms crossed, stretched out stiff and cold and heavy, covered
with a white sheet. And then her body changed into Robert's
body, female to male, youth to age, doubter to prophet, with
only the head visible above the cover. His eyeglasses were
shining in the light. The floor beneath her began to rock back
and forth like the waves of a great river on which the coffin
floated. The river carried them along, Robert Treadwell and
Elizabeth Mordew, dead; and Mrs. McMillian and the other,
dead; thousands of others, ten thousand times ten thousand,
without anyone truly knowing how humankind was borne
along by a rag-and-bones drift until dead and sealed and
marked for the feasting of maggots. How strange that all the
differences had the same end.

She focused again. It was Robert's body lying before her.
She thought she could reach down and touch his still-open
eyes. There was no locket. He was painted with some em-
balmer's pink cake, his poor hand hidden beneath his side.
But those eyes . . . she didn't know if the light came from the
reflection on his glasses or from the stars only he could see—
his burning eyes, they were still bright.

* * *

On Sunday one of Mrs. McMillian's friends gave them a lift across the border through Rosman, North Carolina, to Lake Toxaway, where snow began to fall. It was early November. Robert used the money Elizabeth had earned to pay for two cheap motel rooms. "It won't be long," he explained, "until we'll have a hard time finding shelter. But we might as well spend this money now. No use saving mammon." At the door to his room, he fiddled with his Bible and the key while the snow powdered his hair, leaving only a few black specks around his brow. She knew not to help. Finally he pushed the door open and turned around, his left hand half-buried in the pages of his Bible. But before he spoke, the awkwardness of his wounded hand fell away, stilled by the silence of the snow.

Her vision of Robert laid out in the trunk had made Elizabeth begin to see him differently. She saw that at times he needed his own Michelangelo, who could capture his massive, scarred torso as well as his proud, troubled, linear bearing. On a great canvas of prophets, heroes, and gods, he would be a figure to stop and study, to gaze up at the way his clean-shaven face turned toward an ancient scroll unraveling in his hand, his snow-white hair blown back by the wind of prophecy, this Bible-educated Alabama farmer.

"We begin again tomorrow," he announced.

Elizabeth didn't risk asking about supper. In her room she sat by the window and watched the snow fall. It came clean and pure and sad. The separate flakes drifted from the gauze-like sky down to the freezing earth. Over the still, gray lake hovered ripples of vapor, lingering like dreams. A few lost snowflakes spiraled toward her window and stuck, until their designs melted and an ever-expanding circle of ice crept over the glass and blinded her vision, of the storm and the night closing in. She was left alone with a motel room. She went to sleep without eating.

The next morning Robert waited outside her door, his face pink in the cold, soft enough to touch, though she didn't dare, and his cheeks like smooth petals opened from dark, secret eyes. The snow had stopped, but it was terribly and unexpectedly cold. Theirs were the first footprints of the morning, side by side across the blanketed lawn and along the highway toward a diner, the foremost building in a single row that billed itself as the town of Lake Toxaway. Across the road a bold cliff shot straight up, obstructing half the low sky. The snow of the ledge high above rained long lines of water, like gray poles, and behind them the drilling marks in the face of the cliff, top to bottom, screened them from the earth like a tall black iron fence. Nearer the diner Elizabeth smelled coffee. Robert stood by the door. In a few minutes a small truck pulled up, its chains sounding like flat tires, and four men bundled in plaid wool jackets and stocking caps closed the doors and hurried toward them.

"Good morning," Robert began.

"Mornin'. An icy one it is."

"I wondered if you'd like to talk about God."

The first two men swung open the diner door, indifferent. The third lowered his head, embarrassed, and followed the others, lured by the warmth and by the smell of frying bacon. The last man sneered before he entered, and said, "Amen, brother."

The first called back from inside, "Get one of his pamphlets there, Wilbur."

In an instant Robert and Elizabeth were alone again, while the others laughed about them over their coffee. After five more carloads, Elizabeth knew what to expect and, surprisingly, wasn't bothered by the rude remarks. A few were polite, but all declined Robert's invitation, far more concerned with scrambled eggs, grits, red-eyed gravy, and the weather than with any spiritual food those two fools could feed them. Robert said the lead-in was the problem: no one cared to stop because the word *God* threatened their safe little worlds of habit; it was *the* taboo in a civilization claiming it had no taboos. Soon the owner of the diner came out. Elizabeth smelled the bacon grease as the door opened. A tight black bow tie squeezed the man's collar, and his face burned red from the grill fire he tended. Stains spotted his white apron, which he untied before he spoke.

"I'm sure as shootin' sorry, sir, but you'll have to take yourselves somewhere else. I can't have none of my customers bothered on a Monday morning by some evangelist. I allow there's plenty of time due the Lord God Almighty on Sundays."

"I beg to differ with that."

"To everything a season—the Good Book itself says so."

"But—"

"I'm sorry."

"Shall I shake the dust off my feet?"

"This here you're standing on, friend, is a welcome mat you can scrape the snow off your feet on, and the feet of the lady. Far as I am concerned, you are welcome to come in and pay for the finest breakfast Toxaway knows, but not if you're gonna start preachin' when no one's even had time to yank up the shutters of his eyes."

"I am baptizing in the spring."

"Fine, you do that."

"And you tell them inside. I am baptizing in the spring."

By early afternoon the temperature reached the fifties and the rooftop snow, melting first at the ledges, dripped an insistent daylong curtain along their path to and from the storefronts. Elizabeth went out twice on her own.

"Please come hear a man tell a story about God," she said, to no response. Or, "Listen to a story about a modern-day Abraham."

One man offered her a dime. An elderly lady told her she had no business on the streets, and her friend said they were a nuisance and a sacrilege, profaning the name of God by saying there could be such a thing as a modern-day Abraham. Another man said that Robert would kill a man by trying to baptize the poor fool in a mountain stream—even in the summer the water'd freeze him straight to hell. A few people stopped and listened as Robert told his story twice, but Elizabeth always suspected they were only being considerate of a person whose hand was missing two fingers and had stubs for a forefinger and a middle finger. By the end of the day, every storeowner, each one a churchgoer, had threatened to have them arrested for loitering, and that night the sheriff claimed he was doing them a favor when he drove them all the way to Glenville.

The day in Lake Toxaway began a four-month journey through the mountains of western North Carolina. They walked or hitchhiked from a diner to a warehouse to a barn choked with nuggets of hay. From a filling station and grocery store, a restaurant or a five-and-dime, to a feeding trough, a Cherokee souvenir store, a town hall. They stayed away from churches, but met just as many pharisees in the marketplace. Elizabeth caught a cold at the end of the first week, and kept it, off and on, for the rest of the journey. About a third of the time she slept outdoors. Robert developed great skill at building fires, but nights in an abandoned railroad car or an aborig-

inal shack tore at her health. The chain she still kept around
her thigh provided continual mortification—although mortification for what, she often never knew. She lost fifteen pounds.
She survived, being young.

Being obsessed, Robert also survived, even at his age. He
woke up every morning at dawn, and though his muscles must
have ached even more than Elizabeth's, he didn't lie there
hoping for added sleep. Stiffer than a corpse and in nose,
mouth, eye, and bladder clogged up with the abominations of
the body, he nonetheless scrambled up to a full stretch when
he saw the first light and shouted his prayer loud enough to
wake the few, frigid birds. "Let the words of my mouth and
the meditation of my heart be acceptable in Thy sight, O
Lord, my strength and my Redeemer." He extended the final
syllable until he heard it echo against the nearest trees. He was
put in jail for a week in Franklin; behind bars he memorized
the Beatitudes, ten parables, and fifteen psalms. "God knew I
needed more material," he explained. Past Franklin and
Aquone Lake, by the third week in Cullasaja, he gave away
the last of what little money they had.

A blind man was the recipient. He sat on a street bench in
the cold, wrapped in a long overcoat the color of his unshaven
face, which was pitted with red scars. A paper flower was stuck
in his lapel and dark glasses wrapped around the wounds of
his eyes. The man felt their presence beside him, and gripped
his cane. "I know the Lord God Almighty," he said.

"Amen," Robert answered.

"I have not forgotten. Once I lived in another room and I
was sure that it was all of the house. But then the room burned
to the ground. Nothing was left but the ashes, and then I discovered that the ashes themselves were a mansion with a
weather vane that rises far above the earth, into the sky."

Robert knelt before the man and gave him every bill—they
had about three left—and emptied his change into the man's
coat pocket. Then without asking he crooked his arm around
the man's legs, one by one, and with his left hand massaged
the man's calves. The blind man did not object, quietly waiting for him to finish. Robert looked at Elizabeth. "Off the
mercy of strangers—it is how angels live. I've often wondered
how they were dressed on the plains of Mamre."

Suddenly the man rapped Robert with his cane. "Leave me
alone, pervert," he shouted.

Robert stood up.

"This man is trying to rape me!"

"I am baptizing in the spring," Robert said again, and walked off.

From Cullasaja they turned north to Andrews and headed on through Robbinsville. In a Stecoah backyard he gathered together an audience of eight, standing atop a floorless, rusted Packard the talkative owner refused to junk, having already displayed and given them the history of his collection of hub-caps, an old plow and mule, an original Coke machine, and a pink flamingo statue he bought on his honeymoon in Florida. He said he couldn't bear to throw anything away—it was such a waste. Elizabeth thought of Mrs. McMillian. Robert told the story of the prodigal son, but only two of the eight stayed until its end. Both Robert and Elizabeth felt two of eight estab-lished a little momentum, though. And one man offered them a ride to Bryson City.

"You're lucky you're in the mountains," he said before dropping them off, "where there's a history of people like you. Anywhere else you'd been done for."

The sheriff provided free beds that night as a friendly ges-ture; he said he had a few female cousins as fanatical as Rob-ert and Elizabeth were. He also told Robert that the best place to baptize in the spring wouldn't be there at Deep Creek—it was too cold—but farther east toward Brevard, in the French Broad River, which was near where they had started.

By this point in the trip, Robert was encouraging Elizabeth, if she wasn't still rounding up people for his story, to lead off with a solo hymn. He had increasing respect for her stamina and courage, and realized how much her musical talent could help him focus a crowd. Why not? she told herself. It would give her something to do. Sometimes a few people joined in, especially at the choruses, but often they only listened to her rich contralto singing "Amazing Grace," "I Need Thee, Pre-cious Jesus," and "Jesus, Lover of My Soul." The man was right: the mountains bred people who understood. When she looked out over the few wizened, shivering faces, she dimly saw the fervor that once wrote and sang those simple hymns over a missionary sea. She lost herself in shaping phrases that would please them and seem authentic to their blood; and during these times, and these times alone, she forgot her doubt.

Occasionally Robert drifted from his own gift. He scoffed at city people who decided they no longer needed to plant their own gardens because grocery stores would provide them with proper nutrition. He lambasted that "disease called Madison Avenue," as he put it, and claimed that marketing ruined the very fabric of life—there was absolutely nothing good in it. He even nailed up a few of the ubiquitous mountain roadside signs; his read, "Romans 3:23," nothing else.

But soon he would return to his work on the stories. He tried to begin with just one sentence about grace and love and the repenting of sins, and then quickly proceed with his story line. He wanted those three words—*grace, love,* and *repent*—to pass into the listener's mind so the story could reinforce those ideas with episodes of everyday life. Without those initial words, he told Elizabeth, the story lost direction; with too much philosophizing, the listener would lose interest.

Elizabeth kept silent, though she wondered if he really knew why his stories weren't working. Once or twice she tried to persuade him to tell the story by itself. They were good and getting better, she said, and more than enough. He added stories about Joseph in Russia, David as an American general, Cornelius Vanderbilt as the rich man of Asheville, the local grain merchant and his talents, and Senator Saul the Communist-hater. Each story improved, but few people listened to the end. Most thought him foolish. Some argued.

"God does not put us to the test of sacrificing a son," one man said.

"Sure a father should welcome a wayward son back home, but he has a responsibility to teach what is right and wrong and reward a son when he does right," said another.

"An American should never have to serve any other country. We've saved this world—don't forget that!"

"God honors those that honor Him."

"What is wrong with making money, just so long as you tithe?"

"The Bible justifies interest! Look at the gain from the talents."

"Christians are *not* Communists. You should be shot for that."

"You are a complete and utter fool, Mr. Treadwell."

That winter in Elizabeth's life was a muddle. She had once dreamed of the artistic life in New York; she had visited a cathedral in Reims where the cut and light of the stained glass rivaled the religious sensibility of any place on earth; she had strolled arm in arm through the streets of Paris with a man she treated like a god; she had also given herself to a devil, her own sister's husband. But even with feet sore from the rocky, uncivilized land, and with the hunger she soon wore like a cloak, sometimes for long stretches of a day she felt, as she had not in New York or France, an inner knowledge that her heart was beating with a life that extended far beyond what her immediate senses testified to. What was she doing to possess this strange wisdom? Parading after a crazy old man who thought all the stories of the Bible were the same stories people lived in the present. The "here and now," as he put it.

But by late January the strain became too intense. By then she could not sustain those moments in which she felt a purpose to her life. She was lying to herself when she said she was growing accustomed to the strain; that her soul was confident she was doing God's will; that the hunger, the cold and exhaustion, the loneliness, humiliation, and uncertainty were amending and reforming her life and state. Elizabeth eased the sharp necklace off her thigh, which to her touch was a good two inches thinner. The little uncertainties of each day began to bother her. Would she trudge fourteen miles uphill, stand still eight hours in the snow, fight carsickness, or be able to eat? Washing her hair in a shower was only a luxurious memory. She never met the same person twice, and Mrs. McMillian was the last person with whom she had spent the eternity of a week. She knew no confidant— certainly not Robert—and she hated the inner voice that soon whispered in her ear if she let it. "You're wasting your valuable life in this foolish humiliation," it said. "You have only one life. You know and appreciate more than all these hillbillies combined, and yet you sing country hymns with an old man who hardly knows you exist. Tell me—what are you doing?" When she heard this voice, she imagined that the sin that most offended God—if she could use the word *sin*—was mere self-consciousness.

Some people never believed she was Robert's daughter. Their arch looks became nightmares to her because the greatest strain hid in the silence of her heart: she didn't know what her true relation with Robert was. She tried not to think about it.

* * *

When all seemed lost, the unforeseen struck. From Bryson City they trudged nonstop through Whittier, Beta, Balsam, and Cruso, eastward because either God sent Robert a cloud by day and fire by night or without realizing his mistake he wandered worn and confused back toward where he started. Robert grew even quieter and more frustrated, and quick-tempered, as if she were his true daughter and he had a right to victimize. Then his rage made him guilty and his guilt made him question the seeming indifference of God toward those straining to do His will. Perhaps it was time, he implied, for him to fast alone in the wilderness. They stopped at Penrose, where he told his story of spending talents to a crowd of ten. Halfway through the story, a black limousine pulled over to the side of the road. The side and rear windows were darkened, but the chauffeur cracked his window enough that whoever was inside could hear Robert's voice.

Later on, down the road at Pisgah Forest, before Robert began he glanced at Elizabeth, his face written with uncertainty. Elizabeth was also unwilling to speak of it, for fear that mouthing the words might ruin the unexpected, but in the group of twelve were five people who had come from Penrose to hear him again, including, at the edge of the crowd once more, the dark shape in the limousine. A second time. There were also the same plumber and his assistant, a carpenter and a woman. Robert told the story of Mary Magdalene—Elizabeth's least favorite. Afterward the plumber came to him. "I heard you up the road. You're very good. I've never thought of life the way you do."

"I will baptize soon."

"Will you take a second go-around?"

The woman in the group stood away from the others and listened. She was beautiful, more beautiful, perhaps, than any woman Elizabeth had seen. Her body was ample but graceful, her wavy hair auburn, her skin lamblike, and her stunning green eyes shone like emeralds. She was too substantial to be a fashion model, but any artist would have suffered torture to set her half-dressed or naked in front of his canvas. There was simply some quality about her that was a challenge to capture. She waited for a moment, then walked across the street to a Cadillac and drove away.

A new hope flickered, which scared them. Five people had followed them to hear another story, but Robert didn't want to assume too much. It was a sin to anticipate God. Still, he wondered—if God would allow him—whether the French Broad might be his river Jordan.

At the edge of Brevard, the manager of an icehouse let them stand atop his platform and preach to a multitude of eighteen, including eight from Pisgah. Both the limousine and the woman were in attendance again. Elizabeth sang. They applauded her. Robert told the story of David and Bathsheba, and after he was finished a few more came up to talk, the woman last. "My name is Molly Connor," she said. She had a low, gruffy voice. "I would like to invite you and your daughter to stay with us while you're in Brevard." Robert accepted.

Molly Connor had lived a normal, successful, and wretched life. She had grown up in a churchgoing Brevard family, the second of six children, one of four daughters of a well-to-do businessman and socially connected mother, who raised them to believe in the strict and equal holiness of social grace and the family pew. As a child Molly was active in the First Baptist Church Sunday School and Training Union and was especially proficient in sword drills, flipping so quickly and in such proper order that she won the convention's state championship in Raleigh. With her parents' consent and a conference with the pastor, at twelve she accepted Jesus Christ as her Lord and Savior. The summer she turned fourteen, she retreated to the mountains with her youth group and came home proclaiming that God wanted her to be a missionary to China, like Annie Armstrong. She made a public profession the next Sunday morning. Her parents and her pastor, though, encouraged her to put her decision off until after college. She was the number one student in her high-school class (but careful never to make a boy feel dumb) and she received a scholarship to a women's college in the eastern part of the state.

Her miniature college rebellion was not quite as appropriate as it should have been, however, and put a real scare into her family, especially since she was so beautiful. Her parents easily accepted her announcement that she was not going to be a missionary but an English teacher instead. They felt confident she would marry after a year or two of teaching. The short hem of her skirt was endured, and her father was even able to calm her mother down when Molly admitted she had once had a drink. But one day her roommate unexpectedly found Molly reading a pirated copy of Mr. D. H. Lawrence's *Lady Chatterley's Lover*. It was, of course, totally inappropriate that

Molly was reading a book about sex. But the lengths to which she'd gone in order to get a copy of the banned book raised serious questions about her moral character. The roommate turned her in and she was kicked out for a semester, to be granted readmission only if she consented to a series of conferences with her pastor and if afterward he wrote a letter testifying to her renewed moral convictions.

At home her mother wouldn't speak to her for a week, and when she did, Molly discovered that the family had never borne a single stain, a single blemish, a single sin so despicable as that which she had so thoughtlessly shackled it with. It was animal.

Molly survived it, though. The pastor wrote the letter, her father made a contribution, and upon graduation she was hired in Brevard to teach English—Tennyson, Waldo Emerson, Emily Dickinson, and the book of Job. She fell in love with a GI journalist, a hometown boy, and they married and bought their first house, on Poplar Street. He wrote for the Brevard and Hendersonville papers, worked his way up to copy editor, and moved her to three successively larger, better situated houses. He also bought a summer camp. She quit her teaching. She had babies. It was a normal, successful, and wretched life, and she had come to realize it. For weeks she had taken to long afternoon drives through the mountains, leaving her children to the mercy of the maid. It was on one of these afternoon wanderings that she first spotted Elizabeth and Robert.

They stayed with the Connors until the baptismal day. The three-story mansion outside town abutted the summer camp, where there were plenty of beds for off-season friends and guests. Even without heat, Robert and Elizabeth had not slept in such luxury since Caesar's Head. The French Broad meandered along the opposite edge of the property. Beyond, the mountains rose into the blue, rolling distance. Derek Connor was a man of average size, with puffy hands, a cherubic face, and prematurely balding head (he swept his brown hair up and over from a part just above his ear). His brown eyes were dull and his smile superior, and most of the time at home he wore an off-white, open-collar shirt, pleated pants, and gray Hush Puppies. He worked late the first night they stayed, but the second night he headed the supper table, listening to his children's news of the day and helping his wife direct the maid, who, after the children were excused, brought in coffee.

"So now—the two of you. What's this I heard my wife tell my children, Mr. Treadwell—I can call you Bob, can't I?"

"I prefer Robert."

"Oh. Okay. Have it your way. You're a modern-day troubadour and this young lady's your abigail?"

Robert studied his smile for a moment and glanced at Molly, who hid her reaction by sipping her coffee. "I tell stories about repentance and love and grace. Elizabeth accompanies me. She sings hymns, and if a piano is available, she plays. And gives moral support, too. We've been traveling through western North Carolina."

"How so?"

"Walking. Sometimes people give us lifts."

"How charming." Derek lit a cigarette and buried it between his forefinger and middle finger, his skin puffed up around the ash like white dough. "A regular Quixote and Sancho Panza. You must have a thousand anecdotes about all the characters you've met and the quaint little scenes of life you've discovered. Have you kept a diary?"

"No."

"But you should, you must. Think of all those moments under the stars when you could reflect. Those of us in the workaday world don't have such time, you know, or make the time, as busy as we are. But you! You've had the time to measure the width and breadth of man—what a piece of work is man!" He smiled, blowing his cheeks full like sails.

"Cream?" Molly asked, pushing the silver pitcher past Derek to Robert.

"I can see it now—"

"Derek."

"No, I'm serious, Molly. This man could win the Pulitzer for a series on his quest for windmills. 'American Quixote in the mountains.' How's that? Or 'La Mancha's Call to Repentance.'" He laughed.

"I don't think you—"

But he interrupted. "Do you know that there are actually people who would like to see Dorothy Day win a Pulitzer Prize? Dorothy Day! Can you believe that? She can't write a traffic fine. Of course you probably don't know who Dorothy Day is."

"Do you publish articles like that?" Elizabeth asked, disregarding Robert's frown.

"In the Sunday magazine. When people come home from

church all inspired, they want something inspiring to read. Think how great it would be if you wrote poetry. You do, don't you, Bob? We could do a series on America's bohemians on the road and back home—you know, you the evangelist and the beatniks and the Village and San Francisco. The lead could be 'What is Truth?' That's what Pilate asked Christ, you know, and he didn't answer."

"He kept silent," Robert said.

"Of course he kept silent."

"I don't think Robert and Elizabeth came here, Derek, with the idea of being material for your newspaper career."

"Oh, I know that, woman. I know you have a purpose, Bob. We all do. It is admirable to ask the question. But surely we all need to hear a little irony and humor, don't we? Wouldn't you agree, Molly? It might help us all if we suffered a little irony and humor, including husband and wife. Besides, people consider what you're doing charming, Bob."

"I don't."

"Nor I," Molly added. Her eyes, like burning green beacons across the table, fastened on her husband. "Perhaps it would do you good to realize that."

"That was not my point." He rubbed his cigarette stub into the bottom of his coffee cup.

"Anyway . . ."—Molly addressed her question to Elizabeth—"didn't you say you wanted to ask me something?"

"The limousine."

"Oh, yes. That black limousine," Molly said. "You know, you're not going to believe this, but I don't know. I should. It seems everyone knows all there is to know about everyone else within fifty miles, but I've never heard of the man."

"Who?"

"I thought you weren't interested, Derek."

"Maybe I know him."

"A man in a black limousine who has attended Robert's last two stories."

"Huh. I've heard stories about the old man outside of Candler, but he hasn't been seen in years, they say. It's poppycock anyway."

"Who's to say?"

"It takes courage, you know, Bob." Derek obviously wanted to change the subject. "It takes the radical courage of the Left Bank, standing up against the establishment. It's all very dramatic, don't you think, young lady?"

"I don't see what the Left Bank has to do with it," Elizabeth said, astonished at his unintentional hit on her past.

"For some of us a lot, I imagine."

"You don't seem very interested in what we believe, Mr. Connor," Robert said.

"Oh, but I am, Bob, I am. I think about the truth every day, especially when it comes to getting the paper out on the streets. But people like my beloved Molly develop such a prejudice against the business world that no one believes a businessman thinks about anything but cash flow and interest. Well, I am a writer. The difference between me and you is that I have deadlines. And a few other things. A fellow named Einstein does live in this century, for one."

"God be praised."

"Sure, go right ahead. My wife is more interested in the fringe matters than I am, to tell the truth." He tried to stroke his hair from his ear across his forehead, but the strand wouldn't stay in place, curling back to the side like smothered grass. "She has the time, too—the kids are in school now. I have mouths to feed. By the way, what about your family?"

"I have left them."

"My goodness!" He glanced at Molly. She leaned forward.

"I have a ministry. 'I come not to bring peace, but the sword.'"

"And your wife sits at home?"

"She has a store, a son who hates me, and plenty of friends."

"What an interesting plot twist! The prophet without a home. The evangelist leaves behind his family—Christ is not known in Galilee—and only one daughter sees the truth. She then becomes the daughter of the spirit, is that it, young lady?"

"What's the script in your family?" Elizabeth asked.

"Nothing so interesting. We're too normal."

"And unhappy," Molly added.

"Oh, we are *not* unhappy, Molly. You're just tired, honey, I told you that. You've been working too hard. A little rest and you'll feel fine."

She lowered her head.

"Well," he said, folding his napkin and lighting another cigarette. Then he stood up. "I've got some work to do back at the office. You're welcome to stay as long as you like—anything to further the cause of truth. And, Molly, you make sure

Betsy cleans up. Don't you lift a finger. I'm serious about you resting."

In the middle of the night, Elizabeth heard Robert awake from his sleep screaming. She sat up and leaned her ear against the wall. For about ten seconds he panted like a hysteric and screamed again. Then he stopped. He got up, groaning, and paced along the wall between the two cabins, another sound following behind his footsteps, but higher up. She considered calling out to him, but didn't. She had heard these nightmares before and knew he didn't want to be asked. He would pace for as long as an hour, slowing down when his mind's horror somehow eased and the darkness no longer brought on the memory of whatever it was that tortured his sleep.

As Elizabeth lay awake in bed, listening, she recalled the one night Robert had discussed what he did to his hand. It had been colder, she thought, than any other time; they were still dressed and wrapped in two blankets apiece and trying to sleep in a single cabin room with five other people—a couple and their three children—somewhere in the backwoods mountains outside of Andrews. Neither of them could sleep. They had sat by the dying embers of the fire, whispering. He was bitterly ironic about the failure of his mission, holding his mangled hand before her as he spoke.

"At least I will not murder my own son again."

"Robert, please."

"What do you mean, 'please'?"

"I feel responsible for the whole cursed thing."

"Oh, come on, Elizabeth." He jammed the poker into the ashes. A small flame shot up. "Don't you understand yet? Sooner or later it was going to happen. He was going to accuse me no matter when we met again, and I was going to strike him for telling the truth."

Elizabeth watched the ashes of the fire fall away. Though he surely guessed, Robert had never asked her why Will had come to the Worthington Home in the first place. Robert was a man obsessed with confessing the truth about himself, but he didn't press the same urge on her. And she would never volunteer.

In a strange, horrific gesture, Robert had turned his mangled hand over in front of the fire and then raised it to her face. "Here, look," he said. The ax had hit at an angle. Two fingers were completely gone; the middle finger and the fore-finger were stubs, the former shorter than the latter, and the thumb was complete. "I intended to chop it off at the wrist. It was to be a good clean cut. I really didn't think about whether I would live, but it just seemed right that the cut should be a clean one at the wrist—that's what it means to cut it off, doesn't it? I can't explain to you how important it was to me, but look at this—I can't even cut my hand off right. It seems too perfect, Elizabeth. I have these ideas about what I should do with my life, and look—all of them end up like this mangled monstrosity."

Elizabeth fell asleep in her cabin cot before she heard Robert go back to bed. The next morning she indulged her face when she washed. Molly lent her some facial soap, the water was hot, and the sunlight through the cabin screens promised a warm spring day. Robert was whistling next door, his nightmare lost in the bright morning. She rubbed the suds along the edge of her brow and down to her ears, massaging as much as cleaning, and on around her nose and down to her neck. She buried her face in the towel for at least a minute. It smelled of pine trees. White pines. That smell gave her a new sense of the life of the spirit, for some reason, and served as a premonition that the horrors of the night and the deprivation of the road would be relieved. She could not explain why. He was planning to baptize. He believed there was hope. How far from his misshapen hand to that promise.

She was right. The great day did finally come. Beginning that morning, Robert and Elizabeth paraded through the streets of Brevard for another three weeks, dawn to dusk, telling stories and singing of pure, unbounded love and the new creation proclaimed through the waters of baptism. Robert announced that any river, including one with a name like the French Broad, was the river Jordan, and that any time was the time of Christ. Baptism committed to the here and now.

Elizabeth couldn't believe it, but no one kicked them out. They talked with people in front of their houses, strolling along the storefronts, and waiting in the courthouse. Everyone's spirit seemed changed. The new green and blossoms of the trees, the songs of the mockingbirds hidden in the azaleas, and the bright sky and warm sun gave the people the patience and loving-kindness to listen, which was all Robert asked. He was convinced he had words to speak for those who had ears to hear.

Molly stayed with them every day until midafternoon, when

she picked up her children from school and returned home, preparing with Betsy one supper for her family and then another one for Elizabeth and Robert when they hobbled in. Elizabeth watched Molly suffer a mortification of her own. At great risk to her reputation in town, she insisted that her friends listen to Robert. Supporting the message in her own Galilee, as Derek phrased it, was in effect saying that she believed the supernatural existed among them there in the everyday—except that the man who preached this message was poorly dressed, handicapped, and obviously unconcerned with whose house was larger, or whose name led back to a Virginia family, or who shopped in Atlanta twice a year and had more than one car. These were his unpardonable sins, which Molly, of all people, should have recognized.

At times Elizabeth wondered if people endured them simply because of their connection to Molly—no one would risk crossing her—and not because of the generosity of spring or Robert and Elizabeth's message, but she talked herself out of such a cynical fear. All the while Molly seem to revel in the attention, and Elizabeth knew they never would have accomplished what they did without her. She smothered Robert in a way another man's wife should not, but Elizabeth forgave her that offense, considering who her husband was. When Derek once suggested it might be time for them to hit the road again, Molly made it perfectly clear to him that he would have nothing to do with that decision.

The baptismal day was wondrous. Four people, including Molly, assured Robert they were coming, and he and Elizabeth hoped for as many as ten. They walked across the Connors' camp early on the announced morning, before the others were expected to arrive, over a dirt road and down a slight hill to the bottomland that stretched to the river. The field was edged in rose-red phlox, newly blossomed, some stems of which Elizabeth picked, twirling the trumpet shapes, and slipped into her hair. The air felt mild and fresh, a slight wind sighing over the open space of earth toward a few tall trees that shaded the river, swaying the topmost branches of tulip poplars and beeches and sycamores, their new green leaves dancing expectantly in the sunlight. Beyond the river and the trees, Elizabeth could see the mountains, where the first green of the spring, bursting out everywhere with the ache of newness, fell in with the sea of redbud, and then the sky stretched blue-ward.

Robert's face gleamed with the joy and anticipation of that awaited day. As they walked across the field, Elizabeth saw in his sparkling eyes the knowledge that they had at least made it to spring. Winter was gone, death behind them. In snow and hunger, doubt and humiliation, they proclaimed theirs an existence for each day, living through the questions of daily sustenance and the lack of sustaining answers only by hoping. Hoping for food, for warmth, for meaning and love. The winter now seemed destined to lead to that spring and the baptismal day. Elizabeth skipped for a moment, looked at him, and laughed.

"Go ahead," he said. His eyes had never seemed more loving.

She felt like a young girl again, when the time to dance comes freely. She extended her arms and slowly opened her palms up toward the sky. The stretch in her breast muscles aligned her head with her arms, and then she moved, at first leisurely, testing the give and touch of her flats, until she could step up on her tiptoes. Then she glided, the rustle of her skirt exciting her legs to remember. The first leap was tentative and scared, but the second and third tore from her memory full and clear as she thrust her legs out from under her and dared the earth to deny her an arched rush into the spring sky. When she cast her head back at the height of the leap, light burned on top of the trees. And finally she gamboled ahead until she could turn in the air and land on bended knee, her back leg stretched horizontal with the earth and her arms extended again, like a swan's artful wings.

"Bravo!" Robert shouted. He trotted toward her, clapping his hands above his head.

"I'm exhausted," she said, laughing and panting. She rested her hands on her hips and tried to pull her breath from the bottom of her lungs.

"I wish I were young enough to boost you over my head and hold you up forever."

"Oh, you do, Robert." She touched his arm.

He was winded, too, from just jogging after her. "All I should do is say a word and then tell everyone to watch you dance. God would be well served."

"Yes—to just about kill me."

He laughed and wrapped his arm around her shoulders. They walked arm in arm through the trees and down the river until he found a sandy bottom, where he could stand, the

water waist-high, and baptize. Farther out the water darkened. When he turned around and looked back over the field,
a few black cars had stopped on the dirt road, the flash of
chrome when the doors opened and closed like a sparkle of
sunlight dancing on the river. Molly was first to come, and the
others followed, some with Bibles in their hands: two couples,
then four women—eight, twelve, until eighteen made their
pilgrims' way to the trees by the French Broad. Robert and
Elizabeth were astonished at the number. No one seemed at
all embarrassed. Handshaking all around, and laughing and
glorifying the day, they gathered with him, standing in wait
and hope.

Robert began with a short prayer, and then Elizabeth led
everyone in "Shall We Gather at the River," keeping the
tempo slow so they could hear the harmony some women sang
and take the jerky edge off the dotted eighths and sixteenths.
Slower, it was much prettier. Their voices sang out from the
trees and rose over the sound of the river's current, asking if
they should gather at the river whose crystal tide flowed by the
throne of God. At the beginning of the third verse, Robert
pointed to Elizabeth, and the assembled crowd quieted and
watched as she stepped forth to sing alone. It was a moment
that only music could crystallize for her. The words were simple:

> *Ere we reach the shining river,*
> *Lay we ev'ry burden down;*
> *Grace our spirits will deliver,*
> *And provide a robe and crown.*

The words and the music and the sudden loss of her denying
self lifted her voice to the heavens and called the saints down
among them, she believed, her faith never more sure than in
those moments she numbered, the full-throated glory of God
around them, a present redemption going backward and
forward through all her life and all lives, and out of time into
another realm. When they joined her on that final verse and
they finished, the silence that followed seemed to move over
all the face of the earth.

Robert began, from memory. "Therefore I say unto you,
take no thought for your life, what ye shall eat, or what ye
shall drink; nor yet for your body, what ye shall put on. Is not
life more than meat, and the body than raiment? Behold the

fowls of the air: for they sow not, neither do they reap, nor gather unto barns; yet your heavenly Father feedeth them. Are ye not much better than they? Which of you by taking thought can add one cubit unto his stature? And why take ye thought for raiment? Consider the lilies of the field, how they grow; they toil not, neither do they spin: And yet I say unto you, That even Solomon in all his glory was not arrayed like one of these. Wherefore, if God so clothe the grass of the field, which today is, and tomorrow is cast into the oven, shall he not much more clothe you, O ye of little faith? Therefore take not thought, saying, What shall we eat? or, What shall we drink? or, Wherewithal shall we be clothed? for your heavenly Father knoweth that ye have need of all these things. But seek ye first the kingdom of God, and his righteousness; and all these things shall be added unto you. Take therefore no thought of the morrow: for the morrow shall take thought for the things itself. Sufficient unto the day is the evil thereof."

Robert took his shoes off, rolled up his pantlegs, and waded into the river. Elizabeth came first, barefoot, the water so frigid her bones shivered. She wasn't sure how long she could stay in. Her teeth chattered; the numbness paralyzed her feet. But he opened his arms to her and she went unto him. He cradled her neck and waist and set her in the icy water, which rushed into her ears and over her face in a clear, pure wave. When he brought her up, the water fell from her eyes, and her soul seemed radiant within before it saw the sea of the heavens above and beyond, and then she stood straight, feet in the sand, people of the shore among the trees. Four others followed. She waited on the bank, the sunlight slowly restoring feeling to her limbs, and watched as Robert baptized Molly. When she came up from the waters, she buried her head in his chest and cried. He held her and led her ashore.

Elizabeth did not hear the sound until it was halfway across the field. When she turned around, she noticed that everyone had been watching an oversize black car—the limousine— ease down the embankment and slowly bounce its way toward them, a cloud of dust trailing. A couple whispered beside her, in disbelief. The car stopped at the edge of the trees and the chauffeur hurried around to the back door. There was no back seat. The shadows of a wheelchair and a bent figure loomed behind the darkened glass. After opening the door, the chauffeur slipped a wooden ramp out to the ground, stepped inside, and rolled the wheelchair down on its rear wheels, the cripple's feet sticking up in the air like those of a baby on its back. The elderly man was dressed in a black pinstriped suit, with a carnation in his lapel, a handkerchief neatly pointed in his coat pocket, and a golden watch chain arching from vest bottom to fob. His face was sharp and contentious, and she thought he smelled like vinegar.

The chauffeur wheeled him toward Robert, who stood barefoot at the water's edge. Twice the chauffeur jerked the chair back and around a rock, and each time his passenger was impatient, until they finally stopped below Robert.

"Baptize me," the man said.

There was silence while Robert stared into the cripple's eyes. He had followed them all the way to the river, but Elizabeth wasn't sure Robert should do it. The cripple looked too much like a rich man angry at his lot, his request only a scornful, half-veiled threat. But why did he bother? Robert backed up into the river. The man gripped the wheels and pushed on them. "Into the water," he said, and then, as the chauffeur hesitated, he turned and shouted, "Into the water! Please God!"

The wheelchair immediately stuck in the sandy bottom. The chauffeur waded around to the front, but Robert touched him on the shoulder and said, "No, I will." He reached down to the man, who wrapped his arms around Robert's back like a boy would his father. Robert cradled the rich man, the gold watch swinging from his vest like a pendulum, and turned toward the crowd on the shore. "With men it is impossible," he said, "but not with God; for with God all things are possible." After he laid the man in the water, he picked him up and carried him toward the others. The man's rich suit and watch were ruined. Like a wet dog, his hair hung in strings off the side of his head. The chauffeur worked the wheelchair out of the sand and back ashore, but the man said to Robert, "Set me down on my feet." Which Robert did.

The man stood, swaying, like a baby learning to walk. He extended his arms before him for balance and took one awkward step. He brought his other foot quickly parallel. He tried again, two and then three more paces. Suddenly he started to laugh to high heaven, which made him fall, straight back on his rear like a startled baby. He waved people away before anyone could help him. "No, no! Get away!" He set his hands firmly on the ground in front of him and lifted his rear up first, and then once again struggled erect, but wobbly. The chauffeur hurried ahead and opened the front passenger door. The man tried again, and this time stumbled all the way there. He started to get inside, but changed his mind and walked around and around the limousine, stumbling and laughing with all the joy a man could bear. Finally, spent, he lurched into the car. The door shut, the chauffeur ran around and drove off, the old man's joyous, exhausted laugh carrying back to them from across the field and up the hill. Then everyone turned in silent wonder and stared at Robert.

12

*F*our days later Elizabeth wanted to run away. Forever. Run from the frenzied coming and going of false disciples, cripples, newsmongers, beggars, and blind men, all of whom sought a man who wouldn't budge from his upstairs room. She had had enough. She needed to get clear of the house and the telephone and the doorbell, and the in-the-right-church-but-wrong-pew feeling of sleeping and bathing and eating as a guest in someone else's home. Especially Molly's. She wanted to think, and if she couldn't find the time to be alone, she would abandon Robert. So she lied: she explained that she felt obliged to write home, considering what had happened. Molly asked, in a patronizing way, if Elizabeth actually thought they would understand, and Elizabeth said of course not, but she still felt the obligation to try. Molly brought her own stationery and told Betsy to search for a pen—she had more important matters to attend to—and Elizabeth took a book to use as a lap desk. The only quiet, peaceful place to write a letter was outside.

The first step into the sunlight quickened her, an injection of warmth straight into her blood. She hurried through the safety of the backyard and past the camp's cabins to the hillside that overlooked the field of phlox. It took an effort of will not to keep running. She let the book drop, stretched on tiptoe toward the sky, and breathed in the mountain air. She was free from her prison. The line of white pines on her right paralleled the field to the French Broad, where the cluster of poplars, sycamores, and beeches towered over the baptismal waters. The sky was clear again; the hills beyond crested at the foot of the heavens. The phlox looked a little darker; but other than that, the scene was about the same, four days later. Too much had happened.

She sat, the book on her lap, and smoothed the fine vellum with the side of her hand. Printed across the top was "Mrs. Derek T. Connor, Windsor Gate, Brevard, North Carolina." What did she imagine Elizabeth's supposed mother would think, writing home to proclaim Dad a miracle worker and say that the rich, wonderful lady whose name is atop this paper takes care of him fine and dandy? In fact, Dad sleeps in the room next to hers. Molly: the first reason Elizabeth wanted to run away. But there were others. She scribbled a question: What happened? Then she numbered the question, feeling more questions coming: 1. *What happened?* For some reason she immediately felt embarrassed, even though she was alone. An inner voice, which she had scrunched into the back of her mind, told her never to ask such a potentially serious question. Was it her Gide voice? If it's serious, the voice continued, then it might be construed as foolish or sentimental.

This is a very old Elizabeth Mordew, she told herself. She wrote a second question under the first: 2. *Was he really and truly unable to walk?* The limousine had obviously been custom-built to accommodate a wheelchair. There was no doubt about that.

3. *Could he have been faking?* And build the car for a lark? she answered. His drama was an awful lot of trouble for a joke among strangers. And nothing about his passion seemed ingenuine.

A birdcall interrupted her thoughts. She recognized the sound, the queedle-queedle hiccup this bird's whole body hops to. A limb danced. She eyed his crest halfway up a white pine, where he prepared himself with a few bars before falling into a siesta. He didn't need to ask questions. Down the hill two robins hopped about, rummaging on the ground. One pecked into the earth; tugged out a long, elastic worm; tossed her head back, and gobbled it. Then a cardinal hightailed it down the hill and over the field, bobbing in flight until, from his lowest plunge, he lifted himself upright to land on a branch of a distant poplar. "Whoit, whoit, whoit," called all the way across the field, and with that sound, a memory.

As a girl Susan had stumbled across a fallen nest of wrens one day in the backyard of their Atlanta house. Even at that age a motherly pathos filtered through her voice. "They're so small," she said. "Look—they're shivering they're so scared." She and Elizabeth settled them in a shoebox. Then they secured a supply of spiders, beetles, and roaches, according to their mother's bird book, and used an eyedropper to feed them water. Their father warned them the babies wouldn't live. The parents would not return, he said, because the babies now smelled of human hands. Elizabeth wondered how human hands contaminated something so innocent. Eventually she grew tired of their constant need, but Susan stayed on, whispering to their gawking eyes and fuzzy little heads. There was another reason Elizabeth began to shy away. She worried that her father was right: they were going to die. She was unable to forgive such cruelty. And yet Susan never said she feared for their lives or that the parents should come back or that it was unfair of God. "They're just going to another life," she said when, one by one, they died. She buried them alone, and somehow seemed content in her effort.

Elizabeth had not thought about Susan. Her sister loved the weak and helpless, but since her marriage she'd grown ever more resentful of those who did not cuddle to her breast. Still, it had been close to a year, and Susan, given that she'd had a life before Will, might be able to find a distanced perspective. Elizabeth decided to write her in a day or two, and even mention Will by name, and ask forgiveness, at first in a general way. Maybe Susan could understand that the life of the birds, and of her son, was the same life her sister shared, and in that commonness someday the sinned against might find forgiveness.

4. *Was he only sick in the mind? Psychosomatic?* But she was sick in the mind, Robert was sick in the mind, so were Molly and Derek and Susan and Will and President Eisenhower. And even Jesus Christ in a way, because he was a man, too, and mankind is sick unto death. Healing the mind is no less a cure than healing a leg.

5. *Has he stayed cured?* Stupid question, she thought, but she found herself wanting the cure to last longer than a moment or two, perhaps to gain lifetime certification, with an eternal signature. Yesterday one of the pilgrims had told Molly that she saw the limousine come and go through town. "What citizen would notta got that there buggy dead to

rights," the woman said. "Why, the windowglass was the privatest you ever would see, just a bent-down creaky old shadow in a chair—believe hit or not. But coming back—I waited 'round for hit, h'aint no way I was gonna miss it—this here old man leaned outta the front window flappin' his wings like some high-flyin' bird, one of them condors or somethin', screaming that 'hit happened! Hit happened!' " What happened? Another rumor said he'd hiked a mile each day since, praise the Lord! But that rumor wasn't verified. It could have been a mere myth already built up around him.

Elizabeth looked up: the cardinal was on his way back. The red wayfarer flew low over the field, dipping and rising like a sine curve across a chalkboard. He glided by and landed on a pine branch, where he turned his crested cavalier's head, oblivious to her questions, and whistled his heart's delight. This time his pitch lowered—"purty, purty, purty." His song carried over the busybody robins and the field to the shaded river and beyond to the mountains and the sky. He was content to live without the questions, to eat, to whistle and sing, to exist and die. But not Elizabeth Mordew. She never seemed content, a measly human being jotting down questions and rummaging through her own mind for worm-infested answers. Where was the wisdom of simply living? There were moments when she knew wonder—the water-parted instant of baptism, for one, when she saw the topless heavens and the turning earth and the people on it as a living whole. But those moments didn't last. They gave way to the pilgrims in the house and Molly and her family and the need to run away and Robert's behavior and all these questions. She looked at them:

1. What happened?

2. But was he really and truly unable to walk?

3. Could he have been faking?

4. Was he only sick in the mind? Psychosomatic?

5. Has he stayed cured?

She wrote another question: 6. *Does it matter?* Yes. Yes, it does. It was a matter of choice, really. She had chosen Robert before; out of the confusion she should choose him again.

She scribbled her final question: 7. *What then must I do?* Molly and the rich cripple took care of that. Molly had the answers, the man the money. Before Elizabeth could decide what action to take or even pray that God's will be done, Molly told her how the three of them would understand the past, make sense of the present, and shake hands with the future. The three of them, mind you. One, two, three of them.

That same night, after Derek shooed the pilgrims away and Molly tucked her children in, she suggested Elizabeth and she sit down and talk in the living room. Not on the porch, in the yard, or in the kitchen, but in the living room, where the conversation must be serious (and posed, ornamental, and stale, like the room). Elizabeth had seen the living room. Molly's three children didn't dare intrude upon the sacred museum; they'd been taught from birth to take their shoes off when they set sail through it or to stay on the runners that crisscrossed the carpet when guests weren't expected. In one corner of the room, a baby grand was flanked by a delicately painted white and gold chest, which was empty; two gold-framed, ornate mirrors; and an unsat-upon felt-cushioned chair. This chair was where Elizabeth plumped down to wait now for the lady of the house, for she expected to be made to wait. The chair guarded a side table and its crystal lamp, six sparkling crystals shaped like oyster crackers dangling below the Empire lampshade. Before the burnished ceiling-high mirror across the way, two similar chairs were displayed; and in front of the floor-length pleated lace curtains, the sofa looked at four antique prints of French sailing vessels anchored on the opposite wall. When Molly came in, she asked Elizabeth to join her there.

Elizabeth attacked first. "I think I can persuade him to leave. All I need is a little time with him alone."

"But that's not the point, Lizzie, don't you see?" Molly moved toward her, as far as the rosette, and embraced Elizabeth's hand, top and bottom, with hers, as a mother would a daughter's, suffering in the serious room to talk her out of an unwise, too early marriage. "Everything is changed. Everything is changed by one event, and you can't think in the terms you thought in before. It's a different world now, for the three of us, and there's no earthly chance you can continue in the way you went."

"Why not? It served us well from Greenville on. It can serve us well from here on out. That's how we made it in the first place."

"But where were you? Poor, lost, almost ready to quit. It

might not have been another week before he went home to
your mother."

"I don't think so."

"He told me himself."

"I don't understand what you're trying to imply, Molly."

"It's time for a new, more dynamic ministry. He has come
into the public eye. There are people who need Robert—he
has been given a special power, and God would not grant him
this power if he were not meant to share it with the world. All
the world. Sure western Carolina is a start, but this healing
power can carry us much farther than these mountains. Listen,
Lizzie. The man who was healed, he has given me money.
Money so Robert can begin his new ministry. We can travel in
a different way now, and find more people to heal and save.
Thousands of people. Big tents, churches, weeklong revivals—perhaps television. Have you ever thought about the implications of television?"

"He gave you this money?"

"He sent it in the mail—cash. Five bills. Bills even I have
never seen before. He wrapped them in two envelopes so the
mailman wouldn't realize what he was carrying. There was
only a little note, and it wasn't signed, but I'm sure it was from
him. Who else would have sent such a fortune?"

Elizabeth was stunned. She had never considered the possibility of money. "What did the note say?"

"Something about being eternally grateful. Robert asked
me to keep it."

"You?"

"You know as well as I do, Lizzie, that he's in no condition
to mess with it himself."

"But you, Molly?"

"I am perfectly aware of what you mean, Lizzie, and that's
something you'll have to come to grips with yourself or take
up with Robert when he's up to it. I am trying to help. I know
I am doing the Lord's will. I have been born into the faith
again and feel that the money came as an answer, yes, an answer to what we should do first—if you're willing to join us. I
have already telephoned some friends in Sylva. They're making arrangements for a massive meeting—I know the newspa-
permen over there, too. And Robert's consented."

Elizabeth turned her face and focused on the sailing prints,
trying to think without looking vulnerable. What could she
say? She had struggled enough with the hoopla around the

house after the baptism, but she had not anticipated it was only the beginning, and a small one, if Molly had her way.

"Perhaps you should ask yourself some hard questions, young lady, about what reason you have to be here. I'm not going to ask you family questions. You know that you have been born again not as his daughter in blood but as a spiritual daughter, a bond that breaks the bonds of family. 'I come to bear the sword,' He said."

"Don't preach to me, Molly. I'm sick and tired of preaching. I will discuss it with Robert, whether he wants to or not." She stood up to leave. "And as for you, perhaps you should discuss it with your husband—I *will* ask family questions—and your children. I have nothing to hide." And she hurried away before Molly could respond, since she had plenty to hide.

After the cripple got up and walked, and his limousine pulled away, Robert had almost collapsed, as if the disease had left one body for another. Molly and Elizabeth took his arms, but he stumbled as they escorted him across the field, as tentative as a postoperative patient testing the floor. A trail of attending disciples followed, whispering to each other in an attempt to confirm the event in history, like pinching flesh. At Molly's car Elizabeth opened the door and tossed the drenched phlox from her hair. On the ground it oozed like blood from a wound. Molly drove them back and announced that the most private and comfortable room in the house was Derek's upstairs study, where there was a bed Robert could rest in. Elizabeth said that such an arrangement was unnecessary, but Molly insisted and Robert was too dazed to understand. Upstairs in the study, he knelt down before a wing chair and stared at his mangled hands as if he didn't believe them real. Then he prostrated himself, facedown. His breathing was quiet.

Elizabeth knelt beside him. "Robert, are you all right? Robert?"

Both his arms looked nailed down, but his broken hand painfully curled into a question, his thumb poised in a message she couldn't understand, other than as an emblem of his suffering and his need to be left alone. She looked at Molly, who nodded. They closed the door on his speechlessness.

Robert stayed in the room for four days, while the news, like a burning wind, rushed to the hearts of the sick. A call to love or forgive had never brought the crowds, but a whisper that a cure had been found brought people out of the air. The witnesses at the river carried the message over fences and hedges and telephone wires, to business partners, customers, patients, deacons, and even tourists, all listening to a story of a cripple made to walk. Letters came, hand-delivered. "Josey has been blind from birth," one began, or "He is a dumb boy," or "The doctor tells us there's nothing he can do." The telephone rang without end. Visitors came asking for him, but Robert kept to his room, silent, dazed, seemingly unaware that the world demanded a repeat performance.

Elizabeth tried to respond to the people, but she had no business being bothered, she thought. It was beyond comprehension. A few times she brought him trays of food, but no matter what meal, night or day, he kept silent and still, eating only bread and drinking water. One visit he was bent over his Bible; another he lay facedown on the carpet; still another he stared out the window at the trees circling up the mountains like tiers to heaven.

As she climbed the stairs the morning after her conversation with Molly, Elizabeth rehearsed the words she was certain would convince him. "As Christ bade men to live. Take nothing for the journey. Two by two." She and Robert had not carried one bit before. They had done it once, they could do it again—just don't sully your vision. She knocked and waited, giving him time to be decent. He was awake, standing alone at the window across the room from the door, his back to her. He was dressed in a white linen suit.

"Robert?"

He turned around and slipped his bad hand into the vest pocket of the suit. Elizabeth couldn't believe the transformation. He looked like a white swan, his plummage linen. He was clean-shaven and he wore a starched white shirt whose stiff collar rode high on his neck. A beak of a yellow tie—his only other color—boasted a pearl pin just above the vest.

"Where did you get that?"

"Molly bought it for me, from the money we got. She told you about the money? I didn't even have to go in to get measured—she knows the tailor."

"My God, Robert, what are you doing?"

"I don't understand."

"You wouldn't have dreamed of buying a suit like this a week ago. It is mammon, Robert, you've said so yourself, thousands of times."

"I didn't buy this suit. It was given, and given for a purpose—for our new ministry."

"I've heard about it. Tell me, what was wrong with the old?"

He looked at her in a different way. All those months, when they had exchanged hundreds of glances, she had felt their ages didn't matter; she had even wondered about love. But he put on his father face, pitying the poor daughter who didn't understand a new direction in the family's life, one that had obvious benefits to an adult sensibility.

"Nothing was wrong with the old. It was true and good and right for its time, and it has led and prepared us for this new ministry. A more dynamic ministry, Elizabeth. The baptism was the turning point. I've been reading Hebrews, Elizabeth, look. . . ." At the rolltop desk he found his worn Bible, closed for once, fingernail marks chiseled into the sides of the fading pink onionskin. He lifted it and turned back to her, his hand fumbling to mark the verse. Elizabeth could already visualize him preaching at a sawdust pulpit, shaking and screaming and banging the truth of Christ out of existence, and in its place sweating the linen suits and calls to be born again and pass the plate.

"Listen. 'For every high priest taken from among men is ordained for men in things pertaining to God. . . .' I am a man ordained by God. I have been given a gift."

"You are ruining yourself, Robert. Do you think you're going to walk out of this abomination of a house and go back to some river, or the tank of the First Baptist Church, and heal a cripple again? Are you serious? A person can do anything in life once. Do you think this event is something you can create on demand?"

"I am following the will of God, Elizabeth. Ministry changes, don't you realize? Christ turned from Galilee and headed toward Jerusalem and the Passover week, where he stood before much larger crowds. He didn't know exactly what was going to happen, but he sure didn't turn back because he was worried he couldn't call up his powers. You've stuck by me all the way so far, and it would crush me if you gave up on me."

He had seldom, if ever, said he needed her. She calmed down, savoring his words. And then she tested the waters. "In Jerusalem he found out the truth about Judas Iscariot."

"You must root out the murder in your heart, Elizabeth."

"Oh, Robert, sometimes I could murder you." A burning swelled up in her heart. Molly had sat with him, whispering in his ear. "Yes, you're right. I should root out the murder in my heart. I should ask forgiveness of God. Thank you for saying you need me. I will stay with you; don't ever worry about my loyalty. But it won't be long before you bend a knee and ask forgiveness yourself. You'll see." She shut the door.

On the stairway she ran into Derek. He had begun to bother her even before the baptism, and since then he had picked up his pace. At first she noticed he'd mysteriously appear, with feeble explanations, where she was spending her days. He visited the camp cabins in the early morning, before he went to work. She remembered Molly once saying he took little interest in the camp, only in the money from the lease. He asked her to inspect the newspaper one day, and on another treated her to lunch while Robert and Molly visited a friend of hers. Two nights earlier he had caught her in the downstairs hallway, encouraging her to step behind the dining-room door with him. She wasn't surprised. But she had never seen him upstairs before, near his bedroom. He smelled of a morning drink. "I beg your pardon, my dear. Fancy meeting you here." Beads of sweat hung on his neck.

"I guess we'll be leaving tomorrow, Derek, with a friend of yours."

He stopped, and spread his bulk across the stairs. "Don't you think, my dear, that this has gone on long enough?"

"If you were any sort of a husband, it never would have started."

"Ah, youth."

"Yes, shrug it off to my inexperience."

He reached for her hand, which she quickly hid from him. "But you see, Elizabeth, I don't think you're inexperienced."

"I don't know what you mean by that, but I'd appreciate it if you let me by."

"Well, what sort of daughter are you, chickadee? I mean do you really expect any person with half a brain to believe this charade?" He tried to kiss her. "I could be your father, too."

Elizabeth slapped him, stinging her hand. He was too stunned to understand what happened, and by then she was down the stairs.

Molly chose the old prophet over this man, understandably. But Elizabeth was true to her word: she did not abandon him. She had made a choice. The next morning she tossed a bag in the trunk of Molly's car and without a word got into the back seat while they took the front. Derek was nowhere to be seen. Molly had lied to her children, telling them they were off on a short weekend trip to her cousins in Sylva. Elizabeth didn't know what she had told Derek. But they left, setting out toward a new, more dynamic ministry.

The departing scene stuck in Elizabeth's throat. She and Robert had stood with Betsy in the kitchen when Molly first told the children. She said Betsy'd take care of them and she'd be home soon. The three children kept spooning their cereal as she talked, milk dripping like rain back to the bowls and splattering on their laps. The cocoon of sleep still spun a crusty-eyed oblivion around them, their mother's words as much a part of their lost dreams as that table and the day ahead. The girl rubbed her eyes. She lifted and turned her face with a birdlike movement, her innocence of the world still alive in her sheltered eyes. "Why?" she said.

"Will you be back for supper?" the middle child, a boy, asked. He pushed his demanding chin out into the space before him, daring someone to punch it. Then, with a child's spontaneity, the corners of his eyes and mouth turned down in sorrow. He looked exactly like Derek. "You promised to help me with my Tenderfoot."

"Why, Mom?" the girl interjected. "I asked you why."

"I will help you as soon as I get back. I told you why, dear. I need to help Mr. Treadwell start his new ministry."

"Then tonight?"

"I won't be back tonight."

"But you promised."

"You'll just have to get your brother tonight."

"But I don't wanna."

The older brother kept silent, with a face furrowed in adult seriousness. His expression said that he was the oldest. This was the time when he must act his age. He stared disdainfully at his brother and sister, narrowing his eyes and lifting his nose in a not so slight sneer at their childish pecking at Mother. He would get along fine without her. And he didn't ask about his father, because he knew, with an unspoken wisdom, the truth about his parents.

Elizabeth leaned against the back window and watched Molly's family wave goodbye as if they were her own. Betsy stood in the midst of the children, a yellowish brown matron with her hair pulled straight behind her head. Elizabeth was

sure no God Betsy knew broke up the home. Her large, graceful hands curled over the frail shoulders of the little redhead,
who cried and waved with a hand held no higher than her
chin. The boys stood on either side. The middle one, the image
of Derek, assumed a blank gaze broken only by furrowed
eyebrows, deep in thought about the occasion and the truth of
his mother's words. Something in them suspected her. It was
best seen in the oldest, as his defenses broke. The adult manli-
ness sculpted on his face crumbled into the rubble of doubt
and horror—it was the moment just before he would yell out,
"Don't go! Come back, Mother! Don't leave us!"

She wondered then, and she would always wonder, how
Christ could have asked who his brothers and sisters were,
and, my God, who his mother was.

The incredible newspaper ads and leaflets Molly wrote,
having learned the craft from Derek, called Robert a healer, a
dynamic preacher, a storyteller, someone new! Once he had
cut off part of his hand, to save himself from sin! Her hired
roustabouts pitched the mammoth green and yellow tent two
days before the first meeting and thus provided the children in
town with a playhouse they thought was heaven itself. She visited each minister in town to gain his blessing, and was given
churchwide assurances that her one-handed man's revival
would be mentioned in the midweek services. Molly's advance
work more than succeeded. Hundreds of people, many of
whom usually shied away from tent meetings, came that first
night in Sylva because it was the most publicized event the
town had seen all year. A one-handed evangelist! Assuming
the congregation would not appreciate a woman on stage,
Molly asked a local minister to lead the singing at the beginning of the service, relegating Elizabeth to the piano. Molly sat
in the back during the sermon, taking notes, but she came to
the front to direct the line when the invitational hymns began.

Elizabeth played a medley the people sang by heart, "Just
As I Am," "Jesus Paid It All," "Blessed Assurance" and so on,
filling the left hand with chords, transposing between each
song, and introducing with the closing bars of the refrains. She
never stopped playing, even if she had to repeat a hymn. Silence was the worst. It let the spirit die. The line of believers
filed by her piano toward Robert, common to their hearts a
hope that a word and a wounded touch might cure.

Jesus paid it all,
All to Him I owe;
Sin has left a crimson stain,
He wash'd it white as snow.

A couple stood by her, last in line. The woman was short, un-
pretentious, wearing schoolgirl glasses and a simple brown
dress, tied at her waistline with a black ribbon. She sighed and
then cradled her husband's waist with both hands. He towered
over her like a lightning-split tree, trunk and all the limbs
leaning to his right. He wore blue pants, a starched white shirt,
and red suspenders that tilted toward his long-legged cane.
His hand teetered on the hooked handle. Above the rubber
foot tip it was specked with red dirt.

"She sure is purty," the woman whispered, stretching her
neck around her husband's arms.

"Yep," he said. "But I never seen no woman in a team."

"This ain't no regular team. Just look."

They caught sight, close up, of Molly, with her red hair
wildly brushed back like a lion's mane. She bowed her ear to
each sin-sick person's petition before ushering him or her with
a condensed history to the evangelist. Always in control.

Robert's new jacket lay long since tossed off the stage. His
cuffs were turned up to his elbows, and his white vest was
stained with the blotches and woes of wayward sheep. Sweat
beads rolled down his pale face, the power of the spirit and the
summer heat, draining away his strength. He knelt on the edge
of the stage preparing to listen to a woman who seemed shy
and impassive when she spoke with Molly. Only a pink cameo
adorned the collar of the lady's straight-hanging navy-blue
dress. But when she reached Robert, she jumped at him, head
down and arms lifted into a narrow triangle like a lunging
diver who believed the waters ran deep. Her blind hands
found him and shook the back of his neck as she buried her
head in the cradle of his lowered arms, sobbing. Elizabeth
couldn't believe the change; the woman tried to drag him from
the stage. He slipped his arms around her back and let her cry,
bent over like a holy man praying to the east. No one in the
tent knew how he would help her. Each time was different.

He began by whispering in her ear. She nodded. For a mo-
ment it seemed that they would just talk and she would leave.
But then he lifted her off her feet and set her back down hard.
He did it again. And again, dragging her against the edge of

the stage on the way up, and then almost dropping her. She
nodded. He talked into her ear as he heaved her up again, a
feat of strength for a man his age, kneeling on the stage, to lift
and shake this woman, as if he intended to squeeze out a
swallowed chicken bone until her neck was limp. He set her
back on her feet and she lifted her arms over her head and
screamed.

"What she say?" the woman next to Elizabeth said.

"I don't know."

"Well, praise the Lord!" She squeezed her husband's side.
Elizabeth played on. Silence let the spirit die.

> *Just as I am, poor, wretched, blind;*
> *Sight, riches, healing of the mind,*
> *Yes, all I need in Thee to find,*
> *O Lamb of God, I come! I come!*

Her fingers could play that hymn in the dark. As the last couple filed past the piano leg, she turned and measured the ominous expanse of the tent. Only three naked light bulbs, hung
from the tent poles, illuminated the space within. The playing
shadows above made the canvas seams stretch down to the
sidewalls like a mammoth rib cage, and the breeze flapped
those sidewalls like the sleeping breaths of a great animal
lulled to sleep, for now, by their song. But even in sleep, lying
in wait. What fear his waking?

Caged within were those who believed in this man, and
those who didn't. During the healing, however, every face in
that dim audience, save hers, was riveted on Robert's simplest
moves. How detached she felt. She heard the doom breathing
in the air, she the single person who bothered to turn away
from the stage and watch the watchers, as if with divine vision
she stood behind a dark one-way mirror looking at the human
fray, this night in particular, the human hope. There were all
kinds of men and women and their children—farm families,
merchants, salesmen and laundresses, truck drivers, railroad
conductors, housewives, teachers. Most people sang from
memory, unaware of the words but in need of the sound.
Some mouthed prayers; others held their praying hands silently together. One or two lifted their arms out beside them,
palms up, as if toward the sun. All manner of curiosity and
hope was drawn on the dimly lit faces, all manner of human
need searching.

Then she saw the two boys Molly had hired to pass the plate. Molly had insisted they wait until the invitation, when this new, dynamic preacher was doing his number. Both looked like invalids. Their skin was especially pale and their eyes almost white, the glaze of those eyes a certain sign that pity was a necessary human response. And money. The two turned up their hats, thumping down the creases in the crowns to make them baglike, and sauntered sidewall to sidewall, smiling dumbly and bowing thanks in and out of the rows of folded wooden chairs. Their shoes splashed up sawdust as coins and folded bills flooded in.

> *Blessed assurance, Jesus is mine!*
> *Oh, what a foretaste of glory divine!*
> *Heir of salvation, purchase of God.*
> *Born of His spirit, wash'd in His blood.*

Molly brought the last couple to Robert, her arms around the woman's shoulders, the man hobbling on his cane behind them. Robert smiled and nodded at Molly, who stepped back to watch with the rest of the audience. Robert looked drained, his face pale and his eyes blank, the power of his spirit on the wane and almost dry. The woman was talking, but he motioned her briefly aside and asked the man to come forward. She held his left arm as he limped to the edge of the stage, a leaning tower of a man teetering toward his bad leg. Robert stared at the woman. She stepped aside.

"Do you love the Lord?" he asked.

The man was embarrassed. He bowed his head and shuffled on his cane a moment. "Yes," he mumbled.

"Feed His sheep."

The man stared up at him again, slightly turning his head in perplexity. He had answered the question. He had answered the question truthfully, from his heart.

"Do you love the Lord?" This time, louder.

The man did not look away. He was obviously unused to so many people; they made him nervous. His brow furrowed and he stared at Robert, a cloud of anger passing into his eyes. What purpose this preacher had he didn't know, but he knew he didn't like it. He'd come there to be healed, not interrupted and embarrassed. The man had no right to ask him that question again. He had no right. "Yes. I love the Lord. I have loved the Lord all my life and I *will* all my life."

"Feed His sheep."

The man gritted his teeth. He had not come to be embarrassed. It was time to go. He would get his wife and leave. It had been a mistake. He'd thought the preacher might help, but it was a vain wish. He gritted his teeth again. Only a vain wish.

"*Do you love the Lord?*" This time shouted.

"*Yes, I love the Lord!*"

The crowd gasped. The man lifted his cane to slug the preacher. The hook hovered next to the man's throat, frozen in the air once the miracle was realized. Robert softly touched it and slipped it out of the man's grasp. He was completely still, until Robert whispered, "Feed His Sheep."

The man turned, tears in his eyes, and stepped meekly toward his wife, who hugged him. His walk was still a limp, a struggling as unsure as a baby's, but caneless. Definitely caneless.

Robert stood up slowly and opened his arms, the hook of the cane in his left hand thrust high into the darkness above his head. He didn't even need to glance at Elizabeth, attuned as she felt she was to his every thought. She quickly softened her playing into a left-hand melody of "I Come to the Garden Alone."

"O Lord and Savior," he began. Row upon row of believers bowed their heads as she accompanied him. "Give us the grace to see and know and feel, our Father, that in the blood of Christ Jesus gouged from his hands, his feet, his sides, we can be made whole, that we can know ourselves for who we are, sons and daughters of Thee, precious Lord. Grant us the courage to live our lives in His. Let us shuck aside the anxieties of tomorrow and follow in His footsteps today, with a faith as beautiful as the lilies of the field and a courage as lasting as the cross, speaking each moment the words he has taught us to pray. . . ." The crowd joined him in the Lord's Prayer and at its amen she finished with

> *Blest be the tie that binds*
> *Our hearts in Christian love.*
> *The fellowship of kindred minds*
> *Is like to that above.*

The crowd neatly filed out of the tent, like ants. She quickly finished her closing medley, shutting the fall board and hurrying toward Robert. Human chatter filled the silence. Molly passed her on the way, hurrying herself, her great flowing red mane behind her gallop. A prophetess bouffant, Elizabeth thought. Molly's eyes slanted toward her with meager acknowledgment, while her face kept purposeful and military, as if to say preface to her mission, "You've got a job to do—now do it!" Everything prearranged, according to her plan.

Robert did look exhausted, though, as Molly had predicted. He hobbled down to the sawdust and leaned back against the stage with his arms extended for support like the tent's guy ropes, his head bowed from the strain. His face was limp. His lips were white and his cheeks and temples a pale blue. His legs kept still, knowing better than to exert one bit more.

A covey of women hovered around him like children begging their daddy for more money. They reached to touch him and, if necessary, rip him apart. "I'm sorry," Elizabeth said, pushing through, "but Mr. Treadwell is tired. We need to give him rest. Thank you for coming. Come again. I'm sorry, he needs rest." She grabbed his arm. It was clammy. Robert looked at her with lifeless eyes. "Come, Robert."

"You are always there, Elizabeth."

A woman laid her hand on his chest. "Oh, Mr. Treadwell," she began, "you know—"

"I'm sorry, he must leave now." Elizabeth squeezed her arm.

"But my goodness—"

"Elizabeth." He was shocked at her, but she didn't listen. He had given enough—there wouldn't be anything left. She almost plowed over the woman as she broke her grip and led him limping into the darkness outside the sidewall, where the headlights from an idling car suddenly flashed on them. Molly pulled it up beside them. Elizabeth helped him into the front seat and hurried to the back.

"You took too long."

On the way back from the tent meeting, they kept silent. Elizabeth assumed Molly didn't talk because there was nothing else to take charge of. Robert sat absolutely still, in need of silence. Healing the sick sickened him; the force that cured fled his body, leaving him empty, pale, and hanging in doubt. He can't deceive himself forever, Elizabeth thought, leaning back in the seat and staring out the window. The stars hung like sequins fixed in the black lining of the sky. There was no moon, but in the spaces between the shadowy clouds, every visible star proclaimed itself, a sequin here, maybe a crushed and polished coin there, dancing spangles, a breaking wave, image after image all captured in the dome of the night. Robert and she, even Molly, could drive ever so long, but they could never drive out from underneath.

But those shadowy clouds were gathering into a storm. Molly turned the car from the dirt lot circling the tent onto the blacktop and back toward Sylva. Past Elizabeth's open window moved elongated flashes of the dark earth, elm trees to pines and oaks, front porches, traffic signs and billboards, telephone poles and their lines that dipped like the flights of birds. The three of them that night were pretending they were going somewhere. Back to Sylva. Back to bed, to healing sleep, to another day, to the end of sickness unto death.

Molly seemed to think she could set the moon and the stars in order. Perhaps stop a celestial storm. From the moment they left Brevard, she had put everything in place. When they arrived in Sylva, they were welcomed into her cousin's house, a bright Victorian mansion with gingerbread trim on the porches and tiny, secretive dormers. Each one of them was given a spacious room with a wardrobe and a shelf of books to read. The linen was changed daily. Baths were finished with large, fluffy towels. And for three meals a day, Robert found an attentive audience, as if he were visiting royalty. Molly introduced Elizabeth as Robert's faithful daughter who needed to spend all her time, like a good girl, practicing on the downstairs piano since she played the hymns at the services. Elizabeth spoke little, biding her time.

After Molly had demonstrated for a few days her constellations of skills and connections in setting up the revival, the same afternoon of this first success she had asked Robert to discuss with her ways he could "work the crowd," as she put it. "I don't mean to be sacrilegious," she said. They were sitting in the backyard. A white picket fence undulated along the boundary to a wooded lot below. "But hasn't religion since primitive times been closely linked with drama? I mean, the person in the audience, when he has a religious experience, has a dramatic experience."

Robert listened. Off to the side, Elizabeth looked away from them, toward the woods, which kept her from speaking.

"If you cut whatever story you tell short," she continued,

"you could catalog some sins of hell just before the invitation. All the time—this is the way I see it—you should be wearing a glove, a white one, over your hand, Robert. Now I want to hear what you think about this, please. Don't just let me decide these matters. But since everyone knows about your hand anyway, what would you think—I mean, it would be dramatic—of finding a way to take off that glove right at the end of the sermon? A sort of climactic effect."

Robert pushed himself up from the chair, hovering for a splendidly righteous moment. He decided not to respond, but walked back to the house, the screen door banging shut behind him. Elizabeth had turned toward Molly then, waiting to catch her eye, and when she did, she smiled.

Elizabeth enjoyed that memory, listening to the humming of the tires on the blacktop deepen as they tried to make it back to the house before the storm. Then they slowed down. When Elizabeth sat up, she saw lightning strike on the horizon. It would not be long. As Molly turned off the road, the car bounced and the sound of splitting gravel brought them up the short driveway to the house, where the downstairs lights shone through the windows like torches. In the two brightest rooms, the living room and the study on the far right, a crowd gathered in wait for the social occasion—the three of them—to come home. Some were seated; others circled in standing conversation, like a Sunday coffee after a sermon. Elizabeth recognized Molly's cousin and three of the ministers she had asked to an afternoon tea.

"I know these people have been so kind to me, but I just can't," Robert said. "I'm so tired. I've got to . . ." His voice tapered off, almost in tears. It was fearful, old and tired. The human had intruded into the silence. How long could he last?

Molly turned to him and her shoulder moved enough for Elizabeth to realize she was touching him. "Make an appearance," she said. "Then I'll come in and give your apologies."

Elizabeth didn't follow them in, quite aware that no one cared about the piano player. She sat on the swing at the opposite end of the porch, hearing even from there the fuss in the parlor over this unlikely star in Sylva's firmament. That he as an evangelist was their entertainment—surely that would make him see. She turned her mind from that scene, trying to let the creaking rhythm of the swing and the distant sounds of thunder cleanse it from futile efforts to understand. But she found herself humming, "The beautiful, the beautiful river." That night was the first time he had preached since the French

Broad. He surprised her: he had done the job, had performed another miracle of sorts, this time in front of more people than all the previous gatherings combined. But it wouldn't last. It was all prissied up for mass appeal. Why, then, was she still following him? Why was she still on this pilgrimage that was no longer a pilgrimage? Mortification? Still? When he collapsed, did she want to be there? She had told herself she'd made a choice. But why?

The screen door eased open and Molly held it a moment, looking first to the opposite end of the porch and then to Elizabeth. She quietly closed it and came toward her like a thief in the night. "May I join you? I just cannot abide these people right now."

Elizabeth slid away from her to one end of the swing. Like passengers traveling together through the strange night, they kept an elbow room of silence between them and stared only to their immediate right and ahead, on a diagonal, at the dark ground and trees and road that common wayfarers see and share without a word. Above them, more visible from what was Elizabeth's window seat, the clouds closed out the stars. What they shared, foot-weary pilgrims, was Robert—and nothing else. He was the common ground, Elizabeth thought, on which they moved, each in singular silence, neither interested in a shared word or experience, both wishing the man and time and the event were hers and hers alone. The swing creaked when Molly shifted.

"I've come to ask you to go home."

"I thought as much."

"You have known Robert for a long time."

Elizabeth stared at the far end of the porch, and beyond, into the darkness, a quiver in her stomach.

"There's no need to keep up the daughter front with me," Molly said. "I've never believed that."

She knew Molly would take advantage of the lie. Any way to manipulate the situation to her own gain. She could always reveal the truth and make Elizabeth's company illegitimate: the very idea, the self-righteous would say, of a young woman, and not married to him, traveling the country with an evangelist—why, she is simply a deceiving Jezebel!

She lied. "I have known Robert the length of time you have known your husband, Molly. You are hiding behind your married state as much as I am—behind mine." She would admit nothing to Molly.

"You don't know anything about husbands and wives. Rob-

ert has relied on you long enough, I think. He seldom asks
your advice—you're too young. You don't arrange anything,
and you're not even the greatest piano player, you have to
admit. You are not a wife to him—he's made that obvious—
but you have been necessary. Sometimes I think you're his
home and family and all he's left behind. You're not his
daughter—I know you're not—but you have a lot to do with
his family, which he has really never given up, after all these
years. He wants you here just to remind him."

"He has said he loves me." She was lying again.

The muted sound of thunder came closer, breaking over the
mountains in the east. A flash of light followed, outlining the
roll of peaks across the night sky, and then the boom reached
them. The air thickened, and a cool wet breeze suddenly swept
over the porch. They didn't move. The conversation was not
finished.

"I have heard him. This afternoon when I was calming him
down—you know how nervous he was—he paced across the
room and swiveled around to say he loved you. He was out of
his mind, literally. 'I love Elizabeth,' he said, 'you know that?
She has gone the whole way with me.' It surprised me at first,
but then I understood. You're not a real love of his. He calls
you his daughter because he wants to believe that someone in
his family might say what he's doing is the right thing. I don't
know why he has this obsession, but he does, and it is time to
end it. If anyone in his family actually believed in what he was
doing . . . well, wouldn't a wife or son be here? No, Elizabeth,
you're not a real love of his."

Robert had said to her, Elizabeth thought, that very night,
that she was always there. At the river he had told her she had
gone the whole way with him. But he had never said he loved
her. She tasted the wetness in the air.

"He was born a monk, Elizabeth—that's the nearest way I
can express it. He said he loved you not only because of his
family obsession but because the two of you shared an
old-fashioned pilgrimage the same way monks did, screwed-
up, fat and balding men indulging in their own perverted
friendships. So you've really never been more than another
man to him—if you understand my reasoning. But now is a
different time. He needs to shed these dreams, and I think he
will, after tonight. Tonight he discovered what fruit his ministry might bear."

The first cool raindrops fell in a whisper. The water tapped on her arm until it gathered into rivulets tracing the summer's ease. But the wind blew up and brought the rain harder, in loud, piercing lances flung from the night. On the inside end of the swing Molly was sheltered when the storm came easy, but then the wind rushed in horizontal, wet gusts and she was suddenly as wet as Elizabeth, their clothes ·in a moment soaked.

Elizabeth got up and the swing creaked and swung back and forth unevenly, the other end still anchored. She hurried to the door, her eyes already blinking from the water, and turned around to keep it open for Molly. But Molly wasn't following. She had not moved from the crooked swing, staring at Elizabeth with still-powerful eyes, angry that the storm had interrupted her. They both knew they wouldn't continue inside. Her great mane of red hair had fallen into a tangled mess clinging to her skull. There were certain things she could do nothing about.

13

Sylva, Webster, Alarka, Bryson City, Almond, Needmore Flats, and Franklin. Tents billowed with the acclamation of Robert's stories, singing uplifted, people came with the summons, and the spirit moved, sometimes. They were a month on the road. Molly wrote home every few days, but she stayed on, too caught up in the power of the spirit and in Robert to consider returning. The well of the cripple's money appeared bottomless, though since Molly alone dipped the silver ladle, Elizabeth never knew how much they had. There was also some cash from the hat-passing, but not enough to live the way Molly had them live. Each night, after they left the tents or churches for a boardinghouse, they stayed up toward dawn drinking coffee and talking. Molly learned that for Robert to survive, he didn't need social gatherings but the shelter of a private place where he might sprawl. At the end of the first night in Franklin, he slumped in a chair opposite the sitting room's sofa, his shoes tossed off and his hands folded on his stomach. His head leaned over the crest of the backrest, like a doomed man gasping for air.

Elizabeth was worried. That very morning he had not come down from his room by lunchtime. He routinely got up early to meditate and read his Bible and then eat a large country breakfast. But no one had heard his footsteps to the bathroom, nor the blinds drawn open to what he called "the burnt sacrifice of morning." Elizabeth was nominated, of course. As she wiped her hands of flour and untied her apron, she glanced at Molly, daring her to try to stop her. Near the top of the stairs, Elizabeth thought she heard faint breathing, which reminded her of the sound that sometimes circled through the tents when, toward the end of the services, her medley was no more than a whisper and the flaps of the tent moved, breathing like a great leviathan. Then she realized he was weeping.

He didn't answer her knock. He never did, as if he imagined privacy was unnecessary among prophets and apostles. She turned the doorknob and peered through the crack, but he wasn't in bed. She heard him whispering, though, from the opposite corner. "Are we . . ." His words were barely audible. "Are we . . . servants . . . of sin?" For a moment she stopped, but did not admit to herself what she was thinking. She pushed open the door and saw him draped over a chair in front of a wide-open window, the late-morning sunlight streaming over his body, his head sprocketed onto the arc of the backrest, and his weary legs staked by his feet. His shirt was unbuttoned. He kneaded his naked stomach, working downward.

When he saw her, he let go of his sides and jerked toward her. "You!" he said, pointing with his half-stub of a hand. "What are you doing here?"

"I knocked, Robert. You didn't answer. We were wondering—"

"Get out!" He motioned her back through the door.

"Are you all right?"

"Get out of here, Elizabeth. Don't you understand?"

She was gone. She told everyone he was fine, but she stayed outside all afternoon.

The mistress of the boardinghouse had hired two carpenters to begin a gazebo at the edge of the backyard, by the border of trees that looked northwest to Nantahala and the ridge. They started sawing around noon. Elizabeth didn't mind their work; she was happy to sit outside in the sun, away from Molly. She watched from a lounge chair on the grass, for a while worrying that Robert wouldn't forgive her for intruding. The two-tone hissing of the saws hid the occasional songs of the birds and made dissonant, in a way, the sight of the forest stretching toward the mountain like an arpeggio. But soon she forgot her worries, as the heat of the sun relaxed her and the hissing faded into the background of her silent unconsciousness. It did not fade, however, for Robert.

Elizabeth had almost dozed off in the warmth when she heard the back door bang. Robert hurried by with his hands cupping his ears. Molly was right behind him. He surprised one carpenter from behind, jerking away the handle of his saw before the man realized what had happened. Like a hammer thrower, Robert wound up and heaved the tool far into the trees. "Is there no way for a man to get some peace and quiet in this place?" he shouted. "I can't listen to that impurity!" Molly stepped between them before the carpenter purified Robert with a punch in the mouth. Robert bent over and held his head as if the sound had burst his eardrums and cut into his brain. The simple hissing of a saw somehow was a sin against his existence. "Is there no way?" he said again, turning from them and storming back into the house.

Elizabeth thanked God the evening came and he could preach, even though he would almost kill himself yelling and gesticulating, trying to make his story come alive for the now steadily declining number of people. When his time came, he began with silence, a space long and still enough for everyone to sit up and focus. He stood erect, lifting his wounded right arm and sweeping it slowly across his body like a clock hand measuring the expanse of the tent.

"You are from Franklin, North Carolina. After the war a great drought comes. The lakes, even Fontana, begin to dry up, and the rivers in their banks look as red as blood. Millions of frogs are left to die. Cornstalks wither and fall, bush beans drop, lice suck the skin of man and beasts, flies multiply, and cattle die.

"Your brother, who grew up in Franklin, sends a letter from where he lives—Colombia, South America. He was always known as not only an intelligent boy but a wise one. You felt he was a favored child, and in your own way you got him out of Franklin so you wouldn't have so much competition. But in his letter there are no hard feelings. He sends for you and the large family, immediate and distant, telling you the rains have moved south, almost as if the world had turned upside down. There are barns filled with plenty, he writes; great, fertile forests; work, fields, and shelter; and the sound of an abundance of rain. He has become a government adviser and is so respected that he can guarantee your safe passage once you reach the continent. Why not? Why stay where the famine kills?

"You go. It is an awful trip, like the Cherokees' across to

Oklahoma. And life, once there, is hard: mosquitoes the size of sparrows; heat that dries up your sweat; malaria; serpents. But you are from good stock, and there is no land in the world, as long as God has not cursed it, that you and your family cannot make prosper. You increase. God helps those who help themselves.

"But in ten years your brother dies. Like all men, great and small, he is then forgotten. And the people of Colombia begin to criticize. 'These white people come down to till our land and make a profit, but they don't even know what to do with coffee or sugarcane or cocoa. They refuse to marry our daughters—they think we are too low for them, unclean even. You know what?' they say. 'They're lazy. They're no-good lazy bums who have to sit in the shade so much, nothing is ever accomplished. They're lily-livered. They're always washing their hands and taking baths. They're nothing but pale gringos, weak, proud, and, my God, uglier than sin!' "

The silence was suddenly gone; the folding chairs creaked from the audience's discomfort with that part of the story. No one cared to be called ugly or lazy.

"You and your friends are then told that more of your labor will have to help the state. You are ordered to serve on a public building project in Bogotá, the capital. You are building statues of a famous Colombian dictator when the foreman of the crew hits a distant cousin of yours. In a rage you attack him, and before you know it you've thrust your pocketknife into the man's throat and killed him. Yes, you've killed him. You know you could kill a man. You know you could be angry enough. I don't care who you are—you could be full of enough fire to push that point into the taut skin."

Elizabeth watched Robert demonstrate. He stood on the edge of the platform for a moment, and then in slow motion lifted his left hand toward the audience. He swung his battered right arm around his imaginary victim and quickly plunged the knife into the man's neck and stopped, slowly turning it for effect. He was sweating with his performance, his coat tossed off, as usual, long before. Elizabeth wondered at the relish he showed in acting out the murder. The anger of this man, this Moses Robert was talking about, was an anger Robert easily felt, too easily felt.

"A friend calls you a murderer," he continued, "and you run deep into the rain forest and the mountains. You hide for months, barely living, until you stumble into a mountain village where no one knows you. A young girl nurses you back to health, and soon—you have no other option, really—you marry her and become a part of the small, poverty-stricken community, learning to farm the difficult, steep land. But it becomes an unhappy life. You remember the mountain ranges of western North Carolina, the soft blue lines that slant along the clouds. Life forced its hands and days on your dreams, exiling you to this wild, rocky mountainside.

"But one day, wandering along a mountain path, the air thickens and crackles and you turn to see a wildfire leap through the grasses. You don't move. You stare at a single flame, there and not there, dancing through the air like nothing else but fire. But this fire is not like other fire. It doesn't consume itself. You kneel, untie your shoes, and prepare to die.

"It is only at death that you seem to know. In-moving flames crackle with a voice, that God is, that God is. *I Am that I Am.* How suddenly you see! God is not a God of the dead, but of the living. And the voice tells you to take up the staff and lead.

"And so you return to Bogotá and announce your vision to your family. 'We are to go, make a straight way home, where God will bless us with the honey of the bee, goat's milk, and crops bursting with fruit. But only if we go.' Hear yourself say to the rulers, 'Let go, let my people go.' But the dictator says no, and as a famine moves into his land, he becomes all the more resistant. 'Let go,' we say. God makes the famine worse, until the dictator finally tells them that because they are so worthless he will let them go.

"It is all a sham, of course. Those who love the material world and gain their self-respect in it must hate those willing to give it up. A ruler of this world cannot be at peace with himself when he is ruled by death. If a man is not ruled by death, then he chooses not power but powerlessness."

These were the most difficult moments for Elizabeth, when he would say something that would still move her, no matter how resentful she was about Molly. He paced back and forth across the platform, the sawdust a thin layer of gold dust on his fancy shoes, and he could not see, did not realize, that the woman who managed this whole charade loved the material world he still preached against, and that the evangelist himself, decked out in his new clothes, was now the target of his own sermonizing. Elizabeth believed he was right: those who loved the material world hated those willing to give it up. But Molly thought of him as material, which she might prune and polish as she wished, until it was time to spit him out like a rotten bite of an apple.

"We set out what clothes, mementos, and supplies we plan to take for the journey." Robert stood still in the center again, measuring the crowd with his mangled hand. "The caravan winds along the highway out of the city, west and north toward the distant homeland, the sound of mountain folk songs at different points along the line like a great heavenly chord.

"Silence soon follows, descending like a cloud over the quickly weary walkers. Spirits keep up, though, since you have tried to squelch any deceptions about how larkish the trip will be. The first troublesome report arrives after three days. The rear guard sees a rising haze of dust.

"'Keep going,' you say. 'God is with us.' A thought comes into your mind, but some fearful part of you interrupts and makes you forget it. There is no reason for alarm. You are a peace-loving group. No harm to anyone. A powerless exodus, that's all. But an hour later, when you see the winded young man running toward you, this time you know.

"'The dust comes from a great crowd of soldiers,' he says, too loudly, so others hear. 'They follow in jeeps and trucks.'

"'Keep going,' you say. 'God is with us.' You reason to yourself that it's an escort, a good deed, providing protection for the wanderers until they cross the canal. You tell yourself the leaders are worried: it would not look good if bandits ambushed us, or the neighboring countries refused us. They are concerned about international opinion. They need money. . . . But you know.

"A smell is borne in the air, brisk and salty. Over a rise you come upon a great expanse of water, the tangled field angling down to the shore. The water is calm, sun-spangled. Oh for a hand that would part the waters! The others hurry up beside you and watch the trailing enemy. The convoy splits and drives off each side of the road, truck by truck, across the bumpy fields until the vehicles turn, stop, and empty a close rank of gun-toting soldiers. They begin to walk toward you.

"'Gather your children,' you say. 'Go to the shore.' You watch as your followers, without thinking, hurry down to the water, where you hear a mounting chorus rise up and implore Jehovah. You stand and wait. The barrels of the guns sight you.

"Speak within yourself. Do you still believe in your vision? A voice answers, 'God is not the God of the dead, but of the living.' So you walk down to be with your friends and look out over the suddenly rippling water. Some begin shouting that the water is parting. But you know that doesn't matter. Even if you die, do not ask pardon of this world. God is with us. No one give in, for He is within and among us. Both now and forever. Alive or dead."

After they finally escaped the tent for the closeted sitting room, Elizabeth watched him droop his failing body over a chair. His heart would never survive, she feared. His nerves were only beginning to sight land, like a kite bobbing before a headfirst fall. He talked and talked, though he didn't move, sobering down from the pace and shouting pitch of the sermon. "Each someone who limps down that sawdust aisle is a child of God," he said. "I tell myself that no matter how deformed, each comes to speak with me in whatever way he can. Though our inheritance varies in measure, it exists for all of us as the common gift of living in the here and now. We must greet each other, then, face-to-face, as children of God, not gossips, adulterers, tax gatherers, or publicans, though of course all of us are."

Molly had changed into her royal-blue housecoat. She reached for his empty cup on the side table between them. "No thanks," he said, touching the top of her hand. "I need to go easy. It eats at my stomach late at night." She smiled at his touch and curled into the corner of the sofa, her legs folded under her like a lamb's, but such apparent meekness was a lioness's trick. The lamplight half-illuminated her face, its diagonal brushstroke painted to highlight her full-falling, springy red hair and to darken one eye and a cheek. She was as beautiful as a queen. Elizabeth had to admit it. Molly and Robert turned daily toward a closer relationship, but Elizabeth still wasn't convinced. Molly would never be satisfied.

"Have you ever wondered at the differences among people, though?" he continued. "We believe in the common inheritance, as I said, but how wondrously varied the ways we stumble and are borne up to this common inheritance. You think you know all there is to know about a person. Then one simple word so surprises you that you realize how totally misconceived your impression was."

"I know that feeling," Elizabeth said, without looking at Molly.

"All people, no matter how evil, can be angels of God, without even knowing their own God-sent words. At any moment that angel might visit me, and his trumpeted word be 'Enough!' I might not have the spirit. I have to be prepared for that angel."

"This is true," Elizabeth answered again. She did not remind him of her warning, at the very beginning of this jaunt, up in Derek's study, that he would not always be able to call up his powers.

"Does a carpenter, for example, like those two I maligned this afternoon, does he ever feel that way? Does he ever just not know what to do? Every motion that for years lived as instinct is in a moment forgotten. He just doesn't have it, and he wasn't prepared."

"I know exactly what you mean," Elizabeth said in an excited voice. "I'll be in the middle of a piece I memorized years ago, something as simple as "Just as I Am," which I've played thousands of times since, and suddenly I realize my fingers are moving on their own. My mind can't say which notes are right. I look down at my hands and feel them dance the right steps, but all I can do is watch. Then I get scared. I'm afraid I'll forget the rest, and that's when I'm sure to mess up."

He smiled. "I've never heard you mess up."

With her fingers Molly combed the hair away from her face and let it hang over the sofaback. Her long white neck was exposed. Before she spoke, Elizabeth knew she would change the subject. She couldn't allow Robert and her such intimacy. "How has all this success of yours come to pass, Robert?"

"Has it been?" Elizabeth asked. Molly was fishing for praise.

"What do you call the lines of people, Lizzie, and the sick healed?"

Robert answered: "Oh, it is their belief, not my success. Christ was amazed by how few miracles their belief worked in Nazareth. Notice that it wasn't his power, but their belief. Where he wasn't known, the people accomplished the cures. They healed themselves by faith. I try to make myself the instrument of their awakening, that's all. I wait taut as a string, but inwardly silent and still, I pray. When the words come, I know they are not mine, but the speech plucks them out."

He yawned. He was finally slowing down, letting himself

sink further into the chair and accept the limits nature imposed on his strength. "To bed, I think," he said. "Though I never can be sure. It's good of you both to stay up with me."

Molly stretched, her lifted arms rounding her breasts full into her housecoat. She walked up with him. She always did, just in case. He looked at Elizabeth after he unfolded and stood up, and right in front of Molly said, "Thank you for everything. You've stuck with me through it all. Whatever comes of this, beyond this string of nows we're living, I will always love you for what you've meant to me."

She did not forget. All week she thought about those words.

At the next stop, Andrews, about the same time of night, with a full moon, and stars visible beyond the corona of moonlight, a summer's breeze came down from the mountains like springwater and cooled the air. Elizabeth said goodnight to Robert and wandered out behind their boardinghouse to a long, narrow yard. At the far edge of the expanse, under the shelter of a giant, reaching oak, a circle of fireflies burned. She stopped and watched, waiting for one to grow bright again, but distracted by another, and then again one more, until she simply withdrew her focus from any single firefly and marveled at the whole dance. Beyond the oak, the outline of the mountains rolled across the brilliant heavens.

She took her shoes off and, as she walked toward the lightning bugs, felt the cool grass slip into the pleats of her toes. The voice of a dove cooed three times, and then a fourth, at a lower pitch. At its base the roots of the oak spread across the earth and thrust into it, each day deeper, anchoring itself so its face of branches turned ever upward toward the same broadshouldered sky she sensed herself desiring. The memory of the baptism came over her, found her in a moment emerged and brought up wet and shining toward the sky beyond and the only moment of meaning she had known. All because of him, both then and there, in the event by the river, and here and now, in the remembrance.

Another memory flooded over her, an older one she couldn't detail. She was physically moved by it, as if it were some unseen person with his hands pushing her hips. She quickened her pace, into the fireflies. Around the tree she glided on the grass, asking herself where this other memory was born, the discovery possible, it seemed, only in the movement her body made. But it wouldn't say. The hands on her hips told her to look, though, see the world! Nothing was constant—not this tree or the grass or the lightning bugs; not her dance, the mountains, moon or stars, even prayers for grace. Only, always aspiration. But for what she couldn't imagine.

Her feet began to run. She measured the oak from root to crown and felt the grass cushion the soles of her feet and the mountain breeze blow down from the heavens themselves. She leaped. Those hands set her free to leap toward the sky, and she leaped the full moon and the stars, thrusting her feet up and out into the air and tossing her head back to see. And when she touched, she ran and leaped again and then again, caught in the burning circle of fireflies, until she suddenly remembered the movement in her muscles and turned in the air to land on one steady foot, her arms extended like the wings of an eagle and her leg borne straight into the air behind. Then she happened to look back toward the boardinghouse.

He was watching. From behind the window of his room, where he waited, a single, second-story light silhouetted his figure. He didn't say a word, though he must have realized when she abruptly stopped that she saw him there. For a moment she felt violated. Like a voyeur he peered into her secret life with silent, lustful eyes, until she stood up straight and stared back at him. Her chest wanted to bend over to breathe, but she kept erect, panting from the exertion: She would meet any challenge he gave. The light kept his features indistinct, like a shadow projected onto a screen. She didn't know if he was laughing or crying, or beckoning her to him. The motive of a smile, the glance of an eye—any physical sign—was lost in the dark. And he was still enough to be dead.

She walked away from the fireflies and out from the oak to position herself in the middle of the yard, which, though the night was cool, burned like a bed of coals. She began to consume herself with her own flame, from her heart through her legs to the ground, where that fire of hers threatened to make the earth a burning censer. Alone in a silent expanse, more easily seen, she waited for some word or motion from him. His move. But he didn't stir, staying a shadow in the window, bathed by moonlight and the stretch of stars. She thought better than to call to him. It would ruin the suspense.

She would go to him. She would go to him and kiss him. She would kiss him with the kisses of her mouth. She had left Atlanta and traipsed into the mountains because it was he whom her soul loved. None of her past hesitations were worthy of restraint, for his silent, solitary figure beckoned her see, taste, and—know. She was certain. The unseen hands touched her hips again. "Go. Go to him and kiss him with the kisses of your mouth. He is what you've been searching for." She looked up and began to walk toward the door, slowly, looking to see if he recognized what she was doing. Her fingers fiddled with the button of her blouse.

She tiptoed into the house and up the stairs. The muted light under his door beckoned her. She was certain. He would lie the night betwixt her breasts. Nothing could stop them now from their love, not the judgment of pharisees, the power of Satan, nor the height and depth of age. The steps creaked, but she didn't care—she would trumpet over Jericho's army to get to his door.

It was closed. She heard his breathing inside. He knew she was coming, and when she fell into his arms, he would say, "Thou art fair, my love, the rose of Sharon and the lily of the valley." She heard his whispered words, "Thou art fair, my love," and she understood and gave herself up. She didn't knock. There was no need. He knew she was coming. She eased the door from the jamb—it was unlocked as she imagined—and peered in.

Robert still pressed himself against the window, his chest heaving. The breathing Elizabeth heard from outside his door was not the breathing of a man bewitched by her approach, but she didn't understand yet. He didn't see her for a moment, which gave her time to push the door farther along and without thinking start on another button of her blouse. When he did see her, his eyes swelled in shock. But she was certain he loved her, she told herself; she had never been more certain in her life.

Her hand released the door, and then she followed his gaze back to another corner of the room. The doorknob clicked against the wall. Elizabeth was then a witness. She should have known, really. She had simply discovered seventy times seven reasons not to believe. The clothes piled on the floor, the regal hair falling over bare shoulders and firm hips, in his bed Molly turned toward her, in all that disciple's naked majesty.

The next evening a man and woman walked down the aisle on either side of a boy. There was an air of the inevitable about them. The child looked to be twelve, his body no more than a rib cage perched on chicken-bone legs knocking at the knees. He shuffled his feet, resisting their path through the sawdust. His freckled face had once puffed up like that of a sandy red-haired cherub, but it was losing its innocence. And something was wrong with him. His light-green dumb eyes stared down the aisle to Robert uncertainly, as if at any moment he might make a break for it, and when the three of them moved directly under a hanging light bulb, those eyes turned white and lost focus on the world, as if he foresaw an apocalypse of fire and water.

The couple was ancient and proud, come down from the mountains and out of another century. The woman wore a simple dress, unadorned, to be purified of the world's frivolities. She had folded her gray hair into a bun, crowning a head that seemed carved in stone, each etched wrinkle a commandment testified to by a life as honest as her posture. And as she escorted the boy, she measured with challenging eyes the people watching them. At any moment, because of her stature in life, she could pronounce all of them failures and simply turn her back. He was a farmer, the overalls he slopped manure in clean as virtue and stiff as a board. He wore his collar high on his neck, stiff, too, with a little black bow tie for the occasion. What this country needs, his walk proclaimed, is our respect for the laws of the land and more crop rotation, as the Good Book says. They did not hold the boy's hand, but watching them gave Elizabeth the distinct impression they fenced in the devil in him.

Forward they went to the evangelist. Robert waited on the platform, a poor imitation of himself, his coat not only dry and pressed but still on his back, and his face so old and pale that his usual flush of the spirit seemed a questionable memory of another man, another time and place. Elizabeth hadn't seen him all day. She'd stayed in her room, in a chair by the open window, where she gazed over the trees and the mountains and empty sky, its traitorous blue a fatal wound to all she held sacred. In the evening before the tent meeting, she had packed.

His sermon was awful. The story didn't make sense—it was flat, it jumped around and bored everyone. The few people who attended the service were only following his dying reputation. They wanted not thought or revelation but a chance to say they were part of another person's fame. Soon they would tear that fame down, gleefully, and find some other miracle worker, some other freak to focus their empty beings on. A small group had come down the sawdust aisle after his talk, with much less enthusiasm than was usual. No one played the piano; Elizabeth had sneaked into the back of the tent to witness one more time the humiliation she had given up so much for. Everyone was lost in the silence. Not one single hymn. It made the whole affair naked, which pleased her.

Molly had seen her come in. She continued to meet the professed at the end of the aisle, but she glanced at Elizabeth whenever she could. Her redhead's skin, when drained of life as it was then, turned translucent green like a grape weeks from ripening, and her hair lost its auburn richness for a bleached rust color. She extended her hand to each person and slightly turned her head, as was her custom, expecting each sinner to describe in detail the sins to be laid on the altar, the rededication needed for a life of backsliding and the healing hoped for in the salve of the preacher's hands. Then she would introduce them to the evangelist.

But the old couple led the boy right by her. The man was especially indignant, slanting his face toward the tent top like a downtown lawyer on the way to his club. The old woman actually wagged her finger at Molly. They stopped below Robert, the woman nudging the boy forward with a hand behind his shoulder. He stared up at Robert. His shoulders shook for a moment, and a strange sound came from his mouth, and then again, his arms dangling like rubber hoses.

A look of recognition passed into Robert's face, and his eyes swelled in horror. Like the boy, it seemed he could see straight into some sightless void and predict more than the natural eye could ever see. A line of sweat beads suddenly crossed his forehead, and his shoulders hunched up. He looked old and sick. The boy shook again, and in an instant fell down in the dust between Robert and the old couple, the spasm seizing his whole body. Convulsions held down his stiffening chest while his bony legs kicked madly. His arms jerked as though they'd been amputated, and his neck arched back and strained fiery red to keep his rib cage and head part of the same possessed person. His eyes snapped out of their sockets like marbles full of water, and a white foam edged from his mouth while his teeth were grinding, a helpless, horror-struck child. The crowd pushed toward the front rows and stopped, scared to touch him. Molly came through two men. "His tongue," she said, and then shouted, "His tongue!"

The old man's hand shot up and pointed at her. "Keep away from him!"

By then the crowd circled around the couple and watched. "Oh, my God," someone said. The foam swelled out of the corners of the boy's mouth like the suds of rabies. His faced burned like fire, but he was unconscious, the look of his eyes so fluid that Elizabeth thought he was a drowned boy found washed up on the beach. Robert came down from the platform, his steps tentative and old. The crowd parted to let him through, but he stopped beside Molly and dared go no farther. He stared down at the seizure with scared eyes and a face drained of life.

The old man held his arms out through the length of the spasm, like a policeman keeping the curious from the dead. The woman knelt by the boy, her neck still miraculously straight and self-possessed as she watched him jerk less often, with less violence, and ease the arch of his back. Molly knelt in front of the crowd, barely able to restrain herself from going to the child. In a few moments he was still. The old woman looked up into the crowd and said, "Water." Several people broke away. She eased her hand around the child's neck and helped him sit up.

"How long has he had this?" Robert said.

"Since birth," the old man replied, relaxing his arms and looking down at the boy. "He is the son of our harlot daughter. When she started growing up, I could hardly believe she was a child of my flesh. She was a rebellious soul. She turned from the Lord first in disobedience to her parents. I did not spare the rod. 'He that spareth the rod hateth his son.' But then her disobedience begat dancing; and as sin begets more sin, so dancing begat drinking, until degradation after degradation she became a whore of Babylon. The child of my own flesh! The boy was born on a moonless night, in the barn, alive not long enough before the harlot was gone, but the evil of his birth still seizes him, the curse a mark on any good in life he might live."

"It can't be the child's fault, you old fool," Molly said, standing up. "The child is innocent."

"Molly," Robert said.

She bent down again, opposite the glaring woman, and stared at the boy. Molly seemed completely at a loss, her hands kneading each other in an effort not to touch his forehead, hold him, and carry him away. Molly's sudden compassion shocked Elizabeth, after she had so righteously left her children in Brevard and proclaimed her mission with Robert. "Are you all right?" Molly asked the boy. He looked toward Molly without focus. His face was yellow. Someone handed the old woman a cup of water.

"Slowly now," the woman said, steadying his arm. Water streamed from the corners of his mouth. "Surely the Lord must pity this child," she continued, looking up at Robert. "We heard that God has worked through you. The devil possesses him, but we have faith."

Elizabeth could not breathe. At the edge of the crowd, unseen, she imagined herself come full circle, her mission, from beginning to end and back again. The boy could just as easily have been her child. Her story had begun with the embodiment of her sin, with Will, Robert's son, and then she'd set out seeking deliverance on roads up the mountains, wandering with the hope that taking nothing with her would give her all, hoping that by mortifying her flesh and spirit she would gain the respect of God and herself. But it all got mucked up: the roads had led to Molly, and the woman had built tabernacles in which her naked idolatry brought Robert down. And brought Elizabeth back to her sin. There to the child. She wandered from desire to desire, clothing them only in the here and now. She dared not move beyond.

Robert knelt before the boy. Molly shifted back a little as he set his hands on the child's weakened shoulders. Robert shuddered from the touch. Who could imagine what this prophet saw, face-to-face with the boy? Another child, his own son, came into his life, as if he believed that only in their innocence could he truly search. But his searches—what did they find? He cupped his hands over the boy's head. "O our Father," he began, "have mercy upon us. Help our un . . ." Robert turned dumb and still a moment, and then keeled over.

"Oh my God!" It was Molly's voice.

Robert hit the ground with his legs still folded in prayer, his hands buried under the sawdust. Elizabeth shot through the crowd and fell beside him. "Robert!" People were shouting. Hands pulled at her shoulders. He felt cold.

"Get a doctor!" someone shouted.

He lay still and cold. Tears blinded her, but she looked up at the child, who stared back, his eyes clear and revived.

VI

Luke:
Under the Aspect of
Eternity

14

*A*t the beginning Susan kept the pain from us. She had served me dinner countless times since I came home from what the politicians called the "Korean conflict," understanding better than anyone that I simply wanted to fit back in and not talk about it. Though she waited on me from table to kitchen and back with almost every dish, she never let me suspect she was suffering much more than I was. She came closest to telling Mother, until Elizabeth's letter arrived. She never even considered telling Will, who was at work most of the day and with his cows through the early evening, and who fell asleep quickly and didn't budge the rest of the night, when the pain was its worst.

It was a discomfort in her side. At first she rationalized. Her maternal instinct, she explained to herself, got her to check on her baby three and four times a night. But the discomfort was still there when she eased back into bed. The pain wasn't sharp; the ache distracted her more by its insistence than by its hurt. Soon she couldn't fall asleep. And she imagined the gnawing had a voice: "I am here," it said. "It is three o'clock in the morning and I am not going to leave." She seldom felt it during the day, however. Sometimes in a chair she found herself leaning over the chair's left arm, stretching her right side so as to soothe the discomfort she hadn't noticed until she sat down. But once again at night it announced its return, without fail, and she couldn't find any position that gave relief. She

215

tried lying on her stomach, on her side, and flat on her back. She felt a little better if, like a pregnant woman, she propped herself up with two extra pillows after Will was asleep.

When she admitted something was wrong—only to herself, still not to us—she prayed that the pain would leave her. "O my Lord God," she whispered into the darkness, "hear me. Grant that it be Thy will to heal Thy servant." She knew the body's antibiotic system accomplished some great miracles on its own, and if it failed, perhaps another kind of healing. But then another change—for the worse. She watched herself grow more tired during the days, when the voice became brazen. "I am here in the sunlight now," it said, "and I am not going to leave." She had been able to catnap when Stearns did, but now the voice wouldn't let her. Her prayers seemed answered by more affliction, but she told herself that suffering was a healing process, that to become whole again she needed to be broken apart.

One day Will asked her why she was so tired—she was finding it difficult to walk—but her ready-made excuse was that she was trying to keep up with a two-and-a-half-year-old, if he hadn't noticed.

"Maybe you need Ruby to come another day," he suggested, and then he forgot about it.

Susan kept explaining to herself. Such a brave silence demonstrated her courage to endure pain and wait for healing, she reasoned. This self-serving idea circled around her mind like an animal in a sheltered pen. When she looked up from where she huddled, though, to the field outside the wooden rails, she saw her fear in the shape of two great, shining horns, wider than the brutal reach of Will's Brahman, waiting to burst open that pen and gouge her with a truth she wasn't facing, something about cowardice and not courage. But her rationalization didn't give in. She decided that the lurking fear outside the pen was a fear for her son as much as for herself, as if his body and soul were the ones being torn. And her family life, too, was protected by this insistence that she was doing the right thing not to tell anyone. Their lives together were not as she had dreamed, but since Elizabeth had left town, they were better, she told herself. There was hope for improvement. What they didn't need was a health crisis. It was such bad timing, this diabolic pain!

Later, in the hospital, she told me how Will found out. She had taken to sitting in a rocking chair in the living room after he fell asleep. It was the nearest approximation of rest she ever got. She propped her two pillows on the right side and began the night knitting a sweater for Stearns. She tried to concentrate on the rhythm of the needles until she was so hypnotized she couldn't hold her eyes open. She made it through two nights undetected, but on the third she woke up to Will sitting on the footrest in front of her. The pain in her side suddenly throbbed.

His hair was pressed back over his skull like a wet cowlick. Pink lines, in the shape of a bird's rib cage, touched his cheek where his hand had slept. His crusted eyes straddled the boundary between waking and sleeping, awake enough to realize she wasn't sleeping by his side where she belonged, and asleep enough to speak to her from his unbridled dreams, which like any wise husband he usually kept to himself. "What is it, Susan?" he said. "Must you live your life dragged down into the mud? And ruin mine?"

She, too, was confused from sleep, though hers had not been as deep as his. His words sounded slurred, but in a moment she recognized a too familiar preacher's tone of voice. "Will?"

"Why is it—what is it now, a year, two years?—why must you lower yourself to such suspicions? We've talked and talked about this. I've promised you. I have not lied. I've sworn. I've assured you that I took a vow to you and intend to live up to it all of my life. I have lived up to it every moment of our marriage. I don't know how long I can take these dark fits of yours."

"Will, what are you saying to me?"

"Please, Susan, don't insult me with your pretended innocence. We've suffered long enough not to lie to each other."

She forcefully pulled his hand to her. "I don't know what you're talking about."

"What is wrong with you, then? What in hell's name is wrong with you?"

She paused. "I'm sick, Will. I'm afraid I'm very sick."

I drove her to Dr. Roberts's in Fairfax. Mother could keep Stearns, and I wasn't working yet, so Will was saved taking an afternoon off. No one thought Will was insensitive in letting me escort her. Without one word of discussion, all of us, knowing the kind of person Susan was, expected her illness to be serious, painful, and diagnosed only by extensive tests—a simple office visit would not give us an answer. Since every small-town patient had to suffer until the lab results came back from Atlanta, Will could wait until then to do his duty by her side. For now, Susan might not be as nervous with just me.

After she had completed the office forms and we had shifted in our chairs long enough to be appropriately impressed with and intimidated by medical science, the nurse, a high-school classmate named Louise May, let me accompany my sister-in-law past the first door into the antiseptic odor of a white-walled alcove, where she set about taking Susan's blood.

"Hold still now, Susan dear," she said, rubbing alcohol on a vein and tightening a small rubber hose around Susan's bicep.

Susan slowly turned her whitening face toward the wall. The overhead fluorescent light made her pallid skin appear worse. "How much does he want?"

"Squeeze into a fist. There—now." A dark red gush burst through the syringe. Louise May waited, watching the flow peak at the top, and then hurriedly clamped on another tube.

"I don't see why one won't do. I've got a baby boy to keep up with and I need all the blood I can get."

"He looks just like his daddy, doesn't he, Luke?"

"Oh, no, he's much more handsome than that."

Susan looked paler.

"Are you all right?"

She didn't answer.

"There, that's it." Louise May yanked the needle out and put a gauze pad on the wound. "Bring your hand up there . . . that's it, and hold that. You might even put it above your head. I'll take this off now—and just keep this Band-Aid there . . . that's good." As she turned to leave, she spoke again, trying to make us believe it was an afterthought. "You heard anything from Elizabeth?"

Susan didn't bother to answer. None of us ever bothered anymore. I waited in Dr. Roberts's office, his degrees spread across the wall like one conquered domino after another, while he examined her in another room, kneading her stomach and side and lower back in search of an ailment he could feel with his own hands. He didn't tell us what he found, if anything. He couldn't be sure. She needed an X-ray, he said. If he was certain of anything, it was that she needed an X-ray.

Lying on top of the table as the technician spread two leaden mats over her breast and stomach, she told me, she tried to pray—and concentrate. Concentration was a form of prayer. A purple X on her side marked where the eye of the machine descended, the diseased side, perhaps, but always the side of another person and not herself. How could it really be Susan Mordew Treadwell? As she heard the click, she concentrated on a mental picture of the tumor (she knew what it was without asking). It began to break up like an apple bursting its skin and disintegrating into thin, harmless air. She rejoiced for a moment, thinking her concentration had worked, but then she heard it again: "I am here, and I am not going to leave."

The return appointment came ten days later, after the lab results were mailed back. Susan had not felt any better. Will sat by her side during the diagnosis. His life was hers, in sickness and in health. Yes, their marriage had problems. She could admit those troubles to herself, and later to me. And she could also confess that many of them were her own doing—and worst the way she'd acted with Elizabeth during some house party, and how Will had responded in kind. He had never been the same since all her foolish accusations came spitting out like some demon possessed her. In many ways she was responsible for Elizabeth's going, as much as she could guess about the reasons. But still, he was her husband, no matter what the past, in sickness and in health. He felt close to her, she believed, across the table from the coming news.

Dr. Roberts said it was a lymphoma—a special type of lymphoma, referred to as Hodgkin's disease. His tone of voice was professional, matter-of-fact, as if he had said, "Your body is a microcosm of the work that science does." Except that he said, "You have a lymphoma. You've probably heard of it—Hodgkin's disease." The first symptoms were exhaustion and an inability to sleep because the lymph glands, the spleen, and the liver grew progressively larger. Anemia followed because of the overproduction of white blood cells. More than fifty percent of the patients suffering the disease died—but of all the lymph cancers, the chances of arresting this one were highest. "The treatment is both X-ray and chemical," he said, "and both kill as many, even more, healthy as sick cells. You get nauseated. You lose your hair. You can hardly move. But it's the only hope."

She refused to believe he was talking about her. She had listened to a thousand such stories. She always felt sorry for the sick, and sometimes she'd say to herself, "There but for the

grace of God go I." She tried to imagine their inner distress
and do what she could to ease the pain of worry, but she drove
away from visiting them to a healthy home and forgot—it was
the only way to stay sane, to separate the sick and dying from
the living. Dr. Roberts is not talking about me, she thought. A
voice inside her answered, like the tolling of bells, "Yes he is.
Don't you see? Can't you hear? Wake up, Susan, it's true. It's
really you. 'I am dying'—say that to yourself. 'I am dying.' "
She saw the great horns lurking outside the pen. But she still
couldn't believe the "I" that was dying was really the same "I"
that was thinking, the living "I," that wasn't an object like the
rest of the world.

The day before Susan's first injection, I offered to help Will
with his farm chores, an innocent enough ploy to declare myself. It was a brisk November afternoon, quickly growing
darker. After we loaded the hay into the back of the pickup,
we set across the south forty toward the cows. On the way we
drove past Will's Brahman bull. The beast was a gray hump-
back with pendulous skin and wide, misshapen horns. One
horn faced straight ahead, as if to charge, while the other
veered off to the side and threw his ancient facade off-balance.
He stared at us as we passed, a creature whose blank and colorless eyes made him seem too mysterious to care about siring
calves or about obeying us, his supposed masters.

At the herd we worked in silence. I needed to wait, to stand
next to my brother and feel his presence as a blood-sure, lasting bond. He would not like what I was going to say. He
popped the twine around each bale as I began tossing the
golden-green hay toward the cows, who hurried over and
crowded without fear next to the pickup, densely grouped and
damned souls. They stretched their necks to the ground, soon
lost in the cool, brittle eating, and into the silence of the open
field came only the sounds of the quick snip of Will's knife
and the slow, sloppy munching. When Will joined me in
heaving the last few bales, the straw bounced in wayward
bunches over their backs, the scattered pieces of hay like
tongues of fire.

Sometime since I had last been around Will, for reasons I
could not yet explain, the cows had become to him a great and
glorious obsession. I understand why it is necessary for a man
to escape the company of human beings, especially his wife

and even, to a lesser extent, his mother. But I can't understand why a man would choose the company of cows. Filthy, stupid creatures. But Will insisted that the bug-eyed dunces were not just cows, but *his* cows, the assumption being that his private ownership created a world separate from the hoi polloi of the rising and setting sun, the moon, and the spangled stars. Anyone who questioned this self-serving allegiance—animal to man, and man to animal—Will confronted head on, horns ablazing. He told Susan he would visit his bossies whenever he wanted to; no at-home responsibility could even begin to compare in importance. When Mother asked just how essential cows could be, he told her he'd be a far worse husband without them. When Ray accused Will of believing himself no less than King Solomon, with cows and not women as wives, Will answered that cows were more loyal. The greatest challenge arose from the true master, the Brahman, who according to any other farmer owned the natural right to the harem. But when it came to his cows, Will was not a normal farmer. I had watched him threaten the creature every time he could, spitting in the pen as he fed him. "Goddamn right now, boy!" he'd shout. "Anytime I want to. So you be kind now, ya hear?"

On the way back Will slowed down at the rise above the house, to stand at twilight and look down on the promise his life had wrought. The sight pleased him each time he surveyed it, all the more in my presence because he could remind me of the comparatively meager farm my father lost when we were children. I got out of the truck, needing the open spaces to talk, and he followed, the two of us mesmerized by the setting. The muted ground fell down toward the house and at the last moment swelled up like a cushion proclaiming its jewel. The old-fashioned breezeway darkened with the twilight, but the kitchen window burned like a safe beacon. Susan had insisted I join them, as if this last night before the hospital were the same as any other night. She had not mentioned Elizabeth's letter—more bad news—but I knew Mother had told her. A silent wreath of smoke came up from the chimney and led our eyes farther on, across the quiet blacktop to the obscure land of the New Canaan Farms, fields and forests that stretched from Will's boundary a thousand acres away, toward the horizon line of Georgia pines hooked to the dying sky. Tomorrow evening it wouldn't be the same.

I did not look at him but addressed my words to the scene

below us, and all that it meant to him. "I am going after them tomorrow."

He didn't answer. The sound came first, and then the dim footprints of the headlights along the road, before the car itself followed, west to east, past the house and on to an unknown destination. I turned toward him. A slight sneer laughed on his lips, not angry enough to explode, but loud enough to imply, "I should have thought so." "It is for Mother, of course," I continued. "She is concerned that he will die up there."

"Mother wouldn't dare tell us what she really thinks," he said.

"I guess not. And what does Susan think?"

"Have you been kept up on what they've been doing?"

"All I know is what Elizabeth wrote me after Miss Margaret died." I paused, thinking to myself. I did not want to discuss her with Will. At all. "And Mother showed me the letter yesterday."

"I'm surprised she didn't tear it up."

"Neither of us could understand what happened. Elizabeth was vague."

Will folded his arms across his chest and slowly shook his head, trying to appear as distanced from the fray as a gentleman farmer should be. His sneer was gone, but one corner of his face crinkled up with undisguised tension. I didn't know what was hidden, but knowing Will, I suspected. "I predicted this, Luke," he began. "The moment after Mother telephoned, I realized she would ask you and not me, and that you would agree."

"She didn't ask you because of Susan. I'm available."

"That's not true. Susan could be a picture of health and Mother still wouldn't ask me. She doesn't think I am rational about this. I'm telling you, I've been thinking all night and day—I couldn't do one swath of work today—and I've been trying to understand what is best for everyone, even him. Believe me. All this happening at once . . ."

"I know."

"But listen to me—Mother never has. See if I don't make sense. The man left her and should have to suffer the consequences of the risks he took. She can send you off for him and you can bring him back and she can watch him die, but what good is that going to do? I know you think I'm completely irrational about all this, but you tell me, Luke, what good can you see in the man coming back now? It has been more years than I can count. He is not the same person. He has injured her in ways she could never forgive—not to speak of the rest of us—and still she has this automatic reaction that you should fetch him. Think about it. He has severed himself from us of his own accord. It wouldn't even do him any good— being back, I mean. If he is really going to die, he would probably prefer dying alone. Knowing him, he probably assumes he'll ... Well, it just won't work."

"I don't think it matters to you whether he's living or dying. You've always come down on the side of keeping him away."

He held his breath, gathering patience. "That's exactly the point, Luke. You see, you and Mother and Belle assume I haven't considered this but just reacted as usual—against the old man. Listen, the man's been gone for ages. I couldn't care less if he comes back, because I am sure not going to let the Bible thumper bother me. Don't you think I have enough to worry about?"

"I didn't mean—"

"I am telling you—I'm trying to think of what's best for Mother."

The crimson West darkened into night. Some of the blackening clouds hovered like distant, misplaced mountains under a slight moon that crowned the evening star. We became, to each other, only shadows. I still felt the presence of my brother's body near me, and thus we were more connected than we would have been at two ends of a telephone line. But in the darkness we no longer read each other's face, which made our messages all the more tenuous. Soon Susan would call and we would end this conversation, sitting for the last meal. After sleep I would set off for the true mountains to the northeast, where my father lay dying, with a woman I once loved by his side, and Susan would prepare for the doctor's first nauseating try.

"Mother sat me down yesterday," I said. "You know how she points you into that chair by the window when she gets anxious. I don't think she had talked to you or Susan yet—she never told me when she got the letter, but I assume it was only a day or so ago. Maybe yesterday."

"No doubt—she's the one who's overreacting."

"Well, she went on and on. Not about much of anything, really. But she did tell me this: she doesn't think you understand how much Susan wants Elizabeth to come home. She says Susan feels responsible for Elizabeth's leaving—she doesn't know why. But she's listened enough to believe Susan would feel much better if Elizabeth came back and they could talk out a few things."

"Like what?"

"I don't know, Will. I happen to have been somewhere else, you know."

A long, impatient sigh, like an air leak, burst from him. Then silence. "Susan has always felt responsible for Elizabeth. So have I." No inflection played through his voice; he was determined not to lose his temper. "She is Elizabeth's older sister. They lost their parents when they were girls, remember, and ever since Susan has felt the burden of watching over her. You know what kind of flighty woman Elizabeth is. Admiral Mallery was sure she couldn't take care of herself—just take one look at his will. Susan doesn't want to talk things out— that's Mother's romantic folderol. She has the same problem Mother has, a mothering instinct that wants the foolish child home where she thinks it'll be safe. But it wouldn't help, Luke. Think about it. Elizabeth's presence would only raise a whole 'nother set of worries Susan doesn't need right now. Out of sight, out of mind is better. She has to concentrate on the will to overcome her sickness. Elizabeth would divert her energy. As her husband, I won't let it happen."

I did not respond. In the long silence that followed, Will finally recognized that nothing would deter me from going. For years he had assumed that as my older brother, he had a right to treat me as a son, and thus, couching his words as advice, he tried to tell me what to do, whatever my age. But I was going. His resistance hardened me. The irony was that I was going for reasons we had not discussed, and would never discuss if I could help it. In my refusal to argue with him about what was right for Susan's health, or what was better for Mother and Dad, in my waiting out the silence, he understood.

Will was left, then, with only one other tack. It must have taken him a long time to consider the possibilities and finally decide. He became a chief priest trying to make me a Judas. Like a chief priest and elder, he had tried these other tacks first, a few hints, misdirection, allusions—the stake, just like thirty silver pieces, was risky because it was blood money, tangible proof that he had violated the law. But now he was willing to take the risk. If it backfired, so be it—he was set to bargain, as long as I would join him in crucifying the Galilean, which was in truth, anathema to him.

"Elizabeth," Will said. It was her name, long consi_____
that ultimately penetrated the silence. He tossed it before m___
to roll, unexpectedly, like a piece of silver, and even in the
treacherous darkness shine for a moment and then settle, the
risk taken. "You are going for one reason only, but you are
deceiving yourself, brother. You might think she wants to
come home to this place, and to you, but you are wrong. I am
telling you you're wrong."

Susan interrupted him. She had come out into the breezeway and was looking up the hill toward us. She must have
been there for a while, because she walked into the yard and
waved her hand back and forth until I saw her. She was too
tired to yell. For a moment, in the vague outlines of the night,
her shape reminded me of her taller, graceful sister, standing
alone in the yard and staring up toward the rise and the night
sky that grew fuller behind us. Surely there was some connection there—between sisters, I mean. I would not say to myself,
though I wished I could, between Elizabeth and me. But it was
time for this special dinner. I was concerned that we get there
quickly. I stepped past Will, toward the pickup, but he
grabbed my arm and I turned and looked at him.

"If you go, there will be a great deal of suffering. You just
don't understand. And the person who in the end will suffer
most . . . Luke, don't. Don't."

15

It took me a long time to wake up. The phrase—only the first of many this day—repeated itself from the moment I opened my eyes, like a songbird alighting from dream to reality. But I didn't realize that my mind was chanting these same studied words over and over again until much later. I showered, dressed, and shouldered my bag, and with a cup of coffee hurried through the screened porch and into the pre-dawn light. The hour before dawn mystified me. The air was cool and innocent. There wasn't another sound to be heard. Across the eastern horizon ran a faint blood-red streak, the first color to break from the black of night, and then other colors escaped in groups, until by the time I had driven across town the background of the slate-gray and purple dawn was an aching wash of pink. There was some mysterious connection I could not explain, for when I looked up, stunned by the growth of dawn, I only then realized that since my awakening my mind had been repeating a phrase from Spinoza that I first read one bleak night in college, and then kept at my side through Korea: "Under the aspect of eternity." No other time of the day was better suited to those words. There was a mysterious connection, I knew there was, a connection as human as that between two people, living or dead, because if I ever half-understood what eternity was, it would be, I felt sure, only during the time before dawn.

The phrase kept with me throughout most of the journey

from Lanett up the piedmont plateau to the mountains of North Carolina. Like a figure of music, heard before morning's cacophony forces a few doors closed, it had cut into the back parlor of my mind and set up residence for the day, singing with the same rhythm over and over again. "Under the aspect . . . of eternity." No matter how mysterious and appropriate it first seemed, after a while this repetition bothered me. "Fine and dandy," I said to myself. "I understand. Now leave me alone." But driving a car made it worse. It kept time with the humming of the tires, waiting until I settled into an accompanying cruising speed before it stood up and sang again, stuck on itself like a scratched record. I was surfeited. It stayed with me from Lanett to Newnan and Atlanta, and after lunch to Dahlonega and into the evening and North Carolina. "Under the aspect . . . of eternity." There was an occasional rest, but only when a vivid memory played or the landscape fascinated.

After driving three hours past lunch, I pulled off the road in White County where the highway bridged the Chattahoochee river. Already twice that day I had buzzed over the Chattahoochee, and here I crossed it again, marveling that for hundreds of miles to the south this one stream of water persisted enough to pass by my ghost-riddled departure point on its way to the Gulf of Mexico. I decided I might as well stretch my legs by its bank, checking it out here, and someday everywhere, if I could, from its source on. A path on the other side of the roadside grasses led me through a stand of giant pines that shaded out the underbrush and made the walking to the river mysteriously easy. Then it climbed some moss-green rocks, the first few bordered by elderberry and poison ivy in its fall red. The bushes soon fell away, though, almost magically. At the top, a promontory jutted out toward the middle of the Chattahoochee. Below swirled deep blue water, cooling the air like an overturned mountain of ice. Across the way, around either side of an uninhabited island, white water roared. I watched for a long time, lost in the sound of the cataract, until I spotted a lone sycamore on the edge of the other bank.

Leaning against the tree trunk, as he did one recess after another in the orchard behind the Cusseta schoolhouse, was my fourteen-year-old twin brother. I looked again, to make sure, and watched him shift positions without seeing me, in his lap the wings of his Bible flapping like a bird. He took a bite out of the half-eaten apple in his hand and, dreaming as only he could dream, stared intensely at the white rapids. Then he whispered a few words aloud, probably a verse of some prophet, whch the roar of the river killed.

I must explain. All this, of course, seems terribly fanciful. But I had seen him more than once since he died: reading, usually against a tree in the sun. The last time was at the university, before I left for Korea. And there were times before that.

I first responded as always, without panic. The fear came later. I didn't know what it meant, but when it happened an unearthly calm possessed me, standing across the water, to think the same thought every time: while the rest of us idled about, he was always striving. I didn't say "striving" at first—I came to that word later—and now that I was older and eaten by this memory, I could put other words to that striving, to his belief that a human being could reach his vision if he only kept trying. Even after death. I repeated, and this time welcomed, the phrase. And I knew that something was wrong with me.

Of course something was wrong with me—I had seen a dead person. I looked again—he was gone. Only an image. I retraced my path to the road and locked myself into my car, vowing to stop only when I arrived at my destination. I drove hard, pushing as fast as I could to get away from such unexplainable worries. In every other instance I ran. While it happened I always calmly watched, as if the sight of him were a normal occurrence, and then sometimes for days afterward I dropped into a great depression, unable to understand. This time, night fell a few minutes earlier than I expected, which was welcome, for the cover of darkness helped my spirit push quickly across the state line, into Franklin and on toward Bryson City, where Elizabeth had said they were staying with a family friend of the Mallerys'. Only a few other cars drove the stretch between the two towns; I gunned it around the winding turns and through the cold, dripping rocks, quite uncertain of what I was going to do when I got there.

My hands began to ache from gripping the steering wheel too tightly. It was happening to me again. I could not forget. I could never forget, but I still fought him. This vision, I thought, the spirit of Doug lives. No, it was pure nonsense. I accepted the idea because I was a coward. What was wrong with me? He was eaten by maggots. He was dust. I kept seeing Doug because I was sick. I couldn't forget because I was sick.

The whole daylong sense of mystery worried me. It wasn't mystery, but hallucination, all because I was traveling toward those two Judases who betrayed me and I really didn't want to know what I was going to find out about them. I was a back-and-forth lunatic, one minute welcoming that Spinoza phrase, the next minute hating it; rhapsodizing about eternity, scorning the very idea; believing Doug was a real presence, realizing he was pure fantasy. The problem was my father—that was it, that was always it. I had returned from Korea convinced I would never see Doug again, and I wouldn't have if it weren't for this journey to rescue the old man. There was an inextricable connection between their two spirits.

These visitations had become my history. First of all, a part of Doug had come directly into my bloodstream. It was his sense of striving. I had suddenly developed an ambition, which was always his, not to make money like Will, or to conquer women, but simply to know. Edmund Husserl, the German philosopher, used the phrase "the passion of knowing." To know something about the world, and a consciousness or a system or a philosophy I could study to understand it—though I would not accept the same beliefs Doug did. And to know a little about my confused, duplicitous self. The second part of the curse was Doug's unearthly affection for my father. I did not share his love. I felt an obligation. Doug had left me to care for the old man. Me and me alone. Will and Belle didn't, that was for sure. I didn't want to, and even though I felt like I was hallucinating about all this, I gave up trying to shake it. Korea made me realize that you have to accept certain things about yourself, real and unreal. So there was no way Will would talk me out of going. He might have thought I was journeying to the mountains only for Elizabeth, but, no, it was for Doug. At least I told myself it was for Doug.

I never shared the visitations with anyone—not with my family, Elizabeth, or any of my closest friends at Munsan-ni. One of the earliest came in Germany, at the end of my first stretch of military service. I had wooed and won a refugee named Teresa. It was the first time I had made love. After I finally convinced her, in a language of her own making, Teresa and I found a perfect hollow in the bank of the river outside Rehau. Shrubs disguised the slight indentation, but a sandy space beneath them, just large enough for the two of us to crawl into, provided us the privacy we desired. I cannot remember—there was a buzzing in the air, and a bittersweet taste. We rested afterward, lying side by side. She wanted to stay through the night, but I began to worry—as only I would do—that we would be discovered any moment, two frail humans rutting in a war zone. I slowly turned over and waited, trying to look nonchalant, in a condition that by its very nature makes one look self-conscious and ridiculous. In a few minutes I sat up and scouted the immediate area. Seeing a figure under the nearest tree, I flinched, and then recognized the face. Doug gave me a simple profile, with his open Bible and the apple, his face bent over his salvation. Somehow I wasn't shocked—at least not until later, when I believed I might have inherited from my father some unknown mental disease. It wasn't my fault, I told myself, that I saw a dead person.

When I was shipped home—it was July 1948—Mother could give me little news of my father. I did, however, respond to the other impulse I mysteriously felt, especially since it was so much easier to satisfy. I began to read incessantly—to strive. For many of my compatriots, enrolling in college didn't necessarily imply a profound love of reading. No, for the eighteen-year-olds, attendance meant more a profound respect for a booze bottle, lavalieres, and the forward pass. Most of the other GIs were as serious as I was, but with dreams of self-owned businesses and houses in the suburbs. I read history and philosophy. What else would a man with my background read?

The two and a half years, summers included, passed like an exquisite trance, until one afternoon in January I saw him outside the library, sitting on a bench under a gray, scaly basswood tree. This time he did look up. By the middle of the evening, I was fighting a terrible depression, convinced I needed to lock myself up in some lonely tower, away from those who might suffer my insanity. Who can tell what a man who sees his dead brother will do? After midnight I began to read Spinoza's *Ethics,* soon skipping the demonstrations for the scholia. It was a godsend. First he gave me a word for this striving: *conatus*—that pleased me. But in the early-morning hours I found the phrase "under the aspect of eternity." For some reason it saved me. I did not understand, but I was able to endure. Later, in Korea, the phrase gathered its true force.

During the summer of 1951—an interlude—Elizabeth and I almost became engaged. At least I thought so. From the spring afternoon we picnicked by the Chattahoochee until the morning I left on the train, unattended, I wooed her with all my imagination and courage. I wanted to tell her about Doug—to say, "Look, you must know this about me. These visitations—in Germany, by a river [I would have lied about Teresa], and even at the university, in front of the library of all places." Perhaps she would understand. But I did not find the occasion. Instead I fell into an easy forgetfulness, not necessarily an intentional one, but one that with every passing day, like the acceptance of death, made my life a little more tolerable. I assumed, I guess, that if I didn't think or talk about him, he would go away like the usual maggot-eaten dead person. As for confessing my sickness to Elizabeth, I believed it unlikely she would admire a man whose eyes received trembling visions of the night.

In Korea I found myself hoping that I would spot Doug under that single tree in front of my window, scream my guts out, and be given a medical discharge just to shut me up. I was not a man to pray, not with the father I had. I knew my mind suffered, but there was nothing to do: Others suffered more than I, I would tell myself, and it would help. But sometimes I wanted Doug to come to save me and he wouldn't, not then, not when I expected he would. The tree stood alone the whole time, a single landmark in the procession of the dead. Beyond stretched the endless rice paddies toward the north, where the killing was. Then, like some chant, I repeated the Spinoza phrase, "Under the aspect of eternity, under the aspect of eternity," and I would see one rice paddy after another as generation upon generation, the faithless and perverse, the wicked and adulterous, the vipers and a few of the royal priesthood. The measure of endless time was all I had to put this war and this life of mine in any understandable perspective. But Spinoza insisted that this inexplicable suffering—stretcher after stretcher, arms dangling like limp hoses—had to be seen in a larger context, that all worked for good in the end, if we were only intelligent enough to understand. The larger context I accepted, the good I did not. The idea of the good was false sentimentality.

When I was finally discharged in the spring of 1953, I had no idea who I was or what I was going to become. All I had done for five of my last eight years was take orders. Everyone around me, however—soldiers, housewives, professionals, and even bums—in comparison burned with a purpose, which usually involved capital gain. The prospect of a job, a family

and that new dream of a house in the suburbs made me want
to vomit. My only sense of relief arose from the fact that the
war had forever rid my life of both Doug and Elizabeth. I believed that the presence of death in Korea had exorcised his
image from my mind, and that the distance, time, and experience apart had transfigured Elizabeth and me. We were two
completely different people who could never love each other
again.

But I was wrong. Elizabeth's letter to Mother not only asked
for help—for my father, she said, certainly not for her—but if
at all possible, I was to be the one who came. She asked specif-
ically for me. For me. And then, on this journey after the
Francophile and my father, Doug made himself known again,
as unexpectedly as the previous times. Why was it unexpected? When at last I saw the dim lights of Bryson City huddled between the Nantahala ridge and the Smokies, I told
myself that he had come back to me because of my father, yes,
but probably because of Elizabeth, too. How had I let her in
that window of my soul? It didn't seem possible, especially
since I didn't even know her the few hours after Doug had
crawled out the window and leaped backward into his fate,
and my everlasting burden.

That long-ago night was the first one. After Doug disappeared into the wilderness, I knelt at the window, the cottony
taste of night in my mouth, and watched, wondering if he
might change his mind in a few minutes and hurry back, his
blue jeans and red checkered shirt hardly worn. I knew better,
but the hope kept me for a while from having to decide
whether to wake my father. The dove was silent. His call had
beckoned Doug and accompanied him on his leap, but his
work was done. The crickets kept up a wailing chorus. "It's
hot, it's hot," they shrilled, and then, "He's gone, he's gone."
A whippoorwill sang from deep in the woods, courting my father, for when the old man heard one, he sat on the porch and
answered back without flagging, late into the night. The line
of trees across the south forty underscored a lighter horizon, as
uniform as a single brushstroke above the forest, but higher up
the stars burned like pressed jewels. Somewhere Doug had
stopped, I believed, panting from his escape, and leaning
against a tall pine, stared up at those same stars. "We are
brothers," I told myself, "our blood runs the same."

I did not wake my father. First of all, though I believed
Doug's flight was not only foolish but dangerous, I remained

loyal to my brother. If he had wanted to tell Dad he was setting out, he would have. Instead he chose the secrecy of the night to escape. I honored his wishes. But there was another reason: sure that my brother hoofed it toward serious trouble, I did not want to hurry to my father and see the old man listen and then nod, instructing me to go back to bed, Doug was following the will of God. Even at the outset I suspected my father would be pleased.

I cradled Doug's Buck knife in my hand for a moment, then set it on the night table and got back into bed, expecting to lie there until dawn and feign sleep when my father rose and faced an empty bed. But I fell asleep. And I dreamed. As always, it was a confused dream. No story line revealed itself. I didn't go from one heavenly place to another, or from hell to hell, and discover secrets about myself. I stayed still, in some nebulous garden or field, and saw three aspects of the same appearance, I believe: a very old man with shocking gray hair, who turned into a bull, which I think was our bull Job, who then became a pig, which I identified, whether or not it was true, as the pig Randolph. But I made no decisions about what these three things meant, nor did I feel any compulsion to understand. I was fourteen years old and I was dreaming—that's all. I didn't bother in the dream, or later, when I remembered it, to think there was any relation among the three images. And I remembered this dream much later in the day, of course, because when I woke up there was no way I could have been aware of any past or future time, given what was happening to me in the terrifying present.

At five o'clock I was jolted awake. A pop of electricity exploded deep within my heart and sat me straight up, dumbfounded. I was not conscious of sleepiness, of crusty eyes, aching muscles, or a full bladder—in fact I was not conscious of my charged body as my own body. A breathing not my own crackled from the strange surge pumping within, demanding I wake up and be aware of something I had never experienced. My skin began to burn, each hair aflame like a fire that purified the body of itself and the brain of its very human consciousness, and then my tongue felt scorched and swollen, as if I would never speak again. There was a presence in the room. There was a presence, not another human being, not a ghost, not a nonhuman apparition; it was a presence of being, an awareness—that was all my quickened mind let me call it. I could not define it, but only acknowledge its existence. It was supernatural, I knew that, and it was vital—the true life, dancing hand in hand with timelessness.

But nothing else happened. Nothing. I waited, and, in becoming aware of waiting, felt it begin to fade. It hovered a second, like aftershock, but I felt myself beginning to know who I was again—shaking with fear—and with each passing self-conscious thought, the presence was no longer possible. I was afraid for my life, and then I realized I would live because I was afraid; before, as best as I could remember, I didn't care whether I was alive. And thus I started to sense a great emptiness in my soul—not a depression but a hollowing out of all that didn't matter. I didn't try to think. I didn't want to. I let myself go, then, toward this abandonment, for some reason trusting it as what that startling presence gave me. I felt I was making the right decision, if it can be called a decision, for into that nothingness his spirit came, which—in those innocent days when a boy could say, yes, there is a spiritual world and it is good—was a welcome sign.

With the most soul-wrenching music I have ever heard, a bird sang. The first of the early morning, not a hair's breadth from the window, its notes came into the room and into that nothingness of my soul with a clarity I did not believe possible. Suddenly I shivered. All of my being lost itself in the intensity of the music, and a swelling of tears rose up from my heart and spoke his name. For I understood. I knew nothing of the pagan myths, of cursed kings and raped sisters; nor had I heard the boast that God plays with the leviathan as with a bird. I had not read where a man who wandereth from his place wandereth like a bird from her nest, too young to fly. Nor did I know that the Levites believed that two birds—the living one, along with cedar wood and scarlet and hyssop, dipped in the blood of the dead one, which was sacrificed in an earthen vessel over running water—cleansed a leper of his blemishes. But as I said, I understood. When the sheriff came, later in the day, I knew exactly what he was going to say.

The next morning I asked the motel clerk for directions to the address Elizabeth had included in her letter to Mother. It wasn't far—nothing was far in Bryson City. The town was poor. The courthouse paint was peeling; two of the five stores at the south end of Main Street were boarded shut; and the railroad station, a quaint Victorian structure with a wooden cupola, looked timeworn and depressed. I parked the car a block away and followed the street up the hill until I found a small hedge bordering the dirt road above their house, where I could stand and watch unseen.

From the hill a dull gray, somber sky, not more than a few feet over my head, stretched across the empty town to the barely visible Nantahala. Winter was coming—soon the snow. It was not a day to be outdoors. But stepping from behind the hedge to get a better look, I spotted someone sitting in the middle of the yard, to the side of the house. The man sat perfectly still in an old wooden wheelchair, arms, hands, and legs tightly wrapped beneath a heavy plaid blanket. Around his neck a bandanna poorly imitated an ascot, warmth obviously more important than appearance to the person who had tied it. I immediately assumed, from his position and demeanor, that someone else performed all the basic necessities for him. I was too far away to see the details of his face, but while I stood there it didn't move once, as still and marblelike as a bust—an unusual one, though. From under a beaten-up black hat, his thick white hair stuck straight back and to the side, as if he had suffered a great electrical shock and never recovered. If, in this incredible stillness, he had the consciousness to do anything, it was only to stare in front of him, at the cloud-covered mountainside.

At first, as I watched her carefully close the screen door to the kitchen, a single paper in her hand, I wasn't sure what was different. Then I realized her hair was darker. The blond was going to brown, probably no quicker than any other blonde's aging process, but since I hadn't seen her in three years I assumed the change was a jump, not a slide. There was a far more significant metamorphosis, though, at least in physical terms, which I painfully noted as she made her way to a chair beside the old man. It began at the kitchen. The woman I knew would never have turned and eased the screen door shut; she would have let it bang behind her. And she would not have walked across the yard struggling to keep flat-footed, to force her feet to forget the years. Hers would never be a mundane walk like most women's, for there was still a memory in her movement that I don't believe she ever could have totally forgotten. But much had changed, as if she whispered to herself, "No more, not again."

She sat, straight-backed and formal, in the chair beside the man, who did not acknowledge her as she began to read the letter. I assumed the piece of paper was a letter, and I assumed it was from Mother, who had written to tell them I was coming. I wasn't sure when the letter had arrived—she could have been reading it to him for the first time, or she could have read it to him more than once yesterday, and then again this morning, hoping that its import would sink in and prepare him; people in his condition had to be prepared, of course, to protect them. In either case, he continued to stare at the slope of the mountain in front of him. The words meant nothing. All that could change that insane profile, it seemed, was a chisel and a hammer.

Elizabeth folded the letter and let it fall on her lap, accustomed, apparently, to my father's dumb spiritlessness. I assumed he had suffered a stroke. I still could hardly believe it, but she knew better than the rest of us what he could and could not understand, and she did read to him. I thought about making myself known, but she had a purpose in waiting there beside him, which I wanted to see. For at least five minutes she didn't move, matching his stoic meditation with her own: he looked straight ahead at the muddled horizon, she straight at the side of his face. Five minutes without stirring was a long time, but this weirdly arranged quiescence seemed their only available response to whatever drove them to this place. The two of them—together.

Then, at last, she spoke to him, leaning her head forward for emphasis and, when she finished, lifting her arms from her sides with the greatest of efforts, like an exhausted preacher making one final plea. He did not respond.

She disguised any disappointment with him when she stood up and released the wheel lock, turning the chair, without asking, away from his mountainside and rolling it across the smooth yard to the kitchen. I could better see his face on their way back. Neither side looked paralyzed, though a uniform numbness spread across all of it, especially around his eyes, which even from my distance looked unfaithful to any external reality. The Treadwell jowls hadn't disappeared, but they were thinner, as was his whole face, as thin as a desert saint's, fasting until he won his vision and his early death. The shocking white hair made the impression all the more ascetic. Elizabeth stopped the chair, locked the wheels, and opened both doors for him. He wasn't a complete invalid after all: he slowly pushed the blanket off—which she took and folded as her back leaned against the screen door—and with his feet he swiveled the footplates out of his way. Then he stood up, tentatively but on his own, and hobbled inside.

There was something wrong with his hand.

When I telephoned after lunch, she told me to park beside the sleeping porch and wait. She'd watch for the car. We should talk away from the house, she said, at the Deep Creek Meeting Grounds, perhaps, since the sight of his own son, after all these years, might unnecessarily bewilder my father. I didn't argue, but I was suspicious. On the way I wondered why every single business on Main Street was closed for the afternoon when it wasn't Wednesday. The answer came when I crossed the bridge. Three sparkling black hearses were trailed by a parade of cars that must have stretched the complete width of Bryson City. The low, gray sky made the ritual all the more somber; the sky felt deeper than the ocean, and the winding ribbon of headlights was drowning.

As soon as I turned the corner, she came out, but she walked along the veranda half-speed and even held the top rail as she negotiated the four steps to the yard. Elizabeth looked like the one who had been to war. At first glance, no matter how shell-shocked she appeared, I was unwilling to grant her suffering; it is very difficult for a veteran, even one who saw as little action as I did, to believe that human suffering outside the constant threat of strafing and snipers can in any way compare. It doesn't seem authentic. And of course I bore other resentments, which I planned to discuss. But just before she dragged herself into the car, I saw her framed by the window, almost as still as a photograph, and I could tell. My heart begged to give way. Without my three years in Korea, I would not have recognized the face that kept toward the ground, looking at the world with the tops of her eyes and only if necessary, refusing to maintain contact—what could the eyes of another human being tell her? Without Korea I could not have seen her slumping shoulders and wondered if they, too, bore more than the weight of steel weapons—whatever her weapons with my father had been—but the burden of the act also: a shot, a scream, and then the eyes.

It was hard to believe a woman involved in some half-baked religious quest could be suffering from combat fatigue, but I saw the same weariness in her that I saw in my friends who came back from some numbered hill with years added to the skin around their eyes and a terrible dull look, which immediately warned me not to ask. They were the ones, I thought, who would wake up in the night, years from now, the ghost not exorcised, and rant about something too trivial to believe: "He stole my razor, I tell you! Goddammit, he stole my razor!" He, of course, was a dead buddy. Or I'd hear that a friend had done something stupid, like marry a whore in a drunken stupor. Or he divorced his wife, beat his children, became convinced he could make a million by mortgaging his house and investing in a new real-estate deal. Soon, suicide. They make decisions, I thought, considering Elizabeth, that they believe will guard their souls, when all they're doing is destroying themselves because they're guilt-stricken for surviving.

She leaned over and kissed me on the cheek. "I can't thank you enough for coming, Luke."

"I'm sorry I'm late—there was a funeral procession through town."

"A Mr. Fisher. Mr. and Mrs. Mallery are there."

"An important personage?"

"From what I can tell, the whole town turns out for every funeral."

She directed us down the hill to the lumberyard and along the river on a winding road that grew progressively less traveled. It was crucial to her, she said, that we first talk far away from my father. Before I had a chance to ask him questions, I thought. Why was she with him? What kind of relationship did they have? Or was she trying to prepare me for the way he looked or what he would say?

We passed some farm country and stopped at a small campground in the national park, leaving the car on the opposite side of the field from the one other car and following a muddy trail, marked with hoofprints, along the creek. The tranquilizing white water, climbing deeper into the silence of the mountainside forest, helped to insulate her from the old man, and me from the funeral and the low, oppressive sky. In a while we had escaped the company of the world and found an appropriate place, away from the distractions that would keep us from explaining—or at least keep *her* from explaining, if I could find a way to ask.

"So—you're alive," she said finally, with fatigue even in her voice. "Thank God they didn't kill you over there."

"I'm too yellow."

"Still selling yourself short, Luke. I'm sure you did your duty."

"Typed a hell of a lot of letters. Didn't get many to read, though."

She half-smiled without looking at me, still recognizing my tendency, perhaps my need, to be sarcastic. She wandered from the path and bent over to examine a freshly fallen, slender twig whose leaves were one of the few signs of green. Her plain blue dress tightened around her hips—they were much leaner, almost bony. She broke off a stem and twirled the leaf in her hand as we continued on.

"I should have written more," she began. I waited, and she knew I was waiting. She fiddled with the leaf in her fingers, but then she refused. "Well, I just should have written more."

"You must not have received my most recent letters."

"I guess not."

I guess not, I repeated to myself. How nonchalant. "There is something wrong with my father's hand, Elizabeth. I saw him this morning in the yard with you, before I called. If we can't talk about you and me—there's no reason we have to, or that we should—why don't we come right out, then, and talk about that?"

She looked away from me, toward the creek. "He injured it."

"How?"

"I'm not sure. I wasn't there. You'll have to ask him."

"You know."

"Well . . ."

"But you won't tell me?"

"It's not that at all, Luke." She seemed exhausted by the few questions. "I don't have a right to say."

"What in God's name does that mean? You've been with him for however long and you can't tell me how he hurt himself?"

"I have been with him—that's right. I followed him a little over a year, and now I'm trying to get him safely home. But I don't have any claim on him. I don't speak for him, he doesn't for me."

"But I thought he was in no condition to speak at all."

"Well, you'll have to judge for yourself. He might be in the condition, but he doesn't want to."

I turned from her and trudged along the rooty path, careless of mud or horse dung or ankle-spraining rocks. Who did she think she was? At the moment I didn't care how wounded she looked from her evangelical hike; I hadn't come calling all the way to North Carolina for Elizabeth to play some cryptic game with me. I could just as easily turn my derriere around and speed home—I could forsake any Doug-induced obligation to my father and tell her she wasn't worth the love I offered anyway. I could imagine the worst about the two of them. She had suffered a lot, yes, and I didn't want to hurt her, but I deserved some information, some simple facts, didn't I?

"Please don't be that way, Luke."

"Why did we come out here in the first place, then?"

"I wanted to see you alone."

"Well, I'm not asking for a critique of my father's motives."

"I know, I know. But all these things are in the past."

"When I wasn't around."

"You will know sooner or later. Please don't press me. Be patient. Who's to say you want to hear? It is a great burden to me, believe me, Luke, and at the same time a relief, that one day all of it will be revealed. And I don't mean petty little rumors, but our hearts. I have a feeling the story will come out on its own, now or someday in the future. And it will reveal itself to me as much as to anyone else. It will come out because I was born to a stripping away toward the center of my rotten core."

"You're going to make me believe what people say is true."

"Are they saying that?" There was a pause in her voice again, as if she weren't sure about whom I was talking. "Me—with Robert?"

I nodded. "Good Christians all, dear."

"Well, at least you know better, Luke. You've never assumed the easy route—it's probably your greatest strength, even in your . . . I can't believe how many people misestimate your father."

"No one has seen him in over ten years."

"Well, your mother has, but she probably didn't tell anyone."

"Yes, she did, but not much."

"He says she sent him away after a few minutes."

Around the next bend the path dropped toward the water and widened. We walked through a stand of trees to the nearest rocks. The water broke on both sides and muffled any words we tried to exchange, as if we spoke with our heads turned and our mouths covered with handkerchiefs. We fell into a long stretch of silence.

She was in trouble. Since the day I first met Elizabeth, and fell in love with her, when she surprised Will and Susan and me with her wild, spontaneous dancing on the banks of the river, the complaint against her was that she was too carefree. I remember how Mrs. Mallery and Susan worked on her, insisting that she needed to be more responsible, and more aware—that famous refrain—of "what will people think"; she just couldn't flaunt her New York City pants and walk barefoot down State Line, not at her age. When we were dating, she never wanted me to plan an evening. Sometimes she'd bounce into the car and say, "You decide," and for the rest of the night I'd call every shot and she'd never object. She preferred to wait for the mood she was in, and respond, if something outlandish presented itself, with joy in the unexpected moment. Like the time we broke into the city pool and went skinny-dipping. I don't care how goggle-eyed I was, every single second we swam after each other I worried we would be caught, arrested, and publicly embarrassed. She picked up my anxiety and made me suffer for it later, when I assumed her act had implications. But that was the Elizabeth I loved—it was impossible to predict what she meant.

Now she stumbled with sore, dusty feet, too heavy to plant, one burden after the other, even on a path she stopped to consider before taking. This was not the Elizabeth I knew. Doug was a quick, joyous child who died from the leap he risked, full of my father's faith. With Elizabeth it was a slower process. She sat beside me with her head down, meticulously deveining the leaf she had picked up. With surgical patience she broke the saw-toothed edge and peeled along the vein to the stem, then moved to the next vein, higher up. At the tip she could begin down the other side. I took the leaf from her hand and tossed it into the water, where it was quickly carried downstream and lost beneath the white bubbles. Then I yanked her up by the arm, shaking it to loosen some of her muscles, and pulled her back ashore and to the path headed home. Without explaining.

"I know that you don't want me prying," I began in a few minutes. "I understand that. And I want you to believe that I have no suspicions about you and my father. I do know something about him, more than anyone in my family, I believe, because of my brother who died. Doug, you remember. I can understand why the old man went into the mountains to preach—I certainly heard him enough as a child—and I know he cherished your company for many reasons. I would never suspect you, Elizabeth, whose fault, if you have any, is sometimes a too direct truthfulness. But I am confused. I'm not exactly sure how to phrase this, but my father . . . well, I imagine he has been an evangelist in tents, with people who can't think very well. . . ."

"You want to know how a person with any brains could buy your father's pitch—lock, stock, and barrel?"

"You're too rough on yourself. My father is not unintelligent."

"But he is a mountain evangelist—or was."

"Yes."

"You can imagine the humiliation people have heaped on me because I played the piano for a man who told toothless farmers to repent. Everyone with any education thinks the way you do. Everyone with a glossy style. I thought that way sometimes. But when you sit down and meditate and finally make a decision, how do you explain it? You wouldn't begin to say you talked with Jesus—how embarrassingly literal! I mean, mountain people might make a decision to give what little money they have to their church, or send food to people in mourning, and they would explain it by saying that they were doing what Jesus told them to do. Even if it was picking up a shotgun—Jesus told me to blow the guy's head off, he said so when I tried to go to bed last night.

"But how do *you* express it, Luke? You reason it out, isn't that it? So what you do is talk to your god Reason and he gives you an answer. Isn't it the same thing? What I mean is that the mountain people are innocents, with a literal way of looking at life—which is as it should be, as hard as it is for the poor to assure themselves of the simple necessities like food and warmth. The rich can acquire style and education. And it is so easy to condescend, which more than anything shelters you from real life. Your father preached that Paul wasn't successful in Athens because his message wasn't reasonable. And so the Greeks denied Paul and kept going with their way of reason, passing it to the Romans and then the Europeans. Remember 'Nothing is true for everyone'? Isn't Gide's relativism the final path of reason? You respect education more than anything. I don't as much, not anymore, not after I've seen your father be in touch with things that reach far beyond reason. Besides, he helped me once, when I was in deep trouble. There were times when I felt he needed me, whatever he was doing. He would disagree, but he needs me now to get him home."

Rather remarkable, I thought, unsure of how to answer her.

I was all the more certain that Will was wrong about the two of them, and I was suddenly reacquainted with my father's power over people. "You seem anxious to get him home."

"Let me ask you this, if you need a reason, Luke," she said. "How sick is Susan?"

"I guess you'll have to ask her."

She smiled enough to acknowledge my point, but only out of a sense of deference: I had a strange feeling she needed to know not simply because she loved her sister and was concerned, but because my answer would affect a series of decisions she had to make, none of which she was going to share with me. I had assumed she was coming home for good. "Your mother wrote that she was going into the hospital for treatment."

"She had her first X-ray yesterday. The doctor told Will that any cancer was never more than fifty-fifty, but that Hodgkin's disease had the highest rate of remission."

"Who's staying with Stearns? Your mother?"

"We tried to persuade Will to move in with Mother for at least three days. Or Mother could sleep in the extra bedroom at the farm—I'm sure Susan would appreciate the help. Will's not very interested, though. He drops Stearns off a lot, but doesn't want the boy to spend the night. And he doesn't want to put Mother out, he says, with the store to take care of. Can you believe Will uses the store as an excuse?"

She didn't answer. She stumbled into worry again, this time about Susan. I didn't bother her on the way back. Though she might once have believed all that she said about the evangelism, she didn't believe it now. Her speech about reason felt like a provocation, but I wasn't offended. The way she looked, the tone of her voice, the burden of Susan added—my heart was giving way, crippled by the silent frustration any sympathetic person feels when he tries to decide how to help a friend drowning in hopelessness. And Elizabeth was drowning—I was certain now. A few raindrops fell, and it was late, but the overcast sky hid the sun; the gray was simply growing darker, toward the night. She didn't ask me until we were back in the car and heading back along the tiny road.

"Will tried to keep you from coming, didn't he?"

"Well . . . when—"

She spoke in a monotone, and not in any way to me. She spoke aloud to herself, and to the car window, as if to make a vow. "He need not worry. But I must see my sister."

"I'm afraid he'll object to that. For some reason he thinks

seeing you will upset her too much—I have no idea why. You probably understand all this more than I do. No one explains. . . ." I stopped, hearing myself ask for sympathy, which I didn't want. Elizabeth did not continue the conversation.

I thought of my mother, who had seen my father again. And now Elizabeth said she had to see Susan, which my mother thought was absolutely necessary and Will believed would be disastrous. Will and Susan, probably my mother and the rest of them, even my father—she had said he'd helped her, and that was probably the most crucial revelation—all of them knew something else, about which I'd be goddamned if I had any idea. I'd gone from that stinking town to other horizons and a far more important life, whether they realized it or not, stuck in their little incestuous cookie jar of a place. I felt suspended on a string between two women: my mother at home, telling me to go off into the mountains and bring the two of them home—I was the only one would could do it; and Elizabeth, sweet Elizabeth, former love who even in her pain could still spin me around her little finger—"I can't tell you very much about what happened in the mountains, Luke, but you can prepare me, if you don't mind, for what's going on at home; there's so much more I need to know." Which was why she had insisted we talk alone.

The darkening road returned past the farms to town, winding beside the lumber mill before the turnoff. The sun was setting, though the overcast still kept it away, stretching itself into night. After the last mill building, the river hugged the road, and from a steepled church across the water came the sound of bells, their ringing resonating off the surface of the still, evening water, lingering in the air. I pulled over to the side of the road. Each bell was endlessly mournful, a tortured ghost traversing a river of hell. I expected the ringing to end at six, guessing the time, but the rings kept on, still resonating— ten, eleven, twelve, thirteen . . . I looked at Elizabeth.

"At dusk on the day a person is buried in this town, they toll the number of years he lived," she answered.

On they tolled—twenty-one, twenty-two, twenty-three . . . I heard myself respond, but as throughout much of our conversation, I was one human being speaking to himself, while the other was merely an accompanying presence. "They sound like they'll never end."

*   *   *

On the veranda the next morning, before she escorted me into the living room, where my father waited, Elizabeth told me she had decided not to go home after all. She had stayed up the night thinking about it, and though she badly wanted to see her sister, she knew she was not welcome. I didn't respond. It was Will, whatever the reason. Then she narrated one episode that she felt I needed to know before my father and I met. After her constraint the day before, I was not going to argue about what she should or should not tell me, even if I was being treated unfairly.

It was a quick story. A tall, redheaded woman from Brevard, a false disciple, Elizabeth said, brought an epileptic boy to my father for healing. When he tried to cure the child, he suffered a stroke. At first Elizabeth thought he was dying, but he survived, and recovered most of his motor skills and his mind, though she couldn't be sure how aware he was of the world when he refused to speak. Elizabeth insisted his silence was his own refusal and not a result of the stroke; in the hospital he had talked enough for the doctor to believe he was fine, even if he had not uttered a sound since the day he rose up from his bed and walked. She was convinced he had taken a vow of silence. She pointed out that in the midst of their long journey through the mountains, he had repeatedly quoted a verse about sitting on the ground and keeping silence. He often took the verses of the Bible quite literally, she informed me, as if I were dumb to who he was. Then she finished her story. Soon after he fell sick, the other people in his ministry abandoned him, she said rather enigmatically. But she stuck with him, humbling herself before her relatives for a place of rest and retreat. Once again she did not adequately explain why she stuck with him. She was determined to get him home—that was all I needed to know—where his family might care for him in his last days. But now she planned to let me take him by myself.

"He tried to heal people?"

"A digression."

"How much do you think this stroke has . . . you make me believe that it really wasn't that serious a stroke. I mean, is he himself healed of this evangelism? Does he really want to go home with us—with me?"

"I don't know what his silence means, Luke."

"And you're sure he doesn't need more medical attention?"

"I'm not sure of anything."

Elizabeth apologized for Mr. and Mrs. Mallery's absence from home again. But it was just as well—she'd probably arranged their departure, to make this father-and-son reunion less awkward. We turned from the entrance hall into a comfortable living room, where the height and breadth of the near wall was satisfied by shelves of leather-bound books. Past a circle of chairs and a couch, a writing table pondered the window overlooking the side yard, and at the far end of the room a fire burned in the fireplace. A few feet from it his chair touched the outer hearth. Turned toward the soft flames, the wild hair of his head bloomed like fallen snow. On his blanket-covered lap, he had spread a newspaper, which caught the shavings from a half-whittled bar of soap he held clumsily with his hurt right hand while cutting with his left. His little sculpture looked something like a bird.

I had imagined meeting my father again. For some reason I had always thought we would come face-to-face once more before he died. In my most common scene, I sat him down across a smooth, sand-colored wooden table and said a few magic words that somehow worked their way into his fanatic brain and converted him. "Yes, you're right, son," he would respond, staring out a nearby window. "I've never seen it that way." He asked forgiveness, as he should; I forgave for the family, and he returned home to humble himself before my mother, who also forgave him, of course, and they were reunited the last years of their lives. There were also some nightmares, I admit, when I stepped up and crushed him like an insect. But as I stood across the room from him now, my expectations seemed foolish—the very idea of conversion, or forgiveness. I pitied him, this one-handed, fallen prophet, reduced to whittling a bar of soap. What in God's name had happened to his hand? Someday I would find out, though I doubted I would ever understand. I also found myself wondering, with a cruel detachment, if he was worth it. What cost to us—emotionally and, yes, financially, too—if I took him home.

With the dark and charged eyes of a cornered runaway whose prayers were left unanswered, he watched me, as if, as I walked across the room, leaned over, and kissed him on the cheek, I betrayed him to the waiting soldiers. I tried to calm his fear by softly cradling his neck in my hand. His stubble had softened into an early beard. His smell—right in the crook of his neck, where as a child I had cried or laughed or simply rested—I remembered as if it were yesterday. But he did not look up. I knew he had not lost his fervor, even in silence. I felt his body remain taut as he struggled to keep looking away, toward the fire, to remind me that whosoever did the will of God, only the same was his brother, the same his son.

"Luke," Elizabeth said, her hands bracing the headpiece of a chair she had strategically positioned opposite the fire, facing my father, "why don't you sit here? Then all three of us can talk." She sat between us to form a semicircle before the mantel.

He had never learned to disguise his anger well. I spotted it, in his tightening eyes and nostrils, the moment she spoke; a woman's voice was a curse on him, a damnation of his soul.

"Luke has come all the way from home," she began, "as Mattie said he would. It was good of him to come. He is willing to take you back so Mattie can make sure you receive the kind of attention you need. I can only say again, this time in the presence of one of your sons, that you can't take care of yourself, Robert, at least for now. No one is trying to force anything on you. I don't want you to think that about me, or about your wife. But there is no alternative, and, besides, I think this is the right decision. What you have done here in the mountains has been the will of God—of this I have no doubt. But the place for you now is home. What has happened has happened, and there's nothing either one of us can do about it. I have tried my best, Robert. I know what I am doing doesn't please you—nothing pleases you. But that's the point—what has happened. . . . Luke, you tell him. Isn't the right place for him in his own home, with his wife, who has said in her letter, Robert, you heard it, that she wants him back?"

I was tired of playing Elizabeth's Egyptian handmaid. I had driven all the way to North Carolina and it was not to genuflect. As she talked, he kept a monklike meditation, his austere head lowered and tilted forward over the soap carving to focus on the rug behind our chairs. His hands turned the bar once or twice, but I don't believe he even heard what she was saying. Was this silence despair? Was it anger? Or was he making the world serve him in his usual self-righteous way? "Speak to my silence," I could hear him say, "find grace in my sight for I possess the mystery." I had no intention of being *his* handmaid either.

"I came here more concerned about Elizabeth than about

you," I said. He seemed to be listening. "You made your decision long ago, and I expect you to endure whatever the consequences for leaving your family behind and taking off on this cockeyed journey to hell. I'll take you home, but only because I know Mother wants me to. I disagree with her; taking care of someone in your condition—whatever it is—will drain her. But you know as well as I do that she does these things."

" 'What I desire is mercy, not sacrifice,' " she said, interrupting. "These are your own words, Robert. Making a sacrifice of yourself has lost its meaning. Mercy is offered. You must have the humility to accept."

"As I was saying, Dad, I came here as much for Susan—Will's wife and Elizabeth's sister—as I did for Mother. Mother is only doing what she thinks she ought to do, and I still think she's wrong. But Susan is worried she might die and she wants to see her sister again before she does. She will not discuss with me all the reasons she must see Elizabeth again, but I respect the wishes of the dying, though I pray she is not. I assume you know more than I do about why Elizabeth left home and ended up on your tramp through the mountains, and more about why Susan insists she come back, but it sounds like there is some mercy involved in that, too. Maybe justice—I admit I am a blind agent. But the dying deserve justice also."

"You know as well as I do, Robert, what's involved, and that I can't—"

"So you see, Dad, I came here first and foremost to fetch Elizabeth. But getting her home seems somehow to be involved with getting you home, which is what Mother wants anyway. So if I need to take you home, too, in order to satisfy the rest, I will, but don't think for a moment that I believe you have any right to be there, or that Mother should kill herself, which she might do, taking care of you, as cranky and insane as you are. This silence bit of yours, for example, is so unnecessary. And, I admit, I feel an obligation to Doug."

There was a glimmer of a smile in his eyes as he turned from us and whittled his bar of soap again. His right forearm bulged from his tight grip on the birdlike figure, but his knife barely moved; he was much too clumsy to carve an artistic figure and he knew it. He tried to be as careful and slow as possible, losing himself, I assumed, in the details of the work. The smile remained there, in his eyes, and for a few moments on the edges of his mouth.

I looked at Elizabeth, who was not, as I expected, angry, but close to tears. Elizabeth had always fought with me. If I crossed her, she reveled in letting me know what a blind rattle-brain I was, that of all the men she had ever known, she kid-ded, I was the most obtuse. Then she would kiss me, the victor. But now she came too easily to tears, like a self-pitying victim. This sense of duty, and only duty, ill suited her. Something had happened between them; I did not want to imagine what their relationship was before; I had come to some safe conclu-sions about the limits—that was all. But I knew there had been a change, a falling off, from faith to duty certainly, from hope to some strange sense of responsibility, in which there was only hopelessness, and perhaps, worst of all, from love to alle-giance. It had not been the kind of love I would imagine, but love nevertheless. I could not believe, though, how strong these leftover ties were—the duty, the responsibility, the alle-giance—even if they were not what either of them wanted. She was trapped in them. And I would take advantage.

She raised her eyes and measured me to the quick. "Be merciful, Luke. You don't understand."

Then she spoke to him. "You will go, will you not?"

"And she will," I said, "or I won't take you."

He set the soap down on his lap and stared at the fire, breaking out of his meditation in a few moments and turning toward me. Ever so slightly he nodded. Yes.

16

On the south side of Newnan, we stopped at a country gas station, where the attendant was watering down a small gasoline spill in his new slip. The slick, iridescent beads on the concrete made me cling all the more tightly to my father's arm as he swiveled his legs out of the back seat and stood up, waiting for his always doubtful balance. Without asking, I planned to escort him to the bathroom. Elizabeth, who for the whole trip kept almost as pure a silence as my father, disappeared into the ladies' room before we shut the car door. She had been less than sanguine, shall we say, about this trip.

It took a long time for the old man to maneuver, his short and tenuous steps like a toddler's, his strength shorn away like Samson's hair, but he was nevertheless in much better condition than I had anticipated. After my first sight of him in the yard at Bryson City, I expected the fallen prophet to finish his days compassed about with his infirmity. But we left the wheelchair in the mountains. Once he decided he would speak again, I thought he might pass for a regular half-senile old man with a charming crop of wild white hair. Hope for the best, I told myself. After his first few steps, he slowly got his teetering momentum going and was able to shuffle toward the bathroom on his own. I waited outside until he was finished. The whole process took about ten minutes, by which time the attendant had long since filled the tank, checked the oil and tires, and polished the windshield. When we returned, Elizabeth was still not back.

I steered my father into the back seat and quickly checked the road one way and then the other. As I scanned the shrubbery past the air pump, I suddenly caught sight of her, huddled in a phone booth at the corner of the lot. At that very moment she was turning to see if she'd been detected. She saw me and hung up.

I had no idea what to do. I had no idea whom she was calling. She got back into the car without speaking and, not knowing what to say, I eased us back onto Route 29 for the final stretch to home. I wanted to question her but didn't know how to begin. Finally I couldn't stand it any longer and I came out with my usual feint.

"Reservations at the Waldorf-Astoria, Elizabeth?"

She didn't answer.

"Must you be so impolite? I thought you had made it crystal clear that what I thought didn't matter anyway, so why hide a stupid telephone call?"

"I was talking to Beelzebub, Luke, if you must know. How's that for an answer? He and I have been in close communication for a few years now. I was asking him about a one-way ticket."

"All I'm concerned about, Elizabeth, is that it passes through home."

This time she answered with that wounded voice. "Oh, yes, it surely does. It surely does."

And that was all. If she chose a wounded deceit, so be it—I had to push on home. The three of us, each for different reasons, maintained an injured silence the rest of the way, which lasted a little over two hours and brought us to West Point at sunset. After we passed shantytown and the high school, I glanced at Elizabeth as we slowly mounted the planks of the State Line Bridge, where there was a direct view of the old Mallery place—the new Schnedel and Schnedel Funeral Home—on the far bank of the Chattahoochee. She must have known Will and Susan had sold it—maybe she even consented—but this was the first time she had seen that great house in its adulterated state.

Admiral Mallery's dock had fallen into ruins. Four pylons rubbed their worn heads out of the water enough to ripple it, but the deck had passed away, in slivers and chunks, downstream. An addition leaned against the garage, to hide the limousines. The staircase still came down the side of the house, majestically, as stood the great oak in the front yard, lording it over the front columns and all the trees along the street, but the bedroom windows on the second floor were painted white, to keep the light of day away from the corpses. The result was that the back of the house was one mammoth white wall, broken on the first floor by two plain windows, like peeled patches of undercoating. About halfway across the bridge, Elizabeth turned toward the house for a moment, without a visible response, and then riveted her eyes on the street ahead. I looked in the rearview mirror. My father was no better. He, too, wasn't interested in Lanett or West Point or Admiral Mallery's home. He was bringing his crippled mind and soul home to his wife, a stranger to his family and this town, and probably to himself.

At the railroad station we turned up Cherry Drive, accelerating to the top of the hill and our house's signpost, the red, rusting Coca-Cola disk on the store's front door. I parked in the tire-worn patch of the side yard. After I turned off the ignition, none of us moved. It was almost dark, but I saw a flash of white in the oleander bush by the screened porch—a mockingbird, male. I opened the driver's door and let it stay, my rear too sore to move. "Well," I said, inanely. "I've done it—at least the first part."

"I'll stay here," Elizabeth said.

"You're welcome to come in. Mother wants to see you."

"It's not my place now. You know that."

I limped around the car, trying to stretch a few muscles, and braced his arm as he stood up. I draped his plaid blanket over my shoulder. He wore a green woolen shirt and the same baggy work pants Mr. Mallery had given him when Elizabeth took him from the hospital. In his pocket were his knife and that whacked-up piece of soap. Elizabeth had packed only one small bag, which he carried. In it was his Bible. After more than a decade away, that was all. He and I plodded toward the screened porch, where I helped him up the steps, glancing back at Elizabeth sitting alone in the darkening car. The final task would be to drag that golden shadow to her sister's bedside. At the door I tapped on the windowpane before we entered.

In the dining room we turned and saw Mother on the end of the couch in the living room, reading a book to Stearns, who perched on a cushion and rested his head on her shoulder, musing on the pictures as she spoke. "It was going to be one of Rabbit's busy days," she read. "As soon as he woke up, he felt important, as if everything depended . . ." The boy realized our silent presence first, suddenly sitting straight up, frightened by the stranger. I wondered if he saw the resemblance between my father and me. Mother slowly lifted her eyes from the page and blinked at us, a little confused, like a sleeper awakened from a dream. "I had the strangest feeling," she said, "when I heard the car pull up—that it was normal, that you'd just been out to town or something for a moment."

He kept his silence, expressionless.

She shut the book and cradled Stearns in her arm. "This man is your grandfather, Stearns. Can you say hello to your granddaddy?" The boy stared at him briefly, puzzled, unable to grant all that bushy white, wild hair a place in his world. He burrowed his head back into the blind safety of his grandmother's neck, sneaking a quick look until he saw we were still watching him, and back he went. She patted him on the back and smiled. "You've been terribly ill," she said. "I thought you'd come in an ambulance, the way that letter sounded."

He cocked his head, like a talking bird, as if to say, "Such is life." But he did not speak.

She didn't try again. I wanted to hurry back to Elizabeth and leave them alone, but as he turned and slowly moved past the dining-room table toward the rear hallway, Mother looked at me in a way that asked me to follow and make sure he was all right and settled before I began my next duty. And perhaps she didn't want to be left alone with him. I considered asking her to check on Elizabeth, but thought better of it. She was whispering in the boy's ear as I followed.

He toured the back of the house and the store. He began in the bedroom, shuffling around the perimeter once, without stopping to study the furniture and the faded wall hangings, or to glance through the back windows at the barn and the garden. I saw that it was almost completely dark by then, and I felt anxious about Elizabeth, waiting alone in the car. But I didn't want to interrupt him yet. The rusted latchkey hung by the bedroom door. He lifted it off the peg to unlock the private entrance to Mother's business. He turned on the lights, gripped the banister, and hobbled down the stairs, stopping on each step with both feet.

At the top of the stairs, a wave of cold air curled around my face. A level lower than the house, which blocked the morning sun, and shaded from the midday heat by the tall pecan trees on the western side, the store was always cool, no matter what time of year, and at this time of year it was cold. The air car-

ried with it the memory of taking a break from work as a
high-school boy, hidden from the store's getting and spending
by climbing to the top step of these stairs and leaning my face
against the cool, plain wall, out of sight of the cash register,
where Mother spent most of her time listening to the customers' gossip and billing them for their meager purchases, credit
at one dollar a week. I hardly knew Elizabeth then. I was
dreaming of a girl named Hunsinger—a Jewish girl my
mother was just as pleased I had too much work to do to pur-
sue. In a few minutes guilt would overtake my dreams and I
would push up and gather myself back to the smokehouse or
stock room in the back, where it was too sweaty, too smelly,
too full of the dust of life to dream.

Dad surprised me as he tottered along examining every single item, each a fascinating discovery, as if he had completely
lost his memory of what a small store was. Here was a cooler
churning with soft drinks; over there were packages of flour
and white bread, the pickled pigs' feet, the lard and cornmeal.
He seemed ready to take out a clipboard and inventory sheet
at any moment. I wondered what Doug would think. And
Mother.

At the front door he turned around and started down the
other aisle until he reached the door to the smokehouse, a tall,
wooden, self-contained shack that the previous owners had
backed up to the main house and nailed on, with a steep tin
roof. A small, straight-backed chair wasted away inside the
door. Four meathooks, once bright as silver, hung from the
crossbeams, rusted black. He pulled the chain of the single
light bulb and wandered in a circle under the meathooks,
kicking up some dirt, and then carefully sat in the chair, which
creaked but held him. By this time I was ready to interrupt
him and return to my more pressing business, my grip on
which, with every passing second, felt increasingly tenuous.

I heard a noise and turned around. My mother and the boy
stood at the top of the stairs, poised like an antique, elevated
statue of Madonna and child. It was a strange picture. She
broke the spell when she set him down by her side, but she
kept her arm cradling his shoulders. The boy's facial features
already declared him a Treadwell for life: his eyes were wide
and drooping, with long, fluttering eyelashes; and though his
young skin wrapped his face as lovingly as the skin of a peach
protected its flesh, it was just as soft, and with time and wear
would begin to sag into the godawful jowls, which on me were

now half-grown, and on the man in the chair were full, animal pouches. And yet for now that soft skin seemed innocent, as all of us once were, boys full of faith and trust and naïveté, certain that this life held in it luscious secrets found deep in the woods.

Mother's hair was grayer, and the visible bones of her body—along her fingers, at her wrist and her collar, above her eyes—were terribly fragile. I passed through my life with her, year after year, assuming she was eternal, as all sons must, and then periodically I saw, like the blind awakened, that she was aging—when Will got married, when I came home from Korea, and now, only a short time later, when I brought the Judas back. She had mothered three generations of Treadwells: the man behind me; myself and my brothers and sister; and now my brother's son. A certain dignity still lived in her kind face and piteous eyes, but I couldn't begin to explain why.

Stearns stepped away from her, surprising me. After this stranger barged into the house, I didn't think he'd leave her touch for days. But Mother's eyes were swelling, startled by something behind me, and for a moment completely unconcerned about her grandson's whereabouts. Stearns started down the stairs, for some reason drawn to whatever mystery it was that worried her. "Luke," she said. Her tone told me to turn around, please, and help the man.

He was leaning back in the chair, his head against the wall, like a man strapped to a rock. He grimaced at the meathooks in the crossbeams, tears bursting like sweat from his eyes. There was nothing else there, only the meathooks. I looked again at the ceiling—nothing. He groaned, his fingers suddenly crooked with fear, fending off the hooks in the wood above him, hooks that were the ripping claws of a hawk, a ravenous hawk, chasing him. And then this boy came to his side. I cannot explain it. When Stearns first saw us, like any other child, he hid. But something within him changed, and gave him courage, or perhaps some great spirit in my father, about to die, before either the man's son or his wife moved, brought that kindred child to him, to wrap his little arms around the old man's neck and give him comfort.

In a few moments we persuaded him to lie in bed. I helped him up the stairs, pulled his shoes off, and covered him like a child with his own blanket, and he soon fell asleep, still dressed in his loose shirt and crumpled pants. Stearns sat with Mother in the frayed wing chair she had toted from their bedroom at the farm and never given up on. "Do you think I should call the doctor?" she asked.

"He's just tired, Mother. He's going to be fine. He actually looks a lot better than he did when I first saw him." Telling her about his perpetual silence could wait. I needed to return to Elizabeth, and Mother couldn't stand too much at once. A few steps toward the hallway, I turned around. "Susan's at home?"

"She's still in the hospital, Luke." She sounded worried. "Day to day, according to the doctor. Will said she'd come home by the weekend."

"When does he pick up Stearns?" I glanced at my watch, then caught myself. But she noticed.

"You never can tell. Usually around nine o'clock. But he stayed out last night." She kept from looking at me by rubbing the boy's back. "Aren't you sleepy, honey?"

He shook his head, his gaze still riveted on the old prophet.

"Well, I'll go on to the hospital then. What room is she in?"

"At the end of the second floor. Is Eliz—"

"Yes."

"Good."

But it wasn't. And it was no one's fault but my own. I should have known. She was gone. Of course she was gone; anyone with a squeak of intelligence would have known she would take off, and this time it wasn't simply to make a furtive telephone call and hurry back undetected. The moment she saw me close the dining-room door, she hoofed it out of the car and into the forgetfulness of the night, her one obligation to her past finally accomplished. She would never see me again, because she didn't love me. "Luke," I said, "she doesn't love you, can't you see? She betrayed you. And she would let her sister meet her fate alone." The flesh-and-blood obligation was not strong enough—something had happened to make the prospect of seeing Susan and Will again too horrifying. She had fulfilled her one duty by bringing the old prophet home—the bond I would expect with the sister actually existed with the old man—and now she could get on with the rest of her life, without us.

I stood by the car, uncertain about what to do in response. I was powerless. And the last person I wanted to see would drive into the yard any moment. In the direction of town the horizon glowed a sickly yellow, the streetlights strung toward Langdale, the security lights in the stores, and the lights in the parking lot at the mill and along the top of the turreted buildings only strong enough to spot the hem of the night sky. But above the hem, darkness quickly folded in upon itself; and then higher, at first a few and then, as I lifted my eyes, hundreds and thousands and suddenly countless stars flecked the late-autumn night. There was no way for a man alone, his neck aching from the angle, to find a bearing. Navigators, yes, and astronomers and simply stargazers might say, "There is Orion, and the sweet Pleiades," and one constellation after another, but for me there was always the darkness in between.

My journey to the mountains had been rather a sham, anyway. For a few days I had been swept away with a missionary purpose—to find the man and the woman and rescue them from themselves. As if I knew enough to save someone else. How authentic. It was easy to forget my own being and take on this crusade when there was nothing else in my life, that same nothingness I was left with beneath the black, inhuman sky. I would go to Susan and tell her: "I tried, Susan. I thought it best to follow instructions, to bring my father home and bring your sister back to you. I failed. That is all. It was rather a sham, though, since I didn't really believe." Then I would get the hell out. Leave my family, this miserable town, maybe this very country, as I'd often promised myself.

I drove to the hospital in a daze, unaware of how fast or slowly I was driving, or what streets I took, even if I was in my hometown. I arrived, parked the car, and walked into the building. Inside the lobby a sudden dizziness forced me to lean against a column until it passed. The glare bothered me; I told myself the glare bothered me—the bright lights and the glass at the receptionist's booth and the white walls broken only by the plaques listing the mayor and city council members and presidents of the construction company and everyone else's aunt and uncle. Sara Barker was the evening receptionist. She wanted to speak to me, but someone asked her a question in time for me to sneak by. As the elevator doors closed, I saw her pick up the telephone, looking my way. All the nurses knew me, of course, nodding as I walked past the second-floor station, the sound of my shoes beating time on the drumskin of a polished floor. Susan's door hung slightly open. I knocked, and waited a second after she answered.

She lay against a mound of pillows in a bed angled head-up at about forty-five degrees, trying her best, it appeared, to find a comfortable position that approximated sitting straight up, as she had done those nights in the rocking chair. I could not believe this was the same person I had said goodbye to four days earlier. The doctor had implied she might go home in three days, but this woman looked like she would never leave that bed again. She wore a white turban, which against the background of white pillows seemed larger than it was and thus gave her head the appearance of an elongated monstrosity. Her face had no more color in it than the pillows and the turban, except around her eyes, where a deathly gray closed in. Her collarbone hung from her neck like a coat hanger, and the sheet she had pulled up to her breasts was barely creased by whatever was left of her body from stomach down. This was in four days, after only one treatment—and there was supposed to be a series of treatments.

I tried my you're-going-to-be-all-right face. Without speaking she watched me walk to the side of the bed and lean over to kiss her. Her cheek was cool and damp.

"Did you see the bird feeder?" She tried to lift her arm and point, but she let it fall, exhausted, and simply rolled her wrist over in the direction of the window. The glass feeder stretched from the screen to the ledge, where someone had anchored it with a wide band of electrical tape. I went for a closer look. The windowframe, when cranked up, swung less than an inch past the lip of the feeder, and then the lower part of the inside screen slid up to rest with its partner so the feeder could be re-filled with sunflower seeds.

"I'm surprised they let you put that thing up."

"Connections."

"Isn't it sort of a health hazard—I mean, with the poop all over the window?"

"This place is a health hazard. The birds aren't."

"I guess you're right." I came back to her side, noticing her necklace. I remembered it, but was surprised she wore it. I hadn't seen the rose leaf since the wedding.

"How do you like my bouffant?"

"It must have been awful."

"Oh, some hair's left, Luke, here and there—at least for a while. I'd take it off, but it would embarrass you, the little curls twisting out of a great bald globe. I can't decide if I feel like I'm wearing the whole world as a head, or if my head and my rear have switched positions."

"What'd the doctor say?"

"Well, if you listen to my husband, he swears I'll be out of here by the weekend, back at the stove cooking him dinner. All the doctor says is 'One day at a time.' It's a chorus with him, 'One day at a time.' I don't think he was very pleased with the results—or at least with how I responded. I guess I should have been stronger, or recovered quicker. But you know how it is with doctors. It's a moral offense if you ask them too many questions."

"Our high priests."

"Yes. And Will is insufferable. He's decided that the way to beat this thing is to take a positive attitude. Can you imagine your brother cheerleading? 'Mind over matter,' he says. The next thing you know he'll be saying I need to pray for healing. . . . I *am* praying, though."

I had no answer. She was praying. And talking very fast, exhausting herself. And I had to tell her sooner or later. My fingers fiddled with the edge of the sheet. I watched them from behind my eyes, knowing they were mine—that they were somehow connected, hand to arm to body to somewhere behind the eyes—but feeling they moved through a faraway land on their own. In a moment, searching through the heartsick whiteness of the sheet, they found the faded black markings of the hospital laundry, an imprint of a few insignificant words in the corner, claiming ownership. I could lay the comings and goings of my family across a bed like a sheet marked in some unforeseen corner. Not that we weren't responsible for the anger of our own individual actions, the ache of love and betrayals from birth to death. On the contrary. But at the same time, we didn't burn that imprint into the sheet—goddammit, we did not—nor did we claim we wanted the words that claimed us, words that we are sometimes told amount to love.

The door slowly swung open. Both of us looked up. Will stood there for a moment, not at all surprised by my presence. I thought I caught him taking a quick, nervous breath before he spoke. "I'm glad to see you two have had some time together." And then, as if nothing were wrong, he said, "We can't thank you enough for . . . Elizabeth."

He stepped into the room, but the door did not fall back into place. It stood there, held by someone behind it. When she followed him in, she glanced at me, but not long enough to establish any meaningful eye contact. Instead she stood with him at the foot of Susan's bed, the two posing as a couple—

husband and sister—attentive to the least of the sick woman's needs.

"Luke and Elizabeth just hoofed it in tonight, not more than an hour or two ago," Will continued, measuring Susan with a face as uncorrupt and sincere as a disciple's and pressing his arm around Elizabeth's shoulder. When he touched her, Elizabeth looked uncomfortable, but like a captive with a gun hidden in the small of her back, she smiled at him. "I don't know if Luke told you. Did he?" He suddenly seemed to regret asking that question. Before either of us could answer, he returned to his rapid chatter.

"They brought my father home, too, believe it or not, for now at least. In one piece. I thought he would finally come home in a coffin. Mother has him back at the house with Stearns—he's probably trying to tell a story to the boy right now. Quite remarkable, isn't it, that the old man would actually come back to Mother after all these years? They're not even the same people. Why, it takes time for you and me to adjust to each other again when I'm gone for only three days, doesn't it? Only time will tell. But Elizabeth here . . ."—he squeezed her shoulder again as he spoke her name—"she is the one. She moved mountains to get the codger home, and even if I thought it was the wrong thing to do, I have to give her credit. It took a lot of get-up-and-go, and pure courage, to write and stay with him and, shoot, to put up with Luke on the way home." He laughed. "But that's for sure, we have to give her credit."

I stared at Elizabeth. "I don't understand."

Will answered for her, but I didn't listen to what he said; I watched her as he spoke. She focused her eyes, the eyes I wanted turned to me, on some safe point slightly above Susan's head, also out of direct contact with her sister. She was hiding. There were only three of us, but that spot on the wall was like a break in a massive, brainless crowd she envisioned gathered around a slave dock where she stood, hung out for inspection, the man next to her telling stories about her running away and her coming home. It was clear she felt our presence as threatening as a mob's, and it was clear she did not want to listen to what the man said, even though she felt enslaved by his power. But in many ways a slave to her myself, I could not understand how Will kept her chained.

"Don't you understand? My goodness, Luke, I was coming to pick up Stearns and who do I find sitting all alone in your car but Elizabeth! Why would a gentleman leave a young lady alone in a car in the middle of the night? Surely you have more sense than that. She told me you were with Mother and the old man, and that she had been waiting a long time, so I took her out and got her some food—how long had it been since you'd eaten?—and then brought her here to see her sister, which is where she wanted to go in the first place."

Susan listened to us, and observed, with a gaze so white and impassive that she seemed hidden behind an alabaster mask. She didn't care about any of the questions that plagued the three of us, her mask a face of distance, of the loss of desire, of sickness unto death. We didn't understand, it said; we were only concerned with petty issues. What did the possession of a woman matter? In a moment she pushed herself further upright in the bed—I fluffed a pillow to help—and then measured her sister, who from the beginning was the only one she was interested in; the men were, for now, unnecessary appendages.

"Well, Elizabeth," she said. "Come here and hug your peaky sister."

Elizabeth broke free from her mesmerized stance, suddenly part of the same conspiracy, turning from my brother and me to the essential business at hand, her sister. She circled the bed, surrendering her purse to the windowsill, and bent over to press her cheek against her sister's. Susan brought her bony arms up to gather her sister to her, their embrace, as Elizabeth gave in, soon growing tight and long-lasting, like lovers, sister suddenly sunk in upon dying sister, abandoning their bodies and separate wills to a hoped-for reconciliation. Elizabeth's face remained buried in the crook of her sister's neck as her back shuddered a few times. Then she sat up and Susan wiped the tears from her face. Elizabeth cradled the golden necklace in her fingers. "Look at this," she said, touching her eyes with the back of her hand. Susan smiled, in a sad-eyed way.

17

Dr. Roberts let Susan go home for a week, but at her next appointment he ordered her back to the hospital and this time refused to say how long he expected her to stay. She took another treatment, ahead of schedule. Afterward Will and Elizabeth rotated nights rooming in. I filled in during the days, standing watch by her bed. Whenever she was awake and felt like talking, we began to exchange secrets about ourselves. At first it was surprising, but soon we felt comfortable with such intimacy.

Both of us, in a way, faced death and needed to confess what all our lives we had kept hidden in our conscience-stricken hearts. It was presumptuous of me to compare my death with her death, and at least once a day, always unexpectedly, she scorned my meddling. "Oh, you don't know, Luke," she said. "The very idea that you could begin to know! You can't even imagine. Why, tell me, are you standing there and not I? Why are you not here in this bed? Answer me that." But the rest of the time some sympathy within her accepted my spiritual disease and responded to my desire to cast away all other concerns and sit by her side, listen, and open myself up. She explained the voice within her, for example. I confessed to my vision of Doug. And these two revelations were only where we began.

Because the treatments completely exhausted her, these sessions were short and, as the weeks into the winter passed and the doctor still kept her in the hospital, more infrequent. Susan found talking increasingly draining, though she tried as long as she could stay conscious. But the bond, perhaps founded because of our separate, wounded lives, nevertheless grew and strengthened us against what other people coming in and out of that door would not confess.

Sometimes, when she was asleep, she crawled like a kicking newborn toward the headboard. One day after she woke up from such a thrashing dream, she told me she'd dreamed she was a soldier bellying under the zing of bullets. She had to keep moving, she said. No matter how shooting the pain, she must not stop. The voice told her, "Don't stop!" But she didn't know where she was going. A fire burned along the shore of a river. The pines were black. Rabbit tails bobbed in every direction. Like a scythe, the blaze cut charred swaths across the forest. From the leaning sycamores above her, flames fell like fiery comets into the water. The roar and crackling maddened her, but she kept moving. The river was burning, too. The surface was covered in black, like oil, and the fire leaped up into black clouds hovering over the holocaust. And she was on fire. The fire scorched a path through her veins, through her sight; every taste and thought and smell—all that was human—passed through the fire toward a great, soundless void.

"Keep moving," the voice said.

She wormed her way on through the flames, without direction. She could not stop, though, and let the fire consume her, for the voice possessed her. A spit of land poked out into the river, and she followed it, on elbows and knees, along the burning sand to the burning water, hoping she could cross over and be made new. But there was no escape. The smell of charred flesh drifted from her legs. She sat back on her haunches and stared into the river as the flames curled into smoke. The blaze and roaring black encircled her face. She was sick and dying. Her hair was gone. Her face was whiter than chalk against a blackboard and the fire inside was killing her. Will didn't care. No one did. She looked beyond her face, behind the fire and smoke, to the clouds and the stars, where would come the sudden angel; the quick beat of her heart's wings would kill her.

She heard the voice again and pivoted toward the mainland. "Keep moving!" But the peninsula was washed over. She was trapped on a small island in the midst of the holocaust, and still the voice demanded she push on, with nowhere to go. She was finished with crossing. The voice joined the din of the forest fire and crescendoed until it hurt to think. She couldn't move, and the pain . . . Then she felt herself breathe out, her soul vanishing into the fiery air, giving up, even her own smell dissolving, ember to ember.

When she woke up from these dreams, I turned her over and fluffed up the pillows behind her back and heavy, awkward head. She liked to wake up in this position—I guess she thought it looked more respectable. She appreciated any attempt to make her appear normal. For a while she stared at a wandering crack in the plaster on the ceiling, and then, when she was ready, turned to me, which was the cue to rub a wet washcloth across her forehead. Both of us hated small talk. I never told her she was going to be all right, and I never woke her from a dream saying, "Now, now, you're fine—it won't be long before you're out of here." I kept silent. Silence was the truth she most desired. Soon she realized where she was, and recognized that silence as our particular bond—no one else in the family responded to her in that way. It brought her back, slowly, simply thinking, and hoping, until her face suddenly, pathetically showed me when she heard the voice again, reminding her of the hopeless treatments, the murderous and vile injections. Then she knew for certain where she was—the treatments were her anchor to reality—and she would tell me about her dream.

After she detailed a dream, if she had the energy she narrated a story of her and Elizabeth's childhood, or Will's proposal, or the Mallerys' deaths. I listened to every syllable. I needed to know. It was an obligation. Sometimes in the middle of a sentence she stopped and stared at the bird feeder expectantly. Only a few came—titmice, wrens, an occasional warbler—but Susan was too weak to sing with them. She seemed disappointed with these pedestrians, wanting another kind of bird, an exotic one, I believe, but she never told me its name. Then she would continue with her story, easing her hands up as she spoke until they touched each other on her stomach, reacquainted. Then she slid them along her body's flat, dry surface toward her eyes, where she witnessed their lover's grasp, crossed and cradling her face, with a promise it would last.

Her story about Will's proposal didn't surprise me. He spent four weeks trying. Even the first time, she said, she suspected

his intentions because he telephoned Monday, a day earlier
than usual, and because, full of hearts-and-flowers, he asked
her to go for a spin to Callaway Gardens on Saturday, when
he usually worked. If he mustered the courage, he would assume a garden setting was the storybook place. Fine with her.
It was about time. She didn't mind if he asked atop the Chambers County dump, but she'd believe his mettle only when he
did. So she said yes, she'd love to go to Callaway Gardens—
what a special opportunity! Susan could not believe that all
these years later, lying sick in bed, she remembered the details
of that day more clearly than what had happened to her in the
hospital the day before, or the day before that. She'd been so
nervous she'd spent an extra hour that Saturday morning getting ready, washing with cold cream and twice powdering her
face to cut its oily shine. The rouge and mascara she kept simple, then blotted her lipstick, donned her favorite navy-blue
outfit with a white blouse, brushed her hair, and was pleased
with every detail in the mirror except what she held in her
hand: a red and white scarf.

She had been shopping Thursday for a purse at Taylor's
and bought the scarf instead. It was a weak moment, when she
gave in to a foolish dream about herself: Isadora Duncan had
worn wild red scarfs; one strangled her on just such a motorcar
trip. Susan hung the scarf around her neck and, with a quick,
dramatic movement, bowed her head and tossed the end of
the scarf around and over her shoulders, offering her profile to
the mirror. For a moment a wild red spirit seized her—a freedom to shout out and laugh and let the whole boring world
cheat itself of life. But just as suddenly she was embarrassed.
Elizabeth could pull it off, but she couldn't. She yanked the
scarf from her neck, folded it, and hid it in the back of a
dresser drawer.

Will had chatted cheerfully during the ride, his best grass-
hopper self, as if he meant to shed his earthbound legs and
leap and sing with debonair wings, all for the love of her. He
held her hand, he stared into her eyes and troubled to find
how many ways he could compliment her beauty. She began
to feel sure he would ask. They picnicked according to plan,
but when they strolled along the paths famous with azaleas, a
silence like the cold, deadening air of winter soon descended
over him. She wasn't surprised, three years into the courtship.
She recognized this silence because by then she knew this I-
will-and-again-I-won't character of his. After he had tele-

phoned Monday night, she'd worried this would happen, that
he couldn't cross over the line into commitment. She tried to
warm him up by talking. She commented on the variety of
color in the azaleas, on the hybrids and the miniatures, and on
the best soil preparation, but all the time he kept silent, distracted by her every word.

"The dogwoods are especially beautiful," she continued,
"don't you think?"

He didn't answer.

"Every spring when I first see them, they remind me of
white Japanese pagodas. What about that? I don't know why
they do—maybe the layered effect. What do they remind you
of, Will?"

"Not much of anything."

So she gave up trying. They chose the less awkward path
that circled out of the woods and led straight to the parking
lot. It passed by the lake. Across the water the afternoon
sun cast bright spangles over the surface, gathering them together into a brilliant yellow curtain pinned to the opposite
shore's tall pine trees. While she walked Susan looked back
at the line of shadows on the near shore. As the sun set, the
shadows would creep across the lake and ease up to the sky
that curtain of light, where it vanished as the tapered charcoal
clouds turned and faced the dying west. She and Will had
never openly discussed the issue. There was no way they
could. He was a man and she a woman; he was to ask and
she consider and that was that. He was too weighed down
to ask, though. His burden was his family, she assumed. But
their suns were setting, and hers sooner, past the acceptable
horizons.

When he telephoned again two nights later, he asked her
back to Callaway Gardens for the next Saturday. "The azaleas
were so gorgeous," he said. "I thought we ought to take advantage." Not detecting any smart-aleck irony in his voice, she
accepted. She allowed that asking took courage for any man,
no matter what the circumstances, since the decision was the
most consequential one in a person's life. Will simply needed
another week to set his family affairs in order and cross his
Rubicon. And—she heard about those kinds of things in a
man's youth—it involved a change in moral behavior. She was
certain, however, that in Will's life, the greater obstacle was
his duty to his mother and his family.

The second Saturday was a repeat of the first. Will wolfed

down her chicken-salad sandwiches, walked with his arm
around her, and told her she was as mysterious as the depths
of the silent woods. But slowly the cold fell over him and he
sulked; then in the car on the way home, he turned and stared
at her with flagrant anger, as if she offended him by her very
presence. She faced the window the rest of the trip and cursed
her spoiled, peacock's tears that welled up and blurred the
passing countryside into a map of her despair. How wrong she
had been! How utterly mistaken! How could she have so misinterpreted his every word?

When he stopped the car in front of the house, Susan said,
"Don't bother," and slammed the door. She heard him drive
away while she hurried up the porch steps. Elizabeth was
sprawled over the swing, reading a book in the afternoon sunlight. "I'd like to know where the Heathcliff in my life is," she
said, looking up. Susan hesitated a second, ready to tell Elizabeth she could have the bastard, but she was too shocked by
the word her mind chose and went on without responding.
She flung open the screen door, set her purse down on the
hallway chair, where it shouldn't be, and pounded up the
stairs, each step ringing from the heel of her shoe. In her room
she undid her belt and tossed it onto the bed. Marching to the
closet door, she opened it and stared into the private darkness
of her clothes. She moved a foot farther, across the threshold,
and let go.

"Goddamn you, Will!"

She swung the door closed and felt suddenly better. She was
proud of herself.

Interrupting herself now, she said to me, "And now I am
dying." She reminded herself more than once. Nothing, not
even her own stories, could distract her very long. I never responded, I waited. Sometimes she completely gave up and fell
asleep. Or she rallied from her despair. This time she continued, saying it took him four Saturdays in a row, all at Callaway Gardens. He had to telephone twice before she
consented a third time, and then she made the mistake of explaining to him that one of the garden's flower-lined walks
was the bridal path. That put him in a funk. She went along
the fourth Saturday with the intention of breaking it off. Three
years without a ring was scandalous. But just as she prepared
to tell him, he said, "I've been trying for a month to ask you to
marry me." She didn't say a word in response. He didn't deserve it. She simply let her head sink into his chest.

* * *

There was a catastrophe in the Atlanta hospital in January—I will explain later. Afterward, in February, a snow flurry paralyzed all movement for twenty-four hours and left the soil and the West Point and Lanett streets and even the sky not a peaceful, pure white, but a dirty black. The next afternoon the three of us—Elizabeth, Will, and I—visited at the same time. We stood around her bed like attendant spirits; I kept out of the way at her feet, while Will and Elizabeth waited on either side. I studied Susan's eyes, and for some reason felt that I could read her thoughts better than at any other time I had held vigil by her bed. I could have been translating my own thoughts into her head, but I felt intimate with her after these weeks, now months, of listening.

She granted us, I believe, the swinish perspective the living can't help—that death, our death, doesn't exist. But this day she wanted us to turn from our normal attitude, which imposed on her our desires, and accept her for who she truly was. The way to do that was to say, "Susan, you are dying. This is who you are. You are a dying person—this is your selfhood." For Will had never allowed her a selfhood. In episode after episode while she was living, he wanted her to play dead; and now while she was dying, he insisted she believe she was living.

Susan groped behind her neck, barely able to move her hands. "What is it?" Elizabeth said, bending over to help. I had seen Elizabeth only occasionally since our return in the fall. I don't think she had spoken a word to my father, and of course he wasn't speaking to anyone. The comfort of a nightly bed and a regular diet had washed away the martyr's shadows in her face and added more substance to her bones. She changed her hairstyle; though she didn't suffer the indignity of an Alabama permanent at Dolly's or Polly's or Ethel's Beauty Salon, she had it shortened to the top of her neck and curled the hair around the part. The blond still turned toward brown, but the progress seemed slightly arrested since she came down from the mountains. Sometimes she joined us for the Wednesday meal at Mother's. Or she passed me by in the corridor, still walking slowly, with her feet close to the ground, on her way to spend the night in Susan's room. She seldom wanted to talk, and when she did, she kept the subject Susan's illness. I honored her wishes.

When Elizabeth realized Susan was fumbling for the clasp

on her necklace, she unfastened it and started to take the heir-loom to Will for safekeeping. Susan weakly lifted her head. "It is for you. . . . Put it on."

Elizabeth frowned. "My goodness, Susan. How can you? Mrs. Mallery gave you this from Mother. Just because you're sick doesn't mean you have to do something stupid."

"I want you to have it."

"But, Susan, Stearns's wife should get this when he marries. It was given to you, and you should keep it in your family."

"You are family, Elizabeth."

"I mean immediate family."

"You are."

Elizabeth glanced at Will, who nodded, asserting the awful conspiracy of the living. Elizabeth circled her neck with the chain and hooked it, and then fingered the rose leaf. "You shouldn't do this, sister."

Susan stared at her a moment, and at Will. "You will," she said quietly. "I know you will, and there's nothing I can do about it. What you don't understand, though, is that I don't care. Neither should you, but you're alive." She turned toward the wall and fell back to sleep.

In March Will finally consented to let Susan come home. Dr. Roberts insisted on a live-in nurse before he discharged Susan and let us take her where she wanted to be, home. Mother asked to keep her and offered to make room for Will and Stearns in the store, but Will pronounced that the farm was her home, thank you, no matter how much she ranted in her deliriums about the town house or the Mallery place. Will still carried Stearns to Mother on his way to work, however. Even though the old man hobbled around making a silent, menacing nuisance of himself, Will was convinced Susan wouldn't rest at all if she knew the boy hopscotched around the house and yard, especially with that old bull she had al-ways hated lurking in the pasture above the hill. And it was unhealthy for a child's spirit keeping him in a house where cancer ate away at his mother. More than once Will warned Mother against any damage his father might inflict on the boy's psyche, saying that spending the day near him, whether or not he was talking, wasn't a healthy situation for his son, just as it hadn't been for Doug and me when the teacher/prophet was in full voice.

Elizabeth and I visited as regularly as before, and still sepa-

rately. But Elizabeth, of course, no longer spent the night; she
had rented a small, mill-owned apartment near the river. On
one of my visits, Susan told me she was going to be alive in
May when her son turned three, and she was, though the doctor had taken me aside six months before and predicted she
would be dead by the new year. Living five more months,
though, didn't appear worth it, birthday or not. She seldom
knew where she was, even after I reminded her that we had
followed her wishes and brought her home. "But I don't see
the mirror," she always said in response. I set an oval mirror
beside her bed, but she shook her head. I even moved a mirror
to the wall, but that wasn't the one, either. "I don't see the
mirror." The phrase haunted me.

Drowned in the sickness for almost every hour of the day
and night, she woke up for short stretches of time—five, ten
minutes, no more than fifteen—suffering to find one more
molecule of energy to perform the bodily function of breathing, in and out, without immense pain. She was unwilling, or
unable, to die. But after Stearns's birthday the strangest
change in fortune—no, in the appearance of fortune—happened: she suddenly gained a new, unearthly strength, rel-
ative to her previous condition; that is, she was able to talk,
to sit up, to once again address the question of dying. It was
a terrible mistake, for Will reacted by returning her to the
hospital, of all places, against her will, as if this final strength
meant renewed hope. I did not take part in the decision. I
don't believe the doctor gave Will any assurance that this
strange, ungodly strength was a conquest of the cancer, but
Will decided he would put her back in and convince her
once again she could live. At least this was how I interpreted his motives. It was June. Her first treatment had been in
September.

For most of a Wednesday afternoon in late June, I waited
by her bed hoping she would wake up, if only for a moment. It
was a futile hope, for if she did wake up, she wouldn't hear
what I said—I had a new and terrible suspicion—and if she
did somehow hear, she wouldn't understand, or care. Reen-
tering the hospital had been a ridiculous mistake. By this time
her body was no more than a skeleton wrapped in a foul-
smelling, bleached bag of rags. What Hodgkin's disease didn't
kill, chemotherapy did. The sore-spotted skin on her face, like
a small white handkerchief the width of her eyes to her lips,
was stretched tight to cover from the top of her head to her

neck, with frayed sockets cut out for the dark eyes, the nose and ears, and the salivaless mouth, which she could no longer hold open. Whenever she slept, an animallike rasp eased out with every breath. The bones around her neck and shoulders and hands reminded me of fragile white fossils wrapped in mummy cloth, which with one touch would disintegrate into dust. She was alive, yes, as well as I could ascertain, but I don't believe she understood whether she was living or dead. I would have preferred poison.

A brief rain fell. Afterward a few robins began to hop around the hospital yard, tugging at worms. The bird feeder hung on the ledge again; it didn't matter that Susan couldn't see as far as the window—Will insisted that simply knowing it was there helped her frame of mind. The tray was almost empty, and since I stood an inch or two inside the glass, the birds that came to feed fluttered quickly away. In a few minutes I planned to leave and have supper at Mother's, and then Stearns and I would return to meet his father and aunt this evening. As I leaned against the window, watching the robins, I found myself remembering a dream Susan had narrated to me earlier in the year. I couldn't date the dream—maybe when she was in the hospital in the winter, or in the spring when she stayed at home. The extended illness wore away my sense of time. I only know her dream stayed with me.

Stearns had grown into a tall, graceful man, she began. He tended an orchard on a small strip of land between a river and a rock—that was the only way she could locate the dream in space, between a river and a rock. He worked with his shirt off, the sweat glistening on his back like the shine on a stallion's muscles, and he kept a red bandanna tied around his forehead. For some reason he never felt the desire to leave the orchard. The boundaries of river and rock satisfied him, so all he might accomplish in life was never more than the proper care of trees—peach, apple, pear, and fig. Susan immediately wanted to shout into the dream, "Put your shirt on, son. Go into the world and don't let your life waste away tending trees! Go to college, start a business, raise a family, but do something worthwhile—time's awastin'!" But in her dream her words sounded foolish, and he didn't listen.

Susan watched as the seasons passed, speeded up like the frames of a movie reel. She had the impression that winter, spring, summer, and fall led toward a single end, unlike the cycles of life, when each season came back to itself. It was winter, and Stearns cut back the peach and apple trees, letting the peach spread out quickly from the trunk into wide branches cut off like a flattop, but keeping the apple a single trunk until the limbs could spread like the arms of a candelabrum. He let the pears grow uncut, and trimmed the figs. Then he scraped for peach borer and dug circular trenches around all the trunks.

Soon robins hopped over the spring grass, and the blossoms ached for the bees and pollen. Susan sensed the significance of this fertilization to her son, again as if the expected fruit was somehow sacred, even an end unto itself, and yet final. Stearns didn't need to spray. He continued to work the ground below the trees, watering the roots; but once the fruit appeared, he seemed satisfied no insects hid within the cores, drilling out pencil-thin holes. A wave of heat broke over Susan as the great days of summer passed into fall and the promise of picking.

At harvest time Stearns worked hard. Each day he tested the fruit and the stems, gathering into wicker baskets the bounty when it was ready to fall. He labored from sunrise to sunset and stored the fruit by the rock, where for some reason nothing rotted. In this orchard making preserves wasn't necessary because the fresh fruit waited for its mysterious purpose, which was not to decay and begin the cycle again.

One night when a multitude of stars hovered brightly overhead, a great call sounded across the orchard. In a language Susan didn't understand, names were proclaimed by some unknown voice. Stearns stood by the living rock and prepared to give away every piece of fruit he had labored to grow, giving the food to a procession crossing over the river, coming to feast. But Susan didn't see to whom the fruit was given. She said she woke up just before she could see.

Now I heard her mumble, interrupting my thoughts. Her hands jerked up involuntarily, like the reflex kick of a newborn's nervous system. Her eyes opened wide, stunned awake by this muscle spasm. I hurried to her side and she looked up at me, but didn't know who I was. All these days by her side and she didn't know who I was. Her eyes searched above me and then fell down my face before they came back to my eyes, trying to focus. She whispered something.

"What is it, Susan?" I leaned over to her mouth.

"Hear him?" I think that was what she said.

"What, dear? What is it you hear, Susan?"

I could taste the stale, metallic sickness in the air, as if her very breath exhaled what ravaged her blood into the world she was leaving behind, finally. She spoke again before she shed that muscle spasm and fell back into the sleep she desperately desired.

"Drink your tea."

I slid a pillow under Susan's suddenly still head and left her asleep again, and after asking the nurse to check on her in a few minutes, hurried to Mother's for her usual Wednesday night family supper. Neither Elizabeth nor Will attended, leaving me to honor Mother's cooking alone, and to check on Stearns for Will, making sure my father wasn't feeding him his poison. I also remembered my obligation to Doug, closely watching my father for him. The old man was better, but keeping silent.

After the meal I helped Mother wash the dishes. From the kitchen window I watched Stearns walk across the dimming yard to a stump by the abandoned pen. He had become an excessively quiet child since his mother reentered the hospital. He pulled a mangled piece of soap from his jeans pocket and began to cut away short yellow shavings to make some kind of figure. Will had been too preoccupied to know how much time the old man and the boy spent together, and thus to forbid it. But day after day, more often in an unnatural and much too still silence for a child his age, the boy was learning to carve strange and obscure shapes, each with some semblance, stretching the imagination, to a human form.

The smokehouse door banged shut and Mother and I watched Dad teeter toward the boy. He walked all the time now, though his sense of balance often failed him. He spent most of his silence in the smokehouse, reading the Bible again, praying or sitting still—I don't know. Every day he took an afternoon nap, and this surplus rest, the silence, and Mother's care and patience restored his health, as did his growing friendship with his little grandson. Neither of them spoke as the old man came to him, but Stearns popped up and smiled, cramming the soap back into his pocket as he fell into eager step at Dad's side. They paraded along the fence until Dad swung open the rusted gate and crouched, waiting low enough so Stearns could mount the rails and climb onto his back, the boy's legs harnessed in the crook of the man's arms, his hands locked around his grandfather's collarbone.

"I've durn run out of breath telling that man not to carry the child on his back," Mother said. She slammed a saucer into the dish rack. "Do you know where they're off to? The railroad station, that's where. Near onto a mile to the station and he piggybacks the boy all the way there and back. His heart won't stand it, I tell you."

"He does seem stronger, though, and happier now, with the boy."

"Susan'd be tickled," she said.

They made their way through Mother's corn patch, the boy's head tilted beside his grandfather's so he could see, and the two of them bobbing above the darkening stalks like two nibbled corks drifting away on the river. At the end of the row, Stearns sat up and let go, his head tossed back and his arms flung out like the wings of a bird. Then they turned and disappeared behind a tall hedge, where a path led along the neighbors' backyards to the railroad tracks. All the time in silence, I thought. We still couldn't believe the silence. Only Stearns accepted it, as if he knew perfectly well why Dad chose to sit alone and not speak. I was too well reminded of how Doug had accepted Dad's extreme behavior.

When we finished the dishes, Mother stood at the sink drying her hands. Over the garden and the trees, the sky was still painted a daytime blue, darkening its tone quickly. I felt suspended in a musical rest, waiting. I poured another cup of coffee for both of us, without asking, and she turned and joined me at the table. The ceiling light threw a yolk-colored haze like a fishnet over us, as we remembered another day before the occupations of the night separated us. We were the go-betweens. We always had been.

Then Mother began talking. "I cannot catch sight of him toting that boy off without remembering the time I carried my sister 'cross the branch at Antioch. It came about 'cause of that Hampton woman my daddy hitched on to. Mama'd been dead about a year. This woman figured we were the wildest, most ill-bred country girls on earth, and Daddy'd do nothing to bridle her. She worked us raw, dawn to dusk. One day after we'd been ironing durn near five hours, she paraded on in and found a wrinkle in a shirt and kicked the door open and pointed to the yard, which was swept clean of grass, of course, back then. She flung Daddy's shirts, one by one, into the air and slammed the door.

"I had had enough, and I convinced my sister Cora to run away with me. We had to cross the branch, and I was knee-deep in the cold water before I reckoned that Cora wasn't there. She was still standing on the shore. She wouldn't cross 'cause she'd get her dress wet. No matter how much I threatened, the only way I could get her in was to carry her on my back, which I did, straight 'cross, though I thought both of us would drown and join Mama in heaven.

"We heard the woman screaming at us just when we made the other side. I can't remember what I shouted back at her, but it came from my very heart, and I knew the risk was worth it when I saw how fierce her anger was. I don't think we stopped running for six hours, way past Antioch, all the way to Grandma and Grandpa King's—my mother's parents. They were shocked when they saw us, but they took us in and Grandma King promised right then and there she'd never let that Hampton woman take us away, not unless she was dead and gone, and maybe not then either. They both knew that Hampton woman wasn't fit to be a mother and what a fool mistake Daddy had made, and Grandpa King told him so the very next morning out in the field in front of the house when he came for us, each man—in-laws—lugging shotguns.

"I remember waiting inside the house, huddled in a chair with Grandma King. She comforted me with a soft, singsong voice like I was a baby and not the same girl who had the gumption to get up the day before and run away. I was more fearful waiting for those two men, in their powwow out in the middle of the field, than I was any other time in the whole episode. I don't think I could have put into words why I was scared, but I sure know now what was wrong: everything a woman does in life can be undone by a man, quicker than the flick of a gunlock. If Grandpa King had decided that we ought to return to my father, then there would have been no other choice but to go—I don't care how many rivers I had bravely crossed. The men decided, no questions asked.

"But for once in my life, a man's decision was the one I wanted. He was a tall, gray-haired, handsome man with a sad face. His eyes turned down from the pity of the whole affair when he came back in and set his gun behind the door, waiting, of course, in his male's royal silence until Grandma King couldn't stand it anymore and demanded that he tell us. 'You and Cora,' he said to me as I gripped my grandmother with a life-or-death hug, 'you're our'n now.' And I never saw my father again."

Mother smiled. We sat at the table in silence. Though it was 1954, because of the strange circumstances of her childhood she was in many ways the last of the frontier women. The grandfather who raised her after she ran away was born only twenty years after Horseshoe Bend, a conquest that supposedly civilized Alabama, but he knew a portion of savagery all his life and he passed on to his favorite granddaughter lessons in how to steel oneself against the brutal and the unexpected. "Self-sufficiency," it's called these days.

I watched her entertain once in a while in Lanett, without a husband, attend the coffees and even a few church socials, imitating the ways of our small-town society, but when I saw her smile so fully after this story, I realized that from the lines etched deep into her wide, flat face came a delight in the hardness, bred on a farm, that demanded a woman accept the droughts and the cholera, tie up her dress to feed the swine, and learn to use everything from bone gristle to leftover clothes. She was not like my father. He would remember such a story sentimentally. She didn't. She relished her courage in crossing the river, but she didn't forget her fear and the injustice of that Hampton woman. Her face was a man's face, with a wide, set chin and weather-worn skin, and her shoulders were broad and forearms muscular. And yet her eyes were still warm.

I stood up and walked to the side window, which overlooked the back of the house and store, the smokehouse, and the old barn at the edge of the garden. Mother didn't move. The evening star perched like a bright diamond in the intensifying blue. Below it the embers of the sun's death burned, resigned to the night's curfew. Another day of my life was gone.

"It's hard to believe your father just let you go like that," I said.

"It's easier for men."

"Why do you say that?"

"It seems obvious to me."

"I guess."

"But that was all for me—that one time. You can spend a lifetime crossing rivers."

I heard footsteps and looked up as the smokehouse door opened. "They're back." Mother pulled the cake plate off the shelf while I waited by the window, reluctant to crank up the car and return the boy to the hospital and his father. I often found myself wishing Susan would die and get it over with.

Other stars came out like voices in a chorus, and I looked up at the night sky and imagined each new one a soul at rest, our souls, gathered up like seeds and given a place in worlds we did not know. There was a longing somewhere out there that touched mine. Ah, but what a stupid, sentimental thought.

Stearns shuffled in alone and sat at the table, his right hand gripping some mysterious object only a boy would value, I guessed. He seemed just as hesitant to leave. It was past seven, though, and Will was expecting us. Stearns had told me once that the hospital lights were too bright and the air smelled and he knew his mother didn't like it there anyway. He was a smart, gawky, shy boy with knobby knees and thin limbs and a wild golden cowlick that stuck up like a porcupine's quills. I wondered how much else he understood. As Mother gave him the piece of pound cake, I said, "What you got in your hand, brother?"

"Luke." Mother frowned. *Brother* was a southernism she could do without.

Stearns shook his head at me. It was a secret. But only secret enough to bring to the kitchen, not "real secret," which was secret enough to hide.

"You want some milk, Stearns?" Mother asked.

"Come on, show me." I sat down beside him.

He waited, distrusting the adult in me, then slowly opened his palm. Two shiny pennies were flattened out, bright as mirrors and twice as large as normal size, now worthless copper shapes. The boy stared at them as though they possessed a mysterious power.

"The railroad tracks?"

"Granddaddy gives me three or four when we go to the station. I put 'em on the tracks so the train smushes 'em. And then all-aboard and the train pulls out and Granddaddy lets me run down to the track where it's warm and these eyes of God are left. . . ."

I smiled. "Slow down, son. What did you call them?"

"The eyes of God—that's what Granddaddy calls 'em."

Mother turned around.

"Stearns?" I said.

"Granddaddy says that if you look deep enough, you can see the face of God."

"He tells you this?"

"Stearns?" Mother sat across the table from him and

stroked his hand. "Now, honey, you're telling us that Granddaddy talks to you when you go to the railroad station?"

He nodded his head yes. "He's not sick, Grandma."

"Well . . ."

"I'm not supposed to tell."

"We won't let on," I said, glancing at Mother.

"We sing and talk all the way. If somebody sees us, he says
he can't talk. He doesn't want me to, neither. You can't speak
to someone who is not a friend. You lose your chance to see
God."

"Everyone else in the neighborhood probably knows except
us," I said.

"What is it you talk about?" Mother asked.

"Nothing."

"Well," I said, "you must talk about something."

"Luke."

"We do," the boy said, almost defiantly, as if he'd been
warned. "He tells me stories."

There was a breaking point between Will and Susan. There
had to be, I believe, because he was living and thus driven by
hope and determination, and she knew she was dying. I've
heard stories of people arresting cancer through a will to live,
and stories of miracles brought about by belief and prayer. I
don't deny these accounts. But all of us die, even those who
were once cured, and sometime or another we must accept it.
After watching Susan, I am convinced the dying person knows
more about her own condition than any doctor, husband, or
friend. It was Susan's self-knowledge, perhaps in an unconscious way, that brought us all, but especially Will, to that
breaking point.

In January—I said I would speak of this—the doctor had
sent her to Atlanta for another treatment. She checked into
Saint Joseph's Hospital to take the chemotherapy and then to
vomit and sleep. Will demanded they obey the doctor's instructions to the letter, convinced that they could "lick this
thing, together." By then Susan had fallen under a hundred
pounds. Her shoulder blades etched a line of despair from her
neck to her arms, whose muscles had sunk into the bones that
hung like broken branches to the hands, where the knob on
her wrist bulged like a cancerous knothole. She was never
comfortable in the hospital bed, turning from side to side

when she could find the energy. But she grew so thin she barely disturbed the sheets. The skin of her face couldn't disguise her skull. A cold gray seeped from her eyes across that flat bone, and I had to fight away the dream that I was smelling a dead person. A few strands of hair curled up from her neck like patches of grass bursting through aging concrete. She wore that white turban and hated it.

I stayed with Will the afternoon of the X-rays. He decided to talk with Susan beforehand, to ease her anxiety and help her prepare for the hated event. When we arrived, they had stretched her out on the rolling bed and draped a sheet over her since she had to leave her bathrobe on the bed and her slippers below. The nurse said she'd be right back, but they always said that. During her first weeks of hospitalization in Langdale, every time I looked in Susan seemed worse, her face colder and more ashen, her skull more defined, and the life of her eyes etherized. But after a certain point, the time of which I didn't mark, she looked the same—as close to death as I could imagine, while still able to speak. I never thought I could grow used to the presence of death.

Today I asked her how she was—Will never did—while he straightened the sheets, folded her robe, and lined up her slippers by the bed.

"The treatment's worse than the disease." She turned toward me as she spoke. I was surprised this time by her look. She wasn't complaining; she was telling the truth.

"Now, Susan, you know this is best," Will said. "Dr. Roberts said it was the best option." He walked to her side and gently set his hand on the sheets where hers lay motionless. "I know how terrible the pain is. I've tried to discuss that with you, and told you that I wish I was in your place. But there is nothing else we can do—except lick this thing. And the only way to lick it is to do what the doctor says and have strength and determination. You've got a young whippersnapper to raise. I need you. We can lick this thing with strong hearts and determined wills."

"I am going to die."

"You don't mean that, honey."

After they took Susan away, we walked down to the coffee shop. We waited at a corner table with a chipped Formica top and stared down at the dreary white cafeteria china, each cup and saucer decorated with a monotonous red circle near the lip. On the wall above us a Coca-Cola clock hummed with an incessant droning that did not help. It was 2:15. They'd haul her back to the room by 3:30, when the night shift came on. The X-rays were late getting started, but they never lasted a long time. As I said, Susan hated them. Will once told me she felt offended by them, as if they intruded not simply on her physical insides but on her personal dignity.

We endured the hour and fifteen minutes in silence. Throughout these endless months at hospitals, my brother and I spent substantial portions of our lives waiting. When it was over I forgot, but while it was happening I began to believe that life and death, sickness and health, creation, redemption, and sanctification were all merely a matter of waiting, either in an uncomfortable gray chair by the bed or hunched over cold coffee half-drunk from an unwashed, depressing cup. The droning, mechanical chorus of time passing hovered over my head. The silence was not only a natural response to circles of the second hand but also our particular problem.

Will spoke once during the time we waited. "She simply refuses to try, Luke. 'I am going to die,' she says. How can she say that? She just can't. But there isn't much I can do if she is going to give up on herself. Is there?"

I stared at him for a moment and shrugged. He poured some spilled coffee from his saucer to his cup, and I looked up at the clock: 3:25. We'd go back in ten minutes, after she was helped into bed and was being watched over by the nurse. I never stayed when she began retching, though I know Will appreciated my presence during the other times—waiting at the hospital, staying with his son, keeping our silence over stale coffee. But he couldn't thank me. He was not a man who could express gratitude: thanking me might create an intimacy he didn't want. We also saw Susan's sickness from different perspectives. I suspected Will suffered from the thought that he had a life separate from her. If she died (he had to admit the possibility), he would live on—with her loss and a terrible guilt at simply being alive, but he would live on. He couldn't admit to me or anyone that he felt such guilt.

When we returned, Susan was not in the room. Will waited in the corner while I pushed the gray chair to the window and stared at the passing traffic of downtown Atlanta. For fifteen minutes we didn't worry, expecting a nurse to cart Susan into the room any moment. But no one appeared. It was 3:50.

"I wonder if the change of shifts slowed them up," I said. "Susan'll love that."

Another thought, of a more ominous nature, squeezed into my mind, but I kept it to myself; Will's imagination didn't need my help. He stood in the doorway and peered in each direction. Then he turned around. "You think I should go down there?"

"I don't know. What time'd they say?"

"They didn't. But it never takes this long."

"Surely they'd come get us if . . ."

Will scoffed at my words with a wave of his hand.

We didn't talk for another ten minutes, until we heard her voice in the distance. I didn't recognize it at first. She was screaming. She was crying at the same time, with a chilling waver in her volume, so that one moment her shrieks echoed through the hall and the next her whimpering sounded like a wounded dog. I couldn't believe it. I had never heard her scream or even shout, but what truly shocked me were the vile, incredible obscenities.

By the time I hurried around the door, Will had his arm on her shoulder. She sat up on the rolling bed, jerking, while she gripped the cover sheet to her naked breasts. A bloody rip split the neck of her nightgown. The turban was unwrapped and hanging like a sheet over her head, and her emaciated legs were bare and scratched red from her calves to her thighs. An orderly rolled her quickly into the room while a nurse helped to guide the bed. Will leaned next to her. Her face was bright red and splotched with tears when she turned and tried to spit on Will. "Get me back, dammit—get me back! Damn, damn, Will! Fuck off!" Then she howled.

I held the door open. As the nurse swiveled the bed through the doorway, the room choked with the rancid smell of urine. Trying to be innocuous against the wall, I didn't dare look at her when she rolled by. The sheet under her was drenched with urine. As the orderly lifted her frail body onto her hospital bed, she yanked up the bathrobe to smother a scream, and then cradled it like a child to her breasts. The grim man wheeled the empty bed by me and the nurse followed him out, mouthing the word "Sedative."

"Don't you let that bitch stick a needle in me, Luke!" Susan shouted. "I am so tired of that needle poking in me I could shit in my pants, too."

I hurried into the bathroom and found two clean towels to toss across the room to Will before I left. I had to wait for him to notice me; he was trying to calm her with a snug grip

around her shoulders, but she slapped him in the chest again
and again until her arms hung limply by her sides. "Don't you
understand, Will? Don't you understand?" He looked up and
caught the towels and began to dry her as I shut the door and
stood outside. She kept shouting, asking if he understood,
while he tended to her like a father to a baby. A few patients—vultures—waited by their rooms. We were simply
spectacles for one another's play, from birth to death. No one
really cared.

I stopped the nurse on the way back. She was unsheathing
the hypodermic. "Are you sure that's necessary?"

"You mind your business, mister, while we do ours."

"She'll fag herself out in a moment."

"Not without this she won't."

Susan lay spent, though, breathless from the struggle and
punished by the shock. Dressed in a clean gown and her robe,
she was stretched out on the bed with her face arched toward
the ceiling, fighting to pull air into the fragile lungs that surely
were soon to die. Her eyes darted like those of a frightened
doe, chased through the woods by ravenous dogs. The nurse
swabbed the crook of her arm with alcohol, and Susan didn't
resist.

"Well, she's fine now, don't you think?" I said. "She doesn't
have to—"

"She needs sleep," the nurse said.

Will's stunned gaze told me he didn't understand what I
was talking about, and by then the nurse had poked the syringe into Susan's arm. Susan rolled her face toward the
woman. "Honey, don't ever die. It's no fun."

"You'll be fine." The nurse motioned me out of the room,
but suddenly with one last push of energy Susan sat up.

"Luke!" She pointed a bony finger at my face, and as she
spoke turned it directly toward Will. "Luke, you tell him!"
Then she lay back down and rolled over into a drugged and
welcome silence, turning her face toward the wall.

On the way to the hospital, Stearns rubbed his two secret
coins as if they were powerful charms uncovered at the railroad tracks. He didn't talk to me, each day growing more
comfortable, I felt, with silence—an unnatural silence. I
wasn't concerned with trying to make him talk. Already after
seven o'clock, I was hurrying; Will would be concerned, not

because he would fear we'd broken down or gotten in a wreck, but because he would assume Dad had done something awful—he couldn't say what, but he would immediately blame the man, as if he were some abstract fate that caused the river Jordan to dry up, the cedars of Lebanon to burn, the very air to rot, and humans to die. Even though Will dropped Stearns off morning after morning, from fall to spring, and now into June, he still never spoke to our father. And of course Dad was speaking to no one but, it appeared, the boy. The ways of my family, for all our rallying around Susan, were still troubled.

I remembered that over my mother's protest, Dad also had given Doug and me pennies for the railroad tracks in Cusseta. I took the two Dad handed me and pocketed one. After the train disfigured the one, I claimed the other was lost as I brandished the flattened copper before him like some trophy I'd won. But Doug had never dreamed of deceiving him; he was solely my father's. Buying extra cheese and crackers from those pennies I hid, or saving up for a pair of shoes, wasn't the crown of glory that collecting the shiny coins was, the coins Stearns now called the eyes of God. In Cusseta Doug had hammered thin holes in some and strung them into a necklace, which he fastened to a nail in the wall by his bed. And now this same coin tutelage with the grandson. It worried me—especially the storytelling.

"Uncle Luke?" The boy leaned over the dashboard to watch the mill parapets rise up into the night sky.

"Yes."

"Is Mama going to heaven?"

"Well, son . . . yes, I believe so. She's going to heaven, whatever heaven is."

"Where people go after they die."

"Yes, that's right."

"Why do those buildings have fences around them?"

"Because the mill is private property. Mr. Lanier and friends don't want anyone to get inside and steal all their valuable stuff."

"It's against the law to steal."

"You're absolutely correct. What a smart boy you are!"

He didn't appreciate what I said, sitting back in his seat and turning his head to the side window, where the park lights passed by like white globes adrift in a calm darkness. Will had prepared Stearns after the episode in Atlanta and was careful

not to share his new hope when he put Susan back into the
Langdale hospital. He came to me, too, afterward, measuring
me with his dark eyes as if I were somehow to blame for what
she had shouted, and said, "You don't have to tell me a goddamn thing." His attitude kept us apart, ironically, since
though he did in the spring what I felt was right—take Susan
home—he acted because he believed Susan had given up and
nothing he could do might save her. I thought she only asked
for a few honest words among us. Will and I have never discussed it.

I did piece together the hospital episode. Susan hated to be
wheeled down to X-ray because the nurses told her to leave
her bathrobe and slippers behind. Even with the sheet draped
over her nightgown, she felt undressed. A young nurse on her
first day of work rolled her to the X-ray door at about 3:15 and
left Susan in the corridor while she went inside. Susan had to
go to the bathroom but was too embarrassed to ask the girl,
and of course without a bathrobe and slippers no one with
Susan's sense of propriety would dare get up and hobble to the
bathroom by herself. I can't be sure what happened to the
nurse. She might have thought the shifts changed earlier than
3:15, or that her only responsibility was to deposit the patient
at X-ray, where the technicians would prepare her and call the
next nurse when they finished. The following day another
nurse whispered that the girl went home early because the first
day of blood, bedpans, vomit, and despair depressed her. I
don't know what to believe. Whatever the reason, the young
nurse didn't come back.

A few nurses and doctors hurried by, but they were busy
and assumed X-ray knew she was waiting outside the door.
The technicians never searched for her. Her plight sounds so
unreasonable—that some people saw her and others did not,
while those that did couldn't bother with what her presence
meant. And so accidents happen. Susan suffered in silence, not
only because of her terrible embarrassment and paralyzing
sense of decorum, but because lying flat and cancerous on a
cart she felt like a helpless, doctored animal. Waiting was one
more indignity medicine said would make her well. And of
course Will had told her to be strong.

The next nurse came on duty at 3:30 and soon noticed Will
and me waiting in Susan's room. She asked another nurse
where Susan was. When the woman said Susan was in her
room, the nurse smelled a foul-up and set off for X-ray. I don't

know if Susan had been forced to drink beforehand, but each minute she lay there the pain from her bladder ran berserk through her body and mind. In other circumstances she might have withstood the pain, but the months of mental suffering waited to rush through any carelessly opened prison gate. When the nurse turned the corner of the hall, the sheets were already wet and stinking. Susan was crying but still in control of her senses until she saw the nurse's face, the face of a person who was witnessing such a personal indignity. The embarrassment cut her loose. She screamed and ripped her nightgown at the neck.

After the episode, Susan kept her face toward the wall. She would not speak to Will, any nurse, or Dr. Roberts. She never resisted a pill or an IV, blood-pressure cuff, bedpan, or any other medical marvel, but at the same time she did nothing to cooperate, turning away from us toward the lifeless wall at the first opportunity. Most of the time she slept, and her condition deteriorated. Believing she had given up hope, Will visited Dr. Roberts and persuaded him to terminate the treatments. Chemotherapy wouldn't cure a person who wanted to die, he argued, and so they might as well save the doctor's time and Will's money and meanwhile please Susan, who obviously couldn't endure the side effects. Will explained the decision to Susan, and the next day Dr. Roberts—for different reasons, I believe—confirmed it. She kept her face toward the wall.

Dr. Roberts let Will bring Stearns to her in Atlanta, thinking she would die in the hospital there. Of course Will had not discussed with Susan the wisdom of a young boy attending his mother's deathbed, but when she saw her son creep fearfully to her side, she smiled with the only yes-saying to life I'd seen from her since the fit. Will let loose of his son's hand and watched with me from the far corner of the room. Stearns wavered a moment and then grabbed her arm and stared, horrified by her sunken, cold face laid over a bony witch's shoulders, and by the loss of spirit he always recognized in her eyes. He had never seen her look at him that way.

"Do I scare you, son?"

"You look all eaten up, Mama."

"I am, Stearns. I'm dying. Do you know what that means? I'm going away, to heaven." The boy was puzzled. "You'll come someday, too, Stearns, but after a long time, when you're old and you've lived a full life."

"You're not old, are you, Mama?"

"No. It just happens like this sometimes."

"Is Granddaddy going, too?"

Susan slowly turned her head on the pillow and looked across the room at Will. She wasn't crying. "Take that, husband," she said.

Stearns climbed into the bed with her, kneeling first, and then he carefully set his head on her fragile shoulder. She was shocked by his courage. Her disbelieving, raw hands rose to gather her son in to her withering breasts, while Will came to her side to ease the boy away.

For a brief spell, as I said, Susan seemed much better at home in her own bed. Will moved the bird feeder to their bedroom window because she said she missed them. She sat up a little. She asked for Stearns. She never claimed she would rise up and walk again, as Will began to believe one more cursed time, but she did regain enough interest in life to have a serious talk with Elizabeth and one with me. I don't know what she said to Elizabeth; I suspect, watching Elizabeth in the days afterward, that it was sharp. With me she began by saying I was "poor Luke, the family do-gooder," and then she gave me directives that I had to promise to follow, as if I didn't wear a heavy enough weight from the dead around my neck.

One, she said: someday send Stearns away to boarding school, even if it means selling the farm. Which led to two: Will should buy a house in town. Three: I should marry Elizabeth. I was embarrassed of course, especially with our history, but Susan said she knew I had always loved her sister, since my "salad days," as she phrased it, and I would understand Elizabeth and take better care of her than any other man she was considering—she said "considering" as if it were a current process. I couldn't look Elizabeth in the eye for a week, for fear Susan had told her, too. But Susan was right. Except that I would never understand Elizabeth.

While she was home, Will and Susan lingered at a point of clarification. He no longer tried to force his way with her, giving up his sermons on the will to live, while she apologized for how she spurned him. I was surprised. He had always insisted she stop cataloging her weight loss, her exhaustion, her lack of appetite, her nausea, but now they discussed her disease and discomfort in detail as he sacrificed his beliefs to understand her and to help. For a while it was an encouraging about-face, but he would still not speak of death itself. Instead, after a day when I didn't come and he was alone with Elizabeth for most of the afternoon, he completely reversed himself again. He decided to send Susan back to the hospital, with Dr. Roberts's permission, explaining that he and the doctor thought she looked so much better, there might be a chance.

I couldn't believe it; neither could Mother. Susan simply closed her eyes. But Elizabeth agreed: she said there was hope. I was not about to ask what her role in the decision was, but my suspicion made me remember a scene I wanted to leave forgotten. It was the time in the winter when Susan gave her the rose-leaf necklace. At first Elizabeth had been horrified—a response that seemed genuine. She even turned away, after she followed directions and put it on, so Susan couldn't see her cry. I caught Will staring across the bed at the younger woman: at Elizabeth, with Susan watching, at the girl Susan wanted me to marry. He saw me looking and turned, his close eyes dark as moonless water.

As Stearns and I drove into the hospital lot, I thought that even death could not deliver us and purify away the dross of our sins. Shutting the car door, I looked into the night sky for its stars, but the lights of the parking lot betrayed them and I was left with only an ill-shaped quicksilver moon. Stearns took my hand as we walked to the lobby, where he sat down without saying a word while I telephoned Susan's room.

"Elizabeth's sick," Will answered. "Might be the flu. I sent her home. Can you take Stearns?"

"Sure."

"Let me come down to see him."

Will looked exhausted. The color in his face had drained away into a pale cast, where dark half-circles seemed smeared under his bloodshot eyes. I felt guilty suspecting him. The wear of Susan's illness and the uncertainty cut time out of his body and mind like a sickle whacking away wheat. He gave me a half-smile, not realizing what I had been thinking about him, as he sat down next to Stearns.

The boy began to cry. His face swelled up red and distended as his mouth turned down. His wheezing sounded tubercular and then wet, his very ribs grating against each other as his woe rose like waves from within him. I was shocked. He'd given no sign of distress in the car, but suddenly he exploded with that child's all-out blubbering sense of injury, the sobs wrenching him from the sea depths of his lungs. Will looked at me and I shrugged, at a loss to understand. Then Stearns blurted out, "I wanna see Mama!"

Will put his arm around the boy's shoulders and waited. The crying wouldn't abate. He shook the child for a second. "Come on now, son."

It was worse. "I wanna see Mama!"

"She's asleep, Stearns. You can see her tomorrow, but you'll just disturb her tonight. You don't want to do that, do you?"

Stearns stopped for a second to look at his father, thinking about his words, and then blubbered again.

"If you had come earlier, son . . . You can't stay out running around with your granddaddy and expect to get here before Mama falls asleep."

I set my hand on the boy's knee. "I'll take good care of you tonight, Stearns, and we'll come back first thing in the morning to see her."

"Don't leave me, Daddy!" he cried, and threw his arms around Will's neck. Will leaned over and held him, patting him on the back as the boy wept. "Don't leave me, Daddy. Please don't. Oh, Daddy, please don't go away tonight."

Will looked up from the boy's embrace, startled.

"You'd better take him tonight," I said.

"They wouldn't let him stay here?"

"No."

Will sat the boy straight and wiped his face with a handkerchief. The boy's breathing still sounded like rippling water, though more regular. His face glowed red. "I'll take you home, son. Mother would want that. Tomorrow you'll feel much better."

"I'll stay upstairs," I offered.

Will thought for a moment. "I don't think so. She's so finicky, you know, even now. She'd be embarrassed in the morning." He folded his handkerchief and pocketed it. "I'm sure she'd understand. She'd insist, really. I'll call up there and tell 'em I'll be back first thing in the morning."

I held the boy's hand as Will telephoned from the front desk. Stearns stared across the room at his father. Had we finally quieted ourselves? I wondered. Had we finally quieted ourselves like this weaned child? For surely our souls were even as a weaned child. Let Israel hope in the Lord. I turned to the boy. "What did you and Granddaddy talk about tonight, Stearns?"

He looked at me, guarded in his silence, and turned away.

When Will returned they hurried to go home. Will spoke as they went. "They said they'd look in on her every hour."

"Call me in the morning."

But he didn't answer. He and Stearns, hand in hand, set off out the door, for home. I stood for a moment and watched them, and then headed for my own car.

Early in the morning Susan died.

18

*O*n the third morning, we gathered in Mother's living room before the procession to Schnedel and Schnedel's Funeral Home. I sat in a corner chair apart from the others so I wouldn't have to talk, and waited for Mother to enter and ask all good Baptists and Methodists to hold hands in a circle and recite the Lord's Prayer. Then we'd go. Will had decided that Mother's home would be the house of mourning. The choice was right. Susan lived as a part of the Treadwell family, almost as much a daughter and sister to us as wife and mother to Will and Stearns. Other than Will and Stearns, she was survived by only one immediate family member, her sister, and she would have preferred everyone come to the home place anyway—all of us agreed she would. Besides, the farmhouse lay too far out of town, and was painful for Will, and Elizabeth's apartment wouldn't have sufficed. It was simply easier to accept friends of the family at the home everyone in east Alabama identified with, and Mother, as always, gladly shouldered the burden, our strength and staff in the valley of bones.

I looked around the crowded room and thought that most of the cousins and friends dutifully in attendance hardly knew us, not to speak of Susan. Every face had a name, which I knew, of course, as each knew mine, but some of them I hadn't seen since Doug's funeral gathering. For two days these

strangers graciously filled the house with food and condo-
lence, phrases like "I'm so sorry" and "Surely she's better off
now" and "It is the will of God," each spoken behind some
name and matching face. Mother knew every one. So did Will.
Still, these were strangers to the soul. Mother coordinated all
of them in and about the house, our Martha to Christ, and the
night before at the funeral home, with a stiff upper lip. Will
too accepted these dutiful vultures, unconscious of death, as
they filed by to see his bride raped by cancer, the little bird
painted to imitate life. How well we had done, how well and
proper, because of Will and his standing in the community,
and because of Mother; so much better than the funeral years
ago, Doug dead young, too, and Dad, in heathen rage, beset
behind and before.

The old mountain prophet was even with us, standing
directly across the room from me, waiting to play his part in
the funeral. I don't mean to imply his grief wasn't genuine—
the curse was that he was too genuine—but he appeared unlike himself. He kept his hands behind his back and he
squeezed into the corner by the window, meek as a lamb, his
Amos's rage at social blasphemies passed through the tense air
to me. We had not spoken to him about Stearns's revelation,
but as usual in his life he quit the sham at about the time everyone discovered it. After Susan's death he said one or two
words to us in passing, and neither Mother nor I acted surprised, sure that calling attention to a broken vow would whip
him with chains of guilt. He became remarkably helpful to
Mother, washing dishes with his one good hand, picking up
after guests, and running errands, and he was always watchful
of Stearns in his grief. It seemed such an act to me. Most of the
cousins still didn't come near him, of course, his lifelong reputation keeping him an outcast. So earlier in the morning I was
surprised when one stranger, some third cousin from Wood-
land, did slide through the crowd and speak to him.

"She's better off now," the man said, "don't you think?"

There was no rage in Dad's answer. "She lies in sweet-
smelling arms."

"I'm sorry?"

"A thousand years in thy sight are but as yesterday when it
is past."

"Yes, the Psalmist, right? I hear she was in terrible pain."

"Do we pass judgment on human suffering?"

The man shook his head.

Will still did not speak to our father, even though they kept close company these three days. I suspected he never would. He waited in the back bedroom, preparing himself, as was proper. When I speak of his propriety, I don't mean to question his grief either. No, Will was dumbstruck. No matter how ready he had believed himself to be, the actual loss—she was thirty-two—still wrecked him. But Will hung on to social convention, at all times and in all places, not only because he believed we have a human obligation to maintain civilized behavior, but because he knew himself well enough to grasp his only survival in convention's iron gate, banging back and forth in the face of screaming, dark winds of grief and guilt. Every time in his life he'd let go, he'd regretted it. So he would walk through the funeral with a set face, sad like a toy soldier's, wooden and clad with honor.

Elizabeth was with him. Susan's death thrust the two of them closer together as the primary mourners of the deceased, the husband and the sister. I didn't know of any other relationship. They had not discussed the past in front of me, and I can't be certain they intended to if the circumstances had been more appropriate. Well, it was none of Will's self-righteous business what Elizabeth had done in the mountains—he didn't own her—but I think Elizabeth felt some self-sacrificing, perverse need to make an account. To Will, of all people. She looked like she did. The day after her conversation with Susan, Elizabeth had begun to fall sick, her face soon covered by a pale yellow mask out of Greek tragedy, her eyes empty, her mouth in constant sorrow, as if she bore some unspeakable secret burden. I was convinced, of course, that she had nothing to hide about the mountains. Religion will make a mess of you—it was as simple as that. After Susan was buried, Elizabeth probably would find the time and place to call a reckoning with Will, and then slowly turn back to me, I prayed, with whom she belonged. I had not given up on her. No matter how many times I had warned myself, I still loved her, and I always would.

And then there was Stearns. I believe he was with them also. The day after his mother died, I helped care for him, when people began to call. Dad wanted to take my place, but he concentrated on quietly tending to Mother's work. He didn't think spending all his time with the boy was wise, fully aware of his eldest son's feelings, this eldest who had cursed his running away, scorned his ministry, and not spoken to him since the homecoming. Stearns met a few of the callers that first day, but Will didn't insist. Dressed in Sunday clothes, the boy couldn't do what he wanted to do—lounge on his favorite stump in the yard—but later in the day we did sneak back to Mother's bedroom and sit on the stairs down to the store. Little was said. He perched four of his squashed coins on the step below us while he carved two smooth oak sticks, careful that the shavings fell between his pantlegs onto the newspaper he'd brought. He carved a cross. There was nothing else to make, really. I found some twine, cut it, and anchored the sticks into a tight, final knot. That was all. It was simply a wooden cross, a little slipshod and poor, maybe the kind a medieval peasant carried. I don't know if he understood.

At the appointed time, Mother escorted the three of them into the living room. Everyone who wasn't standing stood. Mother held Stearns's hand while Elizabeth and Will, beginning in my father's corner, with their backs to him, acknowledged each funeral guest with a nod, making their way through the crowd to me. Mother and Stearns followed. I leaned over and kissed the pale, cool cheeks of my sister-inlaw's sister, her graying eyes blank and glassy as she watched me descend to her. I laid my hand on Will's shoulder. Halfway across the room, Mother stopped and whispered in Stearns's ear. He kept one hand in his pocket. Then she bowed her head as a sign to the gathered Christians.

I searched for my father. He looked confused as the lady next to him took his good hand. I felt like screaming at him, "Quit the shamming, Father, it's time!" I had always relied on him to cut through moments like this. He might embarrass me, but I was beginning to think sentiment was worse. It was time for him to cast aside that woman's hand and chastise such a false circle of sinners. "Stop it, hypocrites." That was it; I knew the words. "Hypocrites!" he should shout. "Woe to them that are at ease in Zion!"

But nothing. My father gave me nothing—no righteous zeal, no angry speech, no prophecy. These last few years I had struggled to know what authenticity was, but faced with the stinking hypocrisy of this solemn assembly, I did not object. No, I turned to the old man, as if he were the only authentic soul in my life. I had relied on his truthfulness, but this day he kept quiet and still, smiled at his two neighbors in the prayer circle, and bowed his head with them. I didn't understand. We said the Lord's Prayer and went out.

* * *

We could fritter our lifetimes away worrying about ironies. A funeral, however, encourages a man to think on them. For example, whether my father or mother won the argument that marched us to Cusseta, and all that came of that schoolhouse, has in retrospect become a question of life or death. Or if Lanett High School didn't offer typing, which meant I would not have learned the skill, which meant the Chinese bullet in my neighbor might just as well have found my skull. And then, the Mallery mansion, once full of life, was sold to Mr. Schnedel, who converted it into a funeral home, where Susan, who once combed the hair away from her neck and in those very rooms sent the heart of a young man soaring, lay in state. There were a thousand more. We sow the wind as it is, without having to decide if coincidence means anything, if beyond the whirlwind of happenstance we reap a divine will. But I, for one, can't keep from wondering.

As we gathered in the side room of the funeral parlor, I could not take my eyes off a thin, ornate mirror on the wall by the door. Right by the door, so no one could miss it when he entered the other room to view the corpse. About two feet long, half a foot wide, framed with dark wood and crowned by a finial cut like a setting sun in the clouds. Why was that mirror there? I didn't think funeral homes kept mirrors. Had they never moved it? Swirling day after day down the stairs from her bedroom, a lively, on-the-wing debutante, how many gay and joyous times did Susan pass by this mirror before she made her entrance to the parlor, where she greeted friends and gentlemen callers, one of whom was now her widower? Surely she took one last look at the mirror, to pretty herself before she burst in. Was there ever a passing thought of death? Did she imagine that we would slouch by that mirror into the parlor and view her body for the last time? At the age of thirty-two? The wall still boasted the mirror after all these years, as if it waited for the one time I would pass by, seeing my own face and hoping I could forget who I was.

I wasn't sure what the procedure was—no one was—but correct behavior was a vital issue. Dr. Smith finally stepped to the center of the room and asked us to listen to God's Word. The light through the window sparkled like swordplay on the Masonic pin on his lapel, and his bifocals reflected a gold medallion sun. He was well dressed in a tailored three-piece, his wet hair curled carefully over his ears. He read the passage in John with the verse beginning "In my Father's house are

many mansions," and as he finished he began to pray, with no
pause between, so few of us had hands to hold.

At the "amen" Mr. Schnedel opened the door to the parlor
and stood aside like an attendant in a play, dressed in black
with a white corsage. Rows of empty chairs filled the room. I
realized then what the next move was: as family, we were priv-
ileged to view the body in peace before the others arrived for a
service. We filed in, each of us fated to pass that mirror, and
then stood around, whispering. No one had the courage to
begin the procession, assuming that we were supposed to be
waiting to pass by the body. Mr. Schnedel didn't tell us. There
was a long, embarrassing pause during which none of us
moved, until, in his ill-fitted jacket and worn pants, my father
quietly circled some chairs and stopped at the foot of the coffin to pay last respects to his son's wife. The rest of us, relieved,
followed him.

All her life Susan had been a dark woman. In some not too
distant past, her Anglo-Saxon heritage knew the flutter of
dark blood, which gave her skin a gloriously warm tone, that
beauty made all the more Mediterranean by dark hair and
brown eyes. The sunny summer's day of her funeral was her
favorite kind of day, when like a Greek beauty she could stroll
eternally in the sun without fear, hour after hour bend in her
garden and watch the zigzag of the phoebes across the yard.
When I stood by her coffin, I saw that her body had finally,
after months of illness, lost every brushstroke of its rich color.
Not just the flush of life, from pumping blood, but her natural
skin color, since the disease completely reversed the makeup
of her cells. She lay slightly to the side, begging to get out, her
crooked frame laid to rest on frills of a pillow and a white lace
drop, under an overlay of pink carnations. The white, cakey
cast seemed painted on her emaciated face. The force of gravity widened even its nothingness, so that a few awkward lines
like the parts of a talking dummy's face crossed her white face
at mouth, chin, and eyes. Her wig fit snugly from her forehead
back, but at the neck lay neglected and flat against the pillow.

I walked away and lingered by the door to the side room,
where all of us would wait with Dr. Smith as the parlor filled
up for the service. Past the head of the coffin, in a corner, my
father stood alone, next to the flower arrangements that
turned with the grand sweep of the Mallerys' bay window.
From where he waited he could gaze, absentmindedly, at the
side yard dark with limousines and at the distant oaks that

shaded the edge of the river and perhaps at the peace that lay beyond, past Egypt and the Jordan and the weeping Euphrates. Sunlight flickered over his shoulders. On the opposite side of the coffin from Dad, Will and Elizabeth waited to pay their respects last, as was proper. They stood with a stiff formality, like high priests in black, with their eyes riveted on a middle distance across the room.

Mr. Schnedel brought a platform for Stearns. Will had decided that Stearns was man enough to view the body, but it was Mother who shepherded the child to the casket. Will did not want to lose control. Each passing minute had so far been kept under control, and that was as it should be. After the boy stepped up on the platform, he stood absolutely still, unsure of his balance, as he stared down at the body. Mother spoke to him in a steady, comforting tone, the sound of her voice far more crucial to him than the meaning of her words. He did not reach in and touch her. I was scared he might. He didn't cry. He kept silent and still, and a wave of relief passed over all of us, that the boy was well behaved and didn't make us worry about a scene. At the end he turned toward Mother with a puzzled look.

Then he broke from her. He brushed Mother's hand aside—I heard a slap—and ran full force not toward his father but his grandfather, at the last stride leaping into the old man. We heard only the initial burst of his scream before he buried his face in Dad's stomach. Then the crying was muffled, like faraway nighttime waves. Mother took a few steps toward them and stopped, astonished. All of us were shocked. It was such a sudden change, and such sudden speed. The day was slow and mournful and under control, and now all of us were jolted. The funeral was out of joint.

My father held the boy, his arms bracing the back of the child's neck as Stearns's lungs fluttered like a sparrow's heartbeat. He bent over, keeping the boy tight, his warm body a good comfort against sorrow. After a while he pressed his face to the child's, but he didn't speak, letting Stearns sob and sob, unable to stop. Dad was patient and kind and surely in no mood to whisk the boy away, both of them unashamed of grief, and no one dared interrupt, no matter how embarrassed. Finally, his breathing eased up. Then Dad whispered in his ear. No one heard what he said, but all of us prayed he'd continue to calm down. The boy stopped crying. Dad rested his arms on Stearns's shoulders as the child gazed up at him, at first disbelieving, but then simply to confirm that his grandfather had said what he thought he'd said. My father nodded, yes, Stearns, and then spoke: "Go to your father now."

On command Stearns turned and walked back by Mother and the coffin. He slowed a step as he neared Will and Elizabeth, but he kept on, following directions, until he squeezed his father's hand and moved between them. As he took Will's hand, he pressed it against his cheek and kissed it, and then stood tightly against his father's side, never to leave Will again.

Will watched his son abandon his grandfather and come to him, without moving an inch himself, in disbelief over the sudden turnabout. I'm not sure he realized why the boy had taken his hand, but he smiled at his son as Stearns found him. It was a brief smile. He did not look across the room to Dad then. It wasn't a refusal, though. No, he looked up and away, toward the window, hiding his face from me as he pressed the back of his other hand hard into his quivering eye.

After the service was over, we made our way down the back stairs to the waiting limousines. It was such a relief to go outside. I heard a mockingbird sing and the crunch of gravel under my feet, and the trees and the wind over the river smelled rich and keen, a balm to my soul after the hothouse flowers and mortuary perfume. It was noon. The day was beginning to turn sultry, with high clouds closing in. The black limos reflected the glittering incandescence in the summer air. Will stopped me on the way to the second car. His mouth twitched as he spoke. "Come with us." I nodded, turning toward Mother as I followed. She had seen and understood. I didn't know why he wanted me with Elizabeth, Stearns, and him, but I felt a bond somehow, unworded, blood to blood. Mr. Schnedel and his assistants rolled the finally closed coffin to the hearse in front of us. The cart was level with the hearse's floor, so sliding the casket in was quickly accomplished. I turned my head. Will sat behind me, lost in a silence, his head leaning against the window pillar. Stearns held his hand. In the corner Elizabeth watched the hearse with her deadened blue eyes. It turned through the gravel and led us up the embankment to the street, where the procession waited.

Many of the stores in town were closed for the funeral. We turned onto Main at the corner of State, where Mr. Schnedel's furniture store had cashed in Will's labor since he was a young man. A wreath hung on the door. Elizabeth simply stared, without changing her expression. A strange, rather deadly beauty quickened her, dressed in black, a beauty unlike her former innocent and skyward spirit. Though her face was pale as bleached clay, her black dress and hat made her look darkly romantic, like a poisonous creature soon to die. There in the distance, over silk-smooth black, lay those blue eyes, as fine as crystal. She was earthbound now, grief-stricken but still deadly to sensibilities like mine.

I watched the road, confused. Perhaps it was better, I thought, simply to watch the road. At the railroad station we waited to turn onto Cherry Drive. In the distance, off to the right, Lanett's circle boasted a new Methodist church building, a simple, one-story structure that replaced the decrepit, turn-of-the-century Greek Revival building I had loved, imagining when I passed that its two inset columns looked like the legs of a sphinx burning in the desert sun. Will was a deacon there and the chairman of the Building and Grounds Committee, responsible for the "contemporary structure," as they called the ill-made, boring sight. Since Elizabeth had run away, he had seldom attended. A few of the other men in the church visited him and tried to persuade him to be a regular again. He always promised, said he'd just been lazy, and then came even less often. Susan attended whatever the building, with or without Will, to sit in the same pew and pray for wayward Treadwells.

The procession wound past Mother's house, where our relatives' cars were parked. I hoped they would leave immediately afterward. But they wouldn't, I knew they wouldn't; some would spend the rest of the day feasting on the food and catching up, until someone else died, or the reunion came. The persimmon tree grew heavy, and in the backyard Mother's corn already stood head-high. The awning shaded the front porch, which we seldom used, but the screened porch on the side sat empty, which was a rare sight indeed. When Susan first married into our family, in those summer days when we seemed happy, she sat on that same porch with Mother and Elizabeth after they finished Wednesday's supper, cooling themselves in the evening air while Will and I smoked under that persimmon tree. Elizabeth was part of our family, too, that summer before I went to war.

I wondered about her then and the rest of the way to the graveyard, glancing back every few minutes to see if I could sense in her face what she was thinking. I wanted to know what each familiar place meant to her, because I felt the commonplace resonate with a meaning far more significant than the literal. It began back at the Mallery house, with that mirror hanging on the wall. A great bay window overlooked the bank of the river, where two dark pilons marked the old Mallery dock. Across the water an oak, with a perfect crown, still lorded it over a small patch of dancing grass. These were the places in her life and in mine, and our human spirits in this time wanted to give them more than ever before, and believe. I asked myself if Elizabeth felt the same way I did. Did she, too, feel that in the mirror and the window, the dock, the river, and the oak—in all of the great mansion where they grew up—there lived both a spirit of their lives and of their deaths, at the same time, past, present, and future? When they were girls there was a death in their lives, unbeknown to them, and now, in this death, was there a life we couldn't know?

This procession, too, Elizabeth, I said to myself, was not literal. It was a great snake. Believe me, a great and awesome snake. It stretched from this mansion to the graveyard, birth to death, and back again, where there was a place prepared. I knew in my heart she saw the snake as I did, the hearse the beady head of forked death, and each successive pair of headlights behind us the glittering scales winding through our innocent town, from Fifth Street to Main, our Cherry to the gravesite. The slime of the belly soon left a trail over all of us—there was no escape. The rattle swung like a cord back and forth to touch us, the viper's path binding the quick and the dead.

As soon as we rose up over the crest of the hill, I saw the oak in the graveyard. It stood by itself like the oak at the river, a lone and majestic monarch. Almost all of the cemetery lay treeless, the rows of headstones interrupted only by a few monuments and mausoleums, including a tiny brick house where a three-year-old was buried beneath her dolls. Somehow the oak helped me forget the dollhouse. With a crown exactly wide enough and rounded enough for its height, the tree overlooked the Treadwell plot Dad had purchased when Doug died. It seemed only appropriate that Doug be buried close by the single tree in the place. It may have reminded the others of Doug sitting below the tree, reading. I didn't want to think of that. For me the branches cut away some of the awful indifference of the eastern sky—that was all.

The hearse wound through the cemetery's avenues until it

stopped in a line with the oak, the grave, and the road. The pile of clay was discreetly covered behind a green and white tent. We waited a moment until the casket was removed, and then the driver jumped out to open Elizabeth's door. None of us had spoken. As I opened mine, I heard the sudden slamming of door after door, like gunfire along the line of cars. It startled me—for a moment I thought I was in Korea, and my heart beat against my ribs.

The sun blinded me, and as I stood up a wave of heat came from underneath the engine and off the bright chrome. I thought I might faint. Surely I would see Doug here. I was panicking. I didn't want to see him, not now. I wasn't ready to endure that sight. But what would keep him from sitting beneath that very tree and watching, looking up from his Bible with that questioning look on his face. Luke? Luke? I tried to calm myself, holding my breath for a moment and then letting it ease out of my lungs as slowly as I could. I didn't move until my balance was sure.

The three of them waited for me on the grass. As I approached, Elizabeth's blue eyes measured me from a depth I had never seen, and she took my hand, a touch that would haunt me in my sleep. Then I felt the boy take the other, and the four of us, hand in hand, went on, toward the land of the forefathers, and the place where my brother was buried.

The minister waited for the family to be seated and the crowd to gather. He spoke of comforting all that mourn, but I didn't listen, knowing I'd wake up and hear him when he recited "ashes to ashes, dust to dust." I couldn't sit comfortably on a folding chair in the middle of a sunbaked day and concentrate, but certain phrases in a man's life, like "ashes to ashes, dust to dust," have the power to cut through any daydreaming. "Under the aspect of eternity," "Nothing is true for everyone," "the forgetting of being"—my baggage.

To the left of the tent a robin hopped across the grass. He stopped by a slab and pecked once and again until he yanked out of the earth a long, shiny worm. The light sparkled off the newer, slick stones, and a dead stillness in the air weighed down over the cemetery. My heart had calmed down, but a nervous feeling jumped in my stomach. So I told myself to feel my lungs breathe again. It was a slow, full breath. I was only flesh, I said to myself, a breath that passeth away and cometh not again. I remembered the psalm and said it again: passeth away and cometh not again; passeth away and cometh not again. What else did a man need to say?

". . . and we commit her body to the ground," he said. I was listening, I realized. "Earth to earth, ashes to ashes, dust to dust. The Lord bless her and keep her, the Lord make His face to shine upon her and be gracious unto her, the Lord lift His countenance upon her and give her peace. Amen."

Dr. Smith made his way along the front row of seats. He shook hands and spoke with Will, and then hugged the necks of Stearns and Elizabeth. "The Lord be with you, Luke," he said to me. "We need to see you in church." He continued to Mother and the old man and beyond. We stood up and began to mill around; the more brazen of the crowd—the well-meaning ones, Mother said—came forth to talk to Will and the rest of us. A cousin from Wedowee, whose name I had forgotten, said we needed to see more of each other, that this was the wrong occasion, but it was time to get together, and why didn't I show up for Homecoming? On Mother's Day, ya know, and the second Sunday in October. Dinner on the grounds, ya can't beat that, 'spec'ly for a bach'lor.

Yes, yes, I said, surely and thank you and I will, waiting all the time for Will to lead us back to the limousine so we could speed away. How I hated cousins!

I didn't understand until Mother told me. "Will wants to wait here," she said. "Elizabeth and I will take the boy."

"I'll stay."

It was most unlike her to look to kiss me, her affections seldom public. But I leaned over in response as she kissed my cheek and then held the back of my neck, keeping me for her whispered words: "I believe Robert, too."

I nodded. She didn't need to tell me more. The old man lingered nearby, staying out of everyone's path, but he did say something to Mother as he helped her into the car. She stared at him a moment with stern eyes, and got in alone. Will stood by Mr. Schnedel at the hearse, giving the rest of the bystanders the impression he was preparing to leave. It worked. The limousines pulled away without us, slowing into the traffic jam at the gate, and without my realizing it the three of us were suddenly left alone. It was a pure feeling, free from the crowd, as if hypocrisy drove away with the numbers.

The gravediggers came from somewhere across the cemetery. I had not noticed them until one greeted Will. The four men faced a hot, backbreaking job, for little pay, with a widower watching every move. I'm sure they would have preferred to work alone so they could set their own pace, crack a few dirty jokes, and curse the sun. But Will was determined to see it through, and no one was planning to argue with him. One man began rolling up the back flap of the tent, while the others took the tarpaulin off the mound of clay. The flower overlay was carefully laid aside, waiting to crown the finished grave. The men exchanged a sentence or two and decided to leave the tent standing for shade; it would come down later. Then with wide white cords that looked like strips of sheets, they picked up the casket, kicked away the supporting planks, and, two plots from where my brother was buried, lowered it into the ground.

The man who had first spoken to Will turned toward him, hesitating. The moment felt final. Will stepped to the edge of the grave and stared in. This is my beloved, and this is my friend. All of us kept silent, our heads slightly bowed. Then he took a shovel from a man's hand, turned, and jabbed it into the mound. The sound was like a scissors' cut. The dirt fell on the casket like hard rain.

The task took about forty minutes. The three of us stood by and watched, Will next to the grave, and the old man and I at a distance behind him, in the shade of the oak. Dad had not spoken since Mother left, but he kept a hawkeye on every detail, staying in a straight line with Will's back as if to strengthen him in spirit. (Not one of us had mentioned that other burial, nor had we lingered near Doug's grave. And I had not seen him.)

I stayed to the side, unsure why we were there, and studied my father's face. As I said, he seemed a different man this day, I guess because we had suffered only that one other funeral together, which drove him away from all others. But here, this day, the fire in my father's eyes had softened, the holocaust was quenched. Flames gave way to warm, glowing coals that showed concern and patience, and even tolerance. He still kept almost completely silent, but he looked tolerant: the awful bad taste of funerals didn't bother him; he seemed to say, People are numb, so what? And he appeared merciful toward the sins of his family against him and, most remarkably, merciful toward his own sins, against himself, against humankind, and against his God.

The straight line between them, flanked on each side by

graves, both beneath the large headstone marked *Treadwell,*
stretched much farther than it first seemed. It stretched
through our history like a long, dusty road, and through this
our Sinai that bore no milk and honey, but broken promises,
blood darker than our clay, and lust. At each end of the road
stood father and son. Both had wrestled with the unnamed
one and come away wounded. For my brother the grip was the
love of women. He stood by as the red clay packed down the
body of the first. In his grappling he would turn from one sister to the next, searching for a way to fill his belly, even if he
groveled for only the husks that swine eat. I had to stop him.
My father knew the grip of the love of God, a victim of his
own visions, blinded to the world. One grave was because of
him. Another son had not spoken to him in years. And now he
tried to limp home and be a father.

The tent collapsed quickly. The men covered the plot with
the flowers and stood the wreaths on either side. Two of them
carried a tablet, which, as they turned to set it down, I read:
Susan Mordew Treadwell, born May 2, 1922, died June 24,
1954. Those simple dates almost broke me, that brief candle of
a life. The men wiped their brows with bandannas and nodded to Will, gathering their tools and the wheelbarrow. He
was left alone, standing over the grave. In a moment he turned
around, face-to-face, across that grave-torn expanse, with my
father. It happened suddenly, that they came to themselves.
Will took a few steps, as did Dad, haltingly, and then they
went to each other and embraced. Will fell on his father's neck
and wept.

VII

Elizabeth:
Sometimes a Light
Surprises

19

*E*lizabeth believed that Will was seeking a kind of comfort about his self-worth every time he stopped his pickup at the top of the rise and stepped down to survey his house and land, his foot perched on the running board like George Washington at the prow. He had done well, he told her—more than once—and he would do even better. He had bought a neighboring 100 acres, which brought the total to 450; cut half of it for profit; and cleared it in less than two months. He planted twenty-five acres in lespedeza and another twenty-five in his own special combination of clover, black medic, and Dallis grass, names that he let linger on his tongue like an alchemist's secrets. Next he planned to build a new creep feeder, whatever that was. The hospital was behind him, he said, and with it those days when he had imagined the sky would collapse on his head. And his son Stearns was doing better.

Down the hill Elizabeth turned to the boy beside the pen, watching the Brahman. She was encouraged when Will ticked off his accomplishments since Susan had died—almost four months ago now. The more he boasted about himself, the more she felt he needed her, someone always around to tell him that, yes, he was right, he had achieved a lot and there would be plenty more in store for him, considering the man he was. But she wasn't convinced about the boy. He had inherited the usual Treadwell birthmarks, but he had Luke's, not Will's, particular mannerisms, which bothered Will im-

mensely when he admitted it to himself, and to her. Stearns always kept his hands in his pockets, like Luke. And the boy's
midcarriage, like Luke's, swiveled too much when he walked,
as if his legs reached past his hips to his stomach. Will said it
was girlish. The boy held his arms, bent at the elbows, slightly
behind his body, like an old man backing away from life.
Stearns, and Luke for that matter, never plunged into anything; they sat back and watched. And the boy still carved
soap and stick figures.

The pickup bounced down from the rise and squeaked to a
halt next to the pen, dust spurting into the air. "We gotta get
goin'," Will shouted. "Grandma won't abide us being late to
our first Homecoming in fourteen years. Why, you ain't never
been to one." He hurried into the barn, thrust the basket into
the sack of feed, and took it to the boy. "You ready?"

"He charged me, Daddy."

"Did he now. You see this catastrophe?"

"I just got here," she said. She studied the boy's face, assuming he was lying.

"He did, Daddy, promise. He was over there. I said hello,
then he ran right at me. I'm not kidding."

"Did you stand your ground?"

The boy hesitated.

"Will—my goodness!"

"He stopped right there, Daddy." Tears came to his eyes.
"But he can bust right through that fence, can't he?"

"He's too dumb. Looks like we're going to have to teach
him a lesson or two, aren't we?"

Grinning at the two of them, Will closed the gate behind
him, nonchalant about his courage as he skipped toward the
new concrete stall and its wide trough, whistling all the way.
This covered stall, too, was part of his new life and its list of
accomplishments. He'd once told her it was actually unnecessary; only the mammoth bull ranches in Florida, where each
animal was a prize, needed huts to shade and feed and sleep
the beasts. But he spent the money, he explained, because he
was beginning anew and he wanted every tool rust-free, he
wanted every machine to purr, every structure to stand forever, and all the animals upgraded to perfection. He intended
not only to make good money on the side but to live a new,
upgraded life himself, free of his former imperfections. All except her, Elizabeth thought, smiling to herself. Imperfections
like cigarette smoking, forgotten birthdays, and unreturned

telephone calls. Maybe even lying and guilt feelings—but not the cause of them.

"Did you pull down the window shades in our bedroom?" Will shouted to Stearns from the stall's doorway.

"No, sir."

"Sure?"

"Yes, sir."

"Well, then, fine. You know I like to let the sunshine in during the day. You don't have any ideas about that room, do you? I mean about Mama?"

Stearns didn't answer.

"Here, bull—*brrrh!*"

They watched the great beast amble behind Will toward the stall.

"Aunt Elizabeth?"

"Yes?"

"I don't like Daddy's moustache."

"You don't? You don't think it makes him look handsome?"

"It itches."

"Have you told him that?"

"No, ma'am. He'll be mad at me."

It was too much to ask of the boy, she thought. Nothing she might do could heal the child's grief; she and Will would have to wait it out. He was not yet four, but she knew the greater portion of his life had fallen away, leaving him without the singsong of Susan's voice and the smell of Susan's arms. His relatives were also far past his years, and his father stood atop the rise every day and reminded himself how much more he had accomplished for his beloved cows, but not for his son. Will's major concern about his son was the boy's growing affection for the single friend he seemed to have, Robert, and the influence the old man had always had on boys. Father and son had been reconciled, yes, beginning at the funeral. It was a reconciliation everyone in the family was trying to maintain. But she had her doubts. Serious doubts.

"Stearns," she said, "your father told me you and Granddaddy Treadwell were carving a big log into something—he said it looked like a canoe."

"The ark of the covenant."

"Do you know what that means?"

"*Covenant* means a handshake between God and us. A seat, too—it had the 'holy of holies' on it. It was veiled."

"Veiled?"

"Covered—with a white sheet."

Elizabeth gave the boy a false smile, remembering her own discipleship for a moment, and then, to forget, quickly turned back toward Will and the Brahman. The bull was a Krishna; it had flatter bones than the other breeds and looked uglier and was meaner—so much the better, Will boasted. The left horn curved to a point straight in front of him, while the right one kept off toward the side, their separate purposes making the center of the forehead look off-balance. She watched Will pour the feed into the wide trough and stand to the left until the Brahman, suspicious of the man, safely passed.

"Your mother'll be waiting, Will," she called out. "You said yourself about being late to Homecoming."

"Just a second." He unhooked the harness from the wall. At first she wasn't sure what he intended to do, but as the bull lost himself in eating, Will eased past the animal's left side, where the horn curved face-forward.

He looked up at them, his eyes beginning to burn. "Hey, now—brrrh," Will called, scratching the back of the bull's neck. The beast didn't move.

Will laid the harness rope lightly on the bull's forehead, letting the Brahman feel the fiber at the same time he felt the scratching. What in God's name was he thinking? Elizabeth wondered. He didn't have to prove a thing.

The Brahman lifted up, almost slipping into the harness by accident. He rolled his mammoth neck toward the man, nudging his leg, the horn pointed safely away. The bull seemed to be saying, "Now, none of this. Let's don't." He shook his head so the harness fell off, and he dropped to the trough again. She felt Stearns push against her side.

"Ah, you old horny bastard," Will said. "I'll put up with no crap off of you."

He scratched harder, for a good minute. Then he set the harness on the head gain. This time the bull came hard and quick. His neck butted Will's leg, hurling him four feet backward and almost over, but his sense of balance saved him. Stearns grabbed Elizabeth's leg. She heard herself call out.

The bull was turned toward Will by then, watching. Will moved to the animal's left again, letting the harness out into a rope whip. The first stroke smacked the bull across the eye. Will moved quickly away from the horn the stunned animal faced him with. To the right. He whipped him again—and then again. Will was too quick. The bull backed away, and Will was radiant with his conquest.

He turned toward them. "That'll teach him!" he called out triumphantly.

From the beginning to the end of the sermon, the preacher, one of Will's cousins, sang the praises of the assembled, re-united Treadwell family, perfectly joined together, as Paul said, in the same mind and the same judgment. Elizabeth paid him no mind; she stared through the gaudy stained glass above the pew, its blue and yellow colors swirling like ciga-rette smoke, and found herself thinking about the Lanett fam-ily's reputation among these people gathered at Harmony Grove, Randolph County. Luke had explained once. When Robert lost the farm and moved them to Cusseta, Luke said, the "up-country" relatives—the other Treadwells, the Rampys, the Matthewses, to name only the largest families—screamed that they were running away as far as a foreign land; nothing good ever came out of Cusseta. But it was all country show. It was that they'd never liked Robert. From the time he was a boy, he had been strange, a moonstruck calf who'd walk barefoot through a barn, forget his hat in a field, or set off into the night who knows where, staring at the stars. Nothing Rob-ert had done since childhood had changed their opinion, and Luke believed they were just as glad to get rid of him and just as glad to blame the family's misfortunes on him.

Even though moving away from kin was against better judgment, they declared Mattie a decent, down-to-earth woman. Robert didn't deserve her. She had suffered hard times, but she stuck by her fool, as a death-do-us-part wife should. Contemplating these people, and the social strictures under which Mattie was raised, Elizabeth wondered if she had given Mattie too much credit. She had always believed that Mattie held on out of some extraordinary sense of mission and of love, out of hardly known personal integrity. But maybe she had no choice. What if she had moved out of the county, di-vorced him, or taken a lover or two or three? These were never available options; they were simply too risky. And to prove even further that a woman was bound from birth by her mar-riage oath, all the time Mattie's relatives assumed, of course, that even with her store in Lanett, Will paid most of the bills.

They also categorized the rest of the family. Will was the

hero—Aunt Birdie called him a "who's who." They explained Doug by saying that one of the litter had to be a crackpot, considering who the sire was. And Luke, they stumbled with him. "A nice fellow, though out of whack sometimes." Or, "He wasn't one to beat the gums." But one comment Elizabeth loved: cousin Harry said Luke reminded him of a freak of nature, like a calf born with three eyes. "Why, he looks in so many directions he don't know where to go."

Luke had been on a vacation. He hadn't been working—selling insurance—for three months, and yet he had pursuaded Bob Lanier to let him strut off for a week. He sent a postcard to Mattie from Apalachicola, Florida, of all places. Luke was like that. He probably walked fifteen miles a day, doing nothing—he excelled at doing nothing. And nowadays he probably spent the evenings drunk. He had come home only yesterday, sunburned, just in time for Homecoming. When she asked him if he'd had a good time, he only grunted. She knew he was still obsessed with her and trying to disguise it. But it was just impossible. Not with him.

After the service the women decorated the graves before the group gathered at Grandfather Joseph's home place. In the shaded side yard, between the house and the barn, four long picnic tables spread with checked cloths, which canning jars anchored against the wind, stretched from one gnarled oak tree to another. Soon platters and bowls and plates—and then gluttons—would groan with food. The men circled the benches and a few rockers on the other side of the first oak, in the shade near the pickups and the cars, while the women went inside to work on the fixings.

Since Elizabeth was a visitor, in a way, and younger, Aunt Lonita gave her the least dangerous task—setting the tables and carrying food back and forth, often enough to overhear the men without their realizing they spoke in the company of a lady, which was fine with her. Will spent much of the time answering one good-natured rib after another, especially about his moustache. He fought back by reminding cousin Dennis Matthews about the time Dennis stripped naked and painted himself with turpentine to look like an Indian, and by telling Uncle Queeve he hadn't learned a bug's hair about the stock market. Luke simply smiled and let them kid him about being too highfalutin to come to a reunion; and Robert, before they could get a good piece of him, said, "It is the medicine of the Lord Jesus sent to heal my vain soul," and took off, all one hand of him, to help the women in the kitchen.

The men, predictably, were incensed. Will apologized for him, explaining that the old man had been working in the kitchen like a wounded maid ever since he came home. Or he gardened. Or stayed back in the store, around the smokehouse, reading a few strange books Luke brought him from the library, praying, carving stick figures with Stearns. He hadn't changed much. But the cousins wouldn't let up. It seemed they had been saving up their annoyance at Robert for years and were now eagerly latching on to any slight as an excuse to vent their outrage. It was the worst manners they had ever seen. It was a cowardly retreat. He was a woman. Finally Luke got up and walked right by Elizabeth without speaking and fetched Robert out of the house, where trying to slice tomatoes he had been more of a nuisance than a help, because he was an unwanted, unaccustomed presence to all the women save his wife. Elizabeth watched Luke lead him back to the men's fray, where cousin Leon had begun a story.

"So brother Handsome, Minnie says, bought this mule with the longest ears God ever pinned atop an ass." Leon leaned forward and brought his feet under the chair, close to squatting, which he would have done if he hadn't been Sunday-dressed. "But when Handsome tugged the mule up to the barn, the ass's ears were too tall to get through the door. Handsome a-pondered his dilemma 'til the sun rose and fell three times. Then eureka! He saw the light and up and decided to saw the top off the door, you know, so his ass and his ears could get it. Happy day, he fetched his saw—sort of like Robert Treadwell right 'chere did twenty years ago—and went to whacking away at the door."

"You sure hit weren't no pig, Leon?"

Will laughed, jabbing the speaker playfully in the arm.

"No, Harry, it weren't his pig, it were his ass. So Minnie came prancing up, with her hat on, of course, and asked, 'Handsome, what you doing?' Handsome explained that his mule's ears were too tall, etcetera, etcetera. Minnie pondered the problem a second and says, 'Well, goodness, you got a dirt floor there. Why don't you dig a trench down in the dirt 'stead of tearing up your barn?'

"Handsome gave the once-over to the barn door, then the dirt and his mule's ears, and finally turned back to Minnie. 'Hit ain't his legs that're too long,' he says, 'hit's his ears.' "

"I knew a man once," Robert said, after the laughter, "whose dog was missing a leg. He called him Flat Tire."

"What da we call you, Robert? A right-hand man?"

"I've known plenty of people who go through life like Handsome." It was Nat Rampy III speaking. On Sundays and Wednesdays he preached at Harmony Grove; the rest of the week he painted houses. "Sort of upside down. Leon, I'm going to borrow your story for a sermon. I've known people who believe they have the patience of Job but all they're doing is trying to cut up that barn when there's a much easier solution down below. It reminds me of the camel-and-needle parable—not a very popular one, but misunderstood, in light of the particular gate in Jerusalem called 'the needle's eye.' The mule could have gotten on his knees, like a camel."

"Service is over, preacher," one of the cousins said.

"Yes, you're right." Nat smiled. "Sometimes I forget myself."

"Cutting the door makes perfect sense to me," Robert said. He wore a new pair of eyeglasses with thick black rims, which Mattie had insisted on buying for him. They were one material possession Robert gave in to, a result of the reading Luke had been giving him, back in the privacy of the smokehouse. "The Good Book says," he continued, " 'Set thine heart on the highway.' Besides, any mule I know wouldn't have walked through a trench into a barn door."

"Gol' darn, Robert, you haven't changed much."

"You been 'round that kitchen stove too much, cousin. The heat's got to your brain."

"You see what we've had to cope with all these years?" Will said, gesturing toward Robert. Elizabeth looked up from the cutlery she was laying to see if Robert would smile. He did.

"It's a good thing you don't own a farm no more, Robert."

"Yes, I guess so. Will takes care of that."

Then Raymond, Belle's husband, interrupted. "Will, Belle tells me that besides that new hair on your lip, you got a Brahman bull, too."

Will laughed. "Yeah, I do. The biggest, meanest, tough-skinned creature, you've ever seen, with horns wider than east to west."

"You didn't name it Job, did you?"

"No." Everyone laughed.

"Brahmans are dangerous, Will."

"All the rodeos use 'em," Fred said. "They buck the best."

"Yes, but I don't mean that," Ray said. "They're dangerous because they ain't no mixed breed. They got a history, and any animal with a history has got to be smart, and any animal that's smart has got to be dangerous."

"Sorta like Luke here," Porter said, laughing at his own joke.

"I know what you're up to, Raymond Bonner," Will said.

"What?"

"The turkeys. I'll never forget you and your turkeys."

"Me? Your sister was in on it, too. The way I figure it, Will, you should never have an animal that's smarter than you are. I was pretty safe with turkeys, 'cause I may be dumb, but I was always a mite smarter than a turkey. I remember when Belle and I lived over by the Lanett graveyard, when we had our first flock. One morning I kissed my cupcake goodbye, got in the pickup, and started driving off to work when I heard the 'gobble, gobble, cluck, cluck' right next to me. I looked up in the sky, on the seat next to me, under my feet, until I turned around to see a tom sitting down in the flatbed, just taking a ride and singing. I must have been doing forty by then, but he looked at me as if riding in a truck was the most surefire normal thing a turkey does."

"The Creek Indians," Fred said, "wouldn't eat 'em. They thought you took on the character traits of whatever you ate. They didn't want to digest something that was yellow and dumb."

"You make money on them turkeys, Ray?"

"You kidding? Belle was out one day. It rained, and when I came home, three of 'em had stood under the drain and drowned. I'm not kidding. Didn't have enough sense to stay out of the rain. At least, though, I always knew I was a tad smarter. Will'll never know. That Brahman, he's as old as India—he's got history on his side."

Earlier in the day, as the women were decorating the graves after the church service, Aunt Lonita had taken Elizabeth aside, though not out of everyone's sight, and pressed her hand. The matriarch's fingers were cold and scaly. "Mattie tells me you are responsible for reconciling Robert and Will." Elizabeth objected. But Aunt Lonita insisted. "That's not what *she* says. She told me you convinced Robert to come home and that when Susan was dying, you made Will see how important it was to make up with his daddy. You don't have to deny it. Just you know that all of us thank you. We thank you from the core of our hearts. We have been trying to bring about a reconciliation for years, but it took someone out of the family to pull it off—that makes sense. But you're family now. Don't you forget—you're family now."

A reconciliation, they believed. Robert and Will were certainly civil to one another, if not loving, in public. But as Elizabeth was setting the tables and furtively listening to the men talk, she remembered a night that made her wonder just how permanent this reconciliation would be. After she and Will had lain together, Will as usual came back to her bed with food, this time with a bowl of nectarines. Since he quit smoking, he was gaining weight, which irritated him, but he never could stop himself from fixing a snack before he drove back to the sanctuary of his farm and the propriety of a widower's bed.

"Fruit's good for me," he said, falling back beside her.

He talked incessantly about Susan, and Elizabeth never could derail him from the subject until his compulsion was satisfied. Lately he complained about the arguments he and Susan had, and that evening when he appeared, because they always sat down first and, from self-respect, still courted each other, he told Elizabeth about one of their fights over even something as trivial as the window shades. He wanted to sleep with the shades up and the windows cracked, he explained, so he might listen for any undue noise from his cows. Whenever Susan talked him into closing the window and pulling the shades down, as soon as he woke up in the morning he put them back up, whether the sun blinded them or the rain fell in cold pencil strokes. He felt terribly claustrophobic when the window was closed, as if it implied they lived an intimate life and she owned him. Susan accused him of indecency. He pointed out that they lived in the country, not in the town, but to Susan that was not the point. "There's a certain sense of propriety," she answered, before she finally admitted that no one was likely to see in.

"You could parade buck-naked for fifteen years," he said, "and no one'd see you 'cept a stray cow."

"I don't parade anywhere, Will."

Elizabeth sprawled beside him, patiently listening to his story. It was three weeks after Susan died and Will and his father embraced. Elizabeth and Will had made love before, if only in body, while Susan was alive. Their lovemaking was as spontaneous as the first time, and as violent, but neither of them wanted to make it a habit. After Susan died, it became a habit, as did his compulsion to talk afterward about Susan and his reconciliation with his father. Elizabeth rolled over on her side, still as naked as she was when they began to make love. Susan, he told her, had always pulled the sheet back up over her breasts.

"I do not miss her," he said.

She measured the look in his eyes.

"How can I say such a thing? But it's true. I do not miss her." He spoke the words slowly, weighing each in the balance, judging whether or not he was telling himself the truth. Then he wiped the nectarine juice off his fingers with a napkin. "I say it because this is how I feel and I am finally admitting the truth to myself. It is important for a man to understand the truth about himself. Even if the very idea of not missing a wife of five years makes me Judas Iscariot himself." He spit the core into his napkin and tossed it in the wastebasket next to the bed. "She should have died six months ago. That was when I began not to miss her, you know that— even though she was still alive and I was hoofing it back and forth to the hospital, to Mother's, to work, to home. Thank God that's over. I am quitting a life plagued by lies, Elizabeth. Susan and I lived together for five years. I gave her the farm. I modernized that house with every convenience a woman could want. I sat beside her in those lounge chairs and exchanged opinions with her about whatever she wanted to talk about—friends, symptoms, obligations, you name it—all the time watching her stupid birds. I gave her a son. I have lived a marriage with her. These are truths, not lies. But I don't miss her, I feel free."

"I don't know what to say."

"You don't have to say a word. Unless you want to." He stared at her.

She touched his arm. "Not again—please."

He did not respond to her touch, but began to speak in a mechanical tone, clicking off each syllable. "You must suffer my questions for the rest of your life or until I believe you're not lying about that trip to the mountains with my father. It really ought to be you who's asking yourself, not me. But if we are to love each other, it has to be truthful. Don't you understand that? You seem to think that all you need to do is wait and I'll forget. I'll never forget, Elizabeth."

She would not give in to him. "You don't want me to tell the truth, Will."

"Don't give me that."

"You would prefer that I lie. That way you can say, 'I told you so,' and assume some righteous stance of forgiveness—if that's what you're after. But I really don't know what you're after."

"How can you say that? You always throw it back on me, as if the problem's mine. You always try to make me feel guilty in asking the question. Don't you think I understand that ploy by now, Elizabeth? The best way not to answer the question is to ask another question. You try to get me to believe that just because I'm not naïve enough to swallow some ridiculous story about your Platonic love, I'm the perverse one, I'm the one who sins."

"Sins?"

"Well . . ."

"You're saying 'sin' to me, Will?"

"I'm saying it's time you admitted the truth, not just to me but to yourself."

She repeated his word. " 'Sin,' the man says. I'm the one who sins." The word pierced her side like a sharp horn. She had thought she was under control, that she would be able to endure his spite once again without losing her temper. But whatever it was that animated her, and gave her the foolish strength to love this man, fled from her ruptured side like dammed water broken free. She sat up in bed. She waited. She felt it coming until finally it broke and she slammed the mattress with both hands, and felt it flood through her as she pounded again and again like a hysterical child, cursing the very fate that would bring her to these sheets after everything else had happened, the denial of Luke and the trip with Robert, one Treadwell after another, pounding and pounding again until she was exhausted and her face blood-red.

"Is that what you want me to say? Is that it, Will, you bastard! That I stripped myself like this and took your father to me, just as I took you to me right now and in these god-awful months past, and that it was a terrible sin against you? You want me to say that, whether it's true or false, because you can't understand any other kind of relationship, Will. If it's animal, you can deal with it. If I copulated with him, you can understand. It becomes simple. It was a sin against you—not a spiritual sin, of course, but a physical sin. That's what infuriates you. You don't understand anything else."

Will stared at her with his own explosive eyes. "I understand a lot more than you think, bitch."

"Bitch my ass, Will. That's all you know—bitches and

breeding. And a slaughterhouse. But you know what your father did, Will? He never made love to me, no matter what you think. But he raped me. He raped the very guts out of my soul—that's what he did, Will, and you don't even care."

He descended into a seething silence, keeping still for minutes. Then he got up without another word, dressed, and stormed out into the late night. He had no intention of coming back.

He spun the car out of the small dirt driveway onto Main Street and sped through town, barely slowing down at the stoplights. "Bitch," he said again. "Goddamn bitch." After he turned onto Route 18, he accelerated. His speedometer was broken, but he must have been going 90 or 100. His hands felt the vibration from the steering wheel, and from the steering wheel to the steering column, down to the chassis and the humming tires and the engine, where burned a fire. A vicious, raging fire. He wanted the fire to burn his path over the face of the undulating hills toward the farm, ravaging the land over which he traveled, scarring the enemies of his life forever. He could name his enemies: his father, yes, and Susan, and now—Elizabeth. Enemies for life.

He got to the farm in about fifteen minutes, but kept driving. From the midst of his anger, a sudden fear jerked out of his stomach and began racing through his mind. He couldn't explain it, but it was more than regretting his marriage to Susan and being angry at Elizabeth and suspecting the truth about her feelings toward his father. It was a fear about his life: something terrible was going to happen. He knew something terrible was coming. His mind raced with the possibilities, but all of them focused on past events repeating themselves, as if he were cursed to suffer the injuries of the past over and over again in the future. Then he remembered, involuntarily, an event in the past, when he also felt sure everything was doomed.

Stearns was being born. He had assumed his post in the middle of the maternity waiting room, worrying and waiting for hours, absolutely certain that something terrible was going to happen. Susan and the baby would die. The baby would be grossly deformed, with three eyes or six fingers or an elephant's head or a cripple's legs. Some preacher had once told him that hell wasn't fire and brimstone but waiting around. Forever. And for nothing. He believed the man now, and though hell was a ridiculous idea, hell on Earth wasn't. This was hell on Earth. Then he had to try to convince himself that it wouldn't happen to him—he had survived his father's abuse and a marine landing on Guadalcanal. And bad things at birth just didn't happen now. They just didn't.

At one end of the coffee table in the waiting room, a Gideon's Bible and a stack of magazines, all of which at one time or another he had held in his hands, marked time for those like himself who pretended to read. Then he discovered a penny in his hand. He didn't know when he took it from his pocket, but the face was worn and it felt as warm as a stone snatched from a fire. He wasn't going to worry about it. All his life he had been the victim of unexplainable conspiracies and he simply accepted it: there was an unknown penny in his hand, and he was rubbing it so hard his hand hurt.

On the opposite wall some joker had hung a Nativity painting. The artist obviously had no farming background, but Mary's face was good; her features were of one mind and alive with peace. As Susan's face was, the last few months of the pregnancy. Then Will's memory jumped to another scene. A week before the birth, he had left the store at about 2:30 on Friday afternoon and had taken Susan to the farm, which at the time was only their weekend retreat. After checking his cows, he walked down to the pecan grove by the highway. The blithering idiots in the capital wanted to widen the road so all their blithering cousins could drive to Callaway Gardens faster. He'd lose at least twelve trees and have to lay a new fence somewhere between rows. It made him livid if he let himself think about it. He stepped off fifteen paces, not a penny more, drove a stake and headed back. Susan waited in the rocker on the porch, where she could watch him stride back across the fields from the cows. But coming from the lower grove she wouldn't see him until he was upon her. For a strange moment he wondered what she was thinking. Who was this person he had married, this woman who was about to bear a child? He was walking around the side of the house, until he saw her, and then suddenly he decided to step back behind the corner and spy.

Susan had propped a colander full of green beans against her bloated lap and set a grocery bag for the strings beside the rocker. She wore that golden necklace. She scanned the fields for him, all the time humming a tune he couldn't recognize. He almost made himself known, but then Susan set the beans down, put her right hand on her hip, crooked her left arm, and started singing:

I'm a little teapot
Short and stout;
Here is my handle,
Here is my spout.

When I get all steamed up,
then I shout,
Just tip me over,
And pour me out.

Will slowed the car down, four years later. The mind was strange. First he'd felt an ominous sense and remembered the hospital waiting room. Then, remembering this scene with Susan, one of the few pleasant ones of his marriage, his mind eased a moment and relaxed. There were times, yes, he told himself, when he and Susan loved each other—especially in the months before Stearns was born. He wondered if he would begin to see her in a different way now that she was dead.

He pulled the car off to the right, preparing to turn around and go home. He could decide what to do about Elizabeth after a good night's sleep. But just as the car settled onto the shoulder of the road, he felt a terrible need to piss. He stopped and got out, relieving himself in the roadside ditch. The grass was as high as his knees, and above him he could barely see the outline of the scrub pines against a starless night sky. The barbed-wire fence post in front of him was rotten, even though it was cedar; the field beyond, spread with the mild smell of cow manure, stretched toward the dark outline of a forest.

The second he finished, he was shocked by a terrible thought. When he had been in the waiting room and remembered Susan singing that children's song, his memory had been interrupted first by a strong urge to get up and go to the bathroom and then, while in the bathroom, by a second memory, but a destructive, hateful one. Now, four years later, driving along this road, late at night and remembering that same song, the same physical urge had possessed him, an exact duplication of the experience, as if a powerful memory had control of the nerves in his body. And before he knew it, standing there beside his car, as if he were cursed to live his past over and over and over again, the second memory came again, striking him like the barrels of a shotgun across the face.

He was a five-year-old, a five-year-old with good intentions.

It might be his earliest memory. His mother had carried a
baby in her tummy for a long time, and two women arrived
early in the morning to talk with her about it and see if there
was something they could do to help. The two women and his
mother were still in the bedroom, working on it, after all this
time. Once in a while one of the women would come out and
tend three steaming kettles on the stove, where they were
cleaning towels for some reason—he couldn't imagine what
wet towels had to do with a sore tummy. And all morning a
wet smell, like an August rain mixed with the smell of ammo-
nia, filled the room.

His dad was not in a good mood. He seemed left out in the
dark. He was walking around on the porch, or out in the yard,
rubbing his fingers together like he always did when things
weren't right. Sometimes scary noises leaked out of the bedroom, like a strong wind whistling around the house. And
worse. His dad told him to take care of Belle and make sure
they kept as quiet as the Lord's Day. It was really Tuesday.
"And don't go in that door," his dad said, rubbing his fingers.

Belle hid in a kitchen corner, clutching her rag doll. She
asked him if Mother was going to heaven and he told her to be
quiet—Mother was trying to convince a baby out of her
tummy; the baby was coming from heaven, and that was the
painful part. That seemed to satisfy her. He sat by the window, sweating from the steam, and stared out over the front
field. His dad had gone down by the row of cedars along the
road. It was a gray afternoon, as if God had laid a silent blanket over the trees and made the animals and the earth and the
people keep still because a baby needed to be born. He sorely
wanted to help his mother.

Then he had an idea. She was tired and sick and she hadn't
eaten because of the baby. He would fix her something special
from the kitchen and make her feel better, like she did for him
when his tummy hurt. "This will make you stronger," she always said. "Sip it slowly, and drink all of it. It'll settle your
tummy." He couldn't make chicken soup, but he could pour
tea and cut a piece of bread and go right in there to surprise
her with it. His dad would understand, even after what he'd
said, even with those strange noises, because he was trying to
do the right thing for the family and for Mother, that was all.

He imagined the scene the way it was going to happen,
knocking quietly on the door, with the tea and bread held before him. "Come in," someone would whisper. He would turn

the knob and let the door swing slowly open, stepping in with the tray lifted up like a crown, and his mother and the visiting women would quickly cover their mouths with surprise. "Oh, my word," one woman would say, "look at what this boy has done! How wonderful! Doesn't it smell wonderful!" His mother, her head resting on two pillows, would turn to him and smile.

"This'll make you feel better," he would say, carefully setting the tray on the side table. "Sip it slowly and drink all of it. It'll settle the baby in your tummy."

"My, my, you shouldn't have, Will. But it's just what I need." There would be tears in her eyes.

"It's because I love you." And he would hug her warm body.

So he set about making his dream come true. He slid his chair back from the window, trying to be as quiet as possible, and peered down at his sister. "Help me make tea for Mother."

"No." She snuggled her rag doll closer and scrunched up her face. She smelled like she had gone in her pants.

"Come on."

"No."

He decided he'd better leave her alone. She might throw a fit, and that wouldn't do. He stood by the stove and the cabinet and tried to remember how his mother put hot tea together. He'd watched her so many times he ought to know. But seeing her do it and actually doing it himself were two different things. First he took the rag she always wrapped around her hand and wrapped it around his and swung open the black gate where the fire was burning. It needed to be even hotter. He turned a handle on the side and slipped in a piece of wood, closed it like she did, and budged the handle. He heard a crackle. That was good, because he heard it crackle when she did it.

He moved the teakettle to the one empty black plate on top, careful not to touch the other pots. She always kept water in the kettle. Then he got on his tiptoes and reached all the way to the back of the shelf and slid the tea box to him. But he wasn't sure what to do next. He looked at Belle. She was watching him, but she didn't know either. He spooned some black tea into the spout. That's where it came from, so it made sense that that's where he'd put it. Most of it spilled on the stove. He lifted the tea box and shook it over the snout so a lot fell in. A lot didn't, too. And none was left. He'd make Belle clean it up later.

The bread didn't cut clean, but folded up and crumbled. He was getting worried. He tried five different slices, but when he was finished he stared at a bread heap on the wooden block, each piece torn and ragged. Then he heard her scream. He was sure it was his mother's voice, and it was terrible. And it would not stop, even to breathe, but reached all through the house and into the sky. He looked out the window and saw his father hurrying. Then he smelled smoke. He turned to the stove. Gray puffs snaked out of the sides of the black doors, and out of the pipe on top. And there was a noise like a well pumping. Then a whistle. Dark water full of black specs jumped from the kettle spout. It sprayed the other pots and sizzled on the stovetop.

Belle started crying. "Stop it," he said, the bread knife still in his hand. "We've got to keep quiet." But that made it worse. She started screaming like Mother, hurting his ears so much he thought he'd scream, too. He grabbed the gate handle and burned his fingers. He shook his hand like crazy and grabbed the rag. A burst of gray smoke choked him and flames licked out like snake tongues. Belle screamed even louder. "Shut up!" he shouted. "We can't make noise!"

"Mommy's going to heaven!"

"Stop it!"

"We're going to burn up!"

"Stop it!" He threw the rag at her face, grabbed a wad of bread, and jumped on her. He stuffed the bread into her mouth. "Keep quiet," he said. His hand hurt.

"Will Treadwell!" It was his father's voice. His father ran into the kitchen at the same time the bedroom door opened. One of the women stood there and watched as his father kicked the side handle of the stove and with his bare hand snatched the kettle off the black plate.

"It's all right, honey," the woman said to someone behind the door. "They're just fine—don't you worry. Minnie'll be here any moment."

He felt his father's grip lift him straight off his feet and shake him, rattling the bones in the back of his neck; and before he could speak, his father slapped him. "What are you trying to do, boy, kill us all? Don't you have any consideration for your mother?"

A pain in his hand awakened Will from his memory. He

was gripping the handle of the car door too tightly. If he could take that same insensible grip and find his father's neck, he would explain just how considerate of his mother he was. How could his father not have understood his good intentions? He had been dawdling by the kitchen window, feeling useless, when with all his heart he believed he'd found a way to ease his mother's pain. But blind as a bull his stupid father had stormed in and accused him of murdering his mother. Right then and there Will promised himself he would always consider Stearns's intentions before rashly judging the boy's actions. But he was still angry. He was a father himself, but the injury of that episode still lived in his soul like an insult given the day before. Will remembered every wrong his father had ever inflicted on him, whether monumental or trivial, and he had not forgiven a single one.

It was then that Will caught himself, finally breaking free for a moment from the mad speeding of his brain. His stomach felt awful. He crawled on top of the car and lay there on his back, stretching his arms high above his head and trying to breathe deeply. The black sky gave him no comfort. Susan had been dead three weeks. He was reconciled with his father—everyone in the family told him that, especially his mother, and he wanted to please her. He breathed deeply again. He admitted that the moment he turned around from his wife's grave and saw his father standing there, he felt closer to the man than he ever had, as if there were indeed a strong and sure blood bond between them. At the time his father seemed like someone greater than he was or could ever be, more assured, more consoling, more understanding. And there Will was, racing around the countryside remembering just how violently he hated his father. It was hard to explain. He would try to do better. For his mother's sake. He got back into the car and, barely conscious of what he was doing, drove home to a deep, dreamless sleep and a late morning in bed, disregarding his son.

He stayed away from Elizabeth for two days, thinking he would feel better if he shunned her and all she implied about his father. The occasion of the Wednesday-night supper, however, allowed both of them to save face about their argument and arrange another midnight rendezvous. And the two-day estrangement made their passion all the more indecent.

* * *

Belle and Margaret Rampy came from behind Elizabeth
with the last of the steaming food. Other women followed,
rearranging the platters Elizabeth had moved about the table.
"Gather round!" Belle shouted.

Raymond finished a story about laying brick at a leper col-
ony during the depression, and Robert told them that the
book he was reading said Saint Francis of Assisi kissed lepers
on the mouth. But only Luke listened to the old evangelist; the
other men stood up and stretched, eyeing the food. The tables
were set with duplicate bowls of assorted beans—butter,
snapping green, pinto, wax—greens, squash, beets, peas, cab-
bage, collards, onions, corn, hominy, turnips, and yams,
mixed in with platters of meat and potatoes and pitchers of
buttermilk and iced tea. The aunts didn't want the food to get
cold, but at the same time insisted on a short speech and a
prayer beforehand.

"Okay, listen up now," Leon announced, stepping to the
end of the table. "Before Nat prays, Aunt Lonita's got something special in honor of the Robert Treadwells here."

"I wrote my sister Nancy Ann last month," Aunt Lonita
began, "to tell her how fortunate we would be this day when
the Robert Treadwells came back to us, fourteen years since
their last reunion."

"Hear, hear."

"Amen."

Aunt Lonita was a small woman with weathered, tough
skin, her hands shivering with the paper she held. Everyone
strained to hear her.

"In reply she sent me a precious letter, making me promise
to return it after I read parts of it today. It is an old, old letter—but not as old as me." The gathered clan objected in unison. "All of you know how I've loved my nephew, and how
I've spoken for him all these years he has been away from our
blessed gathering. Some of you men just don't understand, but
you've always had heads like mules. Now listen to this—it's
dated May twelfth, 1913, in Edwardsville, Cleburne County.
From Sara Jane Rampy, Nat the Third's great-grandmother,
to my sister Nancy Ann. I've asked Leon here to read it."

He took the letter from her and cleared his throat. " 'Dear
children. After some delay I seat myself to write you a few
lines.' She doesn't use periods," Leon said, "so please bear
with me—I have to put 'em in. 'We are well and I hope you
still are well. Well, Annie, we went down into Randolph last

Friday and they sure had a big time down there on Saturday. It was their Decoration Day and their regular meeting day at Harmony Grove, so they put in the whole day carrying out dinner as there was a lot of people there'—period, I think," Leon interjected. " 'They had their decoration first and then preached and then dinner, rested one hour, then had a good many speeches and good songs mixed with it so it was all good and nice. I wish you could a bin there to a seen. The way they had the graves all fixed it was the purtiest graveyard I ever saw in my life.' "

"Isn't that marvelous," Mattie said, "that we stand here over fifty years later!"

"Now slip down to this, Leon," Aunt Lonita said, pointing to another part of the yellowed paper.

" 'Well, Annie,' " he continued, " 'I have been thinking if I live 'til fall I would go out there to see you all. I can't go now for Robbie Treadwell is a-boarding here and a-going to school—was here a month before Pa died and made his arrangements to go 'til school was out and then take the examination and get a license to teach if he can afford to go off and leave here—and he is just as good to me as he can be. He won't go off nowheres at night unless I go too. I believe he has a heap of good truth in him all mixed up and one day will do great things maybe in Christ Jesus, for people grow attached to him.' "

"Now, isn't that something? I tell you," Aunt Lonita said, "what a sweet man he was to her when her husband was dying. She knew, too, that Robert was a special man."

"What a wonderful letter, Robert," May Matthews said.

"I had forgotten that you thought about teaching so early on," Leon said, obviously feeling the obligation for at least one man to speak.

"We're so glad you've come—all of you," Aunt Cumi said.

"Yeah, Robert," Harry said. "It's not every day we have so much fun at your expense."

The laughter eased some of Robert's embarrassment. Elizabeth watched him closely. As the letter was read, he kept his head bowed and twitched the fingers of his left hand. Once he removed his new eyeglasses and rubbed his eyes with the half-nub of his other hand. When Lonita finished, Mattie grabbed his arm and smiled at him, but he never looked up and acknowledged anyone's welcome or praise, and his physical shyness brought the conversation to a rather abrupt end.

Nat Rampy III, the preacher, was asked to pray. "O most great and glorious God, we just want to thank you . . ." he began, and then Robert finally raised his head and looked straight at Elizabeth. The new spectacles were bifocals, the lens bottoms cut in the shape of half-moons.

Elizabeth had hardly spoken to him since they came home. She was beginning to believe that nothing had ever happened between them; with more time she thought she could convince herself. But as he looked at her he implored her, and she was surprised, for no matter how much she told herself that she'd never respond to him again, she suddenly felt his beseeching, remembering. She could not escape a year of her life, not when because of this man there were moments she believed her feet washed clean, laced with tinkling ornaments, kissed, and cared for like fine brass. And sometimes her feet danced.

Elizabeth glanced down the table and saw that Will was glaring at her. She didn't care. How different Robert had been throughout that whole conversation among the men, those country spit-vile dunces. They helped her to see again. For a moment she remembered—she could give this old evangelist a moment, couldn't she, remembering, in all its glory, no matter what the world said? So she stared back at Robert, with fervent eyes.

On the porch Elizabeth rocked in a chair and watched Luke, who was old of spirit himself, as he joined Robert in leading the great-aunts to their seats of honor in the circle Leon and Uncle Samuel had set up after the feast was over. Lonita, Cumi, Bertha, Martha, and Birdie sat next to each other; Uncles Parker, Samuel, Queeve, and Baxter, each smoking a cigar, filled in. She stayed on the porch and rocked, along with Mattie, Belle, Ray, and Harry, far enough away to talk to one another without being impolite, and yet close enough to give the impression they were listening. Will leaned against an oak tree in the yard, sulking, she felt sure, because he had seen the way she looked at Robert. On the way up he had told her that the older generation sang because they were weak and sentimental. He was right, but it was their prerogative, she felt, considering their station in life. Seven months would pass before the next Decoration Day, and in the interim at least one of them would die. Everyone understood: singing hymns acknowledged it without having to say so. Many of the

songs they remembered were not in the current Baptist or
Methodist hymnals, which made them even prouder of their
collective memory. As the afternoon waned, the songs spoke
of heaven more often, that tear-jerking by-and-by where
friends call each other by name.

The strangest event of the hymn sing, though, came about
halfway through, when Aunt Lonita persuaded Luke to sing a
song by himself. Elizabeth couldn't believe that ever-shy
Luke, and sometimes scornful Luke, could be persuaded, but
she was glad he was. She had played so many hymns in her
life but had heard this one only a few times; she certainly
couldn't figure out when he had memorized it, not being a
churchgoer himself, but it was a beautiful, interesting song
and he had a pleasant, though not a soloist's, baritone voice.
She overheard him say it was originally a poem by a man
named Cooper, though his name was spelled with a *w*.

> Sometimes a light surprises
>   The Christian while he sings;
> It is the Lord who rises
>   With healing on His wings.
> When comforts are declining,
>   He grants the soul again
> A season of clear shining
>   To cheer it after rain.
>
> In holy contemplation
>   We sweetly then pursue
> The theme of God's salvation,
>   And find it ever new.
> Set free from present sorrow,
>   We cheerfully can say,
> "E'en let the unknown tomorrow
>   Bring with it what it may!
>
> "It can bring with it nothing
>   But He will bear us thro';
> Who gives the lilies clothing
>   Will clothe his people too.
> Beneath the spreading heavens
>   No creature but is fed;
> And he who feeds the ravens
>   Will give his children bread.

> *"Tho' vine, nor fig-tree neither,*
> *Their wonted fruit shall bear,*
> *Tho' all the field should wither,*
> *Nor flocks, nor herds, be there,*
> *Yet God the same abiding,*
> *His praise shall tune my voice*
> *For while in him confiding,*
> *I cannot but rejoice."*

When he finished, Elizabeth glanced toward Will, who motioned for her. She waited a few moments until she could steal away from the singing and the group on the porch and make her way across the yard to the pecan tree, where, with his coat and tie off and his sleeves rolled up over his elbows, he stood by the swing the children had finally abandoned. He tugged on the rope and dusted off the smooth lacquered board, inviting her to sit. She curled her forearms around the rope and let him gently push the middle of her back. While they talked she faced forward; both of them were safe from eye contact.

Elizabeth wasn't going to apologize for herself—she had spent too much of her life apologizing. "Susan told me to marry Luke, Will," she said. "Did you know that?" She felt his eyes burrowing through her back, searching for her heart. He would assume she was lying. "Maybe it was her revenge." She laughed. "Maybe she thought of it right on her deathbed. 'For your own happiness,' she said. She didn't need to give me the idea about you and she knew it. She knew a lot more than you think."

"She didn't know anything, Elizabeth, and she didn't care."

"*Free from the law,*" the hymn-singers sang, "*O happy condition . . .*"

"I'm not naïve, Will, about my sister. Maybe you'd better think again."

"You're right, you're not naïve. My father, for example."

"Will—"

"You know what I mean."

Elizabeth stared at the ground until he stopped pushing her. Finally still, she spoke in a quiet voice. "He demands a lot."

"And I don't? I just demand one thing."

She didn't answer.

"How can I love a woman who believes in that old fool?"

"That's just it, Will—I don't." She stood up and turned around, straightening her dress. A strand of hair tickled her neck. It wasn't worth bothering with.

Another hymn she recognized drifted toward them. *"Where is the blessedness I knew? . . ."*

"Tell me, Will. If you think the way you do about your father and me, why do you keep on asking?"

"Elizabeth."

"What are you saying?"

"Stop it. I just can't believe that you still feel some loyalty to him. If that's what it is. Even if you didn't love him."

"I hate to deceive him. He has never deceived anyone."

"I don't deceive. . . ." He had remembered his promise to himself, she could see. "But do you feel a loyalty to him?" he asked.

"That is the wrong word."

"It makes no sense whatsoever. And there are the words of the vow, remember."

The singers were standing, gathering into a farewell circle for "Blest Be the Tie That Binds," insisting everyone near and far come and join them. He turned away from her, and then decided against it, as if he wanted one more moment together. His eyes questioned her with all his strength of will. She didn't shy away from him, returning his gaze with a sense of corruption that she sent to his very loins. Will had a power she wanted. His was a master's face, and she told herself that she was made to be a disciple. They had taken each other in the silence of the deepest night, unbeknown to the world. She had lost control of herself with a fervent, wild promiscuity only fallen disciples know. And she loved it. And she knew that for Will, the fury and the gain were that her first evangelist was his father.

20

*E*lizabeth eased the door of the store closed. The warmth from the stove's potbelly welcomed her like a friend with hot tea. People don't realize, she thought, how bitter it can be here. How dead the winter.

Lit by two bare light bulbs hanging from the ceiling down to each side of the stove, an aisle divided the folding chairs into sections. At the end of the second row, on the left, Robert ministered to one of the town drunks, a gray-haired but balding black man named Horace. Keeping her coat on, Elizabeth tiptoed her way down the side opposite Robert toward the front, where the piano angled away from his preacher's platform. Robert had evangelized in some strange places, she remembered, laughing to herself. And now the store. Mattie had come home from the fall reunion and announced that she was letting the business go. There was hardly any food left; only a few rows of stacked cans lined the shelves, as well as some scattered cartons of rice, flour, and cornmeal. Over Robert's head loomed the falsely gilded black cash register.

Just for a lark, Elizabeth sat on the piano stool. The chipped white keys were yellowed along the edges and between the black keys; for some reason they always reminded her of the mill's smokestacks, thirty-six of them, which when she played she somehow subdued. She unbuttoned her coat and wiggled her arms out of it and found herself, surprisingly, exercising her fingers over the keyboard. But she hurried her hands back to her lap: she had not come for sentiment: she had come to tell him. Still, there had been a time when a keyboard gave her a sense of place and purpose. She would watch Robert as he preached, always to her left, and follow him when he jumped into the crowd like a tongue of fire. She had modulated the hymns with his every move and word, and had once prided herself on that talent, happily losing herself in the task, her fingers at play without her mind's instructions.

She touched a key. Robert and Horace turned. Robert smiled. She was still surprised by his new bifocals, how the thick black rims weighed heavily on his already heavy face. He pointed at the piano. "I didn't hear you come in. We're just talking, go right ahead. I haven't heard you play in ages."

She smiled and hummed to herself as she faltered through a four-measure line. Then she rediscovered the first chords of each measure, until most of the harmony reawakened in both hands. She played a hymn through once. Another followed—"Jesus Is Calling"—and then "Why Not Tonight," "Pass Me Not," and "Is Your All on the Altar?" Her fingers recognized her old medley of invitational hymns and would not stop, remembering, but teetering, coming home. Molly. Memory, she thought. So much is involuntary. She hadn't thought of Molly in months.

Robert laid his hands on Horace's head. Instinctively Elizabeth wanted to play "Wherever He Leads I'll Go." As Robert prayed, Horace squeezed his eyes shut, tears bursting from the edges and rolling down over his puffy black face. Elizabeth had seen the man about the alleyways and bushes of town, in the same tattered gray work shirt and torn pants, searching through garbage cans for leftover greens and mashed potatoes and cigarette butts. He always wanted to stop people, not to ask for money, he said, but to talk about heaven. Late at night he stumbled along Main Street singing "Mine Eyes Have Seen the Glory." Most of the town ignored him, waiting for him to disappear one day and become part of the barbershop lore.

When Robert finished, Horace opened his reddened eyes. Robert stood up and walked around the counter, where he jiggled open a drawer and pulled out a can opener, giving two cans of sausages to Horace, who scarcely finished chewing one link before he stuffed another into his mouth. Elizabeth wondered if he endured Robert's prayers only because food followed the "Amen." Then Robert led Horace to the row of chairs by the stove and, sliding three together, draped them with a sheet. Horace shook his head but was obviously not adamant. He had finished the sausages and Robert made him sit down and rest and stay warm. Not a minute after Robert tiptoed away, Horace stretched out and tugged the second sheet up to his chin. His reddened, weary eyes closed away the world.

Robert grabbed a chair and set it next to the piano stool. "Let's talk right here," he said, "where you belong." He gave Elizabeth a searching, warm look. "I knew you would come, once you heard I was preaching again."

She ignored that implication, and chastised herself for letting him corner her at the piano, especially when she had come to tell him what he wouldn't want to hear. Somehow it seemed genuine to sit down and play a few hymns when she saw the familiar chairs and the bare light bulbs. All that was missing was sawdust. But sitting at the piano gave him the wrong impression. "What does Mattie think of all this, Robert?"

"Oh, I clean up and sweep every morning. And she said Horace would be the only person to come." He leaned back and glanced at the stairs that led up to the bedroom, speaking in a soft and regretful voice. "I imagine she expected it, sooner or later. She knows me well enough, though I never thought so."

"You're not making any foolish plans, Robert?"

"Planning serves no purpose, you know that. But I miss the sort of cloak I wore. It's invisible, but you feel it more than the tightest-fitting pants. Around here I walk from room to room and say, 'Look, this is ours, and this, and this.' Why? What's the use? It weighs me down. Suddenly I feel like I'm wearing the house itself. But out there in the mountains, after a while you get a security knowing all of it is right there, within touch. This long." He pointed to his stump on his right arm. "No longer. It's what you begin with, and end with."

"Does anyone besides Horace come?"

"Not yet." He laughed. "I've been down on Main Street a little, but I don't seem to have the same effect right now, Elizabeth. You know why? No one considers me a threat."

"It's your hometown."

"Yes, I guess you're right."

"But—well, there's a place here for you, Robert. For all of us. And a time to know it."

She twisted on the stool and got up to sit on a chair. She felt more comfortable separate from the piano and its past. "That stove of yours does the job."

"Yes. Horace'll sleep well."

There was an embarrassing silence. Elizabeth looked away from his expectant gaze. In a foolish moment at the Homecoming, she had met that gaze, affirming that ridiculous journey into the mountains. Now he expected more of her. She had come home, however, to make this decision. She was here—to tell him—because she was duty-bound. Or at least she told herself she visited him out of duty, nothing else.

"Do you miss the mountains, Robert?"

"What is it you've come for, Elizabeth?"

She shifted in her chair, crossing her legs, and surveyed the grocery shelves as she talked to him. "This weather reminds me of the mountains—the nip in the air wakes me up. Remember when we spent the night with that old lady in the shack outside Bryson, the one who sold apple juice with Bible verses written on the label? She had heard about you, Robert, remember? How word passes among the poor, almost as if newspapers and radio didn't exist! She imagined she was entertaining some king disguised in rags." Elizabeth wasn't sure why she was telling this story when she should have been breaking the news to him, but the memory had captured her and made her keep on. "I thought I would freeze to death, until I finally fell asleep—only to wake up and find she had covered me with the most precious quilt I had ever seen. I'm sure it was her single most valuable object. She was already dressed, stoking the fire. And even though when I got up my feet felt ready to drop off, she made the finest coffee I've ever tasted. The second I sipped it I knew I'd never forget the experience."

"She said her daddy recited psalms to her as she grew up," Robert added. "He probably couldn't read."

"Have you ever heard from Molly again, Robert?"

Startled by the question, he stared down at his wounded arm. "No, I haven't, Elizabeth. Never again." There were a few moments of silence, until he lifted his head and once more met her eyes with his searching gaze. "Tell me, Elizabeth, do you really miss the mountains?"

When she talked with Will, she never found herself in such a predicament. As if he had inherited his father's forward nature, Will posed the same probing questions Robert did, but because he asked them in a combative way, Elizabeth never

gave in and answered without first weighing all the consequences. Sometimes she had to lie to keep Will honest. But as
she talked with Robert, even after months away from their
companionship, even after Molly, she found herself relaxing
involuntarily and almost answering freely, just as she feared.
Once they had cast aside posturing every day and discussed
what was most crucial to their lives. But this was not the time,
considering what she had just done, to search too much
within.

"Your life since then has not been satisfactory," he said.

"Has yours?"

"No."

"I'm not ready to admit that," she said. "It is just that we
had to strain so much—there is nothing like it now."

"I will not believe it is over. There are seasons, aren't there?
Rain, shocks of corn, meat, wine, even the sun. 'Canst thou
guide Arcturus with his sons?' "

"You're telling yourself that, Robert. Human beings are not
the seasons of the year. God lets all men die."

"What else, then?"

"I don't know."

Another silence followed. In past times, when Robert and
she had worked themselves up into these conversations, the
silences bore the greatest import. She thought again of Will.
When Will and she descended into silence, they did so from
anger; she rehearsed what to say next, mulling over what he
had said until she exploded out of the silence, panting, with
some vindictive accusation about a trivial, misinterpreted
word. Now she remembered an argument she'd had with Robert in the mountains. It was in Needmore. She had found the
courage to attack him about Molly. Molly was ruining him,
she said, by pumping him with false praise about the millions
waiting for his most insignificant sigh, Christ himself multi-
plying the loaves and fishes. Robert was tired, and himself
uncertain about the turn of events with Molly. For once he
responded bitterly. It had been an awful fight. She had called
him a charlatan, and he had said she was Martha in the
kitchen. They had flung accusations like the manure of Will's
damned cows, until each was blinded with rage. She didn't
want to live another moment. And then they descended into a
long silence.

It was in the midst of this silence, Elizabeth remembered,
that something very strange happened. She was so exhausted

from bitterness and so depressed about their anger that she gave up arguing. Her will to fight died. And into that emptiness, like sudden light, came a strong affirmation. She had never believed her faith could profit at such a time, but after she and Robert had acted inhumanely, after this selfish and murderous behavior, she somehow realized that the values Christ taught were true. She could not find herself without taking them seriously. It was more than lip service—she must try to live them. We must forgive one another, she realized. That is the beginning.

But this was another kind of silence, and all the more painful because of that memory. Her liberating faith was gone. Nothing—not his ministry to the poor and homeless, not the fervor of his eyes at the Homecoming or in this store—could retrieve it, dead in the clutches of another woman, whore of Babylon herself. "What else?" Robert had asked. "What else can a man do?" The silence that answered that question begged with ignorant hands, a child half-dressed in rags, with a stomach bloated from starvation and eyes hollowed out from despair. That was her faith. Robert made her see the truth of the matter, that they were indeed vagabonds. But she didn't want to know the truth. What had the truth gained her?

Now, without warning she felt tears swell within her, and then found herself crying. She wanted to stop, but the bursting within her went out of control and she sobbed. It was awful. She didn't know why she was crying, but she couldn't begin to brace herself. Robert put his hand on her shoulder and waited with her as the anguish ran its course, for a long time, filling her lungs fitfully until they were too tired to comply, and pouring its water from her until she felt empty. Then he kissed her on the forehead. "Let me show you something," he said.

When they stood up, Horace stirred for a moment. They kept still as he snorted, startled himself awake, and opened his eyes to an ignorance of where he was and who she and Robert were, as uncertain of his existence as the risen dead first awake. Then he shifted in the chairs and fell back into a heavy sleep. She took the chance to recover, drying her eyes with tissues from her purse, chastising herself for letting go in front of him. She felt herself rebelling, looking at Horace and remembering that Will had said Robert took better care of the poor than of his own, and remembering what mastery he had over her in the mountains, even in front of Molly. She began to blame it on her condition at the Priscilla Worthington Home, but she stopped thinking about it, not wanting to implicate Will in the chain of incriminations. And now, of all the humiliations, she was crying in front of him.

Robert motioned for her to follow, which she did, along the counter past the stairs to the back corner of the store, where through a slashed curtain a door opened to the old smokehouse. Robert stood to the side after he snapped on the light. The four rusted meathooks hovered in the darkness over the light bulb, a sliver or two gleaming as the light swung back and forth a few inches. Dangling into the light from each hook were long black shoestrings, tied into small knots below each flattened, glittering, pierced copper penny. The strings of oversize pennies, oddly spaced, hovered over a table piled with wood shavings and rising horizontally out of the shavings, like an ancient ship atop waves, was a pine log, completely skinned. The cut ends of the log formed neatly shaped half-cylinders, but from the middle of the log rose a boxlike structure, the four top corners meticulously worked into crosses, each of which was nailed with a coin. Sawdust obscured the floor.

"Robert?"

"Not bad for a boy and a left-handed old man, aye? At first I thought he wondered over the strange shapes—they look like worn stones along an old Roman road. But come here and I'll show you." Robert draped the strings of pennies over his forearm. Elizabeth bent over, pleased that the contraption at least gave them a diversion, and inspected one of the flattened coins like a buyer, weighing it in her palm, checking the opposite side for defects, and holding it up to the light. The others on the string followed like Christmas-tree bulbs. "He's polished them all, you see. It's not the shapes, Lizzie, but the shine. They're as bright as mirrors. He even holds one right up to his eye so he can see himself." Robert's voice raced with excitement. "And this will be the ark of the covenant. It was carried to the people. We're making it to scale, about three by two by two. We can't really attach rings to put the staves through, so we're carving the staves along the mercy seat and painting the rings on, and painting the gold rim, too. Instead of cherubims, we've cut crosses. A different dispensation."

Elizabeth ran her fingertips in a long, slow stroke over the top of the pine box. The wood felt smooth and sensual and warm. Her hand pulled up at the nearest corner cross, in fear of touching it. She had just built her own covenant, and in doing so she broke off the cross. She could not will away the memories, but that way of life was broken off, rent like the veil of the Temple. Robert had taken advantage of her vulnerability—that was it, simply put—but now she was strong enough to live facing the indifferent but clear horizon, in her own dwelling place, patterned to her design and overlaid with gems of her own choosing. She had chopped down that old life—she had. She had.

"Will told me about the ark," she said.

Robert's face darkened.

"Stearns told him, Robert. Did you expect Will to let the boy keep coming over here and not ask him what he was doing all the time? Will is the boy's father—remember, Robert—and he asked."

"We were sworn to secrecy."

"*You're* showing *me*. Certainly you, too, then, are breaking the vow."

"You're the only one I thought would understand."

"Well, now that you're discovered, why don't you take the boy away? Isn't that the next step—to run away? You can teach him how to play the piano and kidnap him into the mountains."

"There is nothing for me to do, Elizabeth, but teach him the truth."

She was glad he had said that. It was easy now. If any one of Robert's sins set her against him, it was his self-righteousness. And this perversion of a boy was absolutely reprehensible. "You teach him the truth so he can live a confused, guilt-ridden life?"

" 'The truth shall make you free.' "

"Ah, Robert, you and your Christ. Who among us is free? Spout, spout your verses, Robert, and teach an imaginary way of living. The problem is that you've been too effective a teacher. This boy believes you. I believed you. And so did Molly, in your bed."

"That's a lie. You don't know what you're talking about, Elizabeth."

"But you see, she did the same thing to you—made you believe her—and made you a fool all the same. Listen to your son for once, Robert. Will has been telling you for years, and, you know, he's right. If you continue to live in a world peopled only by Abraham and Peter, and sanctified by a box you call the ark of the covenant, and falling into the arms of Bath-

sheba, you only do harm. You become satanic, not Christlike.
I am sure Will doesn't understand the extent of this mastery
over Stearns. He knew the boy was hanging around with you
too often, but not this, not to this extent. And I will tell him.
He won't allow it."

The cold silence that came, for its duration, felt final. Elizabeth wanted him to say what he was thinking. She wanted him
to grab the pine log and heave it across the room and shout, "I
can't believe you said that! You've betrayed me, you've utterly
betrayed me!" But he didn't. She felt cold. He looked at her
again, as if to see her soul. He knew, she thought. He knew the
moment he saw her at the piano. He had always read her, but
she would deny him from this moment on.

"I came tonight," she said, "to tell you we're going to get
married."

21

*A*fter they unpacked and changed clothes, Elizabeth and Will took a long walk on the beach. The Gulf of Mexico stretched from lapping waves to blue horizon, where plump cotton-white clouds hovered as still as a distant promise. Elizabeth and Will turned around a pylon beneath the fishing pier and retraced their footsteps, never stopping, even though they had no particular place to go. It was the beginning of a week-long honeymoon; they had married a year and a day after Susan died. On the beach in front of the motel, they began work on a sand castle. While he packed the outer wall, she studied his glistening body. His broad back was beginning to burn, first around his shoulders, where his farm-exercised muscles rippled as he worked. He showed his age around his chin and slack stomach, but he was still an attractive man. And now he was her husband.

She fingered battlements into the tops of the turrets and traced an outline of the gateway on the inside of Will's wall. Then the sunlight sparkled on the waves like reflected glass and she looked up. The flickering stars of light danced over the water toward the horizon. She was no longer comfortable with such extended, open vistas. The sand castle at her feet pleased her more. Faraway places—the horizon, visions, the sea and clouds, dreams—these were let go. She was finished with wild risk taking, content to establish a firm foothold in the here and now, with Will.

Bored with the castle, Will curled a spire of sand on her ankle, the wet, grainy drips tickling all the way up her backbone. She kept still, even though, head to toe, she needed to jerk herself free. The sand hardened into a curling horn of a unicorn—a blessing, it seemed, on their marriage. And when he finished he gave her that look, darkened by the sunlight behind him, and helped her up, laying his hand on her hip as they turned toward the motel room. It was early in their marriage, and she wanted to cry, knowing all the hope she placed in the turn of the doorknob into the already sandy room; the undressing; the moment she first felt him and the scratch of his beard on her neck and the look in his eye, his only giving in when he took her.

Today was one of the few times the bed satisfied him. He preferred the sink counter in the bathroom, the shower, the dresser, the floor, or the woods at the farm, anyplace where he seemed a seducer and not a husband, though now he was. As usual he got up quickly and dressed again, asking her if she wanted to walk to the pier and try fishing. She asked him to wait a few minutes, which he did, on the porch outside that faced inland to the highway and the palmetto swamp. She stood naked at the beach window, edging back the curtain to see the great open spaces of land, the Gulf, and the sky. She searched the shore a few seconds until she found the castle, already half-crumbled.

She didn't enjoy fishing. She wasn't going to admit to Will that she found impaling a worm on a hook repulsive, but she did. She was glad Will didn't have any luck, for he was more willing, two days later, to stroll along the beach for most of the afternoon. Elizabeth's sunburn was hurting and she had thought about taking a long nap, but his enthusiasm made her want to take advantage. As soon as they started out, Will pointed to a brown nub in the distant haze of the shoreline. "All the way round it," he said, setting a steady pace that disregarded shells and wrack and a change of mind.

Even though they hardly spoke to each other, she was pleased that they were walking the shoreline again. Sometimes the sand squeaked between her toes, tickling. An occasional wave broke over her ankles and in its swell and tug slowed her down. Will waited impatiently as, to the accompaniment of sucking sounds, she trudged out of the suddenly deep sand. She wondered how a man could make getting to a pier and back a compulsion, but she followed beside her husband, turning toward the water to watch the waves and keep herself from anger.

She needed to slow down. At her feet she noticed a tall, half-buried spire. It was a broken conch. The spire, though, rose in perfectly layered whorls. The inner lip of the aperture was a beautiful cool pink. As she washed it off in the water and inspected the brown and white body whorl, she remembered reading somewhere about a pattern in nature sometimes found in shells. She didn't recall if the pattern—something about successive layers adding up to each other in sequence—existed in a conch, but she wouldn't be surprised, as mysterious as the shell was.

"Are you coming, Elizabeth," he said, "or do I have to wait all day?"

That evening after supper she tried to read, but she could not forget the way he had looked at her when he spoke. Two pillows propped her up, in a smooth sundress, on the end of the couch below the beachside window, where a soft breeze fluttered the cloth curtains and cooled her sunburned shoulders. The sound of the waves faded from her consciousness, as did the plot of the drugstore novel that lay open on her lap, turned to the same page for at least five minutes. He had shown no interest whatsoever in the broken conch she found. Robert would have. After chastising her for the delay, Will had stared at her with offended eyes and didn't speak for what seemed hours. She still hadn't figured out if she had done something wrong or if he was simply selfish about what he wanted to accomplish, which was to conquer the far pier. This was their honeymoon.

She woke from the trance into which the memory had led her and once again saw the page of the book. But she also felt his eyes on her. She really didn't feel like it. The very idea that stopping to examine a beautiful shell bothered him angered her so much that she felt like spitting. And now he wanted to make love. She took a long breath, exhaled, counting the seconds her lungs took to empty, and heard him—her husband—come toward her.

This time he kept her from the bed. He set her on a small, dirty throw rug in the middle of the sandy floor and entered her from behind. He pushed too quickly—she was dry—and it hurt. She bent her head as he pumped and pawed at her breasts. A dead fly was caught in the hairs of the throw rug, its rigid feet turned up toward her. He slipped out once and she wanted to change positions and get on the bed, but he wouldn't, keeping behind her like an animal, grunting from deep within his throat where he never spoke. Nothing in her body responded to him, which surprised her because before they were married she had made love to him when she was angry, and her body had involuntarily responded. She imagined that was a good sign. But now his brutal passion angered her. When he was finished, she dressed in her bathrobe and stood on the small porch, slowly breathing the salty air and listening to the breaking of waves, and trying not to think.

By midnight neither of them felt like sleeping. Will always grew bored with reading, so a few minutes later he asked her to play gin rummy. From where she sat at the kitchenette table, a side window of the room framed a streetlight the township had placed at the end of the motel court, where the beach began. During the first few games, they said hardly a word to each other, playing each hand like old people, with wasting-away bodies, wasting time as they go. She didn't want to look at him. When she wasn't grouping the faces of kings or numbers of pips, she studied the fluorescent globe in the window and wished her mind might blank out into such a pure, forgetful whiteness. She wondered if some people could raise their minds on command to another level of thought, burning away the everyday pettiness for some renewing meditative flame. She lusted after that forgetfulness.

"At least you might let me win one," he said, laughing. "I'll get an inferiority complex."

She glanced at him and smiled. He tried to gather too many runs, she thought, but what did it matter? It was only a game, a way to pass time until they fell asleep and tried again tomorrow. She won three more games, which made seven straight. He hadn't spoken a word throughout except to grunt when she asked a few questions, simply to be civil.

"Let's quit," she said. "I'm tired. It must be one o'clock."

"You'd like that, wouldn't you?"

"There are a lot of things I would like, Will. One is sleep."

"I bet, Elizabeth, I bet. And I think I could name a few other things you'd like."

"I don't believe you know, Will. Even my most obvious desire. What I want and what I feel are as far from you as the moon."

"Deal the cards, love."

"Don't be ridiculous."

"I said deal the cards!"

She gave him eleven cards and left her ten facedown on the table. As she waited in silence, he sorted his cards, studied them, and discarded the queen of spades. She stared at him. How could a man be so awful?

"Well?"

"Would you grow up, Will?"

There was a knock at the door. The sound startled her. It was too late for anything normal. Will didn't move at first, letting his angry stare burn all the farther into her because of the suspenseful knock, and then he lingered at the door through two more knocks. He could be at the point of death, she thought, and he'd still try to get the upper hand. She overheard the man say there was an emergency telephone call for Will in the office. He didn't speak to her as he left.

Elizabeth began to pack. Some urgent voice told her not to feel foolish about her worry; she should pack because they must rush home.

Terrible white rings circled Will's eyes when he came back and told her that Stearns was hurt and that it was Robert's fault. The white around his eyes was not so much from fear as from the hottest anger. They finished packing in less than fifteen minutes and sped over the hills of the panhandle toward the state line. Elizabeth persisted with her questions, but he had tightened himself into a silent rage. After the monotony of time and the road, however, he began to relate what Luke had told him on the phone. Robert had decided to preach again. The boy had been downtown with him. After they came home to the store, a gang of older boys, who had listened to Robert evangelize, arrived and beat Stearns up. Elizabeth didn't understand, but Will couldn't help her more than that. He was easing up on the accelerator and sharing his rage against his father, though, which was the first time on their honeymoon, she said to herself, that they were truly married. Finally he calmed down and drove on.

A heavy mantle of guilt fell over her. She had begun an argument only moments before he heard about Stearns's injury. She had hated her own husband. But as they slowed down and ran the four o'clock red light in Eufaula's square, she thought beyond that guilt to their new marriage. It was a selfish thought, and she didn't want to believe she was more con-

cerned about the two of them than about her innocent step-
son. But it might be better for them that something terrible
had happened.

Luke found the boy lying on the smokehouse floor. Stearns
had been not only beaten with fists but battered by rocks.
Mattie became hysterical, swearing at Robert even though he
was in the bedroom, fallen into an exhausted sleep both of
them thought was one verse away from death. Luke finally
shouted at Mattie to get control of herself, that the boy would
be fine if she'd just call the hospital and help him clean the
mud and blood off Stearns's face. She finally collected herself,
gathered some of the boy's clothes, and held him beside her
breast as Luke drove him to the hospital, where he was re-
ported scarred and seriously bruised, but without any broken
bones. It was too early to tell how traumatized he was.

Luke and Mattie had him asleep at the farmhouse when
Elizabeth and Will arrived at 7:00 A.M. Will called the intern
at the hospital to confirm what Luke told him. The injuries
weren't as bad as they had first seemed to Mattie and Luke—
anyone bleeds a lot when his face is cut. But just to be on the
safe side, in case of internal damage, Stearns wasn't supposed
to get up for a few days. Elizabeth sent Luke and Mattie home
and prepared the sickroom's implements—washcloths, ban-
dages, soup, juice, aspirin, and extra pillows. Then she sat
down in a rocking chair in a corner of the room, and without
considering sleep even though they had driven straight from
Florida, she began knitting a sweater for Stearns. For the next
day and night she occupied her hands with that sweater while
she waited in the same place for every single beckon, from son
or father.

In contrast Will jerked around, in and out for all of the
twenty-four hours, unable to find a suitable position, in the
room or anywhere on the farm, where he could sit and wait.
He wouldn't consider sleeping, either. She watched him
closely when he paced beside the bed, suddenly freezing for a
moment to stare at his sleeping son, measuring the length and
breadth of the boy's body, the taper of his leg, the rise and fall
of his breast, and the curse of those bruises. He was terribly
confused, far more so, it seemed to her, than when he had circled around his dying wife, her sister. Susan had died, too
young, and now she rotted in the frills of a coffin, meat and

marrow for worms, but this was his son, his own manly flesh. It was only a fight, Elizabeth told him, but Will imagined the boy was close to death. Each time he came in, she could feel sorrow rise like a dark wind. She was worried that once Stearns was all right, a different emotion in Will, of a worse kind, might follow.

The next day Elizabeth tried her best to mother both of them and to continue putting the injury in perspective. She cooked her tastiest two meals and a gigantic breakfast before a checkup, as she called it, at the family doctor's. But the food was wasted: Stearns only wanted to sip some juice and a little of the chicken soup Mattie had sent with Mr. Martin, their neighbor; and Will had no appetite—for food, for her pleasure, for the company of the human race. Many a father, she thought, imagined an injury to his son tantamount to an injury against himself. But Will was even more defensive than most fathers, and she knew he didn't blame the offense on the boys.

She tried to bathe Stearns before they left, but even though he was only four, he was silently embarrassed by his nakedness. She had Will wash him then, but he was awkward, and when the boy groaned from his father's cow-callused hands, Will, of course, blamed her. She didn't argue. Instead she helpfully reminded her husband of his chores—or at least reminded him to call Mr. Martin to do them; and after the trip to the doctor, she met the visitor by herself. He was the father of one of the boys, a mechanic, who said he had tanned his child's behind until it bled. He couldn't believe that his son would pick on a baby boy. She assured the man Stearns was all right.

Elizabeth also stayed in touch with Luke and Mattie. When Will drifted into the backyard that evening, she telephoned Luke at his apartment. She had not slept in over thirty-six hours and could hardly make sense, but she felt obligated to let him know, especially since he had taken care of the boy. Luke then called Mattie, and on Friday at noon Elizabeth herself telephoned her mother-in-law after sending Will to town to run some errands. Luke was having dinner with his parents. She didn't want to speak with him again, but Mattie gave him the phone before Elizabeth could make an excuse. He insisted that both his parents needed to involve themselves with the recovery, or die from guilt over an event that, he emphasized, could have happened to anyone. He admitted that

Robert had been preaching, but pointed out that boys got into
fights plenty of times without adults being able to stop them.
She gave in and arranged a time on Saturday afternoon when
the three of them could visit, but she warned Luke that Will
might completely lose control if he saw one family face. If
anyone understood, it was Luke, she thought, deciding to be-
tray her husband a little and share her fears with Luke
quickly, before Will came back.

"I'm not going to believe this bit about Robert being innocent, Luke," she said. "You know as well as I do that he's been
messing with that boy in ways he shouldn't be."

"Yes."

"But Will is misinterpreting it. He won't talk to me about it,
but I can tell. It's that whole business about his own childhood—you know better than I. Will just can't see it as an un-
fortunate accident, or even as the carelessness of an adult. It's
the history involved. He's absolutely sure that Stearns's
wounds are the same wounds Robert inflicted on *him*."

"The child was defending Dad in a way, I guess. Neither of
them have told me about it, but I assume the group of boys
came to the house to break up that wooden ark."

"I'm not surprised. But Will doesn't have to be told that."

"But Mother has to see him, and Dad, too, really. If he can
see Stearns is all right, I think he'll leave him alone."

"Sure, Luke."

"Can't you fix it so Will's gone when we come?"

"He's my husband. I can't deceive my own husband."

Luke didn't answer her.

It had been a mistake to talk with him. "I'll see," she said,
and she hung up.

After lunch on Saturday she decided to encourage Stearns
to take a nap. She would read to him until he fell asleep,
which was part of her plan. Will would go off to do the farm
chores, and when the three of them arrived, they would not
want to wake the boy, but only tiptoe in and reassure themselves that he was fine. Then they would be gone quickly
enough.

She pulled down the shades to make the room as dark and
cool as possible, and sat down to read by the small bedside
lamp. Stearns was still nibbling on a tomato sandwich, his first
solid food. Without her asking, he told her he could feel the
side of his face again, which both of them agreed was a good
sign. After about fifteen minutes he closed his eyes. She read a

few more words and then tucked the book under her arm. As she rose, however, she felt his hand, soft and faint, barely touch the end of her fingers. Then he whispered, "Thank you, Aunt Elizabeth." He rolled over before she could respond.

Unfortunately he woke up before they arrived. When right on schedule Will left to do the chores, he slammed the pickup door—the noise was as loud as a gunshot—and bounced the truck across the backyard and up the rise to the first forty. Elizabeth was washing the boy's still-startled face when she heard their car pull into the driveway, not two minutes later. Luke had probably been waiting across the road—he knew how legitimate her worry about Will and Robert was. They didn't knock, but suddenly stood there, inside the bedroom doorway. Mattie was already crying, still distraught; Luke waited to one side like the unknown but surely condemned future; and Robert, furrowed and slumped over, his stump hidden between the buttonholes of his shirt, searched for his wounded disciple.

The sight of them brought jealousy to her soul, a small creature curled up in the pit of her heart, monkeylike, with horns and wings, eating the fingers of its own hand. Stearns had thanked her after she read, which made her immensely happy. She gripped his kindness with sharpened claws because since the beginning of her marriage she had not known unfeigned, nor abundant, nor meek and patient love—indeed she had not known any aspect of love. She quickly decided that she and Stearns were on the way, walking down a road together; if the two of them could navigate, they might bring Will along with them. But Mattie and Luke and Robert were roadblocks. She felt that clawing jealousy inside her suddenly fly toward them, ready to land on each one's shoulder and scratch and bite. They brought nothing but trouble; the old man led them to a day of slaughter.

Mattie was the first to move. As she hurried toward her grandson, without thinking Elizabeth held her hand out to stop her.

"Oh, no," the woman said. She whisked by and gently pressed her face against her grandson's. He smiled and hugged her. Mattie held his hand as she turned around. "I brought some more soup—and a ham and a chocolate cake and pecan pie for you and Will."

"You didn't have to do that."

"Don't you think I could help if I just stayed in the guest

room for a while? You've got so much to do, Elizabeth, and I
would stay out of your way—I only want to help. Couldn't
you convince Will?"

"You don't understand, Mother. And besides, Stearns is
past soup now. In fact he's fine." She followed to the bedside
and laid her hand on Stearns's leg. "We're just fine, aren't we,
son? We don't need a bit more help, do we?" But before he
could answer, she continued. "The absolutely crucial thing is
more rest, no matter how well he feels." She was lying—
Stearns could probably get up and go on his way with only a
sore face and stiff muscles, but she wanted to keep him to herself now.

"Yes, of course."

"You heard the doctor say that yourself, didn't you,
Stearns? Don't you agree, Luke—as few visitors as possible?"

"Perhaps—for his physical health." He remained in the corner, trying to keep his distance.

"It's company, Elizabeth," Mattie said. "We're interested in
keeping him company. And you. Certainly you need some
help."

"Will, Mother. You *must* realize." She glanced at Stearns to
make the woman understand. "Don't you think it's better not
to press the issue?"

"I see. I should have known."

"And what else should I be concerned with, Luke, besides
his physical health?" She felt like lecturing him.

"Of course, Elizabeth," Mattie said. "We thoroughly agree.
And we certainly don't want to be a burden to anybody." She
turned back to the boy, who was still smiling at her. "And
more than anything in the world we want this young prince to
get better. You hear me, child? You have one task—to get
well." She measured her new daughter to the quick before
speaking again. "It was so kind of you to let us come over."

Then Robert began to limp toward the bed, still without
speaking. He looked terribly aged, as pale and mapless as he
had appeared the moment before his collapse at Andrews. A
suffering plagued his walk, a spiritual burden so physically
evident that it reminded her of the great depressions he had
endured after his nightly, exhausting preaching sessions in the
mountains when he bowed down before the slaughter and was
spared—at least for another night. The ritual seemed profound to his blood.

She stepped in front of him, muffling her voice from the

boy. "Please, Robert. Don't you think . . . you know Will. My God, have some compassion!"

Luke was not the kind to be insistent, especially with her. But this moment, of all the times he could have chosen, he came to his father's side, supporting him at the elbow, and, like mourners approaching a coffin, escorted him around Elizabeth to the boy. She was ready to object again, but she didn't want to make a scene and disturb Stearns; she was still competing for his affection. And Will would be back soon, blaming her if he found out. She could more easily make them leave if Robert got his foolish words in.

And they were indeed foolish words, more of his jumbled-up biblical indoctrination. She hardly heard his whisper. "The Creator, Stearns . . . their host by number. He called them all by name."

Then the two of them locked hands.

Luke turned him away. For a last moment Robert stared at the boy, through those heavy spectacles, like a man looking down at himself, wrapped in the bed of a pine box. Luke nodded at Elizabeth as he passed again, steering the man out the door.

"Now listen, Elizabeth," Mattie said, her purse strap over her arm. "Tell that son of mine not to jump to conclusions. It was a mistake, really—I should have been watching the two of them closer. But I can't tell you how much they were getting out of each other—and I don't mean just Robert. The boy, too. And when my son scoffs at what I say, and replies, 'Oh it's the man—he's ruined the boy, just like me and my dead brother'—you know all of this is coming, Elizabeth, as we know it's coming—you ask him then about his fatherhood. That's why I didn't do what I should have done. I'm not going to ask you about the kind of two-week husband he is—it's none of my business, and everyone in this county knows the life my husband and I have endured. I'm not going to ask you about my son as a father, either—the same holds true. But since Robert's come home, who has been the boy's father?" She kissed Elizabeth on the cheek and followed the two of them to the car.

Elizabeth turned toward the boy after their car was gone. Stearns had rolled over in bed, his face toward the wall. Of the people who bowed down before the child, even though the others were his flesh and blood, only she truly knew what had passed between the boy and the old man when they locked hands. She remembered how the electrical surge drained away all arguments of the flesh and how time lost itself until, finally, something forced a person to turn his face toward the blankness of a wall, where the emptiness helped the body recover and return to a world where feet trod on solid rock. A spiritual bond is sometimes stronger than either the bond of flesh, as in marriage, or the bond of blood relation. And because she realized what had happened between the false prophet and his unwary, underage disciple, she decided to let the boy lie there undisturbed for the present. She would wait. In the future Stearns would grow out of it, as she did, and behind the scenes she would ensure that he didn't have the opportunity to stand at such risk again with the old man, as Mattie and Luke had allowed. Luke, of all people, whose own twin had died!

She gathered up the washcloth and basin and went back to the kitchen, glancing out the window at Susan's bird feeder. She would take it down. Then she saw the pickup angrily kicking up dust in the backyard, turning almost in a complete circle from too much speed, ducktailing straight back, and then sliding to a stop beside the garage's back door.

Will tramped into the kitchen, slamming the door behind him. She could smell the rotting odor of cows. "You think I don't know what you're doing? I saw the goddamn car, and to tell you the truth, I expected it—from you, woman." He gripped the edge of the sink. A thin red crescent of clay stuck beneath each one of his fingernails.

She slowly filled a pot with water, making him wait. "No— you don't know what I'm doing."

He squeezed her arm with those unwashed, foul-smelling hands. "You're wrong." And then, without warning, he shook her. She felt a twinge in the back of her neck.

"I only wanted to spare you," she said.

"Shit you did."

"Thank you, my love."

"You wanted the boy to see him. You want the boy perverted. Just like you were perverted."

"Your mother, Will. She's the one I was thinking about."

"Did he ask you about our honeymoon?"

"Damn you, Will!" She freed herself from his grip and slid the pot onto an eye of the stove, the stray moisture on the bottom sizzling. She purposely kept her back toward him as she braced herself. She did not want to argue, not now, not after Luke and Mattie and the old man and the way Stearns had welcomed their visit. But Will would not be able to restrain his bitterness; the simple thought of his father seeing Stearns again, and the idea that the boy loved her, maybe more than he loved his father, was too much for him to endure. He was such a jealous man. When she looked at him again, a pale yellow, clammy tint spread across his face. He was becoming a pale yellow ghost, his hair and head and arms oozing a uniform nauseous substance. He leaned over the sink and washed his hands with her dishwashing liquid, and as he dried them—first with four paper towels, and then four more—he stared at her with contentious, hot eyes, hotter than ever before.

"Last night," he said, "I saw Susan standing in the corner of the room, watching us sleep. When I sat up in bed, I saw tears in her eyes. Her love was genuine, you know."

"I appreciate that, Will."

"Well, this house is full of her presence. There's no way you can deny that, Elizabeth. Look out this window—look at that goddamn bird feeder in the yard. Do you see it? I used to sit out there with her and listen to her stories of baby woodpeckers and cardinals and titmice and every sort of helpless creature. We were husband and wife out there. Or the couch in the living room. There's still an indentation where she sat—I swear there is. There's nothing you can ever do to get rid of that indentation. That rocking chair—you know about that. And everytime I get up and walk through the breezeway to the bedroom, I can feel her coming right behind me. And she gets into the bed beside me and puts her face in the crook of my neck, Elizabeth, and she tells me she loves me. She used to do that, woman, every single night. She might have had her faults, but she loved me, and she told me so."

She felt a wind rise up inside her, blowing through the window from the faraway sky, coughing and spitting up and rattling over this house like her dead sister's dying groans. The wind was raging inside his stomach, too. There was a fear between them, not two weeks into their marriage, a fear she had never known, rising up through her heart to her throat, a fear not of each other but of what unseen storms blew across this life—hurricanes and tidal waves and tornadoes and typhoons—that neither of them could do one bit to control. All that was left was to scream.

"You're coming with me." He tossed the crumpled paper towels into the basket under the sink and grabbed her arm.

"Will—"

"I said you're coming with me."

"Don't grab me like that. Get your vile hands off me!"

"I'll grab you whatever way I goddamn want to, Elizabeth. Don't you ever forget that, and don't you ever forget who I am, and what I know about you, woman. You're coming with me because you're a part of it. It's your fault as much as anyone else's." He yanked her toward the door to the garage.

"Stearns, Will. I won't leave him."

"He's fine. He's no concern of yours anyway. Just get your ass in the truck."

She tried to resist him, but he yanked on her arm until she thought he'd pull it out of the socket. Then he slapped her. Stunned, she gave in as he forced her through the garage door and into the cab, slamming and locking the door behind her. His shotgun lay poised in the back window rack. In the middle of the seat was a half-opened box of shells. "What in God's name are you doing, Will?"

"We're going to pay a visit, Elizabeth, just like the three of us got together however long ago. What has it been—almost three years? Except this time, Elizabeth, sweet Elizabeth, we bring the whole goddamn thing to an end." He rammed the stick shift into reverse, throwing her toward the windshield, and then back into first gear, screeching past the garage.

"Will, stop it!"

He stared at her. "My father is never coming near my son again. I'll see to it this time, right in front of your god-awful face, woman!"

It was a day of slaughter. All he held sacred to himself had been defiled, his pride humiliated. He sped them toward town.

By the State Line Bridge, resignation swept over her. She could not stop him. He had cursed her and Robert and Luke and Mattie, his cows and the Brahman, life itself, with a nonstop spewing of bestial obscenities. He claimed he was not going to murder his father—no, he shouted, that would be too good for the old prophet; he was going to rupture his brain, whatever that meant, and he began to repeat the phrase in the midst of his obscenities: rupture his brain, rupture his brain. She realized, of course, with that shotgun simmering in the window, that whatever he planned to do wouldn't necessarily happen. But nothing—not an apology, nor cajolement, nor a warning—even dimly moved him. As a result her resignation was a sudden, physical feeling, like a heavy cloak set on her shoulders from behind and wrapped around her face, weighing her down into a balled-up position, helpless against a world that she was no longer able to resist. She kept quiet; and finally, without her disputing, by the bridge his spewing ceased. When he fitted the car onto the runners, they were silent.

Her peripheral vision blurred, and then narrowed into a thin, elliptical opening through which she watched the river passing under them. It was the mantle, it was the mantle wrapped about her face that tightened her vision into this telescopic slit. Seeing the water through it, with all surrounding distractions brushed away, she experienced a rare sense of history and understanding: the rivers of the earth were its bloodstreams; her own blood ran through the earth-courses of her body; river, blood, earth, vein—all were passing away, like lamb and oxen and young men, toward a very great slaughter. And then, in response, a flood of questions about that river and her life. How many gallons of that brown, slow-swirling water had flowed under that bridge since she was born? Or since they rowed across to the picnic? Since Susan died? Since this very afternoon when Robert came to cause this profound revolt? And the seemingly endless blood running through her own balled-up body, how much of it, the useless waste.

Rising up out of the tangled embankment, the Mallery house beckoned her. Now the dead were embalmed there. The car plopped down off the runners and sped on, her neck whiplashed again. Will turned by Mr. Schnedel's furniture store, then raced down Main Street to the railroad station and Cherry Drive, strangling the steering wheel. The street and station asked her about her past, as did the "Heart of Dixie" license plates and each blurred storefront and supposed friend, turning to flag them down to a safer speed. There were Atlanta and André and the Mediterranean beach and the mountains of western North Carolina, but they were nothing compared to this place, this home. There were her friend Mary and mortification and "nothing is true for everyone" and a medley of invitational hymns, but they were nothing. "Here is the place," she answered herself, "where we have lived." There was nothing profound about that. She desperately wanted her life to possess some historical significance she could put into words, or maybe understand in a wordless way, especially these last moments before the sword and destruction. But it didn't, not since she had come home to bury her sister and marry Will, which was only what she considered the safest option.

Will spun the pickup on the yard's clay patch and slammed on the brakes. The rattle of the cab had been unbearably loud. She waited there in a moment of silence and listened to her own heart throb like a clock in the sudden stillness, deceiving itself into believing now that the breakneck ride was over, relief was at hand. In the afternoon sky behind the house, toward the southwest and the Gulf, the sun fell behind a string of slate-gray, softening clouds. In a moment it would reappear below, close enough to the horizon that the earth's haze would begin to temper it, and eventually define it simply as a seething, faraway orange circle. Later in the day a human might gaze unblinded. Four days ago she and Will had walked on the beach where the sun was setting, hand in hand for a while, trying to make the pier. And now they were here, light-years away.

Mattie's house looked abandoned. Luke's car wasn't there—he must have gone back to his apartment—and Mattie hadn't popped out to the porch to welcome the visitors, which probably meant she was taking a nap. Elizabeth scanned the garden behind the house. The fence gate had fallen down. A few tomatoes hung like bulging hearts on the blackening vines, and bunches of green peanuts lay shook-clean and drying. The okra plants stood as straight as colonels, and the beans were already uprooted and turned over to rot in the soil where once they flourished. Coffee weeds grew tall by then, as did the purple weeds Elizabeth never could name, except they looked like rhubarb. Some onions had been planted too deep and were left alone. They were going to seed.

For a moment Elizabeth thought they were safe, but then they saw a floppy hat Robert often wore while in the garden, inching along behind the back rows of dry, brittle corn, from one stalk to another, as if each scarecrow in a line of scarecrows tried on the hat and passed it to his neighbor.

"Let's go," Will said. He reached for the shotgun, the two cool black barrels staring her in the face as he swiveled it down beside him.

"I am not," she said.

He swung open the driver's door and propped his foot on the running board. He uncocked the gun and set it on his leg while he dropped two shells neatly into the breech and clicked the stock back into place. "I said let's go." He dismounted from the cab and turned back toward her. She did not move.

"I am not."

He lifted the gun from his side and pointed it at her midsection. The two barrels were tapered toward the small, smooth holes. Her stomach quivered, imagining the shot bursting her intestines. "Don't give me any of this crap, woman. You're coming."

She was empty. She was as empty as the oil-slick gun barrels marking her. Whatever spirit had filled her life, whatever blood had pumped through the channels of her body, was dried up and gone, and with it died any desire to save herself.

"Go ahead, Will."

He measured her to the quick. A twitch came to his left eye. She had seen it only once before. It was involuntary, she said to herself. Nothing would go as planned. He hated having someone challenge him, especially if that person was a woman, more especially if she was his wife. But she didn't care. He would kill her because she challenged him. But she was past caring.

Then he lowered the gun. "I'll deal with you later."

"You can't, Will!"

"Oh, I won't kill him." She measured his tight eyes. "But he'll never bother my son again after I rupture his goddamn brain."

He turned and began to stalk the garden. The shotgun, its stock balanced in the crook of his arm, stuck out from his side like a great, ancient broadsword. She scanned the back rows of corn—they were about a hundred feet away—but she could no longer spot the hat. She sat back in silence as Will disappeared behind a row of corn. She was left with waiting. There was nothing she could do—it would be worse if she went and tried to interfere; Will would murder Robert if she showed her face. She was utterly helpless. Robert had brought it upon himself, running away, claiming that his journeys were all for truth. She had told him life would catch him soon enough. Deep within her inner ear she heard the sound of her own heart pumping, faster and louder each time, the blood of her own body bursting its banks as if she were the marked one.

Then she heard voices, immediately loud. Mostly Will, shouting his garbled accusations. And then a silence, which seemed, in its intrusion upon the argument, as long as eternity.

And into that eternity came a picture of her past—a dusty, weed-choked riverbed, empty of the blood of life. She wanted to be safe, she said to herself. She wanted to sit on the side of the river and build her own little house of thatch, content to let the others, like Robert, flounder through the risk-laden crossing—when she had tried, what had it done for her? It was the safest option, Will was, and that precious child; she had thought them a certain choice.

There were two shots. The second followed the first by about ten seconds.

Will ran back from the garden with the shotgun barrels still smoking, jumped into the pickup, and tossed the weapon across her lap. She tried to knock the burning instrument away, but he slammed the buttstock back where he wanted it, almost breaking her leg, and then drove hard, retracing their path all the way to the farm. When he wasn't shifting gears, he pounded the barrels down, over and over again, thinking she might open the door and risk jumping out. A great hysteria gripped her lungs. She breathed once, and when she did, she had to gasp for another breath from her sore and bruised body. She saw in his scrunched eyes that he wasn't finished.

When he pulled off the road into the farm's driveway, he didn't stop at the house. Thank God he was leaving Stearns alone. The pickup spun around the garage and bounced through the backyard past the shed and the empty stall. Then he floored it and sped up the rise toward the first forty. Elizabeth held on to the door handle with both hands and dropped her head forward to keep from smashing it against the roof or the window. He slid to a halt a few yards in front of the cows, and by the time he turned to Elizabeth, ordered her out, and then got out himself, the creatures were innocently sniffing around the tailgate.

He reached back into the car for a handful of shells—seven or eight, she thought—and dropped them into his shirt pocket. Then he shouted: "All right, you bossies! Now's the time, bitches. You first, Baalah."

Elizabeth had never heard him call any of the cows by name. She'd had no idea they even had names. And a name like Baalah. She understood immediately: it had to be because of Robert. She gripped the rail of the truck and lowered her head to the metal, squeezing her eyes shut, trying to get her lungs to open up. She had to breathe in order to escape. She tightened her eyes and told herself to breathe.

The first shot echoed against the curtain of trees surrounding the field; there was a soft flop on the grass and silence.

Then he spoke again, almost lovingly. "Hagar."

With the second shot, a great bellowing began, cow after cow dumbly realizing, ready to revolt. When she opened her eyes she saw them turning to run, but all of them foolishly loped off in the same direction. Will was staring at her. She didn't move. She wasn't going to move, she made her eyes say. He took her deceit as only a possessed man would, jumping over the two dropped cows, pulling two more shells from his pocket—another fell on the ground—and screaming after the others: "Bitches! Goddamn bitches! You're next, Babylon, and then you, Gomorrah, you bitch!"

On both cows the death blow hit the side of the neck—they had turned from him at the last moment. Large ragged holes sank in under their ears. A few bloody strips of hide dangled from the holes like mutilated teeth on a saber saw. Radiating from the mangled centers, dripping red spots of gunshot diminished in frequency, a few cutting the earlobes, some scattering below the eyes, a spot or two at the freshly grass-stained mouth. Their eyes were glassy.

Elizabeth circled the corpses and waited, watching to see if Will would turn. If he saw her standing where she was, away from the pickup, he would be suspicious. She must make a break. There was no other choice. Her lungs, though, said she couldn't. And her bruised legs. She looked his way again. He kept marching toward the retreating cows. There was nothing else in the world but those bellowing animals. He fired twice and missed, the shells popping out of his smoking gun. He kept going, steadily, without running, too far from them to hit one, but confident they could go only so far. And then he would wreak his revenge—on the innocents.

She ran. The ground was uneven and she almost fell in her first few strides, but she kept going, stumbling, flailing, any way to get out of his sight. Each stride killed her battered legs, but a fire burned through her lungs until she could breathe, and with every breath she pushed herself harder. Any moment, she knew, he might try to kill her. She'd hear it first— he'd fire into the sky and tell her to stop. But she wouldn't. She wouldn't give him the pleasure. She kept running across the field toward the drop to the house. He'd have to get into that pickup and come shoot her, and shoot her in the back—for as long as she lived she would run. But any moment . . . any moment . . .

When she heard the two shots, she stopped. Turn around and see how far away he is, she thought, then go. She turned, and saw that she hadn't gotten far, no matter how hard she'd tried. But when she looked she saw that he wasn't turned toward her; she was insignificant, for now. He had felled two more cows, and loomed over them, trying to load his gun again. But he was out of shells—he would have to go back to the truck.

It was a day of slaughter. At the other end of the field, her husband waded hip and thigh in the slaughter he had wrought, four bulging corpses of innocent animals brought down by his insanity. Something inside the man had revolted, and the world was sheep for his sword. She had to go. She had to sprint down the hill and get the boy and lock the house and telephone for help.

Before she turned, though, she saw the Brahman appear at the outskirts. Of course, she thought. Where had he been? The great beast hurried from the edge of the forest, where his cows had retreated, his two great horns, the right one crookedly pointed to the side, bent in the man's direction. Will, as if his life had finally found its completion, saw the beast coming and turned to meet him. When the Brahman was within ten yards, Will lifted his empty weapon and hurled it at the beast. Around and around like a mace it flew through the empty air over the Brahman's head, bouncing on the ground behind the bull. The beast kept coming.

"To the left!" Will shouted at himself. "To the goddamn left!"

But Will jumped to *his* left, not the bull's, and the Brahman thrust his straight left horn into Will's stomach and turned it, and then, like an elephant rearing his trunk, lifted him into the sky, letting Will's own weight impale him.

VIII

Luke:
Purity of Heart Is to
Will One Thing

22

A month after Susan's funeral, I spent two weeks at Apalachicola, Florida, where the Chattahoochee river empties into the Gulf of Mexico. Early every morning I left a dirt-cheap, mildewed motel room and caught a ride on a fishing boat across the bay to Saint George's Island. I must have walked ten miles a day along the shoreline, searching through tiers of broken shells, wrack, and lost and shattered carapaces, listening to the laughing gulls and the incessant Gulf tide, and thinking. The sun burned the back of my neck, and storms tumbled quickly ashore. I ate very little, and at night set a small fan on the end table, sipped gin, and read.

The spirit I inherited from Doug, his *conatus,* was becoming distinctly my own. In response to the reconciliation, the forgiving that surprised all of us and surely Will and Dad, standing over Susan's freshly sown grave, Doug would have beat the timbrel, strummed the harp, and rejoiced. I did not. I kept silent, not because I wasn't thankful but because I was doubtful and I didn't want to be. Faced with this anxious doubt, my own sense of striving sought a different answer.

But searching for an answer, I had long since learned, was not the way to inquire. It was finding the right question. The first was simple enough: why did they embrace each other? Will had been at the weakest moment of his life, grieving, broken by a sense of injustice and guilt. My father had longed for a return to his family. Thus two men, since they were unlike their usual selves, fell on each other. My mother, Elizabeth, Belle, Raymond, and everyone in the valley who had a chance to beat his gums and Doug's spirit alive in my bones praised my father and Will for the forgiving. All assumed a completion. I did not, asking the next question: how could the two of them sustain the reconciliation?

The walking along the island beach and spending time alone, away from my family and the clay hills of eastern Alabama, helped me to focus. The reading at night was mostly in the motel's Gideon Bible and a collection of writings of the early Church, which I brought with me, distrustful of the canon. In the biblical stories, none of the reconciliations of fathers and sons was successful, because in each situation it was clear that the father held power over the son; only then was the father able to forgive. Only in Christ's parables—in other words, in the realm of the imagination—did true forgiveness seem possible. In the case of brothers, the only successful example was Esau and Jacob, but Esau could forgive Jacob because they could split up Seir and Canaan between them. The prodigal son's brother could not forgive him. In my readings of the early Church, the two greatest apostles, Peter and Paul, no matter how Clement of Rome tried to soften their split, remained at odds throughout their lives.

I came away from the beach, then, with three questions. If a person is not powerless, is it truly possible for him to ask forgiveness of another? And if a person does not have control over someone else, can he truly forgive?

And this: can the heart be pure?

When I returned home I decided to stay for a while, taking a job as an insurance salesman. Selling insurance was a questionable choice, but I didn't care; there were few other options in the valley. I would leave Alabama soon enough. For the time being I felt an obligation to Mother. And I must admit a certain sense of the grotesque and macabre delighted me when I sold insurance: there is no lasting and real insurance against death. Nor—though I seldom thought about it—against the loss of love. Most important, though, the job gave me cash for an apartment of my own and nights to sit by the window and read.

The events of the year after Susan's death passed quickly. Mother and everyone else in the family tried to reinforce the reconciliation between father and son as often as possible. I noticed a strain on it at the Homecoming we attended in Harmony Grove. In the winter and spring, Stearns spent more and more time with my father, even though Will knew the boy was carving painted idols with the old man. Will was too occupied with Elizabeth to focus on his son. He married her on June 25, a year and a day after Susan died. It was a small civil service. He asked me to be his best man again, but I refused. Neither my father nor I attended. Afterward, Elizabeth and Will left Stearns with Mother and Dad and took off on a two-week honeymoon.

Since West Point was built on the edge of a wide, capricious river, the sidewalks on all three of the downtown streets were elevated. If I were to stand on one of the promenades and lean against a parking meter, I would look down on car roofs and the bald spots of pedestrians like a preacher thrust against his pulpit, measuring the stolen glances in his sin-sinking congregation. And every few years, at odd intervals, I might safely watch the channeled sweep of the Chattahoochee flooding its banks.

As a youth I was fascinated by those high sidewalks; I felt tall, mature, and somehow regal when, for as many minutes as I could steal from work, I scanned the wandering adults below. Many of the buildings lining those sidewalks were fifty- to seventy-five-year-old brick-and-cast-iron structures, some signed with their original owners' names and the date of erection in the broken pediments and Italianate ornaments along the tops: Mitchelle, 1878; Blair, 1890; Carter, 1903. These massive, unfeigned storefronts, however, were slowly giving way, in the name of quality and progress, to other up-to-date styles, ornament sacrificed to utility. A gorgeous balustrade above the furniture store had been taken down. Mr. Mitchelle's fretwork in his window corners gave way to larger, brighter, and more modern windows that were better for display. A tin-roofed portico stretched out from Mr. Blair's feed store, obstructing the second-story keystones that protruded from the windows. And Kresler's, the oldest store in town, had covered its brick front with wavy sheet metal and a red neon sign.

On a Wednesday morning while Will and Elizabeth were on their honeymoon, at about 11:30, Stearns and my father, carefully balancing one of the wooden poles on the stub of his right arm, arrived with their pinewood ark at Kresler's. The two of them perched that strange, coin-studded contraption on the edge of the elevated sidewalk and stood behind it, waiting for the passersby to slow down, eventually stop, and ask questions. My father's timing was flawless; there was no busier half-hour all week: the buyers in town would finish their shopping and the sellers close up their stores and everyone would go home for the traditional Wednesday afternoon off, which had not yet gone the way of the town's old architecture.

It was a humid, still day in June. Doc Michaels was the first person to come to a complete stop. He pumped my father's hand and listened a moment, smiling smugly at the explanation, and then, while the old evangelist was still talking, wished him good luck and escaped. Mr. Carter knelt beside the box, investigating the flattened coins firsthand. He ignored whatever implications my father wanted to give the ark, stood up, and told a story of his own, belly-laughing on his heels at the punch line. Mrs. Johnson did not speak a word to my father but wagged her finger and pointed to Stearns as she passed. Another fifteen minutes of traffic zigzagged by. Most people, even in a town small enough for everyone to know one another, veered off to the side with lowered heads, too embarrassed for my father and nephew to speak with them. No one wanted to discuss spiritual matters in the middle of the day on a street corner.

School had been out for two weeks; the town fluttered with schoolchildren, who ran from store to store with their pennies; swung around the parking meters, banging each one with a stick; and raced their bicycles along side streets, every one with his spokes choked with clothespins and playing cards. A group spotted Stearns, shot across the street, and hovered around him while my father was accosting someone else.

"Holy smolies," one boy said. "You gonna race this in the Soap Box Derby?"

"It's an ark," Stearns answered.

"A what?"

"An ark of the covenant."

"Does that mean it's Presbyterian?"

Stearns bragged about the finer details, pointing to the painted gold rings, the sanded edges, and the handle notches that made it easier to carry. Two of the boys must have run their hands over every square inch of the thing. They rubbed the sanded pine and the glittering copper of the coins, stopping to stare into their mirrory shine; two others carefully picked up one end to see how heavy it was, but Stearns wouldn't let them move it.

One tough, however, who stretched a head taller than any of the others, did not even deign to march up the sidewalk and inspect the ark, but stayed below, leaning against the hood of a parked car. He was muscular beyond his age, which was probably twelve, three times Stearns's age. The sleeves of his T-shirt hugged his biceps; and his forearms, when relaxed, curved inward like those of some gorilla too strong for his own good. His eye sockets looked as flat as saucers. A toothpick dangled from the side of his mouth, another flat feature on a face crowned by a butch cut.

He began with a few snide remarks, only enough to make his friends beware—they had better stop and look at him, to see which way the wind was blowing. Then he turned his face and lifted his chin up into the air. "Junk," he said. "Pure junk. All you sissies don't know a thing. Look at him, little sissy Stearns up there safe and sound, all worked up over his piece of junk. That's what it is—a piece of junk." He spat on the street.

The effect on his friends was immediate. The more influenced began to laugh, holding their sides in mock pain. Others pointed to the ark as though it were a pool of urine Stearns had left on the sidewalk. And all of them eventually assumed the same disdainful pose their top dog did.

"He's a dumbbell," one sidekick yelled. "I've never seen such a stupid thing, and with an old man like that!" But Robert was still oblivious to the scapegoating going on next to him.

"Yeah," another piped up. "A nincompoop."

"A baby."

"Yellowbelly."

"Stearns is a baby, Stearns is a baby. . . ."

By this time all of them were laughing and slapping their knees in mockery. One boy pushed Stearns on the shoulder, as if he were simply kidding him, just having a good laugh. Then the bully hushed his crowd with a wave of his hand.

From the elevated sidewalk Stearns looked down at the oversize lout. No one stood in the way of the two of them.

The boy pointed at Stearns, one final way to focus attention on himself. With an open fist, like a man throwing a stone, he took a quick swing at the air in front of him.

The other boys guffawed. A boy to the left of Stearns began to pound his fist into his open left hand. The bully began to take up the motion, and the slapping noise served as a catalyst on the others. Soon every boy in the pack was pounding his fist in a mocking chorus.

My father had sealed Stearns for his own. Stearns lowered his head to pray, like a martyr who believed the kingdom of heaven was at hand. But his meekness only encouraged their sadism. My father, ready to pontificate, pulled his new eyeglasses off his face—he was still awkward about them—and suddenly shouted to the assembling people, who began to mill around the scene because of Stearns and the boys, not the evangelist and his ark. The noise—it was close to a whipping sound, in unison—had finally called the adults to attention. The culprits glanced around them and started to scatter. "My friends!" Robert shouted, still oblivious. On the way by, one boy slapped Stearns's face, but then the boy ran blindly into his father's chest. The man picked him up by the waist and carried him under his arm down the sidewalk steps and out of sight behind the store. The boys had hung around a minute too long on a morning when too many parents were in town shopping. The bully himself swiveled around to find his father, Joe Williams, a bent-backed, wiry man, who grabbed his son by the collar and jerked him away from the commotion. As the young Mr. Williams was led to his doom, however, he pointed at Stearns and cursed him.

"People of West Point!" my father shouted as the crowd below him began to thin out. "People of Lanett! Stay and listen for a moment. Before you go home, stop and sit a spell, or stand and listen. I know this is not a part of your routine this day, but give me a moment. You'll never regret it."

Stearns wiped his face with the back of his hand and sat down next to the ark, hanging his feet out over the edge of the sidewalk. When Robert began, there may have been twelve people left. Stearns played with the ark's wooden handle, running his fingers along the soft pine and staring into the starry swirls of the knots in the wood. He looked distracted, but he heard every word my father said.

It was a long, complicated story. A young boy from Ridgegrove, Dad began, was mysteriously given a small black box by a stranger in the woods. Carrying it on his leg, the boy was blessed beyond anyone's expectations, until he became the youngest governor of Alabama. As governor, however, he built an elaborate marble altar for the box to stand on. Because it was no longer on his body, the governor forgot the box and the laws of his God and sinned, most often with women. Soon he was disgraced and exiled to a mill cottage in Lanett. He grew old and sick. Three friends came one day and tried to tell him how to help himself, but he sent them away and set fire to his box, thinking the whole cottage would go up in flames and kill him. It didn't. Only the box burned.

"He saw those ashes," Dad said, finally finishing, "as he had never seen ashes before. He scooped them up and ate them. He knew then why he was first given the box: man's obligation was to recognize that he was ashes himself. When a man truly felt that knowledge in his soul, then he could begin to build a faith, and carry it with him everywhere. God's name be praised."

At the end of the story, three people—two women and a boy, his grandson—remained at my father's feet, staring at the ancient prophet, who kept as still and rigid as a man murdered standing up. Stearns rested his head on top of the ark's mercy seat, reaching his hand out to grasp whatever power still lived in my father's pantleg. The other listeners had walked away while he told his story, puzzled or annoyed with themselves for staying so long. One man, Orville Smith, slammed his car door and sped away angry, considering Dad's show a moral offense to the people of West Point and Lanett. He stopped at my apartment and told me my father was proselytizing again and I had better go get him before someone put him in jail for sacrilege.

Everyone else quietly exited to the side, like churchgoers anxious to beat the crush at the cafeteria. Mrs. Williams—Joe's wife—and a lady I didn't know stayed to the bitter end, but didn't speak to Dad. They nodded when he finished, and then, like people with little to make of their allotted time, ambled down the empty street to their car. My father was a man out of his time. A brother to dragons, he kept as still as a wounded Job, thinking himself less than human, a bone-bruised and afflicted companion to owls.

Stearns picked himself up and wrapped one arm around his grandfather's waist. Dad leaned on the boy's shoulder unawares, still gazing at the distant afternoon heavens, until Stearns shook him and then pulled him to the wooden poles. I drove up just as the old man tried to lift his end of the ark, but faltered. I hurried up the sidewalk steps and picked up one end of the cursed thing myself, supporting him with my other arm. After cramming the contraption into the trunk of the car, I eased my slumping father into the back seat. I stopped at the sudden sound of thunder. Stearns looked up, too, and then hurried in beside Dad. A storm gathered in the southwestern sky—billowing, dark clouds feeding on themselves like unsatisfied desires. Lightning flashed, followed by another rumble of thunder. At one point in the darkness, near the edge, a cylinder of rain fell at an angle from right to left, the hair-thin lines lighter-colored than the rest of the storm, and safe to anticipate. I could almost feel the cool rain, miles away, fall on my face. Storms in that direction delivered, thankfully. Rain would help us all, and maybe help put my father to sleep.

Mother met us on the porch. When she first saw Dad, her eyes sparked with anger and the back of her jaw locked. But she quickly recovered her sense of duty, perhaps her fatalism—I don't know—and guided him into the bedroom, taking off his shoes as we stretched him across the bed. The old man groaned when we let him fall on the mattress, waking for a moment from his walking slumber, but then he turned his face away and fell into an exhausted sleep. His clothes were cold with sweat.

"I said so," Mother whispered. "I told him from the time he rooted in this ground again that he was up to no good once more, but would he listen to me? He's never changed, Luke. He's the same as he's always been, some gray-haired old goat who can't abide being penned up. Oh, he gave me these promises—'I am not,' he said; 'Don't worry, Mattie,' he said—and look at this, this heap of bones ready to die. He doesn't care. He has no sense of other people, only himself, and the stupid story of his own life, which for him has never been anything but destruction, and self-destruction at that."

My father did indeed look ready to die. His turned-away face, from his rigid chin to his white hair, strained like a castaway to cling to the driftage of his body. The skin color on that horror-struck face approximated a ghastly mixture of green and yellow; from his shoulders down, the fight seemed over, his immersed trunk laid out on the bed like the lower part of a drowned corpse. I felt even then that he couldn't last much longer. Stearns, the faithful disciple, knelt beside the bed until Mother leaned over and squeezed his neck, lifting him up and whispering in his ear that it was best to let Granddaddy sleep. She tried to lead him out of the room, but he turned to me instead. A look of expectation came over him.

The ark—that was it. Stearns wanted me to help him take the ark back to the smokehouse.

"Are you sure?" I said, and then immediately realized my mistake. He was crestfallen, a moment from crying. I couldn't undo what my father had done. I grabbed his shoulder and led him back to the car, where we unpacked the box and carried it to the smokehouse and the table where it had been sculpted. The thunder from the storm grew closer.

"Don't you want to come back in, Stearns, and clean up? Maybe take a nap yourself?"

"In a minute," he answered. "Leave me alone."

"Here?"

"Yes, sir."

So I left him with his wooden ark, reminding him to get back inside before it rained and to clean up and take a nap—I was going to check on him in a minute or two. I wanted to nap myself. I felt exhausted just getting the two of them back home. My father and Stearns must have felt drained of all energy. The afternoon air was ripe with the expectancy of rain, the heavy dust turning and turning like a tumbling cloud, each revolution growing wetter, promising relief from the heavy, dull burden of the Alabama heat.

Mother sat in the chair at the foot of the bed. Her eyes looked heavy with sleep also. The old man hadn't moved. I told her to check on Stearns, I was going to take a nap, to wake me if she needed me. Fine, she said. But the moment before I disappeared down the hall, she spoke again. "Do you think I should call the doctor?"

I shook my head and moved on, around the dining room and the living room to the other bedroom in the far corner of the house. I had not slept in that bed since leaving for Korea. Propping myself up on a pillow, I tried to relinquish all thought. The bedroom's two windows opened onto the front porch, which looked out on a "slow" curve in Cherry Drive, slow enough that I understood the words of a song from a passing car radio. The afternoon was still too heavy and hot. God, I wanted it to rain. In the back of my mouth, I still tasted the dust of the morning and early afternoon, the dry red clay flicked up into the air from the roads, the powdery yards, the barren gardens, dust as pervasive as death. The backs of my legs stuck to the sheet.

Then the wind began to rise. Its breath was uneven, up and

down, periodically interrupted by the asphalt hum of tires going somewhere at the last hour. There came an unexpected sweet smell in the room, for only a moment, but it was strong-scented. I wasn't sure what it was—a flower, something cooking—but its sweetness overwhelmed me for a moment, and then the rain came. As I was falling asleep, I remembered that my father had slaughtered that pig when I was a boy, and burned it.

I had a dream. I was running along a dusty, ribbonlike road that grew thicker with dust the farther I went. I took a path across neighboring railroad tracks and into the forest. Wild blackberry vines tripped my feet and stuck their thorns into my hands and through my pants into my legs, but I kept moving, running toward a place ahead where I might hide. When I saw the clearing through a break in the trees, I first heard the words that soon kept repeating themselves like a hammering chorus in my brain. *Purity of heart.* I had read that somewhere. It came again: *Purity of heart.* I pushed on past a stand of gigantic beech trees until I stood at the edge of the clearing. In the middle some pieces of wood were crossed, one on top of the other. *Purity of heart.* The wood lay at the center, carefully built to make a fire, but it was not disintegrating as it burned, and it was indeed burning. Not a single ash.

The cry that came burned into my consciousness with the same singular purpose—a long, gut-wrenching, childish scream that jolted me like an electric shock. I jumped up in bed. The sky was dark, but I had no idea how late it was. Then the single scream fell into a terrible bawling, as panic-stricken as a helpless baby's. I pulled on my pants and took off barefoot, knocking against a table in the living room while I found the light and hurrying past the dining room to the hall. The bawling kept up, rising and falling now like the wind that had put me to sleep. Mother was struggling to get out of the chair. She, too, had fallen asleep. The old man hadn't budged from his corpselike pose on the bed. It was still raining. When I looked out the window on my way, I saw three, maybe four flashes—shadows—scurrying away, one a head taller than the others.

I took the steps down into the store in two strides, broad-jumping from halfway to the bottom. The door to the smokehouse was open. What I saw first was an ax, sunk into the top of the ark. Whoever had thrust it into the box was not going to have an easy time getting it out—the blade was almost completely buried and to be removed would have to be rocked back and forth by a strong man. The floor was covered with muddy footprints; it was hard to tell how many boys had stolen into the smokehouse, but there had been a gang of them. In the open doorway, where the rain suddenly fell harder, a few rocks lay innocently on the floor, a steady drip of water from the roof slowly washing away the brown muck and the red spots. I stood stock-still for a moment, frozen in disbelief. My nephew was sitting against the far wall; I could hardly see him with only the single light bulb dangling from the ceiling. His face was turned away, but his neck was bloody and the sides of his pumpkin-size head were swollen with purple lumps.

I cradled the boy in my arms and carried him up the store's steps to Mother, who, after she stopped hysterically cussing my unconscious father, came to herself and helped me clean Stearns's wounds. The rocks had cut his face badly and the swelling almost closed his eyes. We drove him to the hospital, where the intern said that though the worst apparent damage was the bruises and cuts, the boy should stay in bed for a few days, closely observed for signs of kidney damage. Though the intern felt that in all probability the child wasn't too seriously hurt, I decided to telephone Will.

It was not an easy decision. Since Will and Elizabeth had left on their honeymoon, my cruel mind had punished me with unwanted, nightmarish visions of the two of them strolling along the beach, hand in hand, then turning to go back to the motel room again and rut like Will's Brahman and a cow in heat. Once or twice, I imagined, they had joked about me, the lovesick calf.

When I dialed the number, I told myself that while Stearns's injury was probably not that serious, I had an obligation to let them know. Perhaps I could talk Will into staying.

The motel manager took a long time to get him, but finally Will picked up the phone. "Who's this?" he said.

"It's Luke, Will."

Before I could explain, he blurted out, "What in God's name do you want?"

I almost hung up. He sounded as if I made a habit of calling a man after midnight on his honeymoon. Without thinking, I gave up any idea of smoothing over the news and narrated what had happened, flatly, and told him we were taking Stearns home.

"Screw you, Luke!" he shouted. "Don't you dare take him

back to Mother's! You get him over to the farmhouse immediately and wait for us. We're coming. You hear me?"

I hung up.

After Will's barbaric behavior, I felt he didn't deserve to have heard the news in a more thoughtful way. But when I finally calmed down, I regretted what I had done, and I continued to regret it through the events of the next few days. Will interpreted the episode as sensitively as an unleashed bull would; I believed, however, that there was enough of a conscience in him to hold his rage in check, though not enough understanding to allow him to see the episode in any other way but one: that my father was trying to kill Stearns. After Will and Elizabeth returned and we left the farm, I talked to Elizabeth on the phone twice—Thursday evening and Friday at noon—and she admitted that Will was blinded with anger, though it obviously pained her to confess her fears to me. In addition she suspected, correctly, that Will's tone when he answered my call in Florida told me their honeymoon had been disastrous.

We orchestrated a secret visit for Mother and Dad Saturday afternoon; Will would be out driving around his 450 acres, doing the chores. I insisted Elizabeth let us come because I didn't think it was fair to blame my parents. Bullies will pick on people like Stearns whatever the circumstances, and my parents had overextended themselves thanklessly for the child during the last two years, while his mother was dying and his father was neglecting him. Besides, they loved the boy. I also worried about my father's health. He had slept through the afternoon and the night of the episode with Stearns; and except for an occasional walk in the garden, he stayed in his bed until the only activity capable of waking him—our furtive visit Saturday afternoon to see his little disciple.

The visit was not a good one. Elizabeth was defensive and anxious, and Mother was distraught and irritated by Elizabeth's sudden protectiveness. My father grabbed Stearns's hand and whispered some verse about numbering the stars in the sky. At least we escaped without Will finding out. In another few days Will would finally calm down, and perhaps start paying closer attention to the son he suddenly felt so precious to him. As I drove Mother and Dad back home, I began to feel nauseated. I waited in the car, unable to decide what was wrong with me, when they got out. Mother walked him around the front of the car to my side. "Are you sure you won't come in, Luke? I can fix you a piece of pound cake."

"No, Mother. There's nothing you can do for me."

"Are you sure?" She let go of my father's arm and leaned her head toward the car window.

"Yes, Mother, I'm absolutely sure. Nothing. Absolutely nothing."

I waited until she had helped the lost evangelist navigate the porch steps and teeter through the front door. Before she disappeared she looked my way again, but I didn't respond. I could smell a faint odor—burning rubber—and then I knew what was coming over me. I thought I had left my dead brother behind.

23

*I*t took only a few minutes to drive out of Lanett. My stomach became still. I followed Route 50 west, by Huguley's water tower and the graveyard and the Reverend Mother's palm-reading place, which marked the end of town and the beginning of the fourteen miles of undulating country between Lanett and Lafayette and then, six miles south, to Cusseta. During the summer Elizabeth and I dated, on the day I opened the letter calling my reserve unit to Korea, I got drunk and paid this same Reverend Mother to read my palm. She was a gargantuan, coal-colored black woman, and wrapped around her head she wore a grease-spotted white turban that smelled of fried fish. "Naw, sir, naw, sir," she said. "I ain't messin' with no white man."

"I got good money, Reverend Mother."

She glanced at my proffered bill and sniffed the air, shaking her head with scorn. "You's drunk," she said, "a'n I's a reading adviser."

"I'm waiting," I answered.

She led me stumbling through two doorways strung with rosary beads and I plopped down at a cloth-covered table, the centerpiece the brittle skull of a dog. After she turned the lamp off, she let me sit in the darkness for a while, and took her place across from me. She eased two of my fingers into the vacant eye sockets of the skull and then turned my palm up, flicking on a small flashlight at the same time. Her eyes bugged out like a terrified animal's; when I looked away from her, all I saw was that skull and its gaping sockets. She wobbled her voice like an aging church-choir soprano. "Oh, Lawdie, long life," she told me, tracing my rather obvious life line, "but wit' de very, very bad sickness in de half, I reckon. An' you bees chief of dem men," she whispered, a prediction that guaranteed she was a fraud.

Then she began to shake her head slowly and talk about my royal downfall, playing the suspense for all it was worth. When she finally told me the cause of my collapse, she let the syllables of the word linger on her tongue, delighting in the sound and the shock in my eyes. She did not pronounce the *J* as a hard *J,* but a drawn-out soft one, ignorantly imitating French, I assume. "Je-ze-bel," she said, and then she bared her broken teeth and from the depths of her whale's belly let loose a rib-shaking laugh, and said it again, faster. "Jezebel."

I coasted past the Reverend Mother's, remembering. At that time I had been uncertain about every aspect of my life, from how I would act that very day to the direction my mind and soul would seek in the years ahead. Had this palm reader accidentally cut open my veins and bled their truth—that I was so obsessed by a Jezebel, who could be no one but Elizabeth, that my heart was ruined? How could I have known then that the war in Korea would not kill me instead? But I felt a great sense of certainty this second time I studied the Reverend Mother's shack, not about any direction to my life but about the next few moments, as if my body had a knowledge of its own. A current in my bones began to burn again. It was Elizabeth and Will and my father and the anger that had slain my brother—a queer smell swelling from within me. I stepped on the gas and hurried over the miles between.

Cusseta's railroad station had fallen into disrepair. Across the street a little red-brick combination grocery and hardware store boasted two gas pumps ten yards from the door. The main dirt road in town still turned left at the railroad station, paralleling the tracks for a stone's throw before it narrowed into the deer hunters' trail. The Sutter mansion loomed on the hill to the left, the last Cusseta landmark before the highway blinked and then sped through open country again. Nestled below the fat-columned, flattop house, on the rise between the pecan orchard and the stables, was the former schoolhouse. I parked below it. The simple wooden building was clean and well kept, its windows—four in front, four in back—curtained in white; above them the A-frame knew a new roof, and below, the cinderblock underpinning was reinforced. A slender, ill-lettered sign above the door said COMMUNITY CENTER. The children of Cusseta went to school in Lafayette now.

The door was unlocked. Inside, a coffee urn rested on a white ceramic sink in the rear right corner room where we had hung our coats, on pegs to the left of Dad's. Two benches hugged the back wall. The rest of the room was cleared of furniture, including the potbelly stove, though its outline was still etched like a fossil under the floor's light green paint. I stepped up on the platform and walked across to inspect a poster on the far wall: it was a list of Boy Scout pledges—mental, moral, and physical promises. The late-afternoon sunlight streaked in through the front windows and cast my shadow across that platform where I stood, and where once I had listened to my father teach us his ways.

As I felt my blood begin to quicken, I stepped to the window and looked for Doug leaning against the pecan tree, the wings of his Bible open on his lap. If he was there, I could explain to myself that I knew my past experience was repeating itself and in anticipating had somehow caused it. But he was not there. Nevertheless I felt . . .

And then my feet planted themselves firmly on the floor. My head rested itself against the wall, where it stayed when the surging of blood grew. For a moment I thought I could manipulate, but, no, the I that was thinking behind my eyes and my brain was losing control. My ankles began to turn out and down, as if they refused to hold the weight of my legs, preferring to let my body sink onto the floor. A strong and steady pumping, with the rhythm of my heartbeat, swelled through every part of my body, as if my heart itself pressed against the skin of my legs, my arms, my abdomen, my brain, and in pressing, burned, until the queer smell of smoking rubber oozed from my body like sweat. My tongue turned dry—for a second it shook uncontrollably—and then deepened into the back of my mouth, pressing against my jaw and the top of my throat. Its taste was dry and metallic. My lungs contracted and froze, count after count, past eight and ten and twelve, until suddenly breath returned, filling my body with a whisper that gave way to a long and quickened silence.

I found myself on the floor below the window. There was a full and perfect silence. Nothing came into it. Only, very slowly, I could feel a consciousness of my own control return, not a consciousness of anything outside of time and the suffering that passes with it. I moved my feet and breathed and lifted my head, and then, carefully, knelt against the windowsill, seeing again a pecan tree at the edge of an orchard, the hills of the blue piedmont behind, stretching far away, toward the sky, as the brown rice paddies I had stared at in Korea had also made their checkerboard way toward the eternal horizon. I felt in a kind of control again, but knew I was wrong in believing I could force anything. I could not force my brother to reappear, I could not force him to stay away, I could not force anything into that silence—not a vision of Doug, not the intensity of a bird singing with first light, not a cure for the disease of my mind. As I had escorted Mother and Dad back from Will's farm and felt the touch of that current, long since lost, return to the course of my veins, I had mistakenly imagined I could hurry to the Cusseta schoolhouse, look at the pecan tree, somehow catch this last nightmare in the making, and purify myself of the insanity.

No. I could not. I might have recognized its coming, only because of past experience, but I could not control it. It burned through my body for a moment at the window, of its own accord, and that was all. I could do nothing. Freedom had to come from without.

As I arrived back at my apartment, the first stars appeared, flecks of pearls broken across the evening sky. I lingered a moment under the blue-green of the dome, which darkened toward a blacker, speckled night, with the moon barely a sliver, its lowest point so low on the horizon that it looked balanced on the distant hills. I made my way inside and up the house's creaking stairs to my door. The telephone was ringing; I thought about not answering it. I needed to sleep for a long time, to recover. And Mother had probably tried to call three, four, five times while I was in Cusseta, with some excuse as petty as supper or a half-gallon of milk or two aspirin—anything to get me back over to the house with Dad, who after that trip to see Stearns would surely puff up with one of his willful cut-off-his-hand schemes.

But it was Elizabeth. She was telephoning from the farm. Her voice had an unnatural tone—a forced matter-of-factness that obviously masked a great fear. I couldn't believe what she was telling me. As she spoke, she talked quicker, until I couldn't understand her anymore. "I think Will is dead, Luke," she said. "He's lying in the middle of the field—I saw the Brahman—I'll tell you—but Will tried to maim Robert, Luke—I think—I don't know—but I've been trying to reach Mattie forever—no one answers—where have you been, Luke? I've been trying to reach . . ."

I yanked the phone out of the wall and heaved it across the room as I sprinted out the door and down the stairs into the street to my car. I was a half-mile gone and turning at the railroad station before my mind even registered what she'd said. She had to be the one to see about Will . . . he was her husband, goddamn it. There was no choice for me. I would go to my father.

When I got there I ran through an empty house. Mother's bed looked wrinkled from a nap, but the rest of the place gave no hint of their presence, or their condition when they left. It was still, terribly still. I went to find my father's stuff and search for his Bible. I'm not sure why. It made no sense. What if it was gone? What would its absence mean? That he had taken it with him to the hospital? That he had run away with it again? That he had thrown it away for good? For some reason I imagined that its absence or presence would be a sign to me. It was Doug's; the old man had carried it with him on his journey over the river and into the wilderness.

His bed was made, and the Bible wasn't on the bedside table. The dressertop was cleared, but dusty. Behind the stairway door, however, a small stack of possessions lay hidden away like bank notes and land deeds and diaries—it was all that he owned in life, or at least all that he would claim. A sanded block of pine, half-carved, lay next to his slippers; the pair of pants he wore to see Stearns fell to the side. I had seen him in overalls recently, but they weren't there; wherever he was, he was probably wearing them, looking like some aged farmer wandering toward his promised land. A cosmetic kit, a shirt, and a belt—nothing else. No Bible. At that very moment his fingers probably stiffened around it, locked into an eternal grip. And I wasn't with him.

I hurried out the smokehouse door and called for them. . . . Nothing. But something was wrong in the garden. Even in the starlit darkness I could see that the rows didn't make a steady, consistent stand of corn. The back part had disappeared: trampled. A man wearing his overalls . . . I groped my way along the first row to its end, but I didn't want to look. I stopped two rows over from the commotion and kept my head down: my God, why did I have to find him? Why was I the one who had to bend over my own father? I stepped through the stalks, my eyes still lowered, until I stood in the midst of the fierce scene and glanced around. No one was there. I double-checked. Nothing but Dad's cast-off floppy hat. But someone had been felled. Elizabeth was right. I knelt down to feel two bent stalks beginning to straighten up from the weight of a man's body—behind them the corn was shredded by more than one shotgun blast. I stepped over the bent stalks to examine the others. They were blown to smithereens. It was hard to tell in the dark, but I couldn't detect any blood. I turned back toward the house. Will had marched right over a whole row of corn as he made his insane retreat.

A figure—Mother—stood in the backyard, staring at me. I hurried toward her, but she began to back up, step after step, until I called out.

"Luke?" Mother answered.

She fell into my arms. She appeared close to death, an old woman who had attempted far too much for her age. Her hair fell in wet strings, the side of her face was bruised, and her eyes were dulled from shock. Her whole body was shaking in my hands, in utter terror. I put my arms around her shoulders and guided her back toward the house. She stopped me, though, to speak again.

"He is not dead."

I led her to the porch and then carried her to her bed. On the way she chattered like a madwoman. "I chased after him, Luke," she said. "Will put the gun next to Robert's ear—he was deaf, and crazy, son, because of the garden and the shotgun next to his ear—and I ran into Horace afterward—because he had run away—but I caught Robert first and held on to him, son—I told him to stop, to listen to me, but he couldn't hear and he pushed me away, he pushed me away, he pushed me away and kept running. Oh, my God, he's going to die!"

I telephoned Belle, who said she was on the way out the door at that very moment. Elizabeth had called them; Raymond was headed to the farm—thank goodness. I told Belle to telephone the doctor and then called the sheriff, who followed Dr. Martin by about five minutes. While Dr. Martin and Belle attended Mother, the sheriff insisted we sit at the dining-room table and talk, as if he were skeptical about the very name Treadwell and wanted to cross-examine me face-to-face, sit-

ting down and still. From the moment I first spoke with the
man, I felt the burden of the past take hold of me and, like a
ruptured vertebra send its pain inching through every part of
my body, no matter how distant from the backbone itself. The
pain whispered that we had been through this catastrophe before.

He folded his wide hands and set them on the table between
us, his fingers stacked on top of each other like rolls of
stomach fat. He obviously did not want to be there, and was
skeptical about every word I said, finding it impossible to
believe that Will Treadwell might be dead or that he might
attempt or threaten to murder his own father, let alone actually do it.

"I don't have a lot of time to waste, please. Send someone to
check on Will and Elizabeth—you can believe what you
want—and help me find my father."

"We only got three people, counting myself, who work in
the evenings, and ol' Parsons goes off at twelve."

"I don't care how many you got."

"Now I don't mean to criticize you or your family, Luke.
Your mother is a fine woman and I believe anything she says,
but you know as well as I do that all of us in this town have
heard about your daddy."

"Damn it, fool!"

"Now don't you go cursing at me, Mr. Smarts! I could have
arrested your sweet daddy the other day, disturbing the peace
like he was on a city street. I'm sure your brother would have
understood, but I didn't do it because I respect Will."

"I can't believe you're arguing with me—this is unbeliev-
able! What the hell are you doing? How much you respect
Will isn't worth crap. Are you just going to sit there and let
him die on his farm and my father die somewhere in your
town?"

He ran his fat hand over his face and sighed, got up from
the table and telephoned a deputy and sent him out to Will's
farm. "We don't like to get involved in family problems, you
know."

"I know. You've made that clear."

"Your brother is a friend of mine, though, and you're going
to have to do a lot of explaining if . . ."

Dr. Martin made Mother take a mild sedative. He would be
back early in the morning. We were supposed to watch her
closely and keep her in bed and call him if necessary. The
sheriff decided to follow his deputy to Will's farm and make

Parsons stay on and help me. Old man Parsons drove through the surrounding streets the rest of the night, stopping back at the house twice to say there was no sign of Dad and that he hadn't heard from the sheriff about Will. No one Parsons questioned had seen Dad since his song and dance on Main Street. And the last time anyone had spotted Horace was two days ago—at the dump behind the railroad station.

I waited with Belle until she assured me Mother would sleep soundly and I could begin searching myself; she also knew Parsons wouldn't succeed. Around midnight I got into my car and began to cruise through the neighboring streets, at first randomly, but then with a consistent pattern, along the grids that enclosed Cherry Drive—Sixth, Seventh, Eighth, Ninth Streets on one side; Main Street, State Line, the river on the other; toward Route 29 to LaGrange on one end and Route 50 to Lafayette on the other. The wider the rectangles grew, the closer they approximated circles, until I felt I was spiraling down some mountain, beginning at the peak and descending toward a base wider than any human could master.

Nothing. By this time even a wounded old man, if he walked without rest, might have pushed past the limits I had traced. What was he thinking? He wouldn't think—that was the problem. He had grappled with his bad angel of a son, and probably had run wildly, the gunshots blasting away his logic and the little sanity he knew. My ever-widening circles tried to cover such irrational flight, but failed. They had not caught sight of a lonely old man stumbling through side streets and backyards, nor of a man crumpled into his final resting place behind some tree.

About five o'clock, when I had decided to give up, at the V in Tennessee Street, which leads to Route 50, I saw a black man walking along the side of the road. I had never talked with Horace, but Mother said he came to see my father often, usually drunk. He was an old man, toothless, with gray hair tightly curled around his bald black pate. Though his shoulders were as rounded as a hunchback's, he moved with a steady, purposeful stride, accustomed to traveling on foot. There was no need for an introduction when I stopped and got out. I did not have to explain who I was or what I was doing out the hour before dawn.

"I's afear'd he's dun ben picked up."

"What do you mean? Surely someone would see, especially in his condition." I could hardly discern the outlines of his face in the dark.

"I say he's found hisself dat chariot, Mr. Luke, like 'lijah. You hear me."

"Did Mother tell you what happened? Or which way he went? I mean, could you understand her when she saw you?"

"Of course I's knows what dun happened. Babeelon his throw'd down. Yes, Jesus. Ain't gonna be no mo dem pipers an' bugle-blow'rs an' dem car fixers like Luther Jones, Lawd, ain't gonna be no mo dem bridegrooms an' wick-burnin' an' streetlights an' Main Street merchants like ol' man Kresler. Lawd, Lawd. Babeelon his throwed down, I say. Mmmm, Jesus. In her hit was found de blood of de prophets an' de saints an' all dem that're slain upon de earth. Allelujah!"

I could get nothing else out of him. Nothing but the ramblings of a drunken disciple shocked into some sort of absurd apocalyptic vision. He refused to get in with me and go back, even though I told him we would bed and feed him. No, food and sleep were not important now, he said; he was keeping watch, and he would keep looking until he found the exact spot, as if he expected to cross some river and see the discarded mantle of Elijah. And with an expectant stride he marched on, toward the highway, until he disappeared in the darkness. There was nothing left for me to do but return. I stood by the car door, though, in a moment of contemplation, exhausted by a day that had begun with four of us in Stearns's room and then stumbled its way through the schoolhouse in Cusseta, my mother's garden, and now the emptiness of the night, my father unfound and my brother . . . I didn't know.

I stood on the edge of town, where none of the streetlights could mar my vision of the night. The sky still boasted a host of stars, numberless lights the size of pinheads, all of the same aspect, and beside them the descendants of those lights—more lights—and beside them their descendants, all suspended on the black canvas that was forever black because of the great nothingness between. For me it was an ever-present sorrow. The stars were beginning to fade, as was the eternal darkness of the night, giving way, the moment before dawn, to the wing-thin, delicate flutter of the east. Sometimes . . . sometimes I could imagine seeing the night like he was seeing it, if he was still alive and still able to look up. My father was a medieval anomaly who read those fading stars as the lives and deaths of saints, each one in the numberless, undistinguished, and timeless horde, pitting the imagination of his heart against the real until he was left with nothing save the sacrifice of his own being. The saint simply forgot—that was his glory.

As the ceiling of the dome faded even further, I followed the promise of new light to the eastern horizon, where like a palm's edge of a burning hand the rim of the sun rose, as it did in various splendor every day, even this one, the same abiding, healing phenomenon, for those who would see.

Then my mind was finally jarred. I understood. I got into the car and drove west, with the sun, not back toward home. If he recovered his senses, he would go somewhere significant to his life—I knew my father well enough. He would set off to Atlanta again, and then to the mountains. Or go back to Cusseta. That was it. Cusseta had to be right, the same way I . . . We were the same. But he couldn't make it all the way there on his own. I'd find him facedown in the roadside red clay, or catch sight of him stumbling on his last legs toward a town that, though no more than a crossing of a state road and a railroad, was for him a new Jerusalem. He might have made it all the way if someone picked him up. But surely no one would have taken him. The driver, seeing his condition, would turn around and bring him back. Surely.

It took ten minutes to get to the outskirts, driving full blast. By then there was light enough to see him from the road. My father sprawled against a cedar tree like a drunk who had passed out, sitting propped up against the trunk with one leg rigid, the other half-cocked, and a troubled face stretched toward the sky. I knew he was dead the moment I saw him. I slammed the door and hurried to him, stopping a foot away, as if to touch him were to die myself. My father. My own father. Even with his betrayals one after another, and his corrupted inheritance, a great pity suddenly broke within me when I realized that this ragged, one-handed runaway on the side of the road was indeed my own father.

Two awful burn marks, from a shotgun, scarred the sides of his neck, as if some savage, supernatural creature, larger than a Samson, had grabbed him by the throat and strangled him to death, the nails of the devil's hands carving the man's neck with huge pink imprints, each colored in the middle by a yellow, puslike hole similar to the boils a martyr at the stake might suffer. Considering his health, or any man's heart, only an incredible strength of will, or of spirit, had kept my father alive for those twelve hours or so. But by the time he stumbled to Cusseta, however he made it, his heart gave way.

The Bible was there, tossed off uselessly to the side, face-down. The bent leg looked as if he had been trying to prop the book on it before he died, but with only one good hand he probably couldn't manage it. I touched him for the first time—he was already deathly cold. His face was so cold, those familiar features, my features, the sagging of his face, in death an everlasting mark. I took him up in my arms, the tears finally breaking from me. My father. Cold now. His eyes were still open. For all his faith, in his eyes was frozen an awful look of terror.

The burn marks on my father's neck came from the hot recoil of the shotgun Will set on Dad's shoulders and swiveled toward his ear as he fired, first on the left side and then, while Dad knelt in the crumpled corn, on the right. As best as I can surmise, Will did not intend to kill him, only to rupture his eardrums. With his own illogical resentment, Will reasoned that if the man couldn't hear, he would eventually lose the power of speech and thus never again preach to Stearns, or to anyone else. Will raised his shotgun to my father's heart first, to scare him, and then at the last moment set it on the old evangelist's shoulder and fired. The buckshot flew safely into the corn, but the recoil rubbed the burning barrels against his skin and also accomplished what Will desired: it blew the hearing out of his ear. My father fell to the ground from the shock and pain. Will lifted the shotgun again, over my father's face, and then pinned it to the other shoulder as he knelt below him. He fired again and, finally victorious, ran back to the truck and Elizabeth.

At the farm, the handful of shells Will grabbed from his pickup apparently ran out with the last cow he felled in front of the Brahman. Nine times out of ten, I suspect, an enraged bull won't kill a man, but Elizabeth said that when Will tried to jump out of the way, he mistakenly flung himself toward the straight horn, which penetrated halfway through his stomach. The death blow followed, when the momentum of Will's lunge carried him up on the horn as the Brahman reared his head, the weight of Will's body driving his heart down to its bursting.

We buried Will immediately. He was put in the family plot next to Susan, but with no ceremony except a prayer by the Methodist minister who joined Mother, Elizabeth, and me at the grave. Mother insisted that my father, on the other hand, be given a proper burial. It went well enough, given his standing in the community. There was one strange episode, though, as if my father were still orchestrating the spirits of those around him, whether living or dead.

Many of the evenings Stearns had spent with my father, they piggybacked down to the railroad station to catch sight of the Boston–New Orleans train. On the way they played a game that began with my father asking the boy to count the stars.

"A million and billion and trillion and gillion," Stearns answered.

"Not enough."

"Cillions and dillions and fillions and millions and pillions and zillions."

"Sorry, not quite enough."

Stearns always tried again, with a deep breath. "All those put together a zillion times."

My father laughed, and bounced him higher on his back. "Close, Stearns, but not close enough. You think about it. Maybe next time." But Dad never told the boy how many.

They sang "When the Roll Is Called Up Yonder" until they reached the railroad station, where Stearns jumped off Dad's back onto the bench, and then down to the platform, hurrying onto the tracks. Meticulously he set four pennies on the nearest rail, then scampered back to stand beside Dad, holding the man's good hand. The train stopped only three minutes and then pulled out, but from the boy's perspective the departure was filled with as much steam and trumpets, earthquakes and white horses as Armageddon, the train leaving as mementos one or two glittering golden smushed shapes as bright as the stars.

For most of the evening, while my father lay in state in Mother's living room, Elizabeth kept Stearns outside in the yard, assuming that out there he wouldn't witness Mother's terrible grief. But as Raymond and I, each supporting an arm, led Mother from her bedroom to the coffin, I looked up and saw the boy's face pressed against the window, his eyes wide. Horace stood behind him. When almost every visitor—there were few—had left, Elizabeth finally went outside and brought Stearns in. She could hardly walk from the bruises on her leg, but when Raymond put a small bench next to the coffin, she slowly escorted the boy in and knelt beside him to explain what to do. She let him go to his grandfather alone.

I watched from the nearby wall. As the child reached into

his pocket and slipped out two of those smushed pennies, I told myself to be patient, not to rush over there out of any sense of propriety. My father had taught me about propriety. But then the boy reached down and pulled the thick, dark eye-glasses off the caked-up corpse, and by the time three of us—Raymond, Elizabeth, and myself—got to him, the child had dropped those two starry shapes onto my father's naked eyes and choked out his final question.

"Granddaddy, how many?"

24

Over the next six months, Elizabeth and I saw a lot of each other out of necessity. She sold the farm and, after asking my opinion, agreed that she and Stearns should move in with Mother—for the time being, she said. I stayed in my apartment, sold a few insurance policies, and at night read every essay and book that Kierkegaard wrote. Unexpectedly, I began work on two essays: one on Kierkegaard's *Purity of Heart Is to Will One Thing,* which I planned to submit to *Philosophy and Phenomenological Research;* the other on Thomas Celano's *Life of St. Francis of Assisi,* for the Catholic magazine *Thought,* out of Fordham University. I suspected both essays would be turned down, but the careful writing of them, as if other people would indeed read what I said, satisfied me in a way I couldn't understand. Two evenings a week I ate supper at Mother's.

A dull lifelessness wrapped around the house and the store like a shroud. I ached to find a way out, for three of us were still young and in need of a belief, the simplest one—that he who lives shall live in hope. But all that remained, whether we languished at the supper table or silently rocked on the porch afterward, was remorse, suffering, and evasion—leprosies of our souls. The evenings I visited, we stayed on the porch late into the night. While the moths bounced around the single overhead light bulb, we spent our time listening to the chorus of crickets and tree toads and, without admitting it, glancing at each other out of the corners of our eyes. No one moved or spoke or sighed without considering what the other two thought, as if I were a boy and needed to ask Mother, "Is it right to do this?" or she, because she felt suddenly senile, wanted to ask the same of me, or Elizabeth, like an adolescent girl, felt a compulsion to wonder what we thought of her.

There was only one reference to the events of June. Mother and I did not answer when Elizabeth, without warning, spoke. "It was a mistake in the first place—all of us know it. So much of it—I tell myself—was because of Susan, and yet a part of me knew for absolutely sure that Susan didn't want me to. I just didn't listen. I thought it was the safest option. But if I had come home and told Will I had no business marrying him, that I needed to leave this town and start over again, then none of this . . ."

One evening I coaxed Stearns outside to toss a baseball with me. As the air cooled and softened the sound of the mitt and ball, and the sky slowly darkened, I began a campaign to turn him away from numbering stars as if they were saints in heaven. My father was dead, and the boy needed other idle dreams. First I tried to inspire him to love baseball, arguing with him that it was a much better game than football, no matter what everyone else in the town, the county, and the state believed. Then I led him into making our evenings together a habit, throwing and talking through July and August and, as he became more and more interested, even into the fall. As children in their complete enthusiasm will do, he became fascinated by my decoy and soon learned all there was to know about the Atlanta Crackers and the New York Yankees.

"Moo-ooo-ooo-se," he said one night, imitating the Yankee fans' greeting of Bill Skowron. A little chant he had made up followed: "Bil-ly, An-dy, Mic-key, Ca-sey, Yo-gi." And then faster: "Bil-ly, An-dy, Mic-key, Ca-sey, Yo-gi. Next year Mickey puts it all together. Ca-sey says he'll be as good as the Blipper and the Cabe."

"Clipper and the Babe."

"Well, that's what Ca-sey says. You can look it up."

"I'll believe it when I see it."

"You'll see it."

On the afternoon of October 4, I left work early and listened to the seventh game of the World Series with him. The poor boy suffered a two-day depression after Amoros caught

Berra's fly in the left-field corner and won it for the Dodgers. He brightened a little when I promised that I'd carry him to Yankee Stadium one day for a Series game, telling myself that this was the kind of hero worship and expectation the child could survive with. He was a scarred boy: he would always be introspective—trying to see into the life of things in the same way he tried to look through those copper shapes he set on my father's eyes—and if he suffered the wrong circumstances, he could turn morose. But sometimes I saw a playful fervor in his eyes as he gripped that baseball and flung it at the sky over my head and broadcast the runner coming around third at Yogi and "yer out!" at home, and when I saw him cock his arm and give the whole world that "out" sign, I imagined he might find, someday, a season or two of clear shining.

Unlike Mother. She boarded up the store and abandoned the garden. When she wasn't cooking, she sat in her rocker on the porch, stringing an endless mound of beans her neighbors donated to numb her grief. She never spoke bitterly; in fact she seldom mentioned the immediate past. Instead she began to write letters to her Cleburne County cousins, people she had not seen in over thirty years, exchanging stories about their childhoods. Elizabeth and I concocted a few schemes to brighten up her life, but she resisted each one. In December we thought we had persuaded her to go with us on a two-day outing to Atlanta. I made reservations for two rooms at the Ansley Hotel downtown: I needed to spend some time at the public library and show Stearns the oak tree in center field at the ball park on Ponce de Leon; Mother and Elizabeth could do all their Christmas shopping. But the night before we were to leave, after she washed the dishes, Mother announced she wasn't going.

"I don't have many people to buy gifts for anyway," she said, inching her way around the living-room couch and through the door to her bedroom.

Elizabeth shrugged. "It would have been an expensive trip," she said. "I can just as easily buy Stearns's gifts in LaGrange or Columbus." In the last year Elizabeth's hair had turned almost completely brown, and resignation weighed upon her eyes, as if they had lost sight of even the smallest possibility. The bruises on her leg were also slow to heal. But she remained, for all she had suffered and changed, a beautiful woman, though one who looked older than her age—forty-one, perhaps, not thirty-one.

"Let's go anyway," I suggested.

"We shouldn't leave Mattie alone—you know that."

"Belle will be glad to stay with her for two days, either here or at her place."

Elizabeth looked at me a moment, measuring my intent. It was a rare opportunity to speak directly.

"Your grief is not my mother's grief, Elizabeth." And then I smiled. "Nothing is true for everyone."

She laughed. "Luke Treadwell, sometimes I don't know what to make of you. . . . Well, why not? Let's go—we've got the reservations, and Stearns'll love it. I wouldn't mind getting out of Lanett, Alabama, either."

She didn't realize just how much she'd enjoy getting away until we were fifty miles up Route 29, comfortably out of the valley. She turned to me and grinned. "Georgia's a cruddy state, too," she said. We laughed. The weather was gorgeous, an early winter's day when the sun shines in a crystal, cloudless sky and the last crisp breeze of fall lingers, promising that a little endurance through a short winter will be amply rewarded. Lightning and thunderclouds and relentless overcast skies seemed part of another life. Off and on the rest of the way through the country, we counted cows and white horses, and by the time we passed through College Park, past Fort McPherson and Sylvan Hills to Spring Street, we were singing a ridiculous blend of songs—"The Tennessee Waltz," "Old McDonald," (with me doing a mean imitation of a pig), "Take Me Out to the Ball Game," and Pooh's "It's Very, Very Funny."

Remarkably, this rare, fresh-air spirit didn't wane for two days. The first morning Stearns and I climbed the fence at the Ponce de Leon ball park and ran the bases, in opposite directions, Stearns sliding into home in the proverbial cloud of dust a second before I lumbered over him. In the afternoon we accompanied Elizabeth to Davison's department store, which loomed over the three city blocks near the hotel—Peachtree, Ellis, and Carnegie Way. We hung around the sporting goods while she visited the women's-wear section, but before we left she took us to inspect a dress she was hemming and hawing about. The blue dress was simply designed, but attractive.

"It's just too much. I have no business spending so much money on one dress—my goodness."

"It's not too much, Aunt Elizabeth."

"She's your stepmother, Stearns."

Elizabeth glanced at me.

"It's not, Mother. Buy it—you deserve it."

She kissed him on the cheek and turned back to the mirror, stepping in one direction and another. I lingered behind her. Elizabeth had combed her hair back and let it fall freely to her shoulders, which were as white and fine as lilies. The bodice fit tightly to her breasts, the waist was gathered, and the simple skirt kept close to her hips and legs. I realized a little more, then, about the lure of clothes, how the right look somehow carried us beyond our awkward selves, our gawky nakedness. She saw me in the mirror—a presence standing, as always quietly to the side and rear, waiting. But the blue in her eyes began to resonate with an unnatural power. She did not stop looking at me, one moment questioning, another imploring, and then measuring me. I was quickly possessed by a far more profound feeling than the one that always had me simply say to her, "You are beautiful."

"A triptych," I said.

"You mean an altarpiece?"

"Except it's glass."

"I never even thought of it. There were two at Reims—I believe they were triptychs—both of the Virgin," she said. "In the best one she holds Christ, dead in her arms. John and Mary Magdalene are on either side."

All that was beautiful about her, from the past, the present, and, I must admit, the hoped-for future, broke in upon me quietly, without any sense of shock or fear, like a surprising light shining through a clear window. The sight was simply the sight of a woman, one I thought beautiful, one I loved, in a blue dress in front of a three-way mirror. For that moment I felt a healing flutter through me, stitching up the wounds of jealousy about my brother Will and soothing over my prideful passion with a calmer affection, which felt more trustworthy, as if I were the believer who, in a dark corner of some great cathedral, knelt in silence before a treasured altar triptych, where the sense of an abiding presence comforted.

On the second day, while I tried unsuccessfully to study in the library, Elizabeth took Stearns shopping. Both of them came back to the hotel with secret smirks on their faces about what they had bought me—object of humor I always have been. Separate from Mother and the valley, there was indeed a new sense among us, of this clear shining; it was never more apparent than that evening, when Elizabeth wore her new dress and we lingered at a nice restaurant and talked about the boy's future for as long as he could stand it, which masked our own interest in the possibilities for our lives. Elizabeth and Stearns needed to move away from Lanett and West Point, and I embraced the hope that with time I could provide the way out. I loved her. I needed her. If I had asked her to marry me then, she would have refused, but I was beginning to believe that as an older, more resigned human being, she imagined me a different person, perhaps a companion for life.

That night, after the two of them went to sleep next door, I bent over a writing desk in my room with the article about Kierkegaard's *Purity of Heart Is to Will One Thing* spread out in front of me. I had to stand up to turn the handle on the old window and pull open the casement. The cool winter air, tinged with the smell of exhaust, drifted in, and I sat down again, staring up to Peachtree Street at the peak of the hill, and the sky beyond. The neon reflection of Davison's sign shone in the glass across the way, where the edge of the building climbed straight toward the dome of the winter sky. I could spot a few stars, though the city lights kept most of them dim. But even a single star reminded me of my father.

And if my father, then Doug. Without telling Mother or Elizabeth, I had taken a day off from work in the fall and checked into Emory's hospital in Atlanta, where I submitted to a series of tests that in their painful thoroughness would surely create a new disease if one wasn't found. There was no disease, however. Given that the last time, in the Cusseta schoolhouse, I had awakened on the floor with my tongue scorched, I had begun to suspect not some kind of insanity but epilepsy. I even mentioned the possibility to the doctor. But I was fine—good heart rate, blood pressure, blood count, body weight, dietary habits, and so on, all according to the latest in medical science. And, more important, after the tests I felt fine myself, believing somehow that the visitations were part of that past I disinherited.

I reconfirmed that feeling at the writing desk, my mind wandering from the manuscript and into the night air around me and through the past. Something within my own heart, I told myself—fear perhaps, or guilt, even pride, some strange imagining—like a live cord touched something outside myself. I could not begin to name what was outside myself and feel it adequate, but I did not then, and believed I never would, question the authenticity of the experience, even if in allowing for my inability to control what happened to me I had to admit that Doug and my father, in their own unsophisticated way, were not completely wrong about what we call the spiritual. I believed all the more in the community of the quick and the dead, that those of us alive should count the dead among us, as the dead, I assumed in a spaceless, timeless realm, numbered us among them. I could understand no more about these events in my life.

Purity of Heart Is to Will One Thing. I wrote in the margin of the last page, "the genuine good." I could not believe, however, that the good would prevail, that all would be well, that the eternal verities would at the end of time ride in on a white horse and be sanctified. In the here and now, my father's verities translated into a chopped-off hand, two broken sons, an ternally grieving wife, and a lost disciple whom I hoped to make my wife. I underlined my margin notes and breathed in the air of the night. There was a car horn and a screech, but no collision. I waited to hear a vicious cursing from the offended driver, but there were no voices, the sounds of the near-accident vanishing. *To will one thing*—my father would have liked the phrase. In these times, when there was no certainty even about theories of uncertainty, to will one thing remained a noble pursuit. I said yes to this pursuit, and in doing so honored my father, whispering his name, Robert Treadwell.

But in my opinion he made one mistake. He should have remembered, throughout his single-minded sermonizing and storytelling and one closely held biblical conviction after another, that the heart, trembling and secret, is not pure.

About the Author

THE QUICK AND THE DEAD is Z. Vance Wilson's first novel. His short fiction has appeared in *Missouri Review* and *Carolina Quarterly*. A native of Tampa, Florida, Mr. Wilson now lives and teaches in Asheville, North Carolina.

SOME OF THE BEST IN SOUTHERN FICTION

by Lee Smith

TA-141